Prais

"This book has just about everything: magic, machines, mystery, mayhem, and all the danger one expects when people's loves and fears collide. I can't wait to return to the world of Evelina Cooper!"

—Kevin Hearne

"As Sherlock Holmes's niece, investigating murder while navigating the complicated shoals of Society—and romance—in an alternate Victorian England, Evelina Cooper is a charming addition to the canon."

—Jacqueline Carey

"Holloway takes us for quite a ride, as her plot snakes through an alternate Victorian England full of intrigue, romance, murder, and tiny sandwiches. Full of both thrills and frills."

—Nicole Peeler, author of the Jane True series

"*A Study in Silks* is a charming, adventurous ride with a heroine who is both clever and talented. The brushes with the Sherlock Holmes mythos only add to the fun of this tale, and readers are bound to fall in love with Evelina and the London she inhabits."

—Pip Ballantine

"In *A Study in Silks*, Emma Jane Holloway has created a wonderful reimagining of the Sherlock Holmes mythos set in a late-Victorian Britain ruled by nefarious industrial titans called steam barons. Holloway's clever writing, attention to detail, and sublime characters forge a fascinating world that combines brass-plated steampunk technology with magic. By turns a coming-of-age story, a gas-lamp thriller, and a whimsical magical fantasy, *A Study in Silks* is the premiere novel of an author to watch."

—Susan Griffith

"Holloway stuffs her adventure with an abundance of characters and ideas and fills her heroine with talents and graces, all within a fun, brisk narrative."

—*Publishers Weekly*

By Emma Jane Holloway

A Study in Silks
A Study in Darkness

A STUDY IN DARKNESS

Emma Jane Holloway

DEL REY • NEW YORK

A Del Rey Mass Market Original

Copyright © 2013 by Naomi Lester
Excerpt from *A Study in Ashes* by Emma Jane Holloway copyright © 2013 by Naomi Lester

Published in the United States by Del Rey, an imprint of The Random House Publishing Group, a division of Random House LLC, a Penguin Random House Company, New York.

DEL REY and the HOUSE colophon are registered trademarks of Random House LLC.

This book contains an excerpt from the forthcoming book *A Study in Ashes* by Emma Jane Holloway. This excerpt has been set for this edition only and may not reflect the final content of the forthcoming edition.

ISBN 978-0-345-53719-5
eISBN 978-0-345-54566-4

Printed in the United States of America

www.delreybooks.com

9 8 7 6 5 4 3 2

Del Rey mass market edition: November 2013

For my parents,
who saw fit to preserve the letter I wrote to Mr. Holmes
when I was in grade school.
I owe so much to your cheerleading, your patience, and
your unabashed gusto for researching obscure subjects—
even if it involves talking to people
who have never actually trod the earth.

Many thanks also to Mr. Holmes's secretary,
who was good enough to reply with a reading list.

A Study in Darkness

CHAPTER ONE

WHAT IF THE SKIES NEVER CLEARED AND HIS QUARRY slipped past, swathed in cloud like a bride beneath her veil?

Or what if the enemy burst forth like a vengeful ghost, spewing a fiery retribution of lead and flame? Indeed, an airship with that much cargo would have guns aplenty on board.

There were a thousand what-ifs the captain of the *Red Jack* could not avoid, but that was the price Nick paid for this new life on the knife-edge of risk. But as an orphan abandoned to the circus—perhaps a Gypsy by his dark features, or perhaps something even less welcome in the world—his existence had been one gamble after another. Plundering a ship twice the size of his own craft was just one more.

Nick had called his magic earlier and raised a vision of where his quarry—the *Leaping Hind*—would pass, but something had gone amiss. By now the *Hind* should have sailed into view, engines groaning beneath the weight of all that wealth. She would be coming in off the coast, flying low and with holds crammed with clockwork, gears, and costly parts from the German states—a queen's ransom in shining brass.

Nick shut his eyes and listened, giving up on sight. The engines of his ship were silent as it drifted with the wind. The creak of rigging was a comforting chorus, as if the *Red*

Jack muttered to itself as it waited. Condensation dripped from the lines. He could hear the footsteps of his men moving around the ship—Digby at the helm, Beadle giving orders to the bosun and the boy, Striker cursing at some piece of equipment. Through the fresh, clear air, Nick caught the scent of gunpowder and grease.

"Athena," Nick muttered under his breath. "Do you sense anything?"

There are birds, the air deva replied from her place of honor at the prow. Devas did not have a voice exactly, or language, though that was how Nick perceived it. *The ash rooks.*

"Anything else?" The rooks were always near, looking for something dead to eat. They were as much pirates as the men.

Captain Niccolo is impatient, Athena chided. *For shame. A successful thief bides his time.*

The elemental spirit—trapped in a half-melted metal cube—seemed female, although she possessed no physical form of her own. Before the cube had been stripped of all its golden decorations, it had been known to scholars as Athena's Casket—an ancient Greek navigation device. Nick had started calling the deva Athena, and the name had stuck. She was the soul of the airship, its intelligence and vital force, and she made the *Red Jack* unique. No other ship, much less pirate ship, had a deva on its crew, and only Nick could speak to her.

Not that those conversations always went smoothly.

"I'm not impatient," he growled. "I'm concerned."

You are *impatient. Your thoughts buffet me like a gale. There is no need.*

"I have buyers waiting for what the *Hind* carries."

All that metal men prize so highly. Dull stuff. But then she was a creature of air.

"Metal makes machines. Machines make power."

And that power—heat, light, pumps to drive clean water into streets and villages—was a necessity of life. The steam barons ran the utility companies as well as the railways, dockyards, and most factories that produced weapons or mechanical parts. They were even branching into the defense industry and the telegraph. And where the barons took an interest, competition was quite literally crushed. No company dared to challenge their monopoly.

To make matters worse, conspicuous consumption of heat and light had become a hallmark of status among the gentry, and that drove up prices and left the poor to shiver in the dark. All this guaranteed an underground market for parts to build unauthorized machines—generators, windmills, batteries charged by wind, and whatever equipment a man needed for his trade. And that's where the pirates sailed in and made their fortunes.

And what did Nick plan to do with all the profit? He wasn't sure anymore. Every man had his dream, but he'd had to let his go. Or rather, his had walked away with a toss of her long, dark curls. Perhaps he was saving up to buy forgetfulness, for surely there must be a sorcerer who could carve Evelina Cooper out of his heart.

He felt a twinge of exasperation from the deva, equivalent to a human woman rolling her eyes. *You must heed your birds, Niccolo. They have found the ship you seek.*

Nick opened his eyes, looking out at the wet expanse that wrapped the *Red Jack*, soaking men and equipment in a clinging mist. If the other ship was invisible, so were they.

Nick's ship was a perfect pirate vessel, small and sleek as a hawk. She had a rigid keel for mounting steam-powered thrusters and a long, thin tail that ended in a propeller. The gondola, wide and shallow, had been shaped to hug the long, thin oval of gray silk, the prow rising into a graceful raptor with outstretched wings. The ship was fancifully carved and painted in shades of white and blue. Its only splash of color was the scarlet flags around the rigging that gave the *Red Jack* its name. Perhaps she was far from the newest in airship design, but she was elegant, and the crew had slaved to make her shine.

"Oy," came the soft exclamation from a few yards away. Striker, his second in command, leaned against the rail, pointing over the side. He wore a long coat covered in pieces of metal—each scrap of brass and steel representing wealth in a land where such goods were hard to get.

Nick joined him, following the line of his pointing finger. It angled down and to the ship's starboard, where dark shapes moved among the clouds. The ash rooks hung in the air like scraps of ragged black velvet, their feathers so dark they seemed more an absence than a concrete form.

They turned, drifting down and to the right in a slow arc. "They're leading us to the *Hind,*" Nick said in reply to Striker's questioning glance.

Athena followed the flock, earning a curse from the helmsman when his careful steering was utterly ignored. Nick and Striker watched the roiling cloudscape, the mountains and pillars of cottony mist a strange and eerie wilderness.

Then Nick's pulse began to speed, and a grin split his face. There, a little way ahead, was a shadow in the mist. The rooks swooped near it in perfect, silent formation until a rifle cracked, the sound muffled by the atmosphere. They scattered in a burst of black wings, darting safely away.

And then the *Hind* tore through the mist and came into view. Her balloon was sky blue striped with gold, the gondola slung below a heavier craft built for hauling cargo. The prow bore the figurehead of a leaping deer leafed with gold. A rich ship, then, flying the cobalt colors of the steam baron known as the Blue King. That was his treasure she carried.

"Got her," Nick growled. His muscles tensed, as if his body was already leaping through the sky to take his prize. They watched as the ship passed between cloud banks, as elusive as a will-o'-the-wisp.

"That's an aether ship," Striker said, his dark face rumpled with concentration. "We can play with things that go boom."

Nick understood. Like the *Jack*, their quarry used aether distillate to keep it aloft. It would have to, with a cargo load like that. Aether systems were finicky but didn't explode as easily as the more inexpensive hydrogen balloons. That didn't mean they couldn't be sunk or burned, but they were less likely to take every other ship in the sky along with them.

"Tell Beadle to ready the attack. We'll get close and give them a shot across the bow."

Striker flashed his teeth in a savage smile, and smacked a fist into his palm before striding off to find the first mate.

"Go," Nick said to Athena, and the single word began a dance they'd done a hundred times before.

At your command, my captain, said Athena. *The hawk stoops to pluck this pigeon from the air.*

"You're gloating," Nick said, unable to stifle a laugh of exhilaration.

All the best pirates have a proper sense of theater. Surely you've heard of Captain Roberts?

"As if I could avoid it." Nick braced himself as the ship banked, sweeping down in silence. The motion was powered by the deva alone, relying utterly on her command of wind and air. The clouds parted below them once more, and he pulled out his spyglass and counted gun ports, estimating just how much damage the *Hind* could do. Then he scanned the deck for lookouts. Their glasses were trained everywhere but at the *Jack*—a gray-on-gray apparition still mostly hidden in the clouds.

There were many ways to catch a ship—flying false colors, pretending to be in distress, or even masquerading as one of the floating pleasure gardens where sailors took their ease. Nick preferred the honest approach—steel and shot first, blood if necessary, and fire if nothing else prevailed.

There was a gun affixed to the *Red Jack*'s deck—a piece of cold black iron mounted on a swivel. Striker had devised much fancier weaponry, but Nick held that back, keeping the element of surprise for when it was most needed. "Mr. Royce," Nick ordered. "Please extend our felicitations."

They waited, biding their time until Athena brought the ship closer. The clouds thinned at the lower altitude, but still a scarf of mist hid the enemy ship for a moment, then slithered slowly away. Beadle swept his arm downward in a silent command.

The gun belched and the ball of lead flew from a plume of

stink and smoke. The gunner's trajectory played true, sending their greetings across the nose of the *Hind*. A cheer went up from the *Red Jack*'s crew, celebrating Royce's skill.

The next move depended on the *Hind*'s captain. He could strike his colors and surrender, or he could retaliate. Nick watched through the spyglass, one foot planted against the side as the deck tilted with the motion of Athena's dive.

And then the *Hind* turned to put its side squarely to Nick's ship, and the gun ports opened, showing the muzzles of half a dozen cannons. They would be small, light guns designed for use on airships—even aether distillate could only do so much to compensate for weight—but they could still blast a ship out of the sky.

"They're not in a mood to chat," Striker said, switching on the engines that drove the propellers. The accelerating churn of gears and pistons seemed deafening for an instant, but they no longer needed silence, and the deva could take advantage of the extra power.

"Mr. Beadle." Nick slid the spyglass shut, part of him glad of the looming fight. "Show them what we've got."

"Hands to gun deck!" roared Beadle. But the order was needless—the crew was already in motion, scrambling below.

The *Hind*'s guns fired, but Athena bounded upward, skipping over the volley of cannon balls as lightly as a child hopping over a puddle. Beadle, Striker, and Nick—staggering a little with the sudden motion—threw open a locker and grabbed weapons. Then they braced themselves against the rail, ready to shoot. Striker held a monstrous weapon—a blunderbuss three times as large as any Nick had ever seen—filled with all manner of metal scrap, ideal for discouraging a mob of attackers.

Nick heard the shouts and rumbles as the *Red Jack*'s crew readied the air cannons below. His stomach churned with a combination of excitement and terror, raising a slick of sweat under the linen of his shirt. His hands tightened on his rifle, and then he gave a nod as Athena dropped in the sky, bringing the *Hind* into view once more. Beadle rapped on the deck—three solid blows with the butt of his rifle, to give the signal to the gunners below. Circling overhead, the ash rooks gave a raucous cry, eager for their meal.

The *Red Jack* opened fire, air cannons spewing, but it wasn't balls of lead they shot. Tightly sewn sacks exploded in midair, and a rain of twisted metal clattered to the deck of the *Leaping Hind,* flipping and skittering as soon as each piece hit the sanded wooden surface. They ran like beetles in a crazy zigzag over the deck, faster than any insect. These were Striker's invention, and the answer to how a crew of eight could overpower a cargo vessel twice the *Jack*'s size. Thousands of the clockwork devices scampered over the deck, driven by a magnetic hunger to find anything made of iron—guns, propellers, boilers, engines, and above all, the aether distillate pumping device.

As the clockwork hailed down, half the cargo ship's crew had no idea what to do. The other half dove for the scampering devices, voices loud with panic. A few of the things were smashed by boot heels, but most found their destination, clamped on, and unsealed the glass vials of corrosive acid inside their clockwork bellies. The devices died by their own poison, melting in minutes, but so did whatever they fastened onto. The engines of the *Hind* failed first, with a gasp, whistle, and then a messy explosion as the metal housing of the boiler gave way. The chuffing propellers whirled once, twice, and then stopped.

Nick was breathing hard, his pulse racing. The sudden silence of the enemy ship was eerie, as solemn a thing as the hush of a sick room. Then the *Red Jack* drifted closer, approaching near enough to inspect the damage, but not so close that the two enormous balloons would touch. Nick stayed perfectly still, waiting until the light in the aether pump winked out. A gust of cold wind struck his face and he could smell the stink of the acid-eaten metal, taste it on the back of his tongue. The *Hind* would gradually descend to earth, steered only by emergency sails and whatever airmanship skills the crew possessed. It was a slow enough affair that there was no need for loss of life—unless they fought back.

Time ticked past, maybe five seconds, maybe a minute,

but it seemed an eternity of suspense. Nick clenched his jaw, hoping the other captain would take the easy road and surrender.

But the *Hind* slowly wheeled, using the little propulsion it had left to turn its guns on the *Red Jack* once more. "Don't do it," Nick muttered under his breath as Athena danced out of harm's way. Surely the other captain could tell what was in store?

Apparently not, because the cannons roared in that same instant. Three of the guns exploded, fatally damaged by Striker's devices. As the smoke cleared, it was plain to see the volley had blackened the port-side gun deck, blowing chunks of the wood away. If she had been in water, the *Hind* would have sunk.

But this time, one of the balls clipped the *Red Jack*, tearing away a slice of her tail. A wave of anger swamped Nick, the scream of the wood as painful as if it had been his own flesh. "Fire!" he roared.

Striker lit the fuse of his enormous weapon, and it thundered, recoiling halfway across the deck. It released a second rain of metal into the air, this one made up of old nails, small shot, and scrap meant to rend flesh. Nick and Beadle fired as well, but theirs were the grappling guns, sending claws deep into the *Leaping Hind*'s side. The prey was caught, and Athena rose in the air until the towing cables snapped tight. She pulled a little ahead, simultaneously angling away from the threat of the *Hind*'s cannons and keeping the crippled ship aloft. The bosun immediately began affixing pulleys to the lines.

And now it was time for Nick to play his part. The gunners were back on deck, readying baskets that would be lowered down to haul away booty. Nick exchanged his grappling gun for a brace of pistols and jumped to the rail, one hand on the rigging as he balanced over a thousand yards of empty sky. Four men would board the enemy ship, but they would not board alone.

"Gwilliam!" he called, and the flock of huge black ravens circled closer.

The ash rooks—for that was what they called themselves—

were a disconcerting sight. They loved shiny things, adornments most of all, and traded their service for glittering loot. And like Striker in his metal-clad coat, they wore as much as they could carry without impeding their mobility. One of them landed beside Nick, his huge, sharp claws easily grasping the thick wood. This one had what looked like a crested helmet and a chain of enameled metal around its throat, and Nick recognized it as the ravens' king. It gave a long, rattling croak.

You are ready at last, wingless one? Gwilliam said, touching Nick's mind the same way Athena did.

"I may be wingless, but I am not flightless." Nick felt a lift in his heart, the excitement before a moment of daring. His body ached with the need to prove his strength and speed.

The bosun had fastened a wooden bar to the pulley on the grappling lines, and Nick grasped it with both hands. In a moment, he had launched himself from the rail and slid down the grappling cable, releasing the brake to rocket through the air at stomach-churning speed. The sky opened beneath him, and with a rush of sheer joy, he was lost in the mist, the wet fingers trailing over his skin and hair. And then his view of the *Hind* opened up below, a picture of men and rooks and the aftermath of the exploded boiler. The birds harried the crew of the *Hind,* using beak and claw to ensure Nick landed safely. He slowed his descent, leaping lightly to land on the enemy deck. Striker, Digby, and Royce followed.

They drew their weapons the moment their feet touched a solid surface, wasting no time leaping into the fray. The fight was near the center of the ship, the combatants clustering together in their eagerness to bash heads. Nick ducked as a blue-coated officer swept his sword through the air, then dodged again to avoid the sweep of an ash rook's wing. And then he was in the thick of it, firing once, twice, and then drawing his knives when the risk of shooting his own men became too great.

There were perhaps twenty crewmen on the *Hind,* all clad in blue and white. One came at Nick with an ax, and he twisted aside only to feel the wind of the blade's passage kiss his cheek. He drove his fist into the man's gut, aiming upward to the ribs, and the airman flew backward, crashing hard against the disabled aether pump. Someone crashed into Nick's back, driving him to his knees, and the next sweep of the ax would have split his skull if Gwilliam hadn't appeared from the sky, claws raking the airman's face. As the man cowered, Nick delivered a boot to his head, knocking him cold.

Someone fired an aether gun, blasting a smoking bite from the rail. Nick swore. Aether weapons were experimental and unpredictable. Striker made them, but Nick hadn't expected to find one in enemy hands—especially not one powerful enough to blow pieces out of the airship's hull. A misplaced blast at the balloon could make the difference between floating gently to earth and dropping like a stone. Unexpectedly— for the sake of the *Jack* and the *Hind* alike—Nick's priority became getting that gun out of the fight.

He grabbed the ax from the unconscious airman, holding it in his right hand; a knife was in the left. There were men down already, their blue and white uniforms stained with red. The boiler and the blunderbuss had taken their toll, as had the rooks—but now the enemy was falling at Nick's hands as he worked his way through the mob. Another crewman raised a barrel over his head, meaning to throw it into the struggling crowd, but Nick kicked his knees out from under him, sending him crashing to the deck. The barrel bounced and rolled away, nearly bowling Digby over. Nick brought the butt of the ax handle down on the barrel-thrower's skull, making sure he didn't get up for a while.

The aether gun fired again with a sound like tearing silk, earning a storm of angry caws from the ash rooks. Black feathers fluttered through the air. Nick forced his way out of the eye of the maelstrom, struggling for room to move and to see what fool had the weapon. Pistols fired, men screamed, and the stink of gunpowder and burned flesh made it nearly impossible to breathe. He had barely broken through to the edge of the fight when he met the captain, easy to identify by the miles of gold braid on his coat. The uniform identi-fied him as a captain of the Merchant Brotherhood of the Air and, like his officer, the captain wore a sword—probably meant more for show than for use. But he also had a pistol, and he held that with the ease of an expert shot.

"Withdraw your men, Niccolo," the captain snarled. He was tall and ruddy, with salt-and-pepper hair in short, tight waves.

It didn't surprise Nick that his adversary knew his name. The *Red Jack* had earned its reputation. "Captain Hughes, I presume," he said. "Give up and you keep your life."

"Not bloody likely, pirate." Hughes jerked the nose of the gun.

Acting on instinct, Nick threw the ax. He was a knife man, not used to the balance of the heavier weapon, and it flew wide. But the distraction bought him a sliver of time, just enough to follow with the blade in his left hand. That struck the captain's fingers, making him release the pistol. It fell to the deck, discharging with a bang as it spun away.

There was a sound behind Nick. He dropped on instinct, avoiding the blast of the aether gun by the breadth of a cat's whisker. Then he rolled to his feet and launched himself through the air, grappling the shooter and bearing him to the ground. Nick had the impression of a brown suit, brown hair, and a forgettable face. They rolled over and over, scraps of broken metal digging into their flesh as they went. Nick thumped the man's head against the deck, then smashed a fist into his face. The man went limp, but Nick hit him again just to be sure. When his eyes rolled up in his head, Nick scrambled to his feet, grabbed the aether gun, and surveyed the situation.

He stood still for a moment, emotions catching up. Fear, triumph, and rage chased through his blood, leaving his nerves sparking with wild energy. Then he was back in the action, waving the deadly gun. "Put down your weapons!" he bellowed.

There were only half a dozen of the *Hind*'s men left standing, including Captain Hughes. Nick caught Hughes's eye, willing the man to see reason, but the captain glared back, fury tightening his face.

The crewmen on both sides sensed the struggle of wills

between the two captains, and the battle slowed to a stop. The last few thumps and grunts sounded, then Striker sent his determined opponent crashing into a water butt. Silence followed.

The officer who had fought with his sword released a low moan of pain. He had collapsed on a coil of ropes, a gunshot wound to his shoulder, his bright uniform giving him the look of a discarded nutcracker doll. Hughes was looking at him with an intensity that said the young man was more than just another officer. Perhaps a relation, by the similarity of their features. The wounded man made another muffled noise, and Nick saw the moment when the captain of the *Leaping Hind* gave in. Hughes drew his sword and passed it, hilt first, to Nick.

"He demanded that you put down your weapons," Hughes said to his men. "I authorize you to do so."

They did as they were told. Nick had won. Within minutes, the able men of the *Hind*'s crew were bound and the best of the cargo was being looted one basketful at a time. Nick stood guard on the prisoners. Royce and Striker did the hauling while Digby kept his weapon trained on the *Hind*'s surgeon, who was seeing to the wounded.

The raven king landed on the rigging in a thunderous flapping of wings. *Hail, Niccolo.*

"Gwilliam," Nick said. "Thank you for finding this ship when I could not."

Do not doubt the ash rooks. This alliance feeds the flock well, and Saria of the silken feathers has agreed to fly at my side. It is to my advantage that Captain Niccolo finds his mark.

There were two dead among the *Hind*'s crew, and the birds were taking their tribute. The rooks were valuable allies, but Nick was doing his best to ignore the sight and especially the sound of the carrion flock at work.

And now I say that you should not tarry. There is danger below.

"When isn't there?" Nick muttered, but the bird had launched itself back into the air. Nick's gaze followed it for a moment, the ink-black arrow of Gwilliam's wings cutting a perfect curve through the mist.

Then Nick glanced over the side of the ship, wondering what the rook had been talking about. Through a patchwork of fleecy cloud, he could see the south bank of the Thames, east of Guy's Hospital and the Tower. It was still the part of London where the steam baron called the Blue King held sway, but more in the country than in the city proper. He froze, a sudden sense of displacement taking him. He knew this landscape, and yet it didn't look the same as when he had passed over just two months before. Now there were large yards—fields, really—ringed with tall, impenetrable fences. Corner towers gave the place a fortified look. Huge sheds stood here and there, hiding whatever was inside.

Nick didn't give the sheds a second thought. What was outside worried him enough. *Great mother of basilisks!*

There were huge monsters of steel down below—gigantic engines, each one trapped in a spherical metal cage. Six of them sat in a cluster, all as tall as houses. And if their sheer size wasn't eye-catching enough, one of them appeared to be rolling forward like a ball, the engine inside suspended upright as its latticework superstructure bumped over the rocky field. His gaze flicked from one to the next, wondering what the contraptions were for.

He wheeled on Captain Hughes. "This is where you were bound, is it not?"

The captain was standing only yards away, hands bound at his back. Hughes gave Nick a cold stare, refusing to respond.

Striker had just fastened his basket of loot to the winch, and it was smoothly rising to the *Red Jack* as an empty container drifted down the other line. Overhearing the exchange, he grabbed the captain's elbow and marched him over to where Nick stood. Then all three of them peered down at the strange sight.

"What am I looking at?" Nick demanded.

Hughes frowned. "This is the place I am contracted to deliver my cargo."

"What are those machines?" Nick said in a tight voice. "Whom do they belong to?"

The lines around Hughes's mouth deepened. "This is the Blue King's property, but I know nothing. I'm under orders to send any unnecessary personnel below deck when we land. Only myself and my first mate are allowed to disembark, and we have given our word to maintain silence about anything we see."

"And that doesn't smell rotten at all," Nick said dryly. "What *have* we got ourselves into?"

Striker gave Hughes a warning look. "How about our friend with the aether gun? That's a rare item for a fellow who looks like a money-changer's clerk."

The captain shrugged, but his attempt at nonchalance failed, pushed aside by curiosity. "Bingham is on the Blue King's business. He keeps to himself."

"And I'd say he was under orders to make sure this delivery got made, and quietly." Striker gave one of his fierce grins, his teeth white against his dark face. "Maybe we should wake him up and ask a few questions."

Nick didn't reply, his eyes still fixed on the machines below. He was no genius with mechanics, but the longer he looked, the better he could see the potential in the device. Twin channels had been left free of the crisscrossing steel bars of the globe. That way, as the superstructure rolled forward, something sticking out from the engine wouldn't catch on the latticework. Nick pulled out his spyglass, taking a closer look at one of the machines. In fact, there was a pair of arms jutting out from the core of each monster. Some pointed their arms straight ahead, some straight up. He angled his view to see the appendages head on. Twin maws peered back at him, like hungry mouths ready to spit death. Nick knew a cannon when he saw it—and this kind didn't just go boom.

Nick's entire body clenched and he let loose a curse. With a hand suddenly slippery with sweat, he passed the glass to Striker. *Athena*, he said to the deva in his mind. *Tow us away from here. Fast.*

"What are those?" asked Hughes.

"Guns designed to shoot at airships." Nick's jaw ached with tension. "Magnetic aether cannons."

Striker swore. "Where would the Blue King get the plans for those? There are only three or four makers who would begin to understand how to build 'em."

"More to the point, *why* would the Blue King have them?" Hughes said incredulously. "Bohemia is the only other nation with a significant air fleet, and they're not about to attack the Empire. There is no threat of war."

"What if he knows about a threat?" Striker asked. "The Steam Council has men abroad."

"Or," said Nick, "what if he's planning a war of his own?"

CHAPTER TWO

August 7, 1888

MAGGOR'S CLOSE

1:30 a.m. Tuesday

IMOGEN ROTH DRIFTED IN A GRAY ZONE THAT WAS NOT
quite sleep. Part of her knew that she was dreaming, and
that a hard bed in a strange house fed her restlessness. But
with the sharp clarity that came only in the dead of night,
the greater part of her dream-mind fixed on the darkness
waiting by the bedposts, the consuming nothingness that
slithered across the room, eager to engulf her.

Of all her nightmares, this was the most familiar and the
worst. It settled over her like a coverlet woven from death itself, trapping her where she lay. A lead weight pressed against
her chest, crushing her limbs against the unforgiving mattress. Movement was impossible, even to take a breath. In a
moment or two, she began to struggle for air.

Helpless, her mind scrabbled like a beast in a cage, frantically hurling itself against the prison of her flesh. It was utterly dark now, no sight or sound or feel of air against her
face. Just the pain of starved lungs, the last rush of heartbeat, an involuntary twitch of a sparking nerve—and then
that was gone, too.

Nothingness. While her body lay deeply sleeping, her
spirit drifted elsewhere, losing all sense of physical form
without even a pulse to mark the passage of time. Silence
stretched backward through infinity, memory shrinking to a
distant pinpoint. And with no memory, the future—floating

like a shipwrecked hull on a still, starless sea—was a moot point.

Worse, she wasn't alone. Something waited in the silent dark. When it would strike, she didn't know. What it was, she didn't know. She had the notion that it was herself, waiting for her own moment of weakness to strike. And while that didn't make sense, it wasn't the business of dreams to be logical. Or maybe she had died after all, and she would remain there, floating forever, robbed of all her senses.

Whatever was left of her mind started to unravel like knitting gone wrong.

Then, unexpectedly, the dream changed. Imogen was standing on a street she didn't know—the kind that her father would never allow her to visit. Rain glistened on patches of mud and greasy cobbles that led between soot-blackened walls. Instinctively, she looked around. There weren't many lights, but in the distance she could see the blue globe of a gaslight. *I'm in the East End, the Blue King's territory.* Pleased with herself for figuring that much out, Imogen took a few steps forward, trying to spot some other clue. She'd never had this dream before, and she liked it much better. At least now there was something to see.

She heard voices, loud with drink. She wheeled around to spy two soldiers—the uniforms looked something like the Coldstream Guards—laughing and jostling with two women. It was the kind of playful push and tug that usually ended in kisses, but in this case the party was breaking up. One couple went to the left, the other to the right. Under some compulsion she didn't understand, Imogen followed the second pair down a narrow street, keeping some distance behind. She wasn't sure why, but the rules of the dream required that she stay out of sight.

About halfway along, the couple found a dark doorway and the woman lifted her skirts. Imogen turned away, embarrassment and disgust curling her insides into a cold ball. There were ugly sounds coming from the pair—sounds that didn't belong with what she'd always imagined the act of love to be. What was this encounter doing in her dream? Why was a good girl like her dreaming this?

Why not?

Imogen stopped. The question hadn't been hers. It was coming from that other thing, the one that hid in the still darkness when it crushed her to the bed. With clammy, horrific certainty, she realized she hadn't escaped the dark place at all. It had just relocated inside her, and now it was speaking. That had never happened before.

She shuddered, wondering what to do. If she spoke to it, would that make things worse? But she was too curious not to ask at least one question. "Who are you?"

The voice didn't respond. She could feel the presence thinking, considering, observing. The man buttoned himself up and walked away, and the woman shook her skirts back into place.

Do you understand?

Imogen couldn't answer. She'd seen money change hands and knew what it meant, but what else was she supposed to know? Imogen's experience of the world stopped far short of these streets.

The presence sensed her ignorance, and made her follow the woman as she left the alley in the opposite direction from the man. Imogen tried to stop her feet, to turn them around, but they wouldn't obey. It was clear the presence had a goal, something it wanted to find out. Something she was going to have to learn, too.

When they left the alley, light from a window above gave Imogen a glimpse of their quarry. The woman wasn't young, tall, or pretty. She had a green skirt and black jacket, a black hat perched on her dark hair. Just from the way the clothes fell around her frame, Imogen had the impression the cloth was limp from long use.

They followed, and followed. The woman went through a rounded archway in a large brick structure. It led to a central courtyard with several stone staircases that led to three floors above. Imogen, who had never lived in anything smaller than a mansion, looked around with a mixture of dismay and fascination. Was this where the poor lived? It wasn't as if she'd never thought about it—the papers were full of opinions about what to do with the impoverished masses of London—

but the specifics had obviously eluded her. The place was dark and dingy and she had a muted impression that it smelled. Forgetting that this was just a dream, she let fear slide beneath her guard. This wasn't a place she wanted to linger.

"What is it you want to know?" she whispered to the presence, as the woman began mounting one of the stairways, her tread weary and slow. And why would this poor woman—who obviously possessed next to nothing—have any information to offer?

The answer didn't come in words, but in anguish. The presence radiated a childlike bewilderment, a sense of displacement Imogen could not begin to name— a knowledge that something was wildly, irrevocably *wrong*. It hit her like a wave, drowning and buffeting her in emotion so strong she lost all bearing. The image of the stairs and the woman vanished, plunging her back into the black, timeless void.

Something is missing.

The statement was followed by searing, violent rage.

With a gasp, Imogen sat straight up in her bed, going from sleep to waking in a single moment. Her head swam, as if someone had struck her. What was that dream about? Why had that presence spoken to her? Why now and never before? Something had changed, and a dark, anxious place opened up inside her. If a person had enough bad dreams, was it possible to lose one's reason?

She was certain—as certain as if she had seen the whole thing during her waking hours—that something terrible had happened to that woman on the stairs. Something the presence had done.

She buried her face in her hands, breathing hard, the slick of sweat on her skin making the gauzy fabric of her nightgown cling to her back and arms. Very soon, the cold air in the room bit through the thin garment and cleared her head. Slowly, slowly the tide of terror receded, its cold touch slithering away.

A candle flickered on the nightstand. She wasn't afraid of the dark in the usual sense, but ever since the nightmares began—she had been little more than six years of age—she'd been afraid of waking up unable to see. The candle was there so that she knew with certainty when a dream was over.

The hideous anger still pulsed in her memory, fading echoes that left her scraped hollow with fatigue. Imogen pulled her knees up under her chin and gazed around, cataloguing the items of barely familiar furniture. The shapes and colors reassured her. She recognized her room at Maggor's Close, Jasper Keating's new country house—purchased so that he might hold shooting parties for his important friends. It might have been the closest thing to enemy territory, but at least it was in the here and now.

What was that dream about? Usually her dreams were of the dark place and the presence, or the even more terrifying one where her soul left her body, wandering away and getting so lost she couldn't find way back. But they rarely involved other people, much less strangers. That was a new twist.

Imogen scrubbed at her face, exhausted. The summer had been bad for nightmares, ever since the difficulties last spring. That had put everyone on edge, and it was a wonder none of them had gone over that edge. The only thing that had kept her sane was the iron will with which she pushed away the images, refusing to think about them once they were over. She couldn't prevent them from ruining her sleep, but she could keep them from cluttering up her waking hours.

Which were apparently starting now. There was no chance of further rest. She slid off the tall bed, her feet searching out her slippers. Then she slid on her quilted robe and paced to the window, cupping her hands to shield her eyes from the reflection cast by the lone candle flame. The moors around them lay in moonlit tranquility, silent but for the hoot of an owl.

And the voices of men deep in the back-and-forth of conversation. Imogen couldn't see them clearly—they were standing too close to the wall below. She picked up the tiny, feminine pocket watch from her dressing table and tilted it to the light. It was two o'clock, the dead of night. Who was up at this hour?

Curiosity riveted her. Perhaps because she was friends with Evelina Cooper, niece of the well-known detective Sherlock Holmes, Imogen wasn't prepared to let that curiosity languish. Besides, anything was better than dwelling on the dream that still gnawed at the edges of her mind.

She crouched, making herself small in case anyone looked up, and grasped the latch of the diamond-paned window. She turned the cold brass handle and gently nudged the casement open a crack, just enough to hear the conversation more clearly. The old wood moved without a sound. After all, since the windows in this dreary place leaked so much cold air, they could hardly be a tight fit.

The first voice she heard was Jasper Keating's. Although he was officially master of the household, he divided his time between Maggor's Close and his London offices, leaving his daughter to entertain his guests for the weeks of grouse hunting ahead. He hadn't been at supper, so he must have arrived sometime that night.

"What are you talking about?" he said angrily. "A bomb in the middle of London? You don't do that sort of thing unless you're ready for a fight."

A bomb? Imogen froze in place, her eyes going wide. She'd been expecting bedroom scandal or maybe chat of a shady business deal, but this was serious. Eavesdropping had suddenly gone beyond an entertaining diversion.

"Perhaps he is. Maybe that's the whole point. In any event, he's planning some sort of splashy statement, and somewhere in your territory." The other voice was deep—Imogen thought she knew it but couldn't call up a face or name. "That's why I came to you. If one of us makes a move to stop him, it will be a long, messy affair—death, property damage, and bad press all around. With two of us, it could be quick and neat. No point in letting rebels take advantage of any lapse in security."

"You're still on about that Baskerville affair."

"So what if I am?" said the deep voice. "I'm still correct. Whoever takes up arms against us—rebels, aristocratic or otherwise—will never succeed as long as the rest of the Steam Council is united."

The Steam Council? That was what the men and women who ruled the great utility companies called themselves. Jasper Keating, one of the key members, was called the Gold King after the yellow-tinted globes he used to mark all the gaslights his company supplied. The steam barons all indicated their territories like that—the Blue King, the Violet Queen, and the rest. At sunset, the multicolored globes turned London into a patchwork glory of light. It was a beautiful sight, even though it was evidence of the stranglehold the council had on London and all the Empire. But the peace that held the council together and the rebels at bay was every bit as fragile as those colored globes.

Now Imogen's blood was fizzing with alarm, making her movements quick and clumsy. As Keating was one of the key members, it made sense that any rebel intrigue would be brought to his attention. But to whom was he talking? Imogen nudged the window open another inch and rose up on her knees to peer out. The angle was wrong, and all she could see was grass.

The Gold King dropped his voice until it was just above a murmur. "What are you proposing? An alliance?"

"Why not? I'll help you take care of this business."

Curiosity was driving Imogen wild. She gripped the edge of the casement and gathered her courage. Then she poked her head out, long braid swinging, feeling rather like a jack-in-the-box. It was the only way to look straight down at the men below. Then she ducked back inside, pulling the window with her so that it was all but shut again.

Holy blazing hat ribbons! The other man was William Reading, the Scarlet King, another one of the Steam Council, and one with his fingers deep into the military might of the Empire. *Two rival steam barons teaming up against a third? Is that what's going on?* And what about the bomb? Who or what was the target?

"And in return for your help?" Gold asked Scarlet.

"We have other interests in common. You, I've heard, had your hands on the only example of an intelligent navigation device. You know, the magic machine called Athena's Casket."

Imogen sucked in her breath, wondering where this twist in the conversation would lead. Even she knew that intelligent navigation was the holy grail of warship design. It combined an air deva with navigational equipment, essentially giving the ship extraordinary lift and a mind of its own, with all the quickness and maneuverability that implied.

Keating made an angry noise. "Only to destroy it. I don't hold with using magic. It's not legal in the Empire."

"Of course," Scarlet replied, though he sounded skeptical. "I understand your position completely. Dodgy stuff, all those glowy orbs and whatnot."

More to the point, machines that used something besides steam power would eventually put the utility magnates on the trash heap. And that was why the steam barons had made hunting down magic the next best thing to a religious crusade crossed with a national sport. Magic was their rival. Anyone claiming to use real power was subject to jail and probably execution or—if there was some suspicion they actually had the hereditary talent referred to as the Blood— a trip to Her Majesty's laboratories for testing.

Imogen's stomach began to ache with tension. She was well aware that her friend Evelina already knew how to put devas inside clockwork machines—exactly the information the steam barons were after. Imogen guarded that secret as if her own life depended on it, because Evelina's certainly did.

"Unless," continued Scarlet in a harder tone, "one of us learns to control magic-powered machinery first. Whoever wins that race wins the Empire. So, friend, what happened to this prototype?"

"It was stolen," Keating growled.

"That's what I've heard." Again, he sounded like he only half believed Keating. "Rumors of pirates using demons to subdue their prey. Making whole ships vanish in a puff of smoke."

Keating grunted, the single sound rich with disgust. "I know who has the casket. The problem is catching him. It's not as simple as it sounds."

"Let me help you," the Scarlet King replied. "I have a fleet of small, nimble airships."

"You don't think I've tried?"

"You have admirable vessels, but my men are trained for surveillance. Wherever it has gone, the device can be retrieved. Discreetly, of course. That's what I want for stopping your bomber. You and I pool our resources and get that device before someone else from the council does. We study it and share whatever technical information we learn."

"It's magic."

"It's an edge. Any one of us will use it if we can, and I plan to use it against the rebels."

Imogen closed her eyes, the ache in her stomach spreading to her whole frame. Evelina's friend—the handsome circus rider Niccolo—had stolen the casket. Had he turned pirate? She hadn't heard that tale, but sometimes the really important news never made it to the papers. Men like Keating wouldn't want the whole Empire after his prize, so they would keep something like that quiet. *Nick as a pirate?* Imogen mused. *He would look good with a cutlass and parrot.*

Imogen's heart pounded as she strained to hear the voices. Angry and urgent, they were almost whispering now, making it hard to pick out words. It sounded like more on the same subjects: rebels, bombs, the navigation device, building an alliance against the other barons. Imogen wasn't a diplomat's daughter for nothing; she could tell the combination of these topics spelled trouble around the Steam Council's table—and that meant trouble for everybody.

Fingers trembling, she nudged the window open again, hoping to hear despite the mumbling. This time, the blasted hinge gave a squeak. She froze.

"What's that?" the Scarlet King demanded. "Look, there's a light above."

Keating replied in a weary tone. "That's Imogen Roth's room. She's a frail thing and always sleeps with a light."

A frail thing? Well, bollocks to you, Keating, I have your secrets.

There was silence, then a scuffle of feet on the gravel, as

if someone was shifting nervously. "Let's go inside," muttered the Scarlet King.

More footfalls. Imogen waited, counting to twenty before she risked making a noise. Then she dove for her bed, burrowing below the covers to find some residual warmth—and to appear innocently asleep if anyone came to check.

But if she hadn't been wide awake before, she was now. Bombs? In London? Ordinarily, one would tell the police, but their supervisors were owned by one steam baron or another. When it came to something like this, their hands were tied.

Still, she had to tell someone what she knew—someone who understood bombs and power struggles, and someone who could warn Evelina's Nick. Unfortunately, there was no one in her family she could trust, and the man she loved was banned from seeing her.

Imogen felt very alone, her nerves worn to nothing, her eyes sandy from too little sleep. She wasn't a swashbuckling heroine who dangled from cliff tops and taught dragons to play fetch. That was more in Evelina's line. Nor was she a brilliant detective; that was Evelina's uncle, Sherlock Holmes. But maybe that was where she should start—by finding a way to contact her friend. Her father had banished Evelina, too—he seemed to take umbrage against anyone Imogen liked—but enough time had passed that maybe she could find a way around his dislike. Then there was still the matter of Tobias and Evelina—now there was a disaster—but that wasn't a question for a tired brain.

It was the start of a plan, and that made her feel better. As Imogen lay in the soft glow of the candle, staring at the moonlit windowpane, she wondered one more time who was meant to be the victim of the bomb. And what kind of man would build such a thing?

The fear she felt was eerily similar to the miasma of her dreams. As Evelina's uncle was known to say, the game was afoot—and it almost certainly had evil in mind.

CHAPTER THREE

THE DOOR TO 221B BAKER STREET OPENED AND A BODY HUR-
tled over the threshold, causing Evelina Cooper to skitter
backward. The body landed with a wheeze on the hot sidewalk, arms and legs sprawling.

In her haste to back up, Evelina stepped into the street itself and narrowly avoided collision with a speeding steam
cycle. With a silent curse, she caught her balance against the
wrought-iron post of a gaslight, wondering what sort of a
mood her uncle was in. Projectile clients were never a good
sign.

The man on the sidewalk moaned. One hand groped awkwardly, as if seeking any solid object to cling to, and fastened on her right foot in its gray kid boot. As the only
weapon Evelina had was her parasol, she swiped at the im-
portunate fingers, delivering a smart tap with the furl of
pale pink silk.

"Sir, unhand my toes." Then she frowned. That hadn't
sounded quite right.

The man didn't move, instead emitting another groan.
She studied him for a moment, the August sun warm against
her shoulders. His limbs appeared to bend in the usual
places and no blood was pooling around the prone body, but
he lay perfectly still. Delicately, she pushed his fingers away
with the ivory tip of her parasol and wondered whether she

should send for Dr. Watson. The good doctor had married and moved out of Baker Street, but he always came at once when her uncle required his services—which seemed to be with disturbing regularity.

Evelina's shoulders hunched. Passersby were giving her strange looks. As she looked up, a lady with a perambulator crossed the street, obviously avoiding the strange tableau.

"Spare him no sympathy, niece of mine, he is but refuse tossed into the gutter." The voice came from the doorway, and Evelina turned to see Sherlock Holmes glowering out at them. Tall and spare, his black-suited form was an exclamation point in the doorway. The long, lean lines of his face pulled into a frown. He jerked his chin toward the sprawling form. "That individual is engaged in a perfidious plot. I suggest you step away from him at once. Quickly."

They hadn't seen each other for months, and one might have expected a hello or a polite inquiry about one's health— but Evelina knew better than to expect social niceties from Holmes when there was a villain adorning the front walk. "A plot to what end?"

"Come inside and I'll give you the details."

"What about him?"

"I'll call a street sweeper," Holmes said mordantly.

Evelina caught a glimpse of movement from the fallen man, but her attention didn't stay on him. Suddenly the house rumbled, and then a cloud of thick black smoke belched from the upstairs study window. There was a female shriek behind Holmes.

"Mrs. Hudson!" Evelina cried, and Holmes turned to check on his landlady.

The man on the ground chose that moment to spring to life. He rolled away from Evelina, coming to his feet in a practiced move. She saw the shape of a gun as his coat swung wide with the motion. Acting on instinct, she thrust the point of her parasol into his spine, the force of the blow splintering the wooden handle of her makeshift weapon. He staggered forward with a grunt, but then he used the momentum to sprint toward the door, drawing the gun as he ran.

Panic bit hard and fast, freezing a cry of outrage deep in her throat. Evelina grabbed for the man, but her fingers just brushed the back of his wool coat. She followed as quickly as a bustle and stays would allow, skirts swinging like a bell, but he was already through the door. She grabbed the frame and hauled herself forward, narrowly avoiding a fall as her heel caught on the sill. She skidded to a stop in the dim light of the front hall. She was alone.

Her uncle had vanished, as had his attacker. Evelina turned slowly, taking in her surroundings. Smoke hung in the air like stinking black breath, but there was no damage she could see. The explosion—for that was surely what had caused the disturbance—had been confined upstairs. And where was Mrs. Hudson?

For a moment the only sound was the clamor of voices outside. A man with a booming voice was explaining that the detective who lived upstairs was a chemist, fond of smelly experiments. An old gent with a wheezy tenor was sure the radicals had struck. No one barged in with offers of help.

"Mrs. Hudson?" she asked in a stage whisper.

"I'm here." The housekeeper materialized at the door leading to the lower apartments. She was still a handsome woman, straight-backed and neat as a pin, but now her face was ashen. "That man chased your uncle up to his study."

Evelina edged toward the foot of the stairs. Pausing for a moment, she listened to the sudden, ominous silence. Her brain wanted to lunge forward, but her feet were obstinately glued to the carpet. Evelina didn't like the fact the armed man had the higher ground and the staircase offered no cover, but there was no alternative—except to do nothing.

A gunshot cracked overhead, echoing ferociously in the tiny front hall. Somewhere on the second floor, a window smashed. Evelina looked up at the sweep of the staircase that led up to her uncle's suite. Feet thundered overhead. Evelina grabbed her parasol more tightly, and then noticed its splintered handle. It drooped like a wilted tulip. She tossed it aside and picked up the no-nonsense broom that Mrs. Hudson had left beside the door.

"You're *not* going up there, young lady!" Mrs. Hudson announced, grabbing Evelina's arm. "I'm fetching the constables."

The landlady was being perfectly reasonable, but the voices inside Evelina were not. She had lost her parents, and Holmes was the one remaining relative who had shown her any understanding. She wasn't about to squeal and run away in a flutter of ribbons—and after growing up in a circus, she had more skills than the average debutante. "You go. I'll do more good here."

"Miss Cooper!" the landlady protested.

"I'll be fine." Evelina heard her voice crack with doubt, but somehow speaking the words broke her stasis. Lifting her skirts in one hand, she took all seventeen stairs in a single, silent rush, the broom poised for action. She crept toward Holmes's study door, staying close to the wall. The smell of gunpowder was thick enough to make her nose run.

Crack! She heard a bullet hit the plaster on the opposite side of the wall, from within her uncle's study. It punched through the wall just above her head and dust rained down, tickling her face. Evelina hurried the last few steps to the study entrance, peering around the carved oak of the door frame. A quick glance told her the path to Dr. Watson's old desk was clear. Watson had always kept his service revolver there. She wondered whether her uncle, who adapted to change with as much ease as rocks learned to fly, had replenished the firearm drawer when the doctor had left.

But the thought went by in an instant, pushed aside by the tableau directly ahead. Holmes knelt on the bearskin rug before the fireplace, facing Evelina. The stranger stood a little to her left, with his back to her and his gun aimed at Holmes's head. Swirls of black particles sifted through the air, eddying on the warm August breeze and settling on the litter of papers and other debris scattered across the floor. The room—never exactly tidy—was in a terrible state, but she didn't take the time to thoroughly catalogue the damage. That could wait.

"We were having a conversation before you threw me out," the man growled at Holmes.

Evelina noticed the accent sounded neither working class nor quite gentry. That made him one of the many in between. These were hard times for men like that, so many trying to scrabble upward while most slid farther behind. And that fit with his clothes—tidy, but inexpensive, his shoes in need of patching. In any other circumstances she might have taken him for a clerk or a lesser type of tutor— almost middle aged, nondescript, and the type one would pass without a second look. Of course, that might have been the whole idea.

Holmes said nothing, his entire body as communicative as the fire screen behind him.

"There's no point in keeping quiet." The man shifted his grip on the gun, as if his hand was growing tired. At the same time, he was using one foot to move the papers around on the floor, taking quick glances to see what they were. More correspondence had landed on the nearby basket chair, and he picked up a handful, quickly scanning the letters and tossing them aside. Clearly, he was looking for something.

At least that meant he was fully occupied. Silently balanced on the balls of her feet, Evelina eased into the room. She saw a minute tightening of her uncle's mouth, but he gave no other indication that he saw her.

Now what? She took another glance around the room. Some of the furniture had tipped over in the blast, but other pieces, like the desks, were still miraculously upright. Watson's desk was directly to her right, just past the dining table. If she moved in utter silence, she could open the drawer, grab the gun she hoped was there—and loaded— and shoot the intruder before he shot her or her uncle. If she remained utterly silent and if she were fast enough, her plan might work.

Or she could creep up and knock him unconscious with the broom handle. She might get shot that way, too, but the whole scheme sounded simpler.

"Even if you think your way out of this with that big head of yours," the man went on while throwing more papers to the floor, "someone else will come. I won't be your only visitor, I can promise you that. The Steam Council is on to you."

So what did the steam barons want with her uncle? As far as she knew, Holmes was in favor with Keating after he had exposed a forgery scheme that had robbed the Gold King of a fortune in antique artifacts. If they survived the next hour, she would have to ask.

Lifting the broom high, Evelina ghosted forward, walking slowly so that her skirts didn't rustle.

"Your brother knows who the members of the shadow government are. But he is a hard man to catch outside the walls of his home or club."

Holmes finally spoke, only the quickness of his words betraying his nerves. "If you believe that I have my brother's complete confidence, you are sorely mistaken."

"Putting a hole in your head might draw him out."

A derisive smirk flickered over Holmes's face. "I think not."

Evelina raised the broom high above her head.

"I'll give it a try anyhow. Unless you want to talk." The man snatched up a calling card, read the name, and flicked it aside. Then he adjusted his aim a fraction, focusing completely on Holmes. "The council has heard the name Baskerville. They'd like to know something about that. It would save time if you pointed me to your correspondence with the rebel ringleaders."

Holmes lifted his brows slightly. "The steam barons have played you for a fool."

Evelina struck. There must have been a noise—a whistle of air through the bristles, perhaps—because the man turned at just the wrong moment. Rather than knocking him out, the broom handle glanced off his temple with a hollow crack, sending him stumbling into the basket chair next to the rug.

Then Holmes was on his feet, hammering the man in the jaw with a hard right hook. The gun went spinning away, clattering under the table. The man dove for it but so did Evelina, using her speed and smaller size to wriggle between the chairs first. For the second time that day, he grabbed her foot, this time trying to use it to drag her out of his way. Then Holmes was on him. That gave her enough time to grab the slick handle of the revolver. It was still warm from his hand.

Evelina kicked the man off and twisted around so that she was on her knees. Holmes hauled the man back and punched him again. This time the man stayed where he fell. Evelina felt a bit ridiculous, crawling out from under the table and trying not to get tangled in her petticoats, but she eventually got to her feet.

She pointed the gun at the writhing man's belly. "Don't move," she said, squeezing the weapon so that it would not shake.

"You bloody hoyden." The man's face twisted as red streamed down his lip and chin, bubbling with his wheezing breaths. "I didn't plan on killing you when I started, but I can see you're an apple off the same tree."

"Confine yourself to answering questions," she said crisply.

He wiped his nose on his sleeve, staining the fabric crimson. Evelina winced in sympathy—there was little doubt Holmes had broken the man's nose—but she kept the muzzle of the revolver squarely aimed. His eyes, red-rimmed and blurred with pain, were still bright with anger.

Holmes, with the air of one who is about to put out the trash, strode briskly toward them. He bent and, quickly and efficiently, searched the man for other weapons. He found a knife, a pocketbook—which he examined, taking out several papers and looking them over—a small flask—which he opened and sniffed—and a ticket stub from a music hall. Holmes set the items aside and took the gun from her. And however little she liked the idea of holding a man at gunpoint, Evelina felt oddly bereft as she surrendered it. A primitive instinct had already marked the intruder as her prey.

"My dear," Holmes said, "would you please reassure the crowd outside that nothing is amiss?"

She suddenly became aware of the hubbub in the street. "What shall I tell them?"

"Whatever you like, but if you see a scruffy young lad

named Wiggins, would you ask him to call for, um, for our mutual friend?"

Evelina stared for a moment, but knew better than to ask for details. Gingerly, she picked her way across the blasted room. Shards of glass framed the view of the brown brick building across Baker Street, with its neat white sashes and bay windows. Mrs. Hudson's lace curtains lay in shreds.

Carefully, she put her head out the hole in the shattered pane. There was a crowd gathered below, their upturned faces all wearing identical looks of bald curiosity. Someone in the street shouted a halloo, and Evelina waved. "Nothing to worry about. Just an accident with the kettle. No need to concern yourself."

A boy of about twelve, wearing ill-fitting clothes and ragged shoes, slouched against the lamppost. "That musta been some cuppa!"

"Yes, it was a very large kettle," Evelina replied. "Are you Wiggins?"

"Indeed I am, miss."

Evelina cast a glance over her shoulder, but her uncle hadn't moved. She knew he employed street urchins from time to time as a kind of messenger service that not even the steam barons could infiltrate. Wiggins had to be one of them. She turned back to the boy. "Mr. Holmes wishes to speak to your mutual friend."

"Right you are." The boy did an about-face and bolted down the street at a dead sprint. Apparently that mutual friend was well known.

She pulled her head back inside, her curiosity getting the better of her. "Who is your friend?"

"Someone equipped to take this charming specimen into custody," her uncle said flatly.

The man swore.

Holmes gave him a freezing look. "Silence. There is a young lady present."

The man shifted, his face sullen.

"Mrs. Hudson already went for the constables," Evelina said.

"Won't find any," their prisoner put in. Perhaps he had

friends who were keeping the local plods occupied. Evelina hoped it wasn't anything worse than that.

Holmes looked unimpressed. "Even so, we dare not waste time." Impatiently, he waved her over and handed her the gun again. "Keep him still."

With that Holmes crossed to his collection of chemical supplies and surveyed the racks of bottles intently, clasping his hands behind his back as if to deliver a lecture on the laws of aether. He stood for so long that Evelina grew bored and longed to let her gaze roam around the room rather than keeping her attention on the man on the floor. She'd caught glimpses of the soot-stained walls, the paintings hanging crooked. The explosion appeared to have emanated from a spot near the window.

"What blew up?" she asked.

"A brown paper package." Holmes finally selected an amber glass bottle from the chemical supplies and then began rummaging in his desk. "It was badly placed and badly made, if the intent was to obliterate my rooms and everyone in them. Although this looks like a great deal of damage, an efficient bomb would have reduced 221B Baker Street to a smudge." Eventually he took out a leather case and opened it, revealing a hypodermic needle. He took it out and began filling it from the vial of liquid.

Evelina's stomach squirmed at the sight of the long, sharp instrument. "I hope that's a sedative."

Holmes gave a flicker of a smile, but otherwise ignored the question as he squirted a few drops out the needle. "This individual—Elias Jones by name, and his pocketbook concurs with that identification—entered the premises on the pretense of hiring my services. He brought with him a package wrapped in butcher's paper and string, and proceeded to spin a tale about a mysterious Dresden figurine I would find inside the box, and how it held the clue to the grisly murder of an elderly aunt and her fourteen cats, and how he had been cheated of his inheritance."

"Fourteen cats?" Evelina echoed in surprise.

"It was not clear whether they were among the victims." Her throat tightened as he turned, hypodermic in hand.

She tried to keep her voice light. "Perhaps the felines conspired to steal the old lady's fortune?"

He gave her a dry look. "My would-be client's laundry needed attention, and the box had a distinct chemical odor inconsistent with fine china. It was evident to me that he was attempting some sort of ruse. Accordingly, I refused his case and told him why. Then he became obstreperous and began demanding information. I summarily threw him out the door for his trouble, before he even had a chance to resist."

"Or draw his gun," Evelina observed, feeling more than a little queasy about what might have happened.

"Quite." Holmes looked uncomfortable. "I apologize for tossing an armed man so close to where you were walking. That was unforgivably careless of me."

"I'm sure you were quite occupied at the time."

"I was annoyed," Holmes replied. "Mr. Jones seems to be under the misapprehension that I know about Mycroft's work simply because I am his brother. He could not be more wrong."

"And the part about the rebels?"

"There is no telling why he assumes we are connected to the dissidents."

That made Evelina's breath catch. *Not exactly a denial, Uncle. What are you up to?* The rebellion against the Steam Council was growing, and had been more and more in the papers over the summer. Anyone identified as a rebel automatically faced the gallows.

"What about it, Mr. Jones?" Holmes asked in a terrifying voice, holding the needle just where the man could see it. "Did your masters give you the order to insinuate yourself into my confidence in the guise of a client, and then search my quarters for evidence of treachery?"

Evelina swallowed hard. Uncle Mycroft worked for the government, but the Steam Council had so many politicians in their power, it was hard to know where the elected officials ended and the steam barons began. Loyalties were nothing if not complicated.

It was far easier for her to concentrate on more immediate

problems. "If Mr. Jones knew his cover story was blown, why run back inside?"

"Indeed, why?" Holmes asked, leaning yet closer.

Jones grunted, flinching away from the needle.

The detective gave a thin smile. "Very well, keep your confessions for now and allow me to speculate. I spoiled your plan when I saw through your nonsense and tossed you to the street. There was no means of gaining information from the curb, so you had to get back inside if you wanted to earn your pay. At that point, direct questioning at gunpoint had to do. Not very subtle, but what does one expect from someone who is little more than hired muscle?"

"I still don't understand the bomb," said Evelina. "Why blow up the very person or place that can provide information?"

Holmes waited, giving Jones a chance to answer for himself, but the man remained mute, holding his hand to his bloody nose.

"That is rather less clear to me," the detective mused. "He was carrying a small amount of a strong sedative, which suggests that he might have attempted to drug me. That would allow him to search my rooms at leisure, find a list of rebel names or whatever else he dreamed would be among my possessions, leave, and set off the incendiary device. Effective, since it delivers a supposed blow to the rebels and covers his deception in the same stroke."

"But what if you had asked to see the figurine in the box?"

"The box might have been constructed to accommodate both a bomb and a prop for his masquerade."

Jones made a noise that might have been agreement, but Evelina couldn't tell. "Perhaps, though why risk setting a timer when there was no way to tell when his search would be over? It would have made more sense to set it once his search was done."

She knew her uncle well enough to see under his insouciant mask. He didn't know the answer to that question any more than she did.

"Accident?" Holmes mused. "Stupidity? You overreached yourself when you went up against me, Jones."

Jones squeezed his eyes shut.

Perhaps he bit off more than he could swallow, but even fools kill people. Evelina's skin pebbled with horror at what might have happened, and she looked down, thinking how easy it would be to pull the trigger on Jones right then and there.

And then, with a look of vague distaste, Holmes pulled a handkerchief from his pocket and tossed it to Jones to stanch the blood dribbling from his nose. As the man grabbed it from the air, Evelina noticed the smudges on his cuffs and understood the laundry comment her uncle had made earlier. "Gunpowder."

"Precisely. Careless inattention to detail."

Jones visibly cringed as he pressed the handkerchief to his face, but then he caught sight of Holmes advancing with the needle, obviously meaning to use it now. He made a low noise and tried to squirm backward. "Please, guv'nor, don't kill me."

Holmes was impassive. "You should have considered the consequences before you walked through my door with violence in mind."

Evelina's shoulders were in knots, the gun shaking in her hands. Elias Jones had tried to kill her uncle and had nearly blown her up in the bargain, but her insides still turned to ice. "Uncle?"

Wordlessly, Holmes caught Jones's arm and began unbuttoning the filthy cuff and pushing up his sleeve. The man struggled furiously, making a choking sound of disgust and fear as Holmes jabbed the needle into his arm. Her uncle's jaw twitched as he depressed the plunger, and Jones quieted at once, his eyes rolling back in their sockets. His silence disturbed Evelina almost more than his fear.

"Did you, uh . . ." she whispered, letting the gun droop.

"No." Holmes narrowed his eyes. "Although that might be his preference by the end."

Her mouth went dry. *What the devil is going on?*

There was a scamper of young feet on the stairs, followed by a heavier tread. A moment later, Wiggins burst into the room, followed by a man. He was about thirty, tall and lean, with curling, sandy hair and small wire-rimmed glasses tinted a pale green. As he surveyed the room, he wore the look of someone who was perpetually amused and slightly dangerous.

"Allow me to introduce the Schoolmaster," Holmes said cordially, stepping away from Jones's still form as if drugging a man senseless was an everyday event.

The Schoolmaster? Evelina had never met a man with a code name before, but in her uncle's line of work she supposed such things occurred—and she would fall on her own parasol before letting on she was anything but *au courant* in the detecting game.

Holmes gave a brisk nod to the boy and tossed him a shilling. "Well done, Wiggins." The lad caught it and was out the door again in a flash.

Then Holmes turned to the Schoolmaster. "Look what my niece has caught for you."

"Indeed." The Schoolmaster grinned appreciatively at Evelina.

His easy smile brought heat to her cheeks and irritated her all at once. She wasn't in the mood for flirtation. "May I put this gun down now?"

Her uncle laughed. "And deprive my friend here of the spectacle of my lovely niece holding one of the prime villains of London at bay?"

"I will point out that I subdued him with a broom," Evelina replied coolly. "If he is a prime villain, then crime in London is in decline."

The Schoolmaster took the opportunity to flip Jones over and pin his hands. Evelina stepped aside to give him room.

"Well, perhaps he is a step or two down from prime," Holmes replied, turning to the Schoolmaster. "You'll be interested in this one. I had to confirm the identification, for I have not seen the man in the flesh for over a decade. Elias Jones is an old hand at the nastiest sorts of thuggery and is currently in the employ of the Blue King. Now there is a match of master and man to make the blood run cold."

Evelina recoiled from the man. The Blue King—better known as King Coal—was the eccentric steam baron who ran the worst parts of East London, squeezing whatever he could from the impoverished residents. Anyone who worked for him had to be either pitied or reviled. Looking at Elias Jones, lying bloody and unconscious on the floor, she decided it was probably both.

The Schoolmaster withdrew a set of handcuffs the like of which she'd never seen before. He snapped a heavy cuff on Jones's right wrist, and then a tendril of steel automatically snaked out to catch the left. The steel was so many-jointed that it was almost ropelike, but it snapped shut with a sharp click. No sooner had the sound faded than another rope sprang out to catch the man's waist, then more slithered down his legs to hobble his ankles. Evelina was transfixed.

"How do those work?" she asked. The need to know was almost a hunger. She loved all things mechanical, and the design of the manacles was elegant, even fascinating, for all that they made her shiver.

The man gave her a teasing look, clearly planning to make her work for the information, and then turned back to Holmes. "Jones? I know this one's reputation—a sly rat, if there ever was one. How long will he be unconscious?"

Holmes gave a slight shrug. "At least an hour."

"Good."

"He is really that fearsome then?" Evelina asked, still eyeing the manacles.

The Schoolmaster frowned, which she took as a worrying affirmative. "Why did the Blue King send him here?"

Holmes answered. "No doubt he wants what all men want from me—answers or silence."

No, thought Evelina, *it's not that simple. They think you know something you shouldn't.* Now that the crisis was past, her mind was churning out questions. She knew that her Uncle Mycroft had his carefully manicured fingers in a great many pies, both literal and figurative—and apparently at least one pie was volatile enough to interest a steam baron and to make Holmes hide that fact from Evelina. *A shadow government? Baskerville?*

The Schoolmaster glanced down at his prisoner. "Shall we take him in, then?"

She wondered where "in" was since she very much doubted that they were referring to the police. If her uncle had wanted Scotland Yard, he would have sent Wiggins for Inspector Lestrade. And who was this Schoolmaster? The steam barons would want to ask him a great many questions about those restraints. Makers weren't allowed to ply their trade without the Steam Council's approval.

Holmes looked critically at Jones. "We'll need a cab. The closer to the back entrance the better."

"I have a Steamer around the corner," the Schoolmaster replied. He turned to Evelina, touching the brim of his hat. "If you'll excuse us, miss."

She nodded mutely and turned to her uncle. "I was planning to have my trunk delivered from the station . . ."

"Oh, by all means," he said with a flap of his hand. "Mrs. Hudson has your room ready. When she's back from her quest for constables, perhaps you could ask her to sweep up and call the glazier. In the meantime, some letters have arrived for you. Invitations and whatnot. I'm sure they will keep you occupied until I return."

CHAPTER FOUR

FEELING SUDDENLY LOST, EVELINA WATCHED HER UNCLE and the Schoolmaster carry Jones out the study door with as much ceremony as if he were a sack of spuds. She had been sucked into the action the moment she had set foot in 221B Baker Street, but had just as suddenly been cut adrift. Hesitantly, she set the gun on the dining table.

Evelina didn't want to sip tea and read letters. Questions needed answering, and there was danger afoot. Besides, after spending the summer with Grandmamma Holmes in Devonshire, the last thing she wanted was one more minute of being polite and quiet. *Come now. Don't be greedy. One explosion should be enough for any afternoon.*

Evelina heard a door open and close downstairs. The back door; the men leaving. With a wave of an inexpressible emotion—maybe loss, maybe relief—she realized that she was alone in the slightly smoking silence of her uncle's residence. As the tension drained out of her, she released a sigh and looked around. *What a mess.*

Evelina looked out the window one last time. The crowd had finally wandered away, and there was still no sign of Mrs. Hudson. At loose ends, Evelina picked up the broom she had used on Jones's head and pushed the debris littering the floor into a pile. The dining table, though still on its feet, had been swept clean by the path of destruction. She recognized pieces of Mrs. Hudson's good Blue Willow china and felt a pang of regret. She bent down to gather some of the scattered papers, careful not to cut herself on the shards of crockery.

The *Times* was splayed across the floor, the charred pages crumbling as she picked them up. Without intending to read, her eyes flicked over the words that were still legible, as if their fragility made them somehow more important. It was the previous day's edition.

> *Yesterday afternoon, Mr. George Collier, the Deputy Coroner for the South-Eastern Division of Middlesex, re-sumed his inquiry at the Working Lads' Institute, Whitechapel-road, respecting the death of the woman who was found dead at George-yard-buildings, on the early morning of Tuesday, the 7th of this month with no less than 39 wounds on various parts of her body. The body has been identified as that of MARTHA TABRAM, aged 39 or 40 years . . .*

And then the paper, and the story of the dead woman, turned to ash. "Thirty-nine stab wounds," Evelina mur-mured to herself, then dropped the crumbling paper onto the pile of debris. It was a horrible image, but her thoughts slid away quickly. After a bomb and a gun and those manacles that seemed to have a life of their own, she couldn't absorb anything that wasn't relevant to her immediate problems. She still had to decide how far she dared to push her uncle for information on Mycroft's activities. And Jones had men-tioned Baskerville. She'd heard the name before, but couldn't remember where.

Then she saw a scattering of envelopes and bent to scoop them up. A few were singed, but most were merely sooty. These must have been the letters Holmes had referred to. She turned them over, reading the addresses. Most were to Holmes, and a few to Dr. Watson—even if he wasn't cur-rently residing at Baker Street. Two of them were for her— one from the Ladies' College of London, where she had plans to apply, despite what her grandmother thought proper. She admired the elegant crest on the envelope, and even the feel of the thick bond paper filled her with eagerness. College was everything she wanted, and she hoped Holmes could convince Grandmamma to let her attend.

The other letter was small and square, the envelope a pale pink sealed with green wax. With a tingle of pleasure, she recognized the graceful handwriting of her closest friend, the Honorable Miss Imogen Roth. Then Evelina frowned. After the debacle last April, Evelina had been sent away from Hilliard House, the Roth's London address, and Imogen had been forbidden to write.

About four months ago, Imogen's father, Lord Bancroft, had been part of a forgery scheme that had robbed Jasper Keating, the steam baron known as the Gold King, of a fortune in antique artifacts. Holmes had uncovered the elaborate crime with Evelina's help. Sadly, while Keating had been pleased and the scandal had been kept out of the papers, the affair had still made her very unpopular with Lord B—so much so that she'd left London until things cooled down.

And I never heard from Tobias again. Evelina had done her best not to think about Imogen's older brother since— not that she had succeeded. That hadn't been the sort of scene one got over in a few short months.

Now here she was, with the square pink envelope in her hand. She almost preferred bombs and shadow governments to this bit of feminine paper that would surely slip past her defenses, no matter what news it held. Friendship, she'd learned, was a perilous vulnerability—all the more potent when that love held deep and strong. Imogen was the school friend with whom she had shared everything from skinned knees and sums to their first real ball. On top of that, Evelina had been practically part of the Roth family for her entire adolescence. She longed to be welcomed back into that fold. For far too long, it had been the only family she'd known—and she'd lost it all last April. It had been like being orphaned all over again—and being a grown woman was no protection from that kind of pain.

So why was Imogen allowed to write her now? *Something new has happened.* A little nervously, Evelina broke the seal and unfolded the letter.

My dearest E,

I have a thousand things to tell you, but let me begin with the obvious. I've heard you're coming to London! I had it from the Duchess of Westlake, who had it from your grandmother, so I know it's true. And I hope your uncle will think to forward this to you from his address, since I'm not sure where you'll be.

It was a fair question, since Evelina was returning to London at a time of year when everyone else had left for the country. She had only come back now to advance her college scheme and—to be utterly truthful—because she longed to be away from her grandmother for a little while. Otherwise, there was little to do in London in August—at least for the fashionable.

High Society gathered in the early spring for the Season— which hit its full stride around Easter, when the debutantes were presented to the queen—and dispersed once the weather grew hot. Right now, the fashionable set was in the North, since August 12 was the official start of the shooting season and the sport was considered superior in or near Scotland—which explained the next few paragraphs of Imogen's letter.

Naturally, I'm dying to see you! We are up here at Maggor's Close, which is a country estate dedicated to the murder of grouse—which began on the Glorious Twelfth and shall no doubt escalate to other feathered victims as the month rolls on. The place was recently purchased by Mr. Keating and the dining room features a great many stuffed stag heads (although, since it's used for hunting grouse, shouldn't there be rows of little bird heads on the wall?). I think it is gloomy, but Papa professes to admire it greatly.

Evelina stopped reading, a bitter taste flooding her mouth. She knew that Jasper Keating had more money than Midas, so a hunting estate wasn't a surprising purchase—but his guest list was. The smart part of her knew it shouldn't have

been, but her idealistic side wanted to deny the twisting cal-
culations that had made Lord Bancroft his admiring house-
guest. However amiably they behaved in public, Jasper
Keating was Lord Bancroft's bitter adversary—after all, it
was his treasure that Lord B had been stealing. Keating
must have felt secure in the price he'd made Bancroft pay for
his deception, if he had the scheming viscount under his
roof.

And it had been a steep price indeed—Lord Bancroft had
more or less given Keating his only son and heir. Tobias was
a talented inventor, just the sort of genius Keating needed in
his steam-driven empire, and Tobias had stepped into the
breach to save his family's honor. It was a decision Evelina
had to applaud, and yet she hated it down to her boot heels.
Tobias had only just started to become his own man when
circumstance had snatched his freedom away, robbing him
of the opportunity to forge his own future. Suddenly shiv-
ery, Evelina returned to the letter, dreading what she would
read next.

> *But this is getting me no closer to my real purpose for
> writing. I have all kinds of fascinating news, so much
> that I can't begin to set it down in a letter. I asked Papa
> if you might spend some time with us again, now that
> everything has settled down. It is beautiful here, but we
> are short of company, and I desperately want to see you
> again. Mama would like you to come as well—I think she
> misses your calm good sense, since none of her children
> has any. Therefore, being the great schemers we are, we
> played our trump card. Mama and I convinced Alice
> Keating, who remembers you fondly, to add her voice to
> the chorus and, as she is our host's daughter, Papa
> could not very well refuse. So you are officially invited,
> my dear. Please, please say you'll come!*

Evelina's breath caught, an ache catching under her ribs.
So Alice is there, too. She had liked Jasper Keating's red-
haired daughter when they first met. Alice was every bit as

smart as her father, but there was one insurmountable thing that kept her from ever becoming a friend.

Evelina had been on the brink of an engagement with Tobias but, as part of the bargain Tobias had made to save his family, he would be marrying Keating's daughter instead. Grandmamma Holmes had found the betrothal announcement in the papers barely six weeks after Evelina left London.

The only mercy was that she and Tobias had kept their growing affection relatively private. She didn't think Alice had ever been aware of it, and there had been no public gossip to endure. But still, even now Evelina's cheeks burned with emotion—though she could not name it precisely. Shame? Anger? Chagrin? The smoldering ash of desire? She would never recover from the wrench of that parting. To say the very least, it had not gone well. She had to blink away the memory before she could finish the page.

> *And now I can hear the gears turning in your clever mind—yes, I realize this isn't the most pleasant subject for you—but there's bound to be talk about the wedding since it's been moved up to the fourth weekend in September, which means planning is going apace. But please don't let that stop you from coming because Tobias won't be joining us until the visit is almost over, and you can leave before then if you wish. The two of you need never cross paths, and I would be crushed if any discomfort between you kept our friendship from continuing as before.*

Weak with disbelief, Evelina dropped to her knees on the charred carpet, barely noticing the last few sentences. Pain shot up her leg when she landed on a shard of glass, but she ignored it. She stared at the page, reading it over again to be sure she wasn't mistaken about the one word that stood out from the rest. *September?* That was next month. It was one thing to know that she'd lost Tobias, quite another to know that tragedy would be irrevocable so soon.

He loves me, not her. After all that had happened between them, her certainty seemed illogical, but she knew Tobias—

perhaps better than he understood himself. Evelina knew the way his face lit up when his heart was moved—when the man emerged from behind the contradictory and complex mask he'd built. Tobias did not love easily, and he'd never looked at Alice in that unguarded, joyous way he had when his heart was open. That look was how Evelina had known he'd loved her, and that his denial of that love had been an act.

With dawning horror, Evelina glared at the letter, trying to read it a third time but too agitated to make sense of the words. Was everything that had sustained her nothing but a lie?

The wedding had originally been set for next spring, and buried as she was in Devonshire, she'd heard nothing of this change of plan. Yet a September wedding tore her belief in their star-crossed love to shreds. Among the fashionable, engagements of a year or more were increasingly common. According to the sticklers, anything less cast doubt on the propriety of a marriage, and especially on the purity of the bride. Keating and Bancroft—both intensely conscious of public opinion—would carefully avoid anything that might give rise to comment. So what had happened?

There were only so many reasons a couple moved up a wedding date. And now it seemed that Tobias wasn't such a reluctant bridegroom after all.

Damn him! Damn him, damn him!

CHAPTER FIVE

London, August 24, 1888

SOUTH BADGER TANNERY

10:15 p.m. Friday

NICK HOOKED A KNIFE AROUND THE MAN'S THROAT BEFORE the fellow even knew he was there. The blade kissed the skin, denting it without drawing blood—though an unlucky twitch could alter that picture. The moonlight gave few details, but sight wasn't everything. Nick felt the man's surprised start and the jump of his pulse as his heart began to race. There was the rasp of breath, the hot slick of sweat despite the chill air. The tall, slender man at the sharp end of the knife was afraid and doing his best not to show it.

Sensing the advantage, Nick's own body tensed with the primitive thrill of the hunt, but he forced reason to the fore. The moment was too dangerous for anything but cool calculation. Maybe that's why the man didn't die when his fingers crept toward the gun strapped at his side.

"Come now, none of that," Nick said in the same low, calm voice he used on nervous horses, and pressed the knife deeper into skin. He was shorter than the man in his grip, but could tell he was easily the stronger. "Gunshots attract attention."

Not that there was anyone around—at least no one that he could see. The stinking tannery—set outside the city for obvious reasons—sat silent. The yard was filled with vats of noxious substances—urine, brains, lime, and who knew what else. Hides cured in the malodorous brews, adding their own rotting scent to the air. Anyone lurking in the yard to catch Nick at this rendezvous had probably passed out.

Except this fellow, who raised his hands in the traditional gesture of surrender. "Right enough."

"Who are you?" Nick demanded.

"The Schoolmaster."

That was the name Nick had been told to expect. "I've never had much to do with school. What do you want?"

"There is a need for your services. An urgent one."

"For me, or for the *Red Jack*?"

"We need you, your ship, and your crew. The job's going to take finesse as well as speed."

Which meant it wasn't going to be easy. Silence fell as Nick allowed himself a moment of reluctance. He heard his second in command moving over the rocky soil, making sure the Schoolmaster had come alone. He wasn't likely to find anyone—there was little to no cover. A few stubborn shrubs grew here and there, but otherwise the land was barren except for the factory walls and its yard full of toxic vats. Even the aether was deserted. Nick had the power to sense nature spirits—the elemental devas that lived in wild places—but no such spirits were anywhere near the place. The tannery had killed the land, and that left him uneasy. No one liked lingering near a corpse.

"Striker?" Nick called.

"There's a vehicle by the gate with some bloke in the back trussed up like a holiday goose." The man's rough voice came out of the darkness, as welcome to Nick as old, comfortable boots.

"The word was for you to come alone," Nick growled into the Schoolmaster's ear. "Or was he the real Schoolmaster and you're someone else?"

"He's not a person," the man's tone was icy. "He's a package for delivery. We need you to take him to where he can be questioned at leisure."

Nick pressed the knife a little closer. "You didn't answer my question."

There was a beat of silence before the man answered. "Then dangle me in front of any member of the Steam Council," the Schoolmaster said dryly. "If you want confirmation of my identity, just listen to their howls for my blood."

"Fair enough. A little melodramatic, but to the point." Nick eased the pressure on the blade just a fraction. "What did your package do?"

"Many things. Most recently, he tried to blow up Sherlock Holmes. If he'd been successful, he would have killed the detective and his niece."

Evie. That got Nick's attention. Even the oblique mention of her made his jaw clench. But there were so many layers of anger and frustration and desire surrounding her memory that he ruthlessly pushed thoughts of her away. That was quicksand he didn't dare step in while there were drawn weapons in play.

"How very uncivil," Nick said sarcastically, lowering the knife and allowing the man to turn around. "Now start explaining what this is all about."

"Do I have your word that you'll hear me out before you refuse the job?"

"I'll give you one minute to state your case. I've found it unwise to stay in one place too long. It's not safe for me, nor for anyone I meet with."

In fact, after cutting the *Leaping Hind* free, Nick had left Captain Hughes and his ship on course for an easy landing just south of the city, but they were never seen again. That bothered him more than he cared to admit, and he wished he'd taken the time to question the man named Bingham.

"Fine. I won't take more of your time than need be." The man turned. The light of the waning moon washed the scene in a ghostly light and outlined the Schoolmaster's long features. He was older than Nick by a few years, his curling hair topped by a low-crowned hat. Wire-rimmed glasses shadowed his eyes and gave him a bookish air. He looked harmless enough, but Nick didn't buy that for a moment. He'd lowered the knife, but he wasn't putting it away.

Striker stepped out of the shadows but stopped a dozen feet away, waiting in case he was needed. His hair stuck out at all angles like a startled hedgehog, framing a blunt-featured face dominated by shrewd, dark eyes. His long coat, covered in bits of metal from top to bottom, glinted dully in the moonlight.

They stood in silence for a moment, but then the Schoolmaster spoke. "Right. We need the package taken to a certain location. There, you'll pick up cargo and take it to another location, unload it in secret, and deliver certain items safely over a land route. But I'll be frank—there are those who would dearly love to get their hands on some of the shipment. There could be danger."

"There's always danger. People don't hire me to deliver the mail."

"You've made quite the name for yourself in a few short months."

"It's a living."

When Nick and Striker met the crew of the *Red Jack*, the vessel had been all but done in. The design was old, the balloon leaky, and the boilers starved for a reliable supply of fuel. The Steam Council's stranglehold on coal had crippled even the pirates. The captain had sold the *Red Jack* and her crew for a pittance. But Nick had money and magic and Striker knew machines. Within weeks they had turned the ship around and made her the new terror of the skies.

"Where do you want me to take the prisoner?" Nick asked. If the man had endangered Evelina Cooper, he'd toss him to his death for free.

"Do I have your word of honor to keep this in confidence?"

Both Nick and Striker nodded. Discretion was just good business.

"North, beyond the Steam Council's reach."

That meant the Highlands—a fair distance to dodge enemy ships, but nothing Nick hadn't done before. "And what am I picking up?"

The Schoolmaster made a face. "Are you planning to do this? If not, you don't need the details."

Nick wanted the details before he made up his mind, but he shrugged. He'd thoroughly researched the Schoolmaster before agreeing to this meeting, and all his contacts had

vouched for the man's credit and his character. He was prepared to move on to the next steps. "What's the pay?"

"We don't have a lot of gold, but we have technical expertise. There are makers who can repair your ship."

It was a good offer, but not one he needed. "I have Striker.
He's as good as any maker alive. We work for expenses and
a cut of the profits. Or didn't they tell you that at the Head?"

The Saracen's Head was the tavern where Nick did his
business in London. It was hardly a gentleman's club, but it
worked just as well for making useful professional contacts.

"We're not selling," said the Schoolmaster. "There is no
profit."

"Then what's the cargo?" Nick asked.

The man frowned, obviously wishing to share as little as
possible. "Mechanical parts. Gears, wheels, springs, pistons—
more or less the type of goods you move already. Mostly German made."

"But you're not selling it?" Nick persisted.

"These are relief supplies," said Striker in a knowing
tone. "You're running parts for the resistance."

For the first time, anxiety showed on the man's face. Join-
ing the resistance was as good as treason. It wasn't something a person let slip lightly. "The parts are relief for the
poor. The nights are growing cold. No one can pay what the
Steam Council asks."

"You know they'll off any backstreet carpenter they find
building a windmill or a waterwheel," Striker said darkly. "I
know. I used to break bones for the Gold King."

The Schoolmaster gave him a sharp look. "I've heard
about you. You're the streetkeeper who bit the hand that fed
him."

"Beat me, more like—and, yeah, I bite."

"Enough to take a job aimed at driving a spike in the un-
derbelly of the council?"

Nick and Striker exchanged a look. Taking a job for rebels
upped the ante. Resistance business meant there would be
more danger, just as the Schoolmaster had warned. All of
the steam barons had combined forces, forging an army
dedicated to wiping it out. That wasn't the same as dodging

the odd excise patrol. It would be a hell-for-leather bolt for their lives.

Plus, there was no real money in the job, and a smuggler had to be practical.

Nick named a sum for expenses. "Plus ten percent of the value of the goods. It's not our problem if you want to give them away."

"Don't you care that the widows and orphans of White-chapel are freezing in the dark?" the man countered.

Of course Nick did, and it was a tribute to his concern that they'd take the job at all. Perhaps that shipment of parts would save a hundred families, but there was a very good chance at least one crewman would die. That was worth something, too. "I'm a smuggler, not your bloody nanny."

"Expenses plus five percent."

"That barely pays for beer."

"I'm not a charity for drunken pirates."

"And I'm the one with the ship."

Nick knew Striker would follow his lead, but he still wanted some assurance the other man was in favor of the scheme. Striker raised his eyebrows, as if to ask what Nick was wait-ing for. His second in command had the kind of grudge against his old master only years of disrespect—followed by a taste of real freedom—can produce.

It was up to Nick to balance a hatred of the Steam Council with the good of the crew—and it was that ability to keep a level head that made him captain. "Seven."

"Done." The Schoolmaster looked pleased, making Nick think he should have gone for eight.

"Not so fast," Nick said. "I still want to hear exactly what you want before we shake on it. I want to know where ex-actly we're supposed to go."

The man let out a sigh. "When you drop off the package on the Isle of Skye, you will pick up cargo—one man and a number of crates. You'll land near Exeter. Your, uh, guest and most of the goods can be left there. Others will take on the task of distribution. But as discussed, some of the cargo must reach London safely, and I know you have the means to achieve that."

"That's a hundred and fifty miles," muttered Striker. "That's a stretch even for our means and ways."

"How much time do we have?" Nick asked.

"As little as possible. There are things which cannot progress until your task is complete."

"What does that mean?"

"Nothing that affects your role—that much I can promise." The Schoolmaster cast a glance over his shoulder. "The next piece of business is getting the package to your ship."

"Can the package walk?" Striker asked.

"He's been heavily sedated. Feel free to use the vehicle. I'll collect it after."

Nick gave Striker a nod. They'd come over fields from where the ship was tethered, but a carriage could follow the road partway there. The big man in his metal-encrusted coat disappeared. Not long after, Nick heard the rumble and hiss of an engine. It wasn't a horse-drawn vehicle then, but one of those Steamers that seemed to be everywhere in London— and which Striker delighted in stealing for recreation. *Interesting. If he has a Steamer, my new boss has money. How did he get mixed up with rebels and Whitechapel widows?*

"Is there anything else you need to discuss?" the Schoolmaster asked.

Nick's body tensed before he even thought to answer. He held up a hand, silencing the man. Then he made a subtle gesture to either side. *Visitors.* They must have been hiding well if Striker hadn't found them along with the Schoolmaster's package.

The other nodded, slowly sliding the gun from the holster under his coat. Nick's skin chilled at the flat anger in his eyes. All of a sudden, the Schoolmaster didn't look so bookish anymore.

They were in for a fight.

CHAPTER SIX

NICK HADN'T PAID A GREAT DEAL OF ATTENTION TO THE tannery, but now he squinted to make out what he could by the vague light of the moon. From his vantage point, he could see through the wide gates into the tannery yard. There were sheds and buildings, but a lot of the operation seemed to be set up outside, probably for the ventilation. Figures were moving around the yard, darting from the shelter of one huge vat to another, and then out through the gates to the scrubland where he stood.

He caught a glimpse of a uniform—a familiar pattern of light braid on dark cloth, barely seen in the uncertain light but still more than enough for alarm. He swore under his breath. "The Scarlet King's men. They're coming from inside the tannery."

"Bugger," the Schoolmaster said in cool tones. "That means they were waiting for us. Probably listening until we told them everything they wanted to know."

And there were more of them than he was seeing. Nick could sense more than hear the footsteps moving in the darkness, as if every shred of his being were suddenly attuned to the fine movement of air. Scarlet's soldiers were good at stealth—he had to give them that. Then again, the penalty for failure was death.

"Do they know we've seen them?" Nick said.

"Hard to tell."

Nick couldn't stop a quiver of panic when he thought of Striker, puttering down the road in the Steamer, or the *Red Jack*, hovering low and vulnerable like a whale trying to hide in a puddle. A curse escaped his lips. Had the soldiers found them? He was the captain. He should know what was happening to his ship. *I have to go. I have to go now.*

His scrambling thoughts were interrupted as the Schoolmaster leaned close and slid something—paper by the sound—into the pocket of Nick's jacket. "When you get to Scotland," he whispered, "the code word is Baskerville."

Baskerville? Was that a person? A place?

But the Schoolmaster stepped away, giving a casual tip of his hat. The long tails of his scarf swung as he turned to go, his eyes sharp with a hellish species of mischief. He raised the pistol in a salute, cocking it with a sharp, metallic rasp. Then he raised his voice in a mocking tone meant for the audience in the shadows. "It's time we said farewell, eh what?"

There was a rustling that said he'd caught their attention.

"Best get this over with, for all it's been a pleasure," said the Schoolmaster. "Safe journey, Captain."

And nothing says safe like a half dozen assassins hiding behind vats of piss and brains. Nick shifted his grip on the knife. Before he'd taken up the life of a thief and a smuggler, he'd been the Indomitable Niccolo, the best trick rider and knife man around—and he'd been no mean acrobat, either. If these fools wanted a show, he'd give them one.

Then the darkness itself seemed to move. The knife left his hand in a graceful arc, anticipating where the gunman would be, and the flash of gunfire blinded him. In the same instant, Nick flew into the air, twisting out of the path of the bullet. He felt it kiss along his thigh, leaving a trail of sharp heat.

"Fardlin' hell!" someone raged.

Nick landed, rolled through a somersault, and came up a foot away from the speaker. A second knife slid out of his boot and into his hand. As he rose, the momentum of his body carrying him forward, he slid the weapon into the man's diaphragm, the slight resistance of cloth and leather giving way to the elastic slide of steel through flesh and the scraping roughness of bone. He felt the man's shudder, the wet, terrified cough as it vibrated through the knife hilt, and then he pulled the weapon away with a sucking jerk.

There was an inarticulate cry behind him, and he whirled, ducking slightly for balance as the wounded man fell to the ground. A third assailant was there, raising his weapon to shoot. Nick kicked that one in the head hard enough to hear his jawbone snap.

The Schoolmaster was trading gunfire with another three. He'd produced a second weapon from somewhere and was shooting two-handed, the ends of his scarf flipping with the recoils. Using the bloody knife in his hand, Nick reduced the man's opponents from three to two.

Suddenly, there was quiet. It had only taken a matter of minutes to end six lives. Nick's knees trembled slightly as tension seeped out of his muscles. The Schoolmaster tipped his hat back with the barrel of one pistol. "Damned fine work. Do you always fight with knives?"

"No." Once, he'd entertained with them, made people laugh and gasp with admiration. Nick slammed an iron door on those memories. "But I like the quiet."

The man's laugh was uneasy. "Well, good luck, Captain. I think we had best go."

But Nick caught his arm. "How did they know we were here?"

The Schoolmaster stiffened. "A traitor, obviously."

That was barely an answer, and not nearly enough to satisfy Nick.

The man must have read it in his silence. "I don't know any more than that, but I'll make it my business to find answers." The Schoolmaster's voice was furred with anger.

Nick released his grip. That was still not good enough, but he had to get to the ship. Then he felt the slippery heat on his fingers. "You're bleeding."

"So I noticed," the Schoolmaster drawled. "Though it's nothing that will keep me from carrying a well-deserved brandy to my lips. Good night, Captain Niccolo."

"Good night, Schoolmaster."

The man was hurt, but was already walking quickly away,

so it couldn't have been any more serious than the sting the bullet had left in Nick's leg. Annoying, but not bad enough to hold him up. Nick paused long enough to collect his knives, then turned and sprinted in the direction of the *Red Jack*. The road looped to the left, but he cut through the rutted field that he and Striker had crossed to reach the tannery. It had been plowed and left in furrows, turning his stride into an ungainly lope. To make matters worse, recent rain had turned the dirt into a boot-sucking mud, but going this way gave him the best chance to catch up to the Steamer. As he crested a rise, he got a clear view of the land.

Straight ahead, where the road jogged, Striker had abandoned the Steamer. The strange-looking vehicle, with two enormous wheels in back and a smaller one in front, looked like nothing so much as a solid-sided birdcage big enough for two people. The engine sat in front beneath a metallic hump that reminded Nick of a snout. A single smokestack puffed out the top, and a round-topped oaken trunk was strapped on at the back for luggage. To date, Nick had declined to ride in one of the vehicles, mostly for aesthetic reasons.

Striker had left the Steamer at the point where the road could take him no closer to the *Red Jack*. Now he had the parcel draped over his shoulders and was trudging toward the far side of the hill where the ship was hovering in a shallow valley. No other airship, however clever the design, could have snuggled out of sight quite so easily, but the *Jack* had a distinct advantage in both its captain and Athena's capabilities.

Nick climbed over a stone stile into another field. This one had a handful of heavy workhorses sleeping in a loose huddle. He ghosted past the animals, breathing in the familiar scent, and then climbed over the fence at the other side of the enclosure.

Now he was standing to the south of the *Red Jack,* with Striker to the west. The Scarlet King's soldiers were crawling over the hills to the northeast, right where the ship's watch would have the most difficulty seeing them. The same little bird that had told them where Nick and the Schoolmaster would meet had also betrayed the location of the *Red Jack*. Who was it?

There was no time to do anything but react. Nick cast out his powers, hoping he was not too far away. "Athena!" he whispered, his lips echoing the thought he screamed with his mind.

What, Niccolo?

"Enemies are coming. Get ready to fly for safety."

Hurry back. Be safe.

"Ring the bell to alert the crew."

You do not need to tell me. I have flown before, my sweet. I have fled the fire of the northern dragons and the claws of the winged lions of Babylon.

"And hopefully the crew was awake when you did it."

Her wordless exasperation reminded him that he was a mere human, and she a powerful spirit who transcended mortal understanding, but Nick didn't give way. The ship's bell clanged, and Nick's stomach unclenched a notch. The crew—by now used to dealing with a presence they couldn't perceive—was warned. Beadle and the others would take things from there.

Nick ran across the next field, casting an anxious glance at Striker's progress. He had set his burden down to rest his back. Anxiety arrowed through Nick, raising the hair on his neck, but he had no power to reach human minds—and no way to warn his friend disaster was closing in.

Piracy carried a death sentence. Magic users—those of the Blood—were burned at the stake or given to Her Majesty's Laboratories for experimentation. Where Nick was concerned, the law—which meant the Steam Council—had far too many choices where his punishment was concerned. And—even worse—he had no idea what that meant for his crew. Death, certainly, but would the council content itself with a simple hanging?

Dark Furies! He leaped a ditch, scrambling to keep his footing, and began running down the side of the valley where the *Red Jack* was hunkered down. He needed to get the ship in the air not just for the sake of the crew but for that of the nearby farmers. He paid them well to ignore the huge ship that paused there from time to time, always at night and for never more than a few hours, but things would not go well if the steam barons discovered they'd been turning a blind eye to smugglers.

Thanks to Athena's powers, the ship could hold its position for an hour or two without the need for mooring lines. It hovered near the side of the valley, close enough that Nick and Striker had been able to climb down the side of the gondola and jump to the ground below. Now Nick slithered down the sloping grass, waving his arms and feeling like an ant trying to signal a buffalo.

The *Red Jack*'s gray silk bulk—the color of rain clouds—filled the valley, the balloon blotting out the stars.

Nick finally caught the attention of Poole, the bosun, who immediately threw a rope ladder over the side. Nick grabbed it and began climbing, his years at Ploughman's Paramount Circus giving him an agility and head for heights equal to his crew. As he got near the rail of the gondola, Poole's anxious face was joined by that of the first mate, Beadle. They grabbed his arms and helped him aboard, then Poole began pulling the ladder up again. Good security meant never leaving the ladder out and unattended.

"We've seen them," Beadle said without preamble. "They're carrying enough firepower to be a problem."

Striker was Nick's second in command and the undisputed king of mechanics, but Beadle knew airships and had flown them into more battles than Nick had birthdays. From his basset-hound face to his large-knuckled hands, he looked like he'd been laundered and left wet in a pile to dry. Now he was turning mournful eyes toward the northeast horizon.

"There are a hundred, at least, sir. They have hot harpoons. We've got five minutes at most before they're here. We'd best leave at once."

Nick flinched. Steam-driven harpoons, wreathed in chemical flame, were an airship's nightmare. They could shred the fabric of the balloon, costing them lift, or worse, there could be fire. In the air, with plenty of wind to fan the flames, it was almost impossible to put a blaze out. About the only good news was that the *Red Jack*—a smuggling ship prone to gun battles—had been converted to run on aether distillate, which was not as explosive as other fuels.

But hot harpoons were not their only problem. "We have to stay low to pick up Striker. I don't leave stragglers. Not when they're off the ship on my orders."

Worry flashed across Beadle's face, saying everything Nick wouldn't. Striker was still halfway across the field and right between the *Red Jack* and the harpoons. "Your loyalty is commendable, sir, but we need distance. Not even this ship can outmaneuver Scarlet's troops if they get grapples on us."

It was true. Athena could steer the ship, providing lift, speed, and precision beyond a normal craft. Striker, ever pragmatic, would understand. But Nick's soul wouldn't. He felt the *Red Jack* shifting beneath his feet as Athena stirred restlessly. "I'm going to pick him up. Tell the crew we're going to stay low and go west."

"Aye, sir."

Aye, sir. Nick felt Athena's mind touch his, drawing out exactly what he wanted to do. It was a connection that had grown since he'd first picked up the cube containing the deva four months ago. At the time, he'd barely understood what it was. Since then, Athena had taught him much about his powers and how they could work together, man and ship, with the precision of trapeze artists.

The ship rose, staying a constant height above the slope of the valley wall. Nick stood by the rail, watching the shadow of the ship blotting out the light of the setting moon. His hand twitched into a fist. To the northeast, he could see the soldiers more clearly now—clumps of men ranging themselves on the other side of the valley, more running for the bridge to get to the west side. In every group, there was one carrying a harpoon gun, the long cylindrical tube like a miniature cannon barrel. With a clench of his gut, Nick tried to guess how far they could reach.

As the vessel rose, he heard a cry go up from the soldiers, then a rifle shot rang out—but the *Red Jack* was too far away for that bullet to matter. Nevertheless, the shot had the same effect as a starter's pistol. Suddenly the deck was seething—men running into battle position, stowing gear, bringing out weapons.

Then the ribbon of road came into view. The School-master's Steamer still sat abandoned, but now it was surrounded. In the midst of the confusion of men, horses, and steam engines sat more harpoon cannons—these big enough to be pushed on wheels.

Black basilisks of hell! None of it made sense to Nick. True, the Steam Council was cracking down on dissent. True, that included catching smugglers—especially those who supplied parts to unauthorized makers. But there had to be a hundred of Scarlet's soldiers and their harpoon cannons out there. Since when did Captain Niccolo and the *Red Jack* warrant that kind of attention? *Since I met with the Schoolmaster.* Who was he? What was Baskerville? And why the blazes was Holmes involved?

Nick shut the storm of questions out of his mind for the moment. *One problem at a time.* The men knew better than he did what had to be done on board, and only he could get Striker and his package onto the ship. *It's time to do what you do best.* Still, he could use an extra pair of hands. "Smith!"

The young man was the dogsbody of the crew. He was little more than a youth, but he was strong enough for what Nick wanted him to do. "I need help hauling in a heavy load."

"Aye, sir. But the baskets are all stowed, sir. Do you want me to go get one?"

Nick tried to envision stuffing an unconscious man inside a basket while dangling alongside a moving ship. It sounded awkward and—from the point of view of someone who'd done his share of aerial tricks—dangerously hard to control.

"No, I need one of Striker's special ropes. The ones with the spring-loaded grapples."

The young man ran to scrabble in a locker.

"You know you can't stop," Nick murmured to Athena. For all he meant to scoop up Striker, they couldn't let the soldiers gain on them. He was the captain, and that meant there was only so much he could gamble, whatever his heart protested. "Keep steady."

I know.

He crossed to the west side of the ship, and there was Striker below, looking up. It was too dark to see his face, but Nick could imagine his alarm as the vessel lifted off without him. Nick tossed the ladder over the side, then Smith produced a dull metal rope fashioned in tiny flexible sections jointed like a lobster's tail. A spring-loaded catch hung from either end. Smith fastened one end to an iron loop on the deck and handed Nick the other. Nick readied himself, crouching on the rail and calculating distance in his mind.

"What are you doing, sir?" Smith's nervousness was plain in his voice.

"I'll need you to haul up Striker's load. Get Poole to help."

"What about Mr. Striker?"

"He can get himself up the ladder if he's not carrying another man."

As the ship drifted toward Striker, moving faster and faster, Nick hopped off the rail, turned in place, and walked down the side of the ship, playing out the rope as he went. On the ground, Striker changed course, angling to intercept the ladder. The moment took Nick back to the circus ring, filling him with a mix of thrill and trepidation. He was dancing on the edge of disaster, but he was good enough to win. *So far, so good.*

Then, from his position halfway down the gondola's hull, Nick saw a fiery harpoon arc overtop the *Red Jack*'s balloon. The sky lit up for a moment, the violent flare of light like a cry of wrath. Nick swore viciously. *Still finding their range.* But the clock was ticking.

Then Striker was in front of Nick, grabbing at the ladder, but the man across his shoulders hampered him. Nick snatched at the trussed-up figure, snapping the catch at the end of the rope into place around the manacles at the man's wrists. He'd expected hemp knots or common handcuffs, but the contraption the man wore was far more secure. Once the catch was secure, Nick glanced up to Smith's face. Poole was looking over the side with wide eyes, his grip on the rope secure. "Haul away!" Nick cried, and then swung to grab the ladder, transferring his own weight from rope to rungs. Smith heaved, and the man jerked into the air, hanging from his wrists. In a moment, the package began a slow ascent up the side of the ship.

But the sudden relief of weight made Striker stumble and lose his grip on the ladder. To Nick's horror, the movement of the ship made it swing wide, lifting Nick into the air and leaving Striker stranded. "Run!" Nick yelled, blinking as another harpoon lit up the sky.

He pushed away from the hull with his feet, swinging Striker's way. But the *Red Jack* was gaining too much in height, and the lowest rung was out of reach. Nick cursed himself for securing the prisoner first, however logical it might have seemed at the time. He cursed himself for—as usual—forgetting anything so mundane as a safety harness. He'd worked without a net for years, but then he'd been the one sailing through the air, not the entire circus ring.

His hand grazed Striker's but not enough to grab hold. There wasn't time to think. He pushed away again, swinging the ladder as far as it would go. He hooked his feet into the rungs, let go with his hands, and let himself fall, reaching out for Striker's outstretched fingers. He grabbed both the man's forearms, felt his friend's lock on his, and then felt the drag of Striker's solid weight as the man's feet left terra firma behind.

Do not move, advised Athena.

Nick swore as the *Red Jack* banked into a turn, picking up speed that left their harpoon-throwing enemies behind. He didn't move. He only tightened his grip on Striker, who was making a noise somewhere between an outraged ox and a whistling teakettle. Hanging upside down by his toes, Nick squeezed his eyes shut as the ladder gently swayed, trying to pretend he was back in the circus with little Evie Cooper cheering him on.

CHAPTER SEVEN

EVELINA TURNED THE OBJECT OVER IN HER HAND, STUDYING its workings. It was small, square, and made of black metal, with a couple of tiny switches on the side. She'd pried off the cover and was peering at the insides, cataloguing the tangle of wires.

She was standing in her uncle's study, bending near the lamp on Dr. Watson's desk. Holmes was reading the paper, saying nothing. That was just as well, as her entire being was focused on the object. Mrs. Hudson had retrieved it from the curb where Jones had fallen. Evelina had seen something similar once before—except that device had been a hundred times larger. She lifted a bit of metal with her fingernail and saw something inscribed on the inside of the housing: Keating Industries.

A flood of angry heat coursed through her. "I know this design. It's a transmittal device. The Gold King developed it first as a means of delivering an electric shock at a distance. It was intended as a means of disciplining the domestic staff."

"How charming," Holmes said from behind the wall of newsprint.

A man named Aragon Jackson had invented the proto-type, but Tobias had taken the theory of remote transmis-sion far beyond the maid-zapping device. "This unit is for sending signals at a distance. Like a telegraph, but without a wire."

Holmes let the paper droop so that he could see her over the top. There was a sharp crease between his eyebrows. "Go on."

"That's how the bomb was detonated," Evelina said urgently. "Jones had this in his pocket, and when he struggled to get up, he triggered it. The timing of the explosion didn't make sense because it was an accident."

Evelina put her back to the freshly repaired window. There was still a lot to fix at 221B—paint, paper, and curtains for starters—but at least the study was no longer alfresco. The memory of the blast and of the struggle with Elias Jones made her shiver. She hadn't slept well last night.

Holmes was silent for a long moment. "Well done, Evelina. What else can you tell me about that infernal device?"

"It came from the Gold King's workshop."

"And yet it was in the hands of one of the Blue King's agents?" Holmes narrowed his eyes. "That's interesting."

Evelina swallowed hard. "It's Tobias's work." There, she'd said his name, and she'd done it calmly. "But you said the bomb was flawed. That's not like him. He doesn't allow his creations out of the workshop until they're ready."

"You forget the gunpowder on Jones's cuffs. Perhaps he tampered with it."

"Why?"

Holmes folded the paper. "Perhaps my death was not the ultimate object of the game."

"He had you at gunpoint," she objected.

"All right, perhaps creating an unrecognizable corpse was not the object. Perhaps the blast was merely meant to obscure evidence. Maybe it was necessary to leave some sort of warning to other detective busybodies. Have a care, my girl. This time, you were in harm's way by chance. Don't allow your curiosity to raise the stakes."

Evelina said nothing, still mulling over the fact that Jasper Keating—and by extension, Tobias—had a connection to the bomb. That was more than interesting; that was significant. She simply wasn't sure how, though she would bet her last shilling her uncle had some theories. But he was back behind his newspaper now, keeping his thoughts to himself even after she'd handed him a particularly juicy clue. She wondered how Dr. Watson—a clever man in his own right— had lasted so many years without bashing his roommate over the head out of sheer frustration.

"You say that young Mr. Roth won't be at the shooting party for a week or two yet?" Holmes asked.

"Correct." Imogen's letter had gone on to give specific dates. "Business keeps him in town."

He snapped the paper straight. "Then perhaps this is an opportune moment to accept Miss Roth's invitation. It's high time you got back into Society, even if it's only a country party. After all, you are young, pretty, and possessed of an unblemished reputation. You're entitled to enjoy yourself for a few days."

"You sound like Grandmamma."

"I am your guardian."

And it all sounded reasonable, except that jealousy had Evelina in its vise. Could she stay civil with Alice Keating in the same room? And if by some misfortune she did encounter Tobias, what would she say?

"Evelina?" her uncle prompted.

Maggor's Close had turned out to be just south of the Scottish border, and the nearest railway station at Pletherow Saint Andrew's was almost two days by train from London. Thus, distance was the first excuse Evelina grabbed at. "It's a very long way away."

"If you were an octogenarian, perhaps," Holmes replied.

"Or I could say the invitation was blown away in the bomb blast."

"In which case you would not mention the letter, since you could not possibly have seen it."

"Naturally."

Holmes scowled at the gossip pages he always read strictly for research purposes—or so he claimed. "I thought you enjoyed Miss Roth's company."

Of course she did. The chance to see Imogen meant everything. Unfortunately, there were complexities. "I don't know why she has to see me now. She could wait until we're both in London." Imogen had double underscored the fact that she had all kinds of news, but what could be that important? "Even if Tobias isn't present, I'm not sure that it's right for me to be there with his bride-to-be." But she was stretching the point, since their courtship had never been publically acknowledged.

Holmes's reply was uncharacteristically gentle. "Perhaps Imogen needs a friend right now. This must be trying for her as well, and she's always been delicate, I believe?"

Mild as they were, the words hit her like a slap. "You're right."

"It happens occasionally."

Evelina felt a stab of shame. "Of course you're right. I adore Imogen. I adore them all. Well, maybe not Lord B, but he never speaks to me anyhow." Her voice was rising, going shrill with panic. "But how can I face Tobias? I still have feelings for him, illogical though that may be. Besides, he shot you. Surely you haven't forgotten that."

"Mm," Holmes replied, hiding behind the newspaper and no doubt wishing it blocked sound as well as sight.

"Or maybe you have," she said acerbically. "It rather resembled the bomb that just blew us up—which he also had a hand in—except it was a tad more direct."

The top of the newspaper drooped, revealing her uncle's slightly wild-eyed face. He hated this kind of conversation. "My dear girl, of course I remember."

"How am I supposed to feel about that? How am I supposed to go visit his family?"

"That is not the question on the tip of your tongue. You want to know if he still loves you, even if he is pledged to another. You want me to tell you to go. Or not go. But until you make up your mind, I cannot give you the answer you wish to hear since you don't know what that is."

Heat crept up Evelina's cheeks. Whoever said her uncle didn't understand the human heart was mistaken. He simply would rather stab himself in the eye than talk about it. "You're quite right. My apologies. I will leave a note with instructions once I've come to a conclusion."

He gave the paper an irritable snap, disappearing behind it once more. "The point is, you cannot have Mr. Roth. For good or ill, he chose another and is therefore not worth losing a moment's sleep over. Someday you will meet him, and it will hurt, but the time after that, it will be easier. The pain fades. Believe it or not, I have some little experience in such matters."

Evelina bit her lip, saying nothing. Her uncle might be making logical sense, but she couldn't get Tobias's features out of her mind. He was smart, talented, handsome—and the subject of many a girlhood dream. A few months' misery couldn't erase everything that had come before. Not completely. And the last time they were together, he'd told her that he loved her. A moment later—the moment she'd figured out he'd shot Holmes—he'd denied any feelings at all. He'd been lying then, trying to save her and his family from Jasper Keating, but what would he say now?

Then she realized with an embarrassed start that her uncle was still talking. "Difficult times do not last. Difficult, obstinate, and impertinent people do. If you're going to raise a flag in academic life, I suggest you cultivate those qualities. A meek manner and clean gloves will get you nowhere in the thrust and parry of intellectual debate.

"Furthermore," Holmes continued, blithely leaping to a new topic, "I would propose that grouse is not the reason Jasper Keating has bought a place so far north."

"Oh?" She tried to scrape her thoughts into straight, logical, nonromantic rows.

"Scotland has so far resisted the Steam Council's influence, not only through an instinct for independence, but also because the mountainous terrain is much harder to control. Consequently, it's become a favorite bolt-hole for the resistance."

Evelina cleared her throat. She was too hot, her chemise sticking to her skin, but it had far more to do with emotion than with the temperature in the room. "You think Keating wants a foothold up north. Someplace convenient where he can start putting out feelers."

"Spies, you mean. You would be right. His new hunting

lodge—every gentleman's accessory come shooting season—
is a nearly invisible means of establishing a base." Holmes
tossed the paper aside. "What a pity you won't be going north.
I would delight in knowing who says what to whom."

"You want me to spy for you?" she asked incredulously.

Holmes made an innocent face. "Ladies don't spy. They
gossip. Copiously. Bring me something useful about Keating's activities."

SO IT WAS she found herself with a first-class ticket going
north. Evelina stared out the carriage window, hypnotized
by the rhythmic rattle and sway of the train. The late summer landscape was still lush, with only an odd field more
tawny than green.

The carriages along the way were as comfortable as one
could hope for, and she was never obliged to endure more
than three other travelers in the car at any one time. It was a
far cry from her early years with Ploughman's Paramount
Circus, when the entire troupe would have to crush into a
handful of the cheapest cars available, animals and all.

They hadn't been bad years. She had been loved and still
too young to understand what her widowed mother meant
when she said that they were poor. Her mother—daughter
of the genteel Holmes family and sister to Uncles Sherlock
and Mycroft—had eloped with Captain Cooper, a low-born
infantry soldier who had risen to an officer's rank through
conspicuous bravery. He in turn had been one of the Fabu-
lous Flying Coopers and a member of Ploughman's circus,
but had run away as a youth to make his fortune in the army.
By the time Evelina was an adolescent, both her parents
were dead and her Grandmamma Holmes had plucked her
from the circus and enrolled her in Wollaston Academy for
Young Ladies. Years later, now a properly educated young
miss who had been presented to the queen and had danced
at the Duchess of Westlake's ball, Evelina kept her early involvement with the circus to herself.

However, it was delicious to be traveling again, indulging
her wanderlust. Of course, traveling in first class was scarcely

a hardship. There was no shortage of personnel to see to her every need, and Mrs. Hudson—off to spend a fortnight with her sister and recover from the explosion—had gone with her as far as York before turning off for Scarborough.

The last leg of the journey found Evelina in the company of a middle-aged woman, a wheezing pug in a wicker cage, and a plump man in a brown suit. The woman was engrossed in a novel and the man was engrossed with Evelina.

"My dear," he said, edging closer to the lip of the worn velvet seat opposite her. "Allow me to introduce myself. My name is Mr. Jeremy."

She rearranged her skirts so that they did not brush his knees. The woman looked up from her book, giving the man a hard stare. Gentlemen did not introduce themselves to young ladies journeying alone. "A pleasure, sir," Evelina said in cool tones—not impolite, but not inviting further conversation. That seemed to shut him down, and then the only sound in the carriage was the pug snuffling against the bars of its cage.

The train slowed as it passed a miserable smudge of a town, choked with coal dust and overcrowding. Seeing it made her chest hurt, as if a fist had closed around her heart. Now Evelina drew back from the window, needing that extra few inches between her and the poverty. Women dragged children away from the tracks, their arms so thin their elbows looked like knots in a rope. Dogs sniffed hopelessly for food, their ribs stark beneath patchy fur. Evelina's life had never been that dire, but some winters had come close enough that sometimes she still had trouble leaving food on her plate, or throwing a garment away before it was completely worn to bits.

"Pathetic creatures," said Mr. Jeremy.

She didn't answer. He'd probably never done a day's manual labor in his life, much less in one of the steam barons' foundries—for she was fairly sure that was what they were seeing. Crates of gears and giant spools of chain sat on the platform, waiting for the barons' own trains to whisk them away to their gas plants or railways, manufactories or perhaps one of the great steam boilers that heated entire neighborhoods through underground pipes. Supplies like these weren't for the ordinary citizen to buy—just to die of the black lung making them.

He leaned forward, his knuckles brushing her knee. "I am sorry such a beautiful young lady is obliged to see such a sight."

She again snapped her skirts back out of his reach. "Better than that I remain in ignorance." She regretted the words the moment she spoke, because speaking had given him an opening for further conversation. He opened his mouth, ready to take advantage of the fact.

"Sir," said the lady with the pug. Her voice said she'd been a schoolmistress at some point in her past. "Pray leave the young lady in peace or I shall call the conductor and have him escort you to another car."

Red faced, the man settled back with a muttered complaint about aging harridans. Evelina shot the woman a grateful look. After that, the train was quiet except for the wheezing of the dog and the rattle of the wheels.

Evelina fell into a kind of fretful daydream, imagining what she'd find when she got to Maggor's Close. Scene after scene played itself out in her mind, reinforcing her anxiety. She still wasn't sure how she was going to face Tobias. *It shouldn't matter now. He is engaged. He's beyond my reach.* And yet some part of her wouldn't let him go.

She had been poised to fall in love, like a swimmer in a fast-flowing river with just one hand clinging to the bank. She had been so eager to let go and surrender herself, had only been waiting for one last sign that everything could work. And then he had declared his love—but withdrawn it almost at once.

Now she wasn't sure how she was supposed to feel. Tobias had shot Uncle Sherlock, but he had been defending his mother and sisters from ruin. Could she despise him for doing a horrible thing when it was for the most honorable of reasons?

She was sick to death of going around and around the question. Evelina closed her eyes, afraid of her own emotions, dreading what the coming weeks would bring. Her

uncle had sent her to spy on the party, and no doubt he wanted
to know which business magnates came and went and what
deals they discussed over whisky and cigars. But, she guessed,
he also wanted her moping presence out of Baker Street. She
couldn't blame him.

The train slowed, the steady chugging growing more and
more arthritic until it slowed to a crawl. A sign that read
Pletherow Saint Andrew's flashed by the window, and Evelina realized she had reached her destination. She slipped
her timetable back into her open carpetbag and edged forward on her seat.

"Do you need help with your cases?" asked Mr. Jeremy.

Before Evelina could reply, the lady with the pug rose and
pulled the cord for the conductor. "We shall request a porter," she said sweetly to Evelina.

As the train stopped with a final lurch, Evelina rose and
tugged at the hatbox on the iron rack above. As she did, her
carpetbag tipped over, spilling the contents across the
wooden floor. Before Evelina could set the hatbox on her
seat, Mr. Jeremy had set about scooping up her things.

"Please don't trouble yourself," she said hastily. "I can do
that."

Matching actions to words, she started shoveling combs,
notebooks, needlebooks, and coins into the bag. She grabbed
the leather train case that had all her supplies for spellcast-
ing and clockwork repairs—neither considered ladylike nor
completely legal—and stuffed it away before it could un-
latch and spill a million tiny gears across the floor. At least
her emergency pair of unmentionables hadn't fallen out, but
that wasn't what she was worried about the most.

"What's this?" The man held up a small steel mouse and
flicked its cleverly articulated tail with one finger. "You're a
big girl to play with toys."

Although it was barely perceptible, she saw the mouse's
whiskers twitch with irritation. *Would you kindly convince
this imbecile to put me down?* it complained. *His hands
smell of stale ham and pickle. It's like being grabbed by
sweaty pillows that have been gently rotting in a trash bin
for six weeks.*

Evelina snatched the mouse out of his hand. "It's a present for my nephew," she lied and stuffed the mouse back into the bag. Then she rummaged around until her fingers closed on her clockwork bird. Good. She had them both. Snapping the catch of the carpetbag shut, she rose and gathered her bags and hatbox.

"Good day, Mr. Jeremy. Have a pleasant journey." Then she turned to the pug lady. "And thank you, ma'am, for all your help."

The woman smiled, a touch of mischief in her comfortable face. She had clearly enjoyed frustrating Mr. Jeremy. "Certainly, miss. And you."

The porter slid open the compartment door and began the process of depositing Evelina and her bags and trunks onto Pletherow's tiny platform. Then, with a hiss of steam, the train chugged forward, gathering momentum until it pulled away in a whirl of cinders and dust. Evelina looked around, taking in the ornate ironwork bracketing the platform roof, the black and white sign with the station's name, and the fact that there was nothing else but heather and scrub grass and tracks for miles around.

She'd seen too many places like this in the past, except back then she would be one of a troupe, stranded in the dust or the rain with a heap of gear and an ever-growing Noah's ark of animals. In the earliest days, there had just been the horses—and Nick, a little more than three years her senior, always holding her hand until the train was safely away. No one knew where he had come from, or his last name, or who his people had been. A Gypsy, perhaps, or some sailor's spawn with a magical Bloodline so different that no one at Ploughman's could teach him to use it. But he had been the best trick rider and knife man she'd ever seen.

And her most loyal friend. If it hadn't been for their incompatible magic, there might have been more. *But he's gone now, too. I can't even think about that.* The pain of it closed her throat until she felt as if she were suffocating.

There was scrabbling inside the bag. Since there was no other human in sight, Evelina set the bag on top of her trunk and opened the catch. Mouse and Bird poked their heads

out. They were both tiny, barely four inches long, but the bird
was the flashier of the two. Whereas Mouse, with its gray
steel fur and velvet-tipped paws, had been made for stealth
and silence, Bird was as beautiful as its wild cousins. She'd
given it crystal-tipped wings and eyes of paste emeralds—but
there were also scars and patches where a streetkeeper named
Striker had repaired it.

But what made them precious to her were the spirits that
gave her clockwork creations life. The tiny creatures were a
synthesis of her mechanical arts and the magic her Gran
Cooper had taught her as a child. Like many circus folk, her
father's family was of the Blood—and Evelina had a unique
gift that could coax devas into inanimate objects.

But no magic—light or dark, high or low—could make
earth devas civil. Bird flitted to her shoulder with a whirr of
wings and looked around critically. *You've taken us to the
end of the world.*

"We're not even to Scotland yet. The end of the world is a
bit farther north." Evelina sat down on her trunk and checked
the watch pinned to her jacket. The train had been on time, so
it was the cart that was supposed to meet her that was late.

Did I hear something about shooting birds?

"You did. This is a shooting party, so don't go flying about
unless you want to end up in someone's game bag."

Or slobbered on by a dog, Mouse added darkly from the
mouth of the carpetbag.

Bird gripped her jacket, driving brass toenails into her
shoulder. *A party for shooting birds? What sort of bizarre,
sadistic impulse prompted you to take me to a mass murder?*

She plucked Bird off, setting it on the edge of the trunk. "I
could have left you with Uncle Sherlock."

*Hardly. Every time he sees me, I can see him thinking
about unbolting my hide so he can see what makes my gears
turn.*

"He looks at everyone like that."

Bird hopped across the top of the trunk disconsolately while
Mouse cleaned its whiskers. The devas had melded so closely
with their mechanical bodies that one would never guess they
were beings of pure energy. The elemental spirits—mostly

small and harmless, but sometimes quite the opposite—were at the heart of the magic her Gran Cooper had taught Evelina as a child. Of all the varieties of devas—water, air, fire, earth, and all the shades in between—the Coopers had an affinity for the devas of the woodland places. They were the ones she could see most clearly and speak to with her mind.

Evelina scanned the landscape around the train station, wondering what manner of spirits lived here. Then she heard the rumble of wheels. Bird flew back to the bag, perching on the clasp.

At first, Evelina saw nothing, but then she rose from the trunk and looked around, finally spotting a two-horse carriage coming up behind the train station. It was far nicer than the dog cart and driver she'd been expecting, but Jasper Keating did everything in style. "Hello!" she called. "Are you from Maggor's Close?"

A female head in a smart green hat emerged from the carriage window. For a split second, Evelina's heart seized, half expecting Alice Keating simply because she was the last person Evelina wanted to see. But her fears were unfounded, because it was Imogen who got out of the carriage. Tall, slender, and with hair the color of pale wheat, she had captured every available heart—and then some—in her first Season. She gave Evelina a huge smile. "There you are. I've missed you so much!"

"I missed you, too." Evelina returned the smile, almost giddy with relief. "I didn't expect anyone besides a driver."

"What nonsense is that? I had to welcome you in person. Anything less would be barbaric."

Evelina glanced down and saw Mouse and Bird had retreated into the carpetbag. Imogen knew all about them, but they had to stay out of sight of the driver. She snapped the bag shut seconds before Imogen enveloped her in a hug. Evelina closed her eyes, happier than she had been for months.

"You look well," Imogen said a moment later, holding her at arm's length. "The country air agrees with you. Far better than it agrees with me, I think."

Capturing her arm, Imogen pulled her toward the carriage, leaving the driver to wrestle with the luggage. Evelina tensed. Nothing could dim her friend's pale, slender beauty, but she did look more fragile than she had last spring. "Have you been unwell?"

"Oh, it's nothing." Imogen waved her concern away. "I think it is just the damp. Or the absence of London smoke. Or perhaps the fact I've been forced to endure gunshots from dawn till dusk for days on end. That's where all the men are now—out slaughtering the landscape. It sounds like a recurrence of the Crimea come to our front door."

"Surely you exaggerate."

"I do that when I'm bored enough to scream. I can't even find a newspaper in this forsaken place. Thank God you're here. I was about to take up a laudanum habit just to pass the time."

Apprehensive, Evelina let her ramble, but she could hear the tension and fatigue in Imogen's voice. Perhaps Uncle Sherlock had been correct about her health. All through their school years, Imogen had suffered nervous complaints and, more often than not, Evelina had been the one to nurse her through fevers and nightmares.

They settled themselves into the carriage, and it set off at a smart clip. "So tell me everything about your summer," Imogen demanded. "How is your fearsome Grandmamma Holmes?"

"As terrifying as ever," Evelina confessed. "It's just as well she'd been a bit under the weather. I truly believe that is the only reason why I could keep up with her."

"Oh?" Imogen leaned forward, the ribbed silk of her sleek green walking dress rustling as she moved. "What was she up to this time?"

Evelina studied her friend. From the dark circles under her eyes, she hadn't been sleeping, and more often than not that meant she was overwrought. Evelina's first impulse had been to tell Imogen everything—the bomb, the mysterious Schoolmaster, and even the detonator that looked so much like Tobias's handiwork, but now she reconsidered. As much as Evelina would have welcomed a comrade in arms, that might not be what Imogen needed.

She decided to begin with a more cheerful topic. "Grand-mamma took full advantage of the fact I'd been presented, and marched me into the drawing rooms of every respectable family in the county who could boast an eligible bachelor. I had to duck three proposals by midsummer's day."

"Good work, Mrs. Holmes!" Imogen nodded appreciatively. "So what was wrong with these three young bucks?"

"Two of them were at least three score and ten, and one was a greengrocer."

"A greengrocer?"

"I exaggerate. He imports food. I didn't mind that, but he smelled like rotting lettuce and had the conversational ability of a carrot."

Imogen blinked. "Heavens, did he have any redeeming qualities?"

"Evidently he can lay his hands on fresh vegetables even in the depths of winter. He has friends who have friends."

Imogen snapped open her fan, plying it vigorously. "Aubergines all twelve months of the year. Is that even legal?"

Evelina sat back against the seat cushions, cringing at her memories. "There was much about this gentleman that should be outlawed, but his produce I'm sure was quite aboveboard."

"How dull."

"Precisely." Evelina smiled. "But once my tour of the drawing rooms was complete, I approached Grandmamma about the question of college again. That was quite the scene. I made the tactical error of bringing it up over an early lunch. I thought she was going to skewer me with her shrimp fork before the meal was done."

"How awful!"

"I made a graceful retreat. Peace reigned once more by the time the trifle was served."

"Thank goodness. Are you forgiven?"

"Conditionally. She hasn't given up on finding me a suitable match."

"And why should she?" Imogen snapped her fan closed.

"Well, I have decided to talk Uncle Sherlock into taking up my educational cause. I'm sure he can make her see reason."

Imogen raised an eyebrow. "Are you sure about that?"

"I don't know, but perhaps I could grow rich wagering on the outcome. There must be a bookmaker willing to help me for a cut of the take."

"But at least you didn't find the summer too dull."

"Not at all." In truth she'd welcomed the change of pace. Her Season—what there had been of it—had been stuffed with more murders, stolen treasure, and magical monsters than a bad opera. There'd even been a sorcerer—and the memory of Dr. Magnus made her shudder even more than Grandmamma and her shrimp fork.

Imogen's face grew solemn, the momentary levity gone. "I have a great deal of news to tell you, but I suppose there are questions you'd like to ask me before we reach the house."

Evelina swallowed, a sudden apprehension drying her mouth to cotton. "What should I know about the engagement?" There. She'd said it. She'd ripped the scab off the wound, and now it could bleed until it was clean.

"Ah," Imogen sighed. "That."

"The wedding is next month."

Imogen stared out the window. "And for all the reasons you suspect. Alice thinks she loves him. Tobias is . . . I don't know. Trying to make the best of things, I suppose."

"I was sure Keating wanted a match between Alice and the Duke of Westlake's son."

"The Earl of Barrington's eldest daughter won that race," Imogen replied.

"Lady Mary?"

"Yes, Lady Mary." Imogen shrugged. "That announcement came two days before Keating made it known that Tobias was to be his son-in-law. I rather think my brother was the consolation prize, as least where the Gold King was concerned."

They fell into an uncomfortable silence, her friend growing more and more grim. Evelina cursed herself. This wasn't the kind of light conversation that she'd intended to have. Nothing about this was going to cheer up her friend. "Will the wedding be in London?" Evelina asked, keeping her voice neutral.

Imogen nodded. "At least, with it being at the start of the

Little Season, some families will be there." The Little Season ran through the autumn and was a smaller, gentler version of the spring's social whirl.

"Others will travel up to London for the honor of attending, I'm sure."

Her friend gave her a pained expression. "After changing the date like that? It's almost certain the sticklers for propriety will call foul. The first set of invitations had gone out only days before we found out about—well, Alice's situation. I thought Mama was going to hang herself then and there. She's never been good with that sort of thing."

Tobias had wasted no time falling in love again—or at least lust. *He couldn't have been that devoted to me.* Evelina swallowed again, forcing herself to be aware of Imogen's distress rather than her own, but it took an act of will. *Hard times do not last. Difficult, obstinate, and impertinent people do.* "Comments will fade quickly enough. No one will dare to say anything against the Gold King's girl."

Her friend waved her fan in a weary gesture. "I never thought I would say this, but I'm glad of it. They'll be married, and then off to Italy for a long honeymoon. By the time they get back, hopefully Society will be tearing apart the reputation of some other happy couple."

Evelina swallowed hard. She couldn't avoid Tobias and Alice forever, but she could keep their encounters to a bearable minimum. She just had to make it through the next few weeks of daily visits with Tobias's future bride at Maggor's Close.

"What makes it all so difficult is that I rather like Alice," Imogen said, half to herself. "I can't help feeling sorry for her."

Evelina felt another irrational pang of jealousy. She looked out the carriage window, willing it to pass. What she saw sent a scuttle of alarm up her spine. "What happened here?"

It had been a village, that much she could tell. The roads were still there, and the stumps of some of the stone walls and houses. But all the roofs were gone, the insides of the buildings scooped out by fire. Bits of broken furniture littered the yards—or so Evelina thought. It was hard to tell what had been the remains of a table or of one of the gates, or sheds, or coops, or the dozens of other structures that had been broken to pieces. A few lost chickens pecked here and there, but the only other creatures she saw were the bloated bodies of sheep.

"Ah," said Imogen. "That was Crowleyton."

Evelina could still smell the tang of ash. The destruction was recent. "Where are the townsfolk?"

"Gone."

Something caught Evelina's eye. She squirmed around in her seat, straining to get a better look. "Those are stocks!"

Imogen's head whipped around to see. "Oh, thank heavens they're empty now. There was a man in there for days and days. I kept the blinds drawn going by."

Days and days? Humiliation was a big part of the punishment, but so was exposure. "I didn't think anyone used those anymore. What happened to the village?"

"They rioted. That was before we got here. I asked Father what it was all about," Imogen replied, her voice strained. "He said Keating was connecting them up to the new boiler he's building nearby. There would have been steam heating for every house, but they weren't having any of it."

They probably couldn't afford it. But once the utilities were installed, no matter which steam baron owned the company, no alternative heat or light would be allowed. Usually, the cost of keeping warm was more than a common man could pay. After that, it was debt or darkness. In any way that mattered, the village became the steam baron's fiefdom. Crowleyton had objected, however, and the Gold King's Yellowbacks had erased it from the map. *Complete with torture. I wonder if the man in the stocks was still alive once they took him away.*

Evelina turned away from the window. She'd heard about the rebellion—bits and scraps of news in the less reputable papers—but she'd never seen anything like this. The violence—even this shadow of it—was terrifying. *And I'm going to be sleeping under Keating's roof.* The thought sent tendrils of cold fear trickling through her limbs, as if a block of ice were melting in her stomach.

Something about the sight reminded her of the bomb in her uncle's apartment, and kneeling in the broken crockery on the floor. The bomb had been Tobias's handiwork, for all it had been used by someone else. He'd never used to make things that hurt or killed. Evelina's throat grew tight with tears, too many shocks robbing her of resolve.

She looked up under her lashes to see Imogen watching her, a crease between her finely arched brows. "It makes you wonder what's going to happen next, doesn't it?" Imogen said quietly.

Unable to find words, Evelina simply nodded.

Imogen reached across the carriage, taking Evelina's hand in her own. Her gray eyes were grave, but her words were sharp with irony. "Did I tell you that I'm glad you're here? There's going to be a party. All the Gold King's friends in the North are going to be there. I hope you brought a pretty gown. I hear they like to flirt. And by the way, the Steam Council is coming apart at the seams. There's going to be a bomb and they're after that navigation device Keating's pet archaeologist found buried in Rhodes. The one your friend Nick has."

Evelina gaped. "I think we need to talk. There was a bomb at Baker Street before I left. Someone tried to blow up Uncle Sherlock."

Imogen's eyes went wide. "Your family visits are always so much more interesting than mine!"

Chapter Eight

THE REST OF THE CARRIAGE RIDE WAS TAKEN UP WITH AN exchange of information. Evelina told Imogen about the explosion, although she said nothing about the Schoolmaster or the identity of Elias Jones; those were details her uncle had asked her to keep to herself. And she said nothing about Tobias's detonator—she could at least spare Imogen that for now.

In turn, Imogen told her about the conversation she'd overheard, and Evelina was so engrossed in the story that she barely noticed Maggor's Close until they were rolling up the drive.

The main house had probably started out as a monastery once upon a time. Gray stone towers flanked the main facade of the house, and the huge arched doorway begged for a portcullis, or perhaps a ghostly guard to ward off unwanted visitors. Jasper Keating had definitely bought himself a Gothic pile.

They'd barely set foot in the house when a tall man Evelina had never met before emerged into the front hall. Somewhere in his forties, he had curling black hair, startling blue eyes, and the kind of roguish dimples that set female hearts aflutter. Fit and smartly dressed in a sports jacket and riding breeches, he wore a startling red waistcoat of figured silk. Evelina would have thought the color flashy to the point of being vulgar—the fashion these days was for sober colors in men's attire—but he wore it so comfortably that it was impossible to object.

"Mr. Reading," Imogen said with a slight tensing of her shoulders.

"Ladies," the man said, his voice deep and pleasant as he lifted his hat. But his eyes were less well mannered; his gaze lingered on Imogen a long moment before it swept over Evelina, beginning at her feet and working leisurely upward. "I see that we have a new arrival to our party."

"Yes, we do. Evelina, may I present Mr. William Reading, of Reading and Bartelsman?"

Dear heavens, it's the Scarlet King! Scarlet was one of the lesser members of the Steam Council, but he still held sizeable interests in London and abroad. Uncle Sherlock had run afoul of the man when he had taken a case last spring in Bohemia.

"Mr. Reading," Imogen went on, "this is Miss Evelina Cooper."

What is he doing at the Gold King's country house? The steam barons weren't enemies—at least not openly—but everyone knew that they were hardly friends. Uncle Sherlock would certainly want to know about Reading's presence here. Tingling with curiosity, she held out her gloved hand, keeping her thoughts hidden and her expression cheerful. Wollaston Academy for Young Ladies had drilled its charges for just such emergencies as this.

She could feel her heart pounding as the tall man bent over her hand. The movement was carefully measured, but spoke of strength and energy. This was no dusty boardroom general, but a man at the height of his physical powers.

"I take it you are here for the grouse?" she asked.

"Indeed I am. I was detained this morning, but now I'm off to catch up to the other gentlemen." He looked up from under his brows, giving her the full force of his blue eyes before he straightened.

He's certainly here to pluck more than the grouse, I think.

He turned to Imogen, repeating the bow. "Though now I am wishing away the hours until we meet again." Then he smiled, showing off healthy white teeth.

"Indeed, Mr. Reading. Until then." Imogen stepped aside so that he had a clear path to the door. "Good hunting."

Perhaps she dismissed him too quickly, because there was a beat of uncomfortable silence. But then, with a polite nod, the Scarlet King gave a final lift of his hat. "I pride myself on always bagging my bird, Miss Roth." And with that, he made his exit.

Evelina turned to Imogen. "You said he was Mr. Keating's guest, but I don't think I fully believed it until I saw him here with my own eyes. Is it open knowledge that they are working together?"

"Not the specifics, but everyone knows there is some desire to forge an alliance between Gold and Scarlet. Ergo, gunpowder and champagne dinners are the order of the day." Imogen bent her head close to Evelina's ear. "He has rather an eye for the ladies, so be careful not to wander off alone. Evidently no female is safe, nor his bed ever empty."

Evelina raised her eyebrows. "I trust he only dallies with the willing?"

Her friend gave her a look.

"You're about to be Keating's relation by marriage," Evelina objected. "Surely Reading wouldn't risk insulting you like that?"

Imogen smiled, but it was rueful. "There is an alliance to be made, and whatever the Scarlet King wants, for now he gets it. At any rate, I'm doing my best to stay invisible, just in case he thinks I'm on the menu."

Imogen was almost certainly exaggerating, but probably not as much as Evelina would have liked. Worse, she'd heard rumors that the Scarlet King had a fondness for exotic poisons— perhaps that was just savage gossip, but it provided one more reason to be on their guard. She took her friend's arm, suddenly very glad she came. "We'll look after each other."

"Like always," Imogen agreed. "Thank you so much for coming, Evelina."

She gave a determined smile. "Well, the men are out killing birds for now. Take me to your tea trolley. I'm famished."

TEA CAME AT a price.

Evelina watched in numb horror as Lady Bancroft produced yet another fashion paper filled with designs for Alice's trousseau. They had been poring over sketches for the last hour. An older, quieter version of Imogen, Lady B had taken on the role of mentor with uncharacteristic zest. Alice had no mother of her own, and Lady B cossetted her as thoroughly as any chick in need of a wing. Even if there was the suggestion of scandal attached to the match, the viscountess seemed to adore her future daughter.

Alice was more reserved, although she clearly returned Lady Bancroft's affection, sitting next to her on the divan in the main parlor of the mansion. Blue-eyed and copper-haired, Alice was dressed in a bright green gown trimmed in looping black braid. She was perhaps the most colorful thing in the room.

Other women were scattered here and there, writing letters, playing cards, or gossiping to while away the time until the shooting party returned for dinner. Imogen had introduced the ladies, but she and Evelina had settled with Alice—who was technically their hostess—and Lady Bancroft. As a newly arrived guest, Evelina was expected to pay her respects. Unfortunately, all the talk was about the wedding.

"If we are to go to Italy," Alice said, "I will need gowns for a warmer climate. I'm thinking of this one." She held up the latest edition of *Godey's Lady's Book,* freshly arrived from Philadelphia, to display a hand-tinted fashion plate of the latest style.

"That's lovely my dear, but what do you think of this one?" Lady B said, holding up one of the Paris fashion papers. "It is very elegant."

Alice looked unconvinced. "Of course you are quite right, but I am not sure about the color. White is difficult for me to wear. It makes me look pink unless I wear face powder—and you know how people are." Respectable women weren't supposed to wear cosmetics.

"Piffle," stated Lady B. "Everyone does it. Find me a single woman in London who doesn't own a pot of rouge."

"Mama, you're in danger of corrupting all the virtues that Wollaston Academy instilled in us," Imogen teased.

Lady B ignored that and pointed to the Paris fashion

paper again. "I know it's not your first choice, Alice, but it is quite the latest thing."

At that point, a maid guided a steam-powered trolley into the room. The scent of Assam tea reached Evelina, and she turned hopefully in its direction. Thank heavens, there were sandwiches! She took several of the little triangles when the plate came her way, sacrificing gentility in the name of hunger.

"A pity the train was so late. You missed a splendid lunch," Lady B said with a smile to Evelina. "I particularly enjoyed the aspic."

"I shall ask the cook to include it again on the morrow," said Alice, clearly eager to please. "Though I'm not sure I agree with this practice of hauling a movable feast out onto the moors just so that the men can keep on blasting away until it's time to eat. It seems less than civilized. Truth be told, the whole shooting business makes me squirm."

Evelina agreed. Hunting for food made sense; killing hundreds of birds a day for sport was grotesque.

Lady Bancroft put a slender hand on Alice's arm. "That's the done thing, my dear, so there's no point in complaining about it."

Alice parted her lips, then closed them with an obedient smile. She had always been overly prone to speaking her mind, but was apparently trying to mend her ways. "Of course."

But Evelina saw the slight flicker of mutiny beneath that demure response, and remembered why she'd liked the red-haired girl when they first met. A generous impulse overtook her, and she took the fashion paper from Lady Bancroft and scrutinized the gown. "I'm sorry, Lady Bancroft, but I don't agree about this dress. I think Alice's choice is correct. The cut is more flattering."

"I'm sure you're right," Alice replied, chewing her lip. "Though now I've agreed with both sides of the argument."

Imogen, who had been through the litany of dresses thrice before, waved the topic away. "Of course Evelina is correct. She agrees with me, after all."

"Don't be a pest," scolded her mother.

Evelina couldn't help a smile. Despite everything, it was

good to be with Imogen and her family again, almost like coming home. Almost, because Alice was the new favorite, sitting in the chair between Lady B and Imogen. *That used to be my seat.*

She forced her thoughts away, refusing to allow herself to dwell on it. "Where's Poppy?" she asked, referring to Imogen's little sister.

"Still with her grandparents," Lady Bancroft replied. "The last thing we needed was to have her daydreaming in the woods while the men were out shooting."

"Is she still infatuated with knights in shining armor? I brought a book she might like."

Imogen made a face. "Not another one of Scott's poems, I hope. I'll break into a rash if I hear about lovelorn lairds one more time."

"She's fourteen," Evelina scolded. "She's the right age for romances."

"And you are too old and jaded?" Lady Bancroft asked Evelina with a sly smile. "There's no one on your horizon?"

Evelina quickly turned her attention to her teacup. The hurt inside welled up, threatening to engulf her. She couldn't let it out—*wouldn't*—because showing that weakness would admit that Tobias had the power to destroy her with his fallen-angel smile. She forced her pain and anger down, willing her heart to freeze to a compact ball of ice. "My plans lie in other directions. It's my ambition to attend the Ladies' College of London."

Alice looked at her enviously. "How marvelous! How lucky you are to have such choices."

Evelina nearly choked on her tea.

"No doubt it's time to dress for dinner," Lady Bancroft replied rather suddenly. "It's important to keep up one's tone when in the country. It's far too easy to forget what's proper."

"ALICE IS RIGHT. You are so lucky to be bound for an education," Imogen said to Evelina a half hour later. Finally, they were alone in Imogen's room and able to talk in peace, Evelina sitting on the edge of the bed, her friend at the dressing table. "I envy you the freedom to learn everything you can and not have to worry about a husband."

Evelina didn't reply. Now that she was back among friends, the whole college adventure felt a trifle lonely. She'd missed Imogen every bit as much as she thought and more. She hadn't talked like this for months.

Mouse and Bird gamboled on the dressing table. They adored Imogen as much as she did, and showed it by playing in her hair ribbons and making a mess of her perfumes.

"Come now, you'll be brilliant." Her friend broke the silence with a smile. She stroked Bird's head, and it preened and bumped against her fingers like an affectionate cat. "I know you will. You'll be inventing new formulae and calculating the distance to Mars while I'm taking tea and playing whist."

"Perhaps I shall fall in love with a professor," Evelina suggested lightly. "That seems to be the fashion in all the novels."

"But they all have mad wives locked up somewhere. That seems a bit of a nuisance to me."

"I think you're mixing up your stories."

"Bah, I know you. You'd prefer Heathcliff in all his doomed glory." Imogen rescued Mouse from the powder box, but he burrowed under her puff again the moment she'd blown him clean.

The statement was innocently meant, but it brought back all the painful feelings Evelina had forced away during their tea with Alice and Lady Bancroft. "Do you think Tobias will ever be happy with Alice?" Evelina asked. "I mean, since we're speaking of doomed love."

"I don't think he dislikes her." Imogen fastened a pearl drop onto one earlobe and studied the effect in the mirror. "She's clever and pretty and nice. For most men, that's more than adequate. And she seems to like him."

"Oh, Tobias." Her throat aching, Evelina picked up the hairbrush sitting on the nightstand, turning it over in her hands. The simple movement helped her to focus. *I will not weep.* "You said he was making the best of things."

"I'm sorry," Imogen said softly. "I know there was something between you."

"Not enough to matter." Evelina cleared her throat. "And I can't afford to dwell on it. That won't help anyone."

"Well, don't think any of this happened because he didn't care for you," Imogen said firmly. "Tobias agreed to work for Keating if he'd forget the unpleasantness about the forgeries, and I think once Keating saw just how much Tobias could do, the marriage was the best way to ensure he stayed with the business. Besides, my brother might not be a duke, but he has a title. That matters to people like the Gold King. His grandson will be a lord."

Evelina nodded, thinking just how quickly that grandchild was going to arrive. Tobias might have wanted Evelina, but clearly not the same way she'd wanted him.

"Whatever happened," Imogen went on, "Father pushed Tobias into sealing a dynastic alliance with the Gold King. He pretends not to care that Keating's money is the only thing preventing the abbreviated engagement from starting a scandal, but I know better."

Evelina gave way to a stab of bitterness. "Doesn't it matter to him that he's uniting your family with the man who burned Crowleyton?" She regretted it the moment she said it. "I'm sorry."

Imogen shuddered. "Don't even mention that place to me. It's just another thing Father acts as if he does not see. In his opinion, if a marriage can shore up the family finances, he's all for it, no matter the cost." The bitterness in Imogen's voice was too obvious to ignore. Bird peeped unhappily, fluttering to her shoulder to tug at her earring.

Evelina put down her hairbrush, suddenly alert. "What about you?"

Imogen clasped a necklace around her throat, saying nothing for a long moment. "My parents have a short list of marriage candidates in mind. I have one."

Evelina felt her eyes widen. "Bucky Penner?" Tobias's best friend had been a surprise contender for Imogen's heart. At least, Evelina hadn't seen his suit coming—but apparently he'd made short work of the competition.

Imogen met Evelina's gaze in the dressing-table mirror. "He came down to the country over the summer and made his feelings plain. He actually fought a duel with Captain Smythe."

"A duel?" Evelina gaped. "Truly?"

A mischievous smile curved Imogen's lips. "The only thing wounded was the captain's uniform."

"And Bucky was the victor?"

Her friend's face grew serious. "He was. And I promised him that I would wait until I am of age."

Mouse popped out from under the powder puff, ears pricked.

"You promised to marry him?" Evelina was glad she was sitting down. Far too much had happened in one summer. "I thought your father . . ."

"Bucky isn't a lord. He has plenty of money, but he's beneath us socially. I don't care about that." Imogen raised her chin, eyes glittering with fierce tears. "Whatever Father wants, I'm not throwing my future away on a man I don't like."

Imogen's frail appearance suddenly made sense. She had been sickly since she was a child and every upset took its toll. Struggling against Lord Bancroft's marriage plans would wear her down fast. "Do your parents know about the engagement?"

"No, they don't." Imogen turned from the mirror, her pale gray eyes almost translucent. Her mouth was pressed into a flat line. "And you can't tell them."

"Of course not," Evelina replied, startled by the fierceness of her friend's words.

"I'm sorry. I know you won't." Imogen closed her eyes a moment. "But they're aware he's the one I want. So they won't let him come anywhere near me."

Evelina rose from the edge of the bed, walking slowly to her friend's side with the sudden feeling that she was approaching a wounded animal. Dismay radiated from Imogen like a sudden heat. "What are you going to do?"

Imogen pressed her palms to flushed cheeks. "I'm nineteen. I won't be able to marry without my father's consent for another year and a half. I hope I can stand up to him so long."

"You'll be fine," Evelina said, kneeling beside her. "I've never known someone as stubborn as you." There had been many times at school when Evelina had nursed her friend through sickness. She'd felt the fierce struggle of her spirit to cling on when it would have been so easy to go. Waiting a year or two seemed such a little thing by comparison, but then it wasn't Evelina's heart at stake. Not in this particular battle, at least.

"But you don't understand." Tears crept out from under Imogen's eyelashes. "It's not turning away other suitors or listening to my father rant that bothers me. It's that I can't ever let myself slip. I want him. I want to be with him so badly that even my teeth ache with it. And I know if I fall, he'll be right there to catch me. If I were reckless, I could have him right now."

"That didn't work out so well for my mother." Evelina took her hand. "Her own father barred the door to her, even when she was widowed."

"I know. I'm trying to wait till I'm of age." At least then Lord Bancroft would have to let her go. He might still refuse to give her a dowry, but Bucky's good name would suffer a little less if they didn't actually elope. Evelina put her arms around her friend, giving comfort because she had no more wisdom to offer. Not about matters of the heart.

"That's the problem," Imogen went on. "He loves me, and he'll do whatever it takes to keep me from hurting. If that means disappointing his own family or disgracing himself in front of all his friends, he'll do it in a heartbeat. And so I have to be the prudent one. I have to be the one to say *not yet*. And I'm afraid I won't be strong enough."

And she started to cry in earnest, spoiling the last half hour's work with comb and powder. Mouse and Bird crawled into her lap, offering what comfort they could while Evelina squeezed her tight. "Let me know if there is anything I can do."

"Can you make me a better person?"

Evelina couldn't stop a strangled laugh. "If I knew how, I'd make myself better first."

CHAPTER NINE

AS EVELINA RETREATED TO HER OWN ROOMS TO CHANGE her gown, she'd heard the men returning to the house. There was a great deal of stomping and rumbling voices, the barking of dogs and cries for whisky and hot water. The big house that had seemed large and full of echoes was all at once crowded.

The evening was to be a dance with a late supper. As Jasper Keating was arriving from London for the weekend, Alice had invited gentry from the surrounding county. It would be much smaller than a London event and much less formal, but probably the most company Maggor's Close had seen for many a year.

Evelina took pains with her appearance, grateful that Alice sent up one of the maids to help with her hair. Her sky-blue gown was mercifully uncreased by its time in the trunk. The fabric shimmered in the gaslight, and with a pearl necklace and ear bobs, it was elegant enough for the occasion. Looking in the mirror, she smoothed her skirts, swiveling one way then the other to make sure the graceful fall of fabric was in place. Her grandmother had bought Evelina the gown for her Season. *Little did anyone know the next time I wore the dress I would be acting as the eyes and ears of Uncle Sherlock because someone tried to bomb his house. Grandmamma was right. One never can tell where the Season will lead.*

She picked up her gloves and fan, and gave a practice smile to the mirror. She thought she might rather enjoy playing the spy. It certainly beat the tedium of trying to catch a husband from among a bunch of men who thought blowing up birds was a fun idea.

As she descended the stairs, she looked down on a parade of musicians, liveried servants, and elegantly attired guests moving from the kitchens and cloakrooms to the party. Several of the main-floor drawing rooms had double doors that could be opened to create one large space for a dance floor. Evelina guessed that at least a dozen couples could waltz with room to spare. Maggor's Close was not a pretty place, but it was definitely functional. In time, maybe Alice could do something about the dark, drab wainscoting. A young mistress was what the place needed.

And Tobias will be master here one day. Even if he did choose her to save his family, isn't he better off? Really, what could I have given him? Evelina clung to the ball of ice she'd made—tried to make—of her heart, and forced the thoughts away. She had a job to do, and that meant she was looking for villains, not logic in love.

The musicians finished tuning, and the room was growing crowded. The calendar in that part of the Empire must have been short on entertainment, because the very air crackled with eager anticipation of a socially important event. The noise level rose with the gabble of voices and Evelina began to feel jostled.

"May I fetch you some champagne, Miss Cooper?" came a deep voice from behind her.

She turned. It was the Scarlet King, resplendent in a dark cutaway coat, but this time with a waistcoat of blood-red brocade. The sheer vibrancy of the color made her blink. He handed her a chilled crystal glass, anticipating her answer about the champagne.

"Good evening, Mr. Reading," she said. "And thank you." She took an anxious glance at the bubbling drink, remembering rumors of his interest in poisons.

"You have a pensive air," he observed. "Although charming in the extreme, I confess that it arouses curiosity."

"Much of the company is new to me," Evelina said, inventing excuses. "There are some familiar faces from London, but many whom I do not know."

"Then allow me the pleasure of pointing out the local fauna," he said in a conspiratorial tone that set off a warning bell. Their acquaintance was far too slight for shared secrets. "Take that gentleman, for instance, the one with the monocle. That is Mr. Hieronymus Williams. He's never seen more than five miles from his factories, but he could purchase half of Westminster without emptying his pockets. I doubt his poor wife has had the chance to put on her dancing shoes for a decade."

She considered Mr. Reading a moment, remembering Imogen's warning not to get too close. But then again, he was a prime source of information. "What do the factories of Mr. Hieronymus Williams make?"

"Airships, after the German models. I have a fleet of them." The Scarlet King spoke with the flat tone of someone who wanted to gloat without being obvious about it. He cast her a sidelong glance, no doubt checking to see what effect his words had. *Vanity, thy name is steam baron.*

"Indeed! An entire fleet!" Evelina accompanied the exclamation with a slight flutter of her fan. Scarlet inflated a little. Uncle Sherlock had once said the baron had interests in Bohemia, and she wondered if that was where he had become interested in German design. "Are your ships meant for passengers?"

"Military use, I'm afraid. The Empire leases them for defense of the eastern borders." He gave her an indulgent look. "But such things could not possibly interest you."

Evelina gave a girlish, insipid little laugh. "Only a little. I was reading a piece in the newspapers about the dangers of airships and how great the risks are to the airmen who fly them."

"Enticed by the uniform, eh? Ladies like a whiff of danger. There's plenty to be found on the deck of a dirigible warship." He drew a little closer, reminding her of a robin redbreast that had crossbred with a shark.

She took an automatic step back. "But no doubt technology has found new ways to make their jobs safer?"

"But of course. Aether distillate is safer than hydrogen, and any future ship I build will use it. Rigid construction

offers stability. There are other improvements in the works."
He sipped his champagne, blue eyes watching her over the
rim of the flute.

Evelina's ears pricked. "Improvements?"

"Perhaps I should give you a tour of my new steamspin-
ners." Reading's gaze strayed from her face to the neckline
of her bodice. "Would you enjoy that, Miss Cooper? There
is a great deal of shiny brass."

"Indeed, Mr. Reading." She almost took a sip of champagne to cover the fact that she was growing flustered, but
stopped herself just in time. A tour might give her a look at
his fleet's technical prowess, but it was clear from his oily
smile that he had other things in mind. Polishing his brass, no
doubt. A rush of loathing clawed up her spine, raising gooseflesh as it went. "Perhaps we should bring Miss Roth. She also
has an interest in dirigibles."

Untrue, but there was safety in numbers.

"As they say, Miss Cooper, the more the merrier," the
Scarlet King murmured, inching closer. "And Miss Roth is
a delectable companion."

He said it as if Imogen were a parfait—but he wasn't done
yet. "I love to demonstrate the principles of inflation. Most
find it engrossing. Would you care to dance a waltz, Miss
Cooper?"

"Dance?" she repeated in a faint voice, just as the Scarlet
King took her champagne away, setting it on the tray of a
passing footman. The musicians were striking the first
chord of the next waltz. "Shall we?"

"Miss Cooper." Jasper Keating suddenly appeared at the
Scarlet King's elbow. "May I have a moment of your time?"
He was tall and straight, with silver hair and eyes of so light
a brown that they looked almost amber.

"Of course." Evelina had heard Keating was coming for
the weekend, but had planned to avoid his notice. Now she
was ecstatic to see him.

The Scarlet King did not look happy. "We were about to
dance."

"I'm afraid this can't wait," said Keating.

"Oh, dear," Evelina tried to sound regretful. "I hope it's nothing dire."

The Scarlet King looked broody, but gave way. "Until we meet again, Miss Cooper."

Keating led her away to the front hall, where it was much less crowded. The focus of the room was an enormous fire-place, with logs ablaze against the creeping chill even though it was only August. The first cool nights came sooner this far north, and with a slate floor and fieldstone wall, there was little to keep out drafts.

Keating gave her a slight smile. "You appeared to require a rescue."

Evelina blinked, not sure how to respond. Gallantry was the last thing she expected from the Gold King, especially with the stink of Crowleyton still in her nose. "Thank you, sir."

"How have you fared since we last met, Miss Cooper?"

"Well enough, sir. I have spent the last several months with my grandmother in Devonshire." In fact, it had been Keating's suggestion that she leave London when the forgery debacle was exposed.

"So I had heard." He considered her for a long moment, his gaze searching. "And you do not find it difficult to be here, in my daughter's company?"

Evelina's mouth went dry, her hands twitching with the urge to wrap her arms protectively over her chest, where her heart pretended to be ice. There was only one reason she'd find fault with Alice's presence. How had Keating known there was anything between her and Tobias?

"Come now," Keating said, his voice edged with impa-tience. "I concede you are a clever girl, so I beg you to re-turn the compliment. I saw you together with young Mr. Roth, and I am not so old that I have forgotten the affections of youth."

Then why crush them under your boot leather? A flicker of anger gave her the strength to reply. "And your daughter is a charming hostess and, I hope, a friend. Tob—Mr. Roth is my best friend's brother; that is all."

"Excellent. I'm sure you understand how Alice's happiness weighs heavily with me."

"Of course." She knew a warning when she heard it.

He gave her another long look while the silence grew awkward. "So what are your plans, Miss Cooper? You do not strike me as one to be contented with the usual social round."

He knew that she had played a key role in breaking the forgery case, which had put her in his good graces, at least for the time being. "I wish to continue my education."

"You are a true Holmes, then."

"I hope to be worthy of the name."

His expression grew almost coy. It was the look of a craftsman spotting a particularly well-made tool, but wishing to haggle over the price. "I have heard much of your scholarship and your skill with mechanics, and I am most impressed. Do not be a stranger to my door. I approve of bright young talent, male or female, and I am far from one to object to female scholars."

Evelina nearly pointed out how inconsistent that was, given that he'd never taken his own daughter into the family business. But then Alice had a dynastic function to fulfill, not a workaday one. "I am flattered, sir."

"Flattery is for lesser minds than yours. I would prefer that you were inspired to excel. I would be delighted to see you at my house when I gather together like minds for an evening of conversation."

"Thank you, sir." She'd never heard that Keating hosted any such events, but then no one in her circle—until Tobias—had come to the notice of the Gold King before. The invitation was intriguing, though she heartily wished it had come from anyone else.

Still, he must have seen that glimmer of interest, because his smile grew smug. "I understand that you have a certain talent for clockwork as well as solving mysteries."

She felt a stab of caution. Only those who had the steam barons' blessing were permitted to build any kind of machinery, however trivial. "I have a little skill. I learned it from my father's father."

Keating harrumphed. "A little skill, eh? That is the standard answer women are trained to give. Tell me the truth."

Evelina bit her lip, her pride getting the better of her. "I trump Tobias when it comes to fine work."

"Then I insist you come mingle with my other guests."

"Very good, sir." Outright refusal would only bring unpleasantness.

This was the man who had burned Crowleyton. This was the man who was after the casket and, by extension, Nick. This was the man who, with a word to the Lord Chamberlain, had erased her mother's disgrace and secured Evelina's presentation to the queen. He had an enormous amount of power.

"Then I hope to see you soon, Miss Cooper."

Evelina curtsied, hating herself for the show of submission. A twist of anger caught her breath and pinked her cheeks. All she could do was hope he mistook her high color for a maidenly blush.

When Evelina looked up, Jasper Keating was gone. Lord Bancroft was staring at her from across the room, a mixture of pity and dislike furrowing his face. When their gazes crossed, he jerked his head away and left the hall.

For the moment, Evelina was alone, her only company the riot of voices in the other rooms of the house. She felt the sudden urge to run up to her bedroom and hide. Like a ruffled cat, she needed a minute or two to lick her fur back into place. But Uncle Sherlock was right. There was a great deal going on, and she needed to find out what it was. This wasn't the time to mull over everything she learned—now was the time to act. She could think during the long, stifling hours of wedding talk and embroidery on the morrow.

Still feeling shaken, she started toward the ballroom, but then trailed to a halt. There were other parts of the house she hadn't explored. Tonight, everyone was at the party. At any other time, guests and servants would be scattered throughout the house, making exploration impossible, and there were places she needed to go. Of particular interest was Keating's study on the floor above, with its mahogany desk and locked correspondence box. She'd been aching to try her hand at that lock since she'd glanced through the doorway that afternoon. *Yes, that's where I'll begin.* Finally feeling like she had a plan, Evelina started toward the staircase.

And she almost made it, but chance—or some devil—made her peer into the modest library next to the stairs. It had grown dark outside, but no lamps dimmed the soft moonlight seeping through the many-paned windows. She stopped to look simply because it was pretty and the cooler air, away from everyone else, soothed her skin and her temper.

Then a movement caught her eye. There was someone standing to the right, a man's figure black against the diamond-shaped leading of the window. Evelina stopped, feeling as if she were the one caught hiding, and not the other way around. Slowly, almost reluctantly, her blood began to tingle with recognition.

"Tobias?" she whispered. "Is that you?"

The figure slipped to the right, disappearing into the shadow cast by the bookcases. All that remained was the moonlight floating through the diamond-paned glass and stealing the color from the thick Persian carpet that muted the figure's footfall.

Had she imagined him? Her breath escaped in a disappointed huff. Then she chewed her lip, thinking maybe she should back away and get on with her plan. But before she knew what her feet were doing they had taken her to the embrasure where the figure had been.

Through the window, she could see the rolling expanse of fields bordered here and there with shaggy pines. An owl flitted over the lawn, sweeping down to strike something on the grass. Then it vanished into the trees, a body clutched in its talons.

The sudden, economical violence broke her dreamlike mood. She turned, her gaze probing the shadows of the room. "Tobias?" She heard movement, a rustle of garments, and the scuff of feet against the carpet.

"Evelina," Tobias replied, turning up the gaslight and flooding the room with a soft glow.

For a moment, she was tongue-tied. She'd always thought

him handsome, but she'd forgotten just how deeply that could shake her resolve. Or maybe it was the memory of his "I love you" that trampled her good sense. Whatever it was, the sight of him caught her off guard.

Tobias looked rumpled, as if he'd been traveling. Like Imogen, he was tall and fair, his eyes a changeable gray. He'd always made her think of a fallen angel, as tantalizingly wicked as he was beautiful, but something had changed. Where he had once radiated a playful suggestion of sin, now he seemed merely weary.

Evelina swallowed, her mouth achingly dry. "I didn't think you were going to be here."

"I wasn't, but then I heard you would be. And I wanted to see you dance one last time."

The simple statement stunned her. "Why?" But in a month's time he would be married, and nothing would be the same.

She should have walked away the moment she suspected he was in the library, but for an instant she had forgotten herself. Now she recovered her wits, too aware of her own weakness where he was concerned. "I should go."

"Don't." He caught her arm. "Let me look at you for a moment."

"Why?" The question nearly burned her tongue. Now painful memories came flooding back—his last cruel words, the fact that they had barely parted when he must have started wooing Alice Keating to his bed. "What do you hope to see?"

"What I've lost." His eyebrows lifted sardonically, every line in his body sharp with mockery. "Maybe understanding, if not forgiveness."

The sound of his voice, so very familiar, made her chest ache. Her mouth worked for a moment, grief and anger tangling her tongue. "You made your pact with Keating. Leave it at that."

"But as you can see, the bargain worked. My father is not in jail and my mother is in a fetching new gown. Imogen and Poppy have their dowries. Our future is intact."

And the sacrifice, judging by the lines that pulled at his

face, was almost more than he could bear. The sight of his misery made it hard to cling to her anger, for all she gripped it like a drowning woman. She'd carefully skirted this abyss of sadness all summer, but his sudden appearance had thrown her right over the brink.

"I understand," she said softly, thinking of her own encounter with the Gold King that night. It made her shudder. She would need her uncle's advice on how to escape that noose—and that was exactly the kind of support Tobias had never had.

His sarcastic air faded. "I had to let you go. I would have dragged you down with me, and that wouldn't have helped anyone."

"So now you make bombs."

"What?" He sounded confused.

"I recognized your handiwork. A remote detonation device."

"When were you looking at bombs?"

She didn't answer, so eventually Tobias shook his head. "I just designed those detonators. I don't make individual devices. And I've designed things for Keating I pray will never be built. Imogen isn't the only one with nightmares."

Part of her had wanted him to grow angry, to protest his innocence. But he didn't even know what she was talking about. He wasn't the one who had built the Baker Street bomb.

"The work isn't what you thought?" she asked, aiming for safe territory.

"When is anything what we think it's going to be?" he asked wearily.

She could summon no words, either to agree or to object. Oh, there were things she wanted to say—should have said—about Alice, about the detonator, about her uncle and a thousand other scraps of unfinished business, but it all fell away like so much ash. Conversation implied a future they didn't have.

He buried his face in his hands. Gas jets flickered from the light overhead, but they had been turned so low he seemed wreathed in shadows. Then he pulled his hands away and drew in a harsh breath. "I'm not like you, Evelina. You're stronger than I am. I don't want to let you go. Do you blame me for coming tonight? For one last moment?"

Last moment. He'd given up the fight to keep her. If there was any hope left alive, its wings finally stilled. Tears blurred her vision, her ribs aching with an unbearable feeling of loss. It was as if her heart had melted, leaving nothing but an empty cavern at her core. *I can't afford to cry. If I do, I'm lost.* Emotions were a fatal quicksand.

"Yes." She groped for something concrete, something factual to argue with, because—but she had nothing left to hold on to. "No."

Tobias closed the distance between them, taking her hands. His touch was warm, his fingers long and a little rough from handling tools. "I'm so sorry."

The finality of it stabbed deep. Evelina squeezed her eyes closed, clamping her jaw to keep her chin from wobbling. The least she could do was carry herself with dignity. She dragged in a shaking breath, summoning the composure to make her good-byes. *Oh, please, no!*

"Don't cry," he whispered. "I can't bear it."

She opened her eyes and Tobias was a blur of light and shadows, but in the next instant he was kissing her, his mouth hot and greedy. And yet he still held back, as if only his mouth had full permission to touch her. His fingers cupped her face as gently as if she were spun glass.

The last of her restraint shattered. Every fiber of her body refused this defeat. She wound her arms around his neck, a noise of encouragement escaping her throat. The effect was instant. As if memorizing her form, his hands skimmed down her ribs, over the flare of her hips, lingering in places that brought heat low in her belly. She made the noise again, pleading without words.

And he pulled her close, teasing her mouth open to deepen the kiss. Yes, this felt right. Evelina's stomach fluttered as excitement and desire raced through her blood. She ran her palms up the soft fabric of his shirt, feeling his heart pound beneath her touch. And then her fingers curled around the edges of the garment, finding the sudden heat of bare skin.

New information flooded her—the silkiness of his tongue, the faint rasp of stubble on his chin, the feel of his chest under her hands. He pushed closer, and she shifted her feet, bracing herself against the force of his need.

Giddiness swamped her, sweeping reason aside like so much crockery. Her own desire awakened, stretching and clawing at her insides, leaving her achy and restless. She met the force of his kiss, body to body.

If only he'd stay with me, I'd give him everything. But the moment the thought formed, she knew she'd still lost. He had already chosen his family over her. Despite this moment of passion, that wasn't going to change. To expect anything else was folly, because the fact that he would take care of his own was one of the very things that made her admire him. *This is wrong!*

Her heart squeezed at the realization, the shock of it deep because it was inarguably true. She broke the kiss, sucking in a breath of air that was almost painful. A look of surprise had barely touched his eyes when a voice ripped through the room.

"Mr. Roth!"

Evelina sprang away from him, her cry of dismay marking her guilt as nothing else could have. As one, they whirled to face the door they had foolishly left open.

Jasper Keating stood there, his entire body sparking with fury. But it was Imogen, standing just behind him, that captured Evelina's gaze. Her face was turning white as paper.

"Oh, bloody hell," Imogen whispered, but no one noticed her curse.

CHAPTER TEN

NICK LEANED OVER THE SHIP'S RAIL, AIMING ONE OF STRIK-er's home-made weapons toward the darkness below. The bosun had spotted a lighter craft dogging their path, but it was hiding in the darkness and using the clouds for camou-flage. The one advantage they had was that their tail wasn't aware they'd been made. The moment the little bugger grew confident enough to put its nose out, Nick would blow it to smithereens. Last night's escapades, nearly losing Striker and all, had been enough to put him in a killing mood. Poole was watching the other side, with the same orders to fire only when he could get a clear shot.

As dawn crept over the horizon, the ground below was emerging into view. Individual features of the landscape gained form and depth from the purple shadows, visible now because the clouds were starting to shred to pieces. Bad luck for their tail, but bad luck for them, too. All ships were exposed in a clear blue sky.

Nick was grateful for the brisk tailwind hurrying them along. The *Jack* could outrun most airships, but the ache in his limbs was a reminder that the best-laid plans could turn to a piss-pot when least expected. He'd only dangled upside down on that damned ladder for a few minutes, but it was as close to a crushed skull as he planned on getting for a good long while.

Striker—who didn't have the best head for heights—still hadn't seen fit to sober up, and Nick didn't blame him one bit.

He thought he saw the shape of a balloon and wheeled toward it.

What is it? Athena asked.

The shape dissipated into mist. Just a suspicious-looking cloud. "Nothing."

Do you wish me to outrun the nuisance?

Nick had thought of that. With Athena's help, they could ascend to heights few smaller ships could reach. Then they could pepper the clouds with cannon shot. "No. I want to see who they've sent after us before I blow him out of the sky."

As it pleases you, Niccolo. But I wonder, what do you expect to learn?

He didn't have an answer for that, so he went back to waiting and watching. The weapon was heavy, and Nick used the rail to support the nose. Striker was one of the finest makers in the Empire, but his inventions were typically small cannons that exploded, electrocuted, or otherwise turned things to a crisp. Some of this was the result of working for so long as the Gold King's streetkeeper and some of it was Striker's own unholy glee when something went up in flames.

On the bright side, he was a deft hand with things like the aether distiller that filtered out the rarified gas during high-altitude flights. It then condensed the distillate in long, copper coils and stored the lime-green liquid in steel canisters until it was released into the ship's balloon. Nick had only the most basic idea of how the thing worked, except that it needed more attention than a high-class whore to keep it running. Perversely, Striker loved it with all the fondness one would lavish on a charmingly wayward child.

Nick ran the crew by letting them do what they did best and tried to learn what airmen's skills he could. He might have been captain, making plans and taking risks, but, on a day-to-day basis, he made sure he earned his keep. Today, that meant watching for annoyances on their tail. The task held the same bizarre combination of boredom and anxiety he'd felt waiting for his turn to take the center ring.

A few yards to his right, the package sat slumped against the water butt, shivering in the gray dawn. A dark growth of beard intensified the hollows of the man's cheeks, and a lack of sleep drew circles under his eyes. Nick noticed that someone had given him a blanket and a mug of tea—probably the helmsman, Digby, who always treated prisoners with courtesy. The *Red Jack* must have run out of custard cream biscuits, or their prisoner would have one of those, too. The thought reminded Nick that he was more than ready for breakfast.

"Captain Niccolo," the package said, his voice hoarse from the damp.

Nick didn't bother to look up. "What?"

"Where are you taking me?"

It should have been a reasonable question, but the paper that the Schoolmaster had stuffed into Nick's pocket had a separate set of destinations than the ones he'd given out loud. Since there was a traitor around, Nick was all for paranoia.

"North," was all Nick said. He frowned at the memory of the fight at the tannery, the silence filled by the gentle *whop-whop* of the tail propeller.

"I know we're going north," the man said acidly.

Nick turned, a little amused by his irritation. "I'm not saying more."

The package narrowed his eyes. "I know we're not going to Skye. The Steam Council blasted the rebels out of that base three months ago."

That was news to Nick, but he kept his expression bland and returned his attention to the clouds. The sun was turning the sky the color of a strawberry cream dessert. Yes, he was definitely hungry. "You talk like we're in open warfare."

"Aren't we?" The man blew on his tea. "You're pointing a gun at something."

"I'm annoyed."

"The Scarlet King's soldiers tried to bake your arse."

A vision of the hot harpoons, flaring so near the *Red*

Jack's balloon, made Nick flex his fingers around the stock of the weapon. "Their mistake."

"Your ignorance. You don't even know who I am."

"I don't ask my cargo's name, even when we give it tea and a blanket."

"My name is Elias Jones."

"Should I care?"

"I care. I'm more than cargo."

"You should have thought of that before taking on Holmes." *And endangering Evie.* "Now you're nothing but a package."

"By accident, not design. You're nothing but a pirate. Was that by choice, Captain? Why take up the red flag?"

Nick almost laughed at the question. *To make my fortune and impress a girl.* It had been that simple, but there had been a thousand complications, too. He'd stolen Athena, and the deva had needed a ship. He and Striker had just killed Dr. Magnus, and he wasn't sure they were safe from the law. Worst of all, Evie was in love with Tobias Roth—tall, blond-haired, handsome, and every inch the English ideal of cultured elegance. Nick had been heartsick and angry, with nothing but poverty and loneliness ahead.

When he'd turned to the skies, it had been an act of defiance. He saw himself swaggering into a drawing room in a suit as fine as Jasper Keating's, showing the world that he'd made enough money to call himself a gentleman. Showing he was every bit as good as Roth.

Somewhere between that moment and now, he'd grown up. There was no way he would ever be anything but an orphaned boy with no last name and skin the color of pale coffee. A vicious mutt from the gutter. "Piracy pays well."

"So does espionage, on occasion."

Conversation ended when something glinted on the brass of Nick's weapon. He looked to the east, squinting into the bright streak of the sun. "Athena, can you sense anything?"

There was a pause. Although the deva was quick to detect any change in the atmosphere, or to track the flight of birds, she wasn't always any better than he was at picking up on approaching vessels. She was a creature of wind and flight, and not attuned to land creatures hauled into the air by machines. *There is something right above our tail.*

Right at the angle where the sun blinded him. "Then move."

No sooner had he spoken than the ship swung around and up faster than it had any right to. Fortunately, the *Red Jack*'s crew was already on the alert. The motion took Nick farther away from the enemy, and he scrambled across the deck to Poole's side. The bosun already had the other craft in his sights. Nick hoisted his own weapon, grunting as its weight connected with his sore shoulder. Both men pulled a lever on the side of the guns that started them humming with a mosquito-like whine.

Through the telescopic scope, he saw the craft come into view as the *Red Jack* sailed upward. It was a small zephyr-class craft, built for stealth more than for power, with a pair of small propellers to either side of the prow and stern. The balloon was striped with the red of the Scarlet King. Then he saw the face of the pilot—no one he knew—and then the mate. That face rang a bell. He'd beat him at a hand of cards—a friendly game in a tavern a month or two ago. Nick wished he hadn't remembered that.

Digby, the helmsman, ran up on his left, thumping against the rail. He'd come to know when Athena took over and his services could be better used elsewhere. "Holy shite. Their gun ports are opening."

Nick had stalled as long as he dared. Any guns the zephyr had would be small, but no less deadly at this range. "Fire at will."

Poole's weapon flared, Nick's an instant later. A jolt shot up his arm, making his boots skid against the deck, and the weapons snarled with a sound like ripping silk. There was a ball of light and rushing air, and the terrified look on the faces of the men. They clearly hadn't been expecting aether guns. And then the entire gondola was engulfed in crackling blue energy.

The two men flew backward, shot across the deck by the charge. The propellers died almost instantly as the connectors inside the equipment melted.

"Go!" Nick commanded.

Going! Athena said, diving away from the zephyr as fast as the *Jack* could fly.

One second. Two seconds. Nick watched the zephyr recede as distance grew between them, his mouth dry as sand. *I gave the order to fire. They had their gun ports open. They meant for us to die.* And yet his guts still writhed with the horror of what was to come.

The corona of blue energy died away as suddenly as it appeared. The zephyr looked dead—no voices, no motion, no threat of violence.

Wind thrummed through the rigging and stung Nick's face. A minute must have passed, the image of the ship now shrinking to the size of a dinner plate from their viewpoint at the stern. Other members of the *Red Jack*'s crew were gathering with doomed expectancy. There was a chance the zephyr's men were still alive, but Nick hoped to hell that wasn't the case because there was no chance of rescue now. Zephyr-class ships used hydrogen.

"No sparks," said Digby, always the optimist. "Maybe they've something worth taking."

They probably did, but Nick knew better. Aether weapons worked through the ship's systems, and sooner or later all that sizzling energy built up a charge, and then sparks. "Wait for it."

They meant for us to die. He remembered the hot harpoons last night—the men to either side of him would have been burned to charred husks. Poole was barely twenty-one, still gangly and unfinished. Red-haired Digby, with his fiddle and tea, wanted to make his fortune and open a tavern. If they were forced to take sides, Nick had chosen these men for his own, and he would defend them to his death. *The package was right. This is no longer the occasional knife in the dark. This is open warfare.*

The explosion came so suddenly Poole jumped—a whoosh of infernal wind and a sheet of flame crawling into the sky, turning their faces to hellish masks with the reflected orange glow. It lasted only seconds, and then the balloon was gone, leaving the gondola a fiery skeleton raining debris into the pearly dawn light. There hadn't even been time to curse.

Nick felt the young bosun shaking. His own insides felt little better. He clapped a hand on Poole's shoulder. "Go get yourself a drink."

Poole didn't need to be asked twice. Neither did the others. Only Digby lingered, a frown on his usually smiling face. "Do you think there are more ships chasing us?"

"Double the watch. I'll split the time on the topside with Smith and Poole." He was one of the few who didn't mind taking the perch on top of the balloon. "I don't think anyone else will be following after that, but I'm not taking any chances."

Digby nodded and loped off to find Smith. Nick slumped against the rail, his mind a blank for one precious moment.

A seagull landed on the deck with a graceless flap. *Fish?*

Nick heard the question inside his head. Since he'd been working so closely with an air deva, he'd started to hear the language of all birds and not just the ash rooks. Unfortunately, they weren't brilliant conversationalists. *Sorry, no fish,* he replied.

The gull ruffled its feathers and sulked.

Still manacled, Jones hadn't moved from his position by the water butt. He took a sip from the mug, his chained wrists making it awkward. "Quite the show."

Nick wasn't in the mood. "Friends of yours?"

The man chuckled softly. "Nobody's friends now. Of course, these days it's hard to tell who's a friend and who's working for thirty pieces of silver. But you knew that already."

He did. "Next you'll tell me you know the name of whoever gave away our location last night."

"Maybe." Jones took another drink of tea, eyes mocking, daring him to knock the tin mug across the deck.

Nick gripped the rail, refusing to play his game even though his guts were hard knots. "Who are you working for?"

Jones finished the tea and let the empty mug dangle. "I'm not saying more."

"Who betrayed me?"

Now Jones smiled, a slippery, unpleasant sight. "I'll tell you if you set me free. What shall it be, Captain? The Schoolmaster's shipping orders or the safety of your vessel and crew?"

Nick weighed the man's words as he watched Smith climbing the rigging to the top of the balloon. Two others patched the deck where a hot harpoon had burned a hole last night. He could still smell the charred wood. Deliver the prisoner, or know the name of the man who had betrayed his friends?

"I've heard you're a rich man, Captain. You're not exactly Robin Hood, despite what the rumors say. You know which side of your bread is buttered." Jones probably thought he was moving in for some decisive stroke of logic.

"That's not entirely true. I help out now and then." And as the steam barons pushed the rebels harder, Nick had found himself giving aid to the poor more often. *I might end up a hero of the revolution yet, for seven percent plus expenses.*

"My freedom or the safety of your ship. Which is it?"

Nick took the tin mug from Jones and tossed it from hand to hand, catching it neatly, although he never took his gaze from the prisoner's face. "You make a good argument, but you also made a serious error."

For the first time, Jones's composure slipped. "What?"

But Nick just smiled, the only sound the cawing of gulls and the creak of wood and rigging. The first mistake was confirming Nick's suspicions that there was a traitor. He'd suspected, but here was corroboration from an inside source. Now that he was on guard, he could be careful. And if the Schoolmaster wanted Elias Jones so badly, the man was worth far more than a traitor's name.

But the real reason he'd never let the man go free was private. *You put Evelina Cooper in danger.* The explosion meant for Holmes could have easily killed her. But he wouldn't say the words. Not to this fool.

While he might be angry with Evie, while she might have shattered his life by walking away, his first instinct was still to keep her safe. No one could ever know that she was his Achilles' heel.

Northern England, August 27, 1888
MAGGOR'S CLOSE

11:05 p.m. Monday

"WHAT IN HEAVEN'S NAME WERE YOU THINKING?" IMOGEN dragged Evelina to her room. She didn't bother to turn on a lamp, but just slammed the door and bolted it, locking them in an envelope of lavender-scented darkness. "How could you do something so witless?"

Evelina wasn't sure there was even an answer. She had wanted—what? Her body felt curiously numb, like she had been injected with one of her uncle's drugs. And yet that absence of feeling was destroying her. Inside, she felt consumed, as if all that was Evelina was blackening and falling away into ash.

"Say something!" Imogen's voice demanded. Only her indistinct outline was visible in the dark bedchamber, her face a lighter patch of gray.

Evelina started to reach for Imogen's hand the way she'd done a hundred times over the years—wanting comfort, offering it—but she cut the gesture short. *This is my fault.* "I'm sorry," she whispered.

"I'm sure you are." Her friend's voice was weary. "Do you still love him then?"

"Yes."

Evelina heard the scratch of a striking match, and Imogen lit the candle on her dressing table. A simple taper was an interesting choice, since they were in the home of the man who owned every gas plant in the West End of London. There was something rebellious in the tiny pool of warm, intimate light.

"What makes you think he loves you?" Imogen asked, keeping her attention fixed on the jars and bottles on the table. The candlelight turned her pale hands the color of new ivory.

The question caught her short, but she understood the question. Tobias was nothing if not complicated. "He told me so."

"I'm sorry." Imogen's eyes were bright with tears. "You know that nothing can come of it now."

"I know." Evelina's chest hurt, as if the air was too heavy to breathe. "I want him to be happy. I know he's not."

"I was hoping things would get better." Imogen sagged onto the tasseled stool that sat before the dressing table. Her image in the mirror did the same, head bowed with sorrow. "Alice needs him now."

"I know, and I'm sorry. I didn't think he would be here. You have to believe that I didn't intend to even see him, much less kiss him."

A tear slipped down Imogen's cheek, glistening in the candle's glow. "I believe you. I don't know if anyone else will. You'll probably have to leave."

Evelina's eyes burned, but no tears would relieve them. "I know." She also knew that her reputation was in grave danger if news of that careless kiss spread.

"Then why open that wound?" Imogen looked genuinely bewildered.

Why, indeed? The wavering candle made eerie shapes on the flocked wallpaper, as if all her childhood monsters had come out from under the bed and were clustered around the room. He had come to see her dance one last time. He still desired her—and she still felt the heat of his answer in her blood. But that wouldn't bring either of them peace.

Evelina closed her eyes. The numbness inside was fading, and it felt as if she were falling into a bottomless cavern. "I should have known better."

Without replying, Imogen rose from the stool, the candle-light catching the faceted jewels in her hair combs. Her silence was the same as agreement, and somehow it was worse than a fight.

Evelina touched her burning face to discover it was wet. "I'm sorry," she said again weakly. Her stomach ached with tension as she looked up into her friend's face, realizing that Imogen was caught between being loyal to her brother or her friend. It wasn't fair.

A voice thundered from outside the bedroom door. "Miss Roth, is Evelina Cooper in there with you?"

Evelina's breath caught at the threat in his tone. *Keating is furious.* He'd been pouncing on Tobias when Imogen dragged her away. Unfortunately, now it was her turn. Visions of Crowleyton rose up to haunt her.

The doorknob rattled. She cast a glance at Imogen's frightened face. *He could destroy her in a blink.* There was a reason that Tobias had bowed to Keating's will. Above all else, he'd been afraid for his mother and sisters. He'd put everything on the line not just for their happiness, but for their survival.

And Keating might have been pleasant to Evelina because she'd helped Holmes crack the forgery ring, but now Evelina had crossed him. More than that, she'd wounded the daughter Keating loved more than anyone else in the world.

Her stomach felt like a corkscrew.

"Miss Roth!" Keating's knock became an insistent pounding.

Imogen tried to hold her, but Evelina pulled her fingers free and turned to the door. She drew back the latch and pulled it open before she could change her mind. The sight of the Gold King's furious face nearly stopped her heart.

She sucked in a breath that sounded eerily like a death rattle. "Here I am."

CHAPTER ELEVEN

"I THOUGHT YOU AND I HAD AN UNDERSTANDING ON THE topic of Mr. Roth," Keating growled. "Now you've hurt my daughter, and I won't have it."

He'd dragged her into his study, one hand clutched around her wrist like a pincer. He shoved her inside and locked the door behind them, then turned and faced her, arms folded.

Evelina loathed being handled like a child. Without thinking, she braced herself, feet apart, ready to fight back. Keating saw the move and raised his eyebrows, daring her. Evelina bit her lip, forcing herself to relax. Her heart pounded with fear and anger, but she'd gain nothing by antagonizing him further. Besides, Keating had a right to be angry, and that knowledge burned worse than anything else. She backed away, putting distance between them.

Unlike Imogen's room, this place glowed with gaslight, and the sudden brightness hurt her eyes. The room was stark, decorated in shades of white except for hideous tartan furniture. The crazy pattern of reds and greens reminded Evelina of the bars of a cage, and the room seemed to shrink with each tick of the clock.

She wet her lips, trying to steady the thundering of her heart. "I'm sorry about what happened. I didn't expect to see Tobias here. I didn't intend to be alone with him."

"Bloody hell, is that supposed to be an excuse?" Keating said hotly, cursing even though she was a young gentlewoman. But then again, she hadn't behaved like one, had she?

"I know it's not an excuse." *How do I reply?* She opened

her mouth to blurt something—anything—out, but he cut her off with a growl.

"Does the fact that he is betrothed *to my daughter* count for nothing?"

Heat flared in her cheeks. *You trapped Tobias. Does that count?* But Keating's wrong didn't erase hers. Guilt slithered through her, devouring her courage. "I know I am at fault, sir. I forgot myself. I should not have come here in the first place."

He advanced a step, his eyes narrowed. "Tobias said much the same thing. If either of you breathe a word of this indiscretion to Alice, if either of you give her a moment's unhappiness, I will personally throttle you!"

She inched backward, keeping the space between them constant. "I understand. Yet please know that I wish I could make it up to her."

"You wish to make amends?" he asked with an edge of sarcasm.

"If there was a way, I would." Then Evelina swallowed hard, realizing she'd made a mistake. She'd given him an opening of some kind. She didn't know why it mattered, but knew she would find out soon. Anxiety skittered through her stomach.

"To her or to me?"

It was a question writ in quicksand, bound to trap her no matter how she jumped. "To either of you, sir."

"I'm pleased to hear it." Keating regarded her with calculating appraisal. "You owe me an apology, and I will collect it on my own terms."

Evelina raised her chin. She deserved to be upbraided for breaking the social rules. She would do penance for endangering Alice's future happiness. But Keating was turning this to his own ends. "What do you want from me?"

He narrowed his amber-colored eyes. "Hm." Then he circled around the study to sit behind the desk. The leather chair sighed and creaked with his weight. Keating picked up a pen and rolled it through his fingers. He'd left her standing like a maidservant, a less-than-subtle assertion of his power over her.

"I'm aware that there was an incident involving an explosive device at your uncle's address," he said in a much calmer voice.

The change of topic was so unexpected that she nearly started. But then she smoothed any emotion from her reply. "You are?"

He gave a chilling smile, his lips the only thing to move. The rest of him stayed utterly still. The clock ticked, dragging out the moment, and Evelina's attention wandered. At one corner of the blotter sat the correspondence box that had tempted her to the stairway in the first place. She felt a deep-seated urge to smash it.

Finally, he spoke. "I hired the man who did the job."

Evelina felt her face go numb with shock. Not that he had done it—it had been his detonator, after all—but that he had admitted it so freely. *But then Imogen said Keating was the one trying to stop the bomber, so was he lying to the Scarlet King, or is he lying now?* She was growing confused. Something about the exchange seemed like a test and she bridled, letting her temper rise. "Why are you telling me this? Why kill my uncle?"

Keating smiled, clearly fascinated by her distress. "But I didn't. Your uncle has special talents. I was extremely grateful to him for the service he performed with regard to that forgery situation last April. It would have been a great shame to lose his talents, and to have such a valuable asset exterminated within the boundaries of my territory would have had the effect of throwing down a gauntlet. I would have had no choice but to go to war."

"With whom?" she demanded. "And where do I come into this?"

He gave another one of his long pauses, and that allowed time for her fear to rise again. Fear came, but so did fury. "Mr. Keating, please explain yourself!"

HER IMPUDENCE WAS all it took to unleash a storm of anger inside Keating, the muscles of his neck turning rigid as steel. He was not a man who sentimentalized domesticity, but Evelina Cooper had struck at the very core of his home. At his daughter's happiness.

"Why should I explain myself to the likes of you?"

"You began this topic, Mr. Keating." She turned pale, but didn't cry or tremble. The Cooper girl was brave.

His anger turned to avarice, and the instinct to collect her—the way others bought horses or hunting dogs— pushed away his wrath. In purely rational terms, Alice had served her purpose and was a bullet spent. Evelina Cooper was fresh ammunition, with her own share of mechanical expertise, impressive intelligence, and far more wit and beauty than any of his male operatives. Keating had done his research. She had had an usual upbringing, to say the least, and had done an excellent job of hiding it—a large point in her favor.

And without meaning to, Tobias had handed over the girl as surely as if he'd put her in handcuffs. He'd compromised her, and that flutter of guilt and alarm was all Keating had needed to make his move. Now there was no need to woo Evelina Cooper with flattery and invitations to after-dinner conversation among the mechanical savants. He only needed to convince her that serving the Gold King was her only possible choice.

And once she was accustomed to his service—and he could make that happen very, very quickly—she would be conduit to a great deal of information. What her uncles did. What really went on at Hilliard House. And she had known the Gypsy who took his device, had she not? According to his information, they had been childhood sweethearts, raised together in the circus. The Cooper girl could be extremely useful, not just on her own account, but as bait in his plans to retrieve Athena's Casket.

Now Keating watched her face, enjoying the look of helpless rage. *Good.* She was far too self-possessed for his liking, and he needed a way past that armor. But then her look turned suspicious, and he knew he hadn't made any headway at all. "What war?" she asked in a low, tense voice.

It was a fair question. He studied her, wondering how much to say. That was always the trick with underlings.

They had to know enough to make intelligent choices, but it was unwise to tell them everything. "How much do you know about the Steam Council?"

Her eyebrows lifted. "I know what most people know. Your names and districts. I know that you are generally regarded as the most powerful, with the Blue King second, and Green third. Then there are the Scarlet King and the Violet Queen, and then the Black Kingdom. I don't know much about them."

The Black Kingdom ruled London's underground passages. Where they fit in the hierarchy of kings was an open question. "No one does. They don't matter, at least not yet."

She waited, her expression almost blank. In a strange way, she reminded him uncomfortably of Striker. Fear widened her eyes and sped her breath, but there was a similar self-reliance that he found disconcerting. If he wanted results from her, he would have to treat her as firmly as he would a man.

But first, he had to prepare the ground. "The Steam Council is held together by mutual self-interest. Together, we are strong enough to run our companies without interference. There are forces in the Empire who do not appreciate what we do for the good of the nation."

"Those the newspapers refer to as rebels, you mean," she said evenly, but he could tell there was a barb hidden in the polite words.

It rankled, and he set down the pen with a firm click on the desktop. "Yes. The council's unity keeps them in check, and so the Empire remains at peace. Do you understand me so far?"

"Perfectly."

"Good. Then you will understand my problem. King Coal—the Blue King—is making a move against the council—against me, to be precise. My own residences are too well guarded to make for an easy target, so his intention was to begin his campaign by attacking someone who has done me a conspicuous service. Your uncle's masterstroke in the matter of the forgery ring is still fresh in the public mind. In addition, Holmes has locked up many of the Blue

King's best men with proofs so decisive that nothing could sway the outcome of their trials. In other words, the Blue King dislikes your uncle sufficiently that his murder was an obvious choice."

Evelina's jaw tightened, the color draining from her face. Keating felt a surge of petty satisfaction. "Sit down, Miss Cooper," he said, waving at the chair on the other side of the desk.

She complied. "You said that you hired the bomber. Where does the Blue King enter into this?"

"Elias Jones, the man I hired, was the Blue King's operative, and the bombing was originally the Blue King's plan. I bought Jones off and altered the bomb so that it still exploded, but not at full strength. I don't want your uncle dead. I can bluster my way around a scare, but a death means I have no choice but to retaliate at full force."

"Then why have the bomb at all?"

"That is where things grow more complex. Pay careful attention to this part." He paused, waiting until she looked up from twisting her fingers in her lap. "To put it simply, Blue can't know that I'm on to him."

"Wait." Evelina raised a hand. "I just want to be completely clear. The Blue King sent Jones, who pretended to be a client. Under his original orders, Jones was to leave the bomb, then detonate it once he was clear of the building?"

"The bomb had a timer. I replaced that when I reduced the charge."

"And you replaced it with a device of Mr. Roth's design."

Keating's eyelid ticked in annoyance. Of course she recognized Tobias's work. But then again, that kind of knowledge was one of the reasons he wanted her talents. "Yes. Less was left to chance that way. But the operative was to carry out every other aspect of the job as if he were in the Blue King's employ."

"Including questioning my uncle at gunpoint?" A sharp edge crept into her words.

"Yes." Because Keating wanted the answers every bit as much as his rival.

Over the summer, he had begun to entertain suspicions

about Mycroft Holmes's involvement with the so-called Baskerville group—and Sherlock's, for that matter. The detective might have served him well once, but was far from a willing employee. The only reason Keating had left the two brothers at liberty was that he had something in mind for each of them. But that was information he wouldn't share with Evelina.

Instead, he waved a defeated hand. "Unfortunately, in the end, the operative botched the job and vanished. You wouldn't know anything about that, would you, Miss Cooper?"

"I'm afraid not, sir."

He frowned, unable to tell if she was lying. Jones was a weasel, and had probably bolted for a hole somewhere, afraid of facing either his old master or his new one. But Keating had men searching high and low just in case. "At any rate, there you have the broad strokes of the picture. The Blue King wants a war. Unfortunately, he started it at your uncle's address. Fortunately, I secretly averted it."

"Thank you for informing me."

"I am merely setting the stage for the important part of our discussion."

He rose from the chair and paced the room, her wary blue eyes following him. There was more he hadn't said. The rebels' true strength remained a mystery. If the Steam Council fractured, it put them all at risk if a rebellion turned out to be more than a few angry mobs. However, giving the *appearance* of a rift in the council—presenting a weakness that would serve as bait—could draw the rebel leaders out where they could be captured and questioned.

Once the rebels were gone, he could turn his attention to crushing the other council members without risking a war on two fronts. But all this required a complicated dance—luring insurgents into the open while conducting a war without committing his forces too soon. He still wasn't sure how that last part was going to play out. Each member of the Steam Council had to be distracted—Green with money, Violet with intrigue, and Scarlet with women. Reading had already been asking about Imogen Roth like a dog licking its chops in hope of scraps. But King Coal—the Blue King—was a deadly old soul, and a much craftier opponent. He would not be so easily fooled.

Ultimately, Keating wanted that war—a war for control of the whole Empire—but he also wanted a guarantee that he would win. And winning was where Miss Cooper came in. "You said you wished to make amends, and I will hold you to that."

She regarded him levelly, but the skin around her eyes and mouth was tight with apprehension. "I'm sure you shall, sir."

"The first service I need from you is simple and well within your scope. Consider it an exercise to limber up your faculties. I need to see how well you perform."

"First service?" The words were precise.

He ignored them. "I need you to deploy your uncle on my behalf. There is information I require about the Blue King's resources. It should not surprise you that all the steam barons have makers on their staff, just like I have Mr. Roth. Those makers create machines. While most of us are proud to show off our talent and the richness of their inventions, King Coal is not. But if he is planning war, this makes perfect sense. Why show his cards, so that we can mount an effective defense? Ergo, I want to know who and what he has at his fingertips."

"Can't you find that out from whatever men you've bought from the Blue King, like Elias Jones? They work for King Coal. Don't they know who his maker is?"

"No. He's kept his plans secret even from them. That's why I need someone with your uncle's talents."

She blinked. "My uncle can't just walk into the Blue King's territory. How is he supposed to find this out?"

He could detect fear in her voice, and anger, but also curiosity. It was what he'd wanted to hear. There were some who could not look at an impossibility and resist the urge to find a way around it, no matter how distasteful the situation. From what Tobias Roth had said, and from what he'd been able to learn about her involvement in the forgery case, Evelina Cooper was every bit as addicted to puzzles as her uncle.

But there was no point in letting her know exactly how pleased he was with how the conversation was going—and that he actually wanted her, and not Holmes, to spy on the Blue King. She was the better tool, and it wouldn't take long to make her see it. And that would neatly serve two purposes: he got his information, and it got Evelina miles away from Tobias Roth.

And, if he was very lucky, she would—all unknowing—draw the pirate Niccolo into a trap. Scarlet's airships were all very fine in a battle, but when it came to catching a man, they couldn't hold a candle to the enticement of a pretty girl—especially since the chit didn't even need to know that she was staked out like a goat to lure the tiger.

God love her, Alice still hadn't figured out that he'd meant to leave her unchaperoned all those long summer days.

CHAPTER TWELVE

KEATING GAVE HER A LOOK THAT SAID SHE WAS ASKING A stupid question. He was pacing, looking down on her. She wanted to stand up and even out their heights, but she wasn't sure her legs would hold her.

"Holmes is a master of disguise, a virtuoso of ruses and deceit," he said. "Tell him to get the information on the Blue King's forces, but keep it secret and keep it silent."

Anger spiked, loosening her tongue. "Forgive me if I am being slow, but why not ask him yourself?"

"For two reasons. From what I understand from Mr. Roth, your expertise in clockwork and mechanics is greater than your uncle's. Your evaluation of his findings is key. And you are far more vulnerable. If I apply pressure to your uncle, I need to exert effort. Holmes is a difficult and irritating man, and the last time I requested his assistance he tried to refuse. But if I apply pressure to you, he will undoubtedly rush to your rescue at once. It's so much more efficient this way."

That was too much. Evelina's anger drowned under a flood of remorse, bringing a sting of tears to her eyes. But when she spoke, her voice was filled with horrified incredulity. "The Blue King has already tried to kill my uncle. I can't ask him to walk into danger."

Her uncle might have the ability to disguise himself as one of the ragged men who wandered the London docks, but no disguise was perfect. He was a fine actor, but he was gentry. Sooner or later, he'd make a mistake. And then, once he was in King Coal's hands, a bomb might have been the merciful option. She'd heard the stories.

"Don't put him in danger." She was pleading now, a catch

in her words. Fear crawled up her back, running cold fingers up her neck and through the roots of her hair. "Please don't."

"Oh, Holmes is safe and secure for now." Keating stopped his pacing and lowered his voice to a dark whisper. "I've had his house surrounded by my men. Every door and window is watched, every delivery, every letter. No one is going to reach him without my permission, so he is perfectly safe."

He's got Baker Street under surveillance. That meant there would be no chance to sneak her uncle away for a long visit abroad.

"You're going about this all wrong," she muttered. "He's not the right man for the job. You need a maker, and someone who understands the people there."

Since the steam barons had forbidden the sale of parts to private citizens—they didn't want the rabble finding ways to generate their own power instead of buying it—a black market had sprung up. She'd gone to such places often enough with her grandfather, looking for this or that part to repair something at the circus. The first trick would be to find that market—it could be a shop, or the back of a house, or a tavern, or even a literal market—and then figure out who were the gossips. However much secrecy King Coal kept around his plans, makers loved to talk, and if something interesting was under construction, the place would be abuzz with it. All one needed then was the price of a pint and ears to hear.

Keating shook his head. "Holmes is the man. The Blue Boys know my Yellowbacks and their streetkeepers." Each of the barons had their army of thugs, and they guarded their territory jealously.

Evelina jumped from her chair. "There's got to be someone else."

"Are you sure? If I'm wrong and your uncle is of no use to me, then if the Blue King sends another assassin—which he surely will—should I stop him?"

Evelina closed her eyes, fighting the wave of panic that bubbled up inside her. She had to do something to get her uncle out of harm's way. After all his kindness—his acceptance of who she was—it was the least she owed him.

"Holmes did well enough last time," Keating said derisively.

The words brought back a scatter of images—her uncle shot and bleeding on the floor of the Roths' dining room; the gallery opening where the forgeries had been exposed; and Keating offering her his own carriage to take her back to Hilliard House after everyone else had left her behind, including Tobias.

Hard on the heels of that was her fear of falling back into the gutter. She'd struggled so hard to raise herself from the circus to the drawing room, giving up the only family she'd known and mastering every impulse until she could pass as one of the gentry. Falling back into the mud had always been a danger, but that she was in danger of falling because of Tobias—who had said he'd loved her despite her birth—stung doubly hard.

She opened her eyes, barely managing to hide the loathing she felt. Her stomach writhed as Keating leaned forward, putting his face so close to hers she could feel his breath. "Well, Miss Cooper, what is it to be? All you have to do is ask your uncle to perform for me."

"I will not."

She'd seen fruits that had rotted from the inside out, the skins unblemished until somebody poked them and they collapsed into a ruin of stink and mold. Someday, she was going to expose Keating's putrefied core—but it wasn't going to be that night. As much as she balked at admitting it, he had won this round. *First he took Tobias, now he's taking my uncle.*

"Then do you propose another method of obtaining the information I require? Surely you have some suggestions. As I understand it, you have something of an acquaintance with, shall we say, the less affluent rungs of society. You had a colorful start in life for a young lady of your class."

Shock coursed through her, so sharp that she actually jumped. *Bollocks, he knows about Ploughman's!* It didn't matter how he'd found out. With one word, he could destroy her reputation once and for all. Society drawing rooms didn't welcome the sequined daughters of the high wire—

and whatever was said of her would rebound on the rest of her family.

Keating had every card. Evelina fell back into her chair, suddenly dizzy. "You would ruin me."

He shrugged. "I wouldn't ever say something about you that wasn't true."

She swallowed, and it felt like shards of glass sliding down her throat. "You would let the Blue King have my uncle."

"The Blue King, or someone else. Your uncle, or someone else. I'll leave that to your imagination. I don't like to put limits on the future."

Her fingers curled into the glossy fabric of her skirts, leaving angry creases. She'd gone past anger into some other state where the edges of every surface appeared far too crisp, almost as if she had a fever. But her mind was racing, her thoughts as clear and logical as if driven by elegant mathematical equations. Or maybe it was sheer madness.

"I will get you your information," she said in a crisp voice that hid the wailing panic inside her, "but not the way you propose." *And I will find some way to make you pay.*

"How?"

"I'll go myself."

"You?" His eyebrows rose, the expression almost amused.

The plan wasn't as preposterous as it sounded. From years of traveling with Ploughman's, she knew the kind of people who lived in the Blue King's district. "I can live in the East End without anyone noticing I'm there. It won't be a disguise for me, so I won't make the mistakes an outsider would. I'm just as much one of them as I am one of you." The last words came out in a rush, half mumbled, the specter of her Grandmamma Holmes looking on in angry shame. *Forgive me, but I have to do this.*

"Indeed. How fortunate that you can move so efficiently between two worlds."

"If I do this, will you keep my uncle out of it?" Her body was tensed, quivering like a drawn bow.

Keating gave her one of his mocking smiles. "With certain conditions . . . but yes, I think we can come to an arrangement. You're dealing with this most reasonably."

And then she understood. She arrowed out of the chair, rushing forward until she stood inches from him, her hands in fists. "You wanted me to do this all along!"

"Did I?"

She was breathing hard, split between wanting to bolt and aching to lunge for this throat. "Why didn't you just ask? Why threaten my family?"

He shrugged, lifting his chin so that he looked down his long, patrician nose. "As I said earlier this evening, I prefer that you are inspired to excel. And now that I've done my part, what happens next is up to you."

THOSE FATAL WORDS were still echoing in Evelina's head when she boarded the train back to London the next morning, and they were still there by the time she reached the smoky outskirts of the city the day after that. The journey home had passed in a haze of disbelief. She'd left London to rejoin Imogen and to report to her uncle about the goings-on at Maggor's Close. Now she was exiled again from her friend and burdened with a very different task.

It pained her that she couldn't stand by Imogen, who was alone and vulnerable. And Keating was only one danger. There was the Scarlet King, and the strain of standing up to her parents. If her brother was giving in to a marriage of expediency, they would expect her to as well. Evelina didn't know Bucky Penner all that well, but if Imogen had chosen him, she would do everything she could to support that decision. Except now she couldn't be at her friend's side. The only thing she had been able to do was to leave Mouse and Bird at Maggor's Close to offer what comfort they could.

Evelina cursed under her breath. It was her own fault she'd landed in this mess. Tobias might have come all the way from London to see her, but she could have walked away. So why had she kissed him?

The question echoed through her with every rattle of the wheels on the track. *Why, why, why, why?* Evelina's gaze lost focus as she watched the trees and rooftops slip by, the forms melting into one shapeless mass. She leaned against the window, her chin in her hand as hot tears slid down her cheeks and soaked her glove.

She'd kissed Tobias because of the misery in his eyes. Because he had once been hers, and a part of her wanted to reclaim what they'd almost had. Mostly because he had been right there and so obviously needing her touch.

But Tobias was still caught in Keating's trap, and now—thanks to their kiss—she was, too. And that was the reason, above all else, that she had to forget Tobias Roth. *I had to let you go,* he'd said. *I would have dragged you down with me, and that wouldn't have helped anyone.* But he didn't love her enough to keep his resolve, even though he'd known it was the one way to keep her safe.

But it's not that easy. She had faced the exact same thing with Nick. A low cry escaped her. *I gave him up, too, but he found me.* Until she'd forced him away a second time. The danger had been entirely different, but the only way to save them both had been for her to walk away. Twice.

But even if he never forgave her, Nick would tell her to fight like a rabid dog. The first priority was always to keep her loved ones out of harm's way. And that meant she had to take care of business if that was the best way to get Keating out of her—and her uncle's—life.

But what if I've agreed to do more than I can manage? Worse, what if she were captured by the Blue King's men? Dread washed over her, so thick that she felt sick to her stomach. She was caught between two steam barons, and it was hard to say which one presented the greater danger. *It's like Keating knew exactly what I would say and when I'd say it.* The man was a master manipulator, and their encounter had left her with a fresh objective. If she survived this adventure, her next would be finding out a way to smash Keating like one of his own gold-tinted gaslights.

Her carpetbag was on the seat next to her. She opened the clasp, looking inside, checking the contents obsessively. She'd repacked, loading it with only the items she'd find the most useful. The train case with her tools and supplies for tinkering with clockwork was there, as well as a selection of plain, practical clothes.

There was also a small, worn purse. Among the gentry, servants and men of business generally handled day-to-day transactions, so Evelina didn't have much cash on hand. She'd asked Keating for a supply of money in small coin, and it was stashed in a dozen places, sewn into clothing, into the lining of her bag, and in the bottom of her toolbox. Only a few coins were in the purse for show.

Keating had also given her a small Webley revolver with an ivory handle as well as a knife in an ankle sheath. She'd never actually owned a gun or a knife before—and fervently hoped she wouldn't need them—but Nick had taught her how to use both.

They'd made other arrangements. If she needed to contact Keating, she could write to him in care of the Oraculars' Club, but not directly to any of his residences or regular places of business. Keating would see to it her trunks were sent home in due course. The people at Maggor's Close—with the exception of Tobias and Imogen—would be told that Evelina was needed back in Devonshire as her grandmother had suddenly taken ill. And as far as her uncle knew, she was at Maggor's Close. If everything went right, she would return to Baker Street on schedule, with Holmes none the wiser. With luck, she might even keep her reputation intact.

But relying on luck is a tall order. I'm trusting my safety to the man who paid Elias Jones to put a bomb in my uncle's house. And now I know too much for him to let me back out. She huddled against the shabby fabric of the train's upholstery, grateful that she was alone in the compartment so she didn't have to hide her misery.

Keating had placed an additional condition on their arrangement. She had until Tobias's wedding to complete the task. The choice of date—as far as the Blue King's affairs were concerned—was arbitrary in the extreme, and Keating wasn't one to waste a good twist of the knife. He'd no doubt picked it to remind her why she was in his clutches, and just maybe to keep her out of the way until Tobias was safely wed. And if she missed the date, all Keating's threats—about revealing her past, about her uncle's safety, about

never being free of his chains—would come to ugly frui-
tion.

"Damn and blast." Evelina blinked the view outside the
train window into focus. It only made sense to have a
contingency—a backup in place in case Keating decided
she could stay lost in Whitechapel, never to be heard from
again. The thought sent a chill crawling through her, leaving gooseflesh in its wake.

Her fingers shook as she rummaged in her carpetbag for
her notebook and a pen. She tore out a clean page and started
to write.

"Dear Uncle, I write to you with the heaviest of hearts.
Alas, the advice you gave me when I left on this holiday I
followed all too well, and I have been taught my lesson by
the All Powerful." She stopped and chewed the end of her
pencil. She was fairly sure he'd get the idea she meant the
Gold King.

"His angelic hosts watch over us night and day, knowing
all that passes in our lives." And by that, Holmes should
know 221B Baker Street was under surveillance—which
was why the letter had to be written obliquely. There was a
good chance their mail might be read, and tipping her hand
would be counterproductive if the Gold King changed his
mind and decided Evelina was more trouble than she was
worth.

"If you do not hear now, you will hear soon of my disgrace, for which I can offer no excuses but the weakness of
a young girl's heart. Grandmamma always predicted that I
was made of the same material as my mother, but I am
afraid that I am even worse. I threw away my reputation by
kissing a man who is promised to another, and now I am
making amends." And that much was no more than the
truth.

"It is best that I go to someplace where I am unknown,
and where my shame cannot follow me. Please, do not look
for me, for this is the bosom of your enemies. Know that I
will do my best to earn a blameless life in hopes of redemption in the eyes of the All Powerful. Your dutiful niece, Evelina." It was a little harder to communicate that she was in

the Blue King's territory at the orders of Keating, but her
uncle was good at codes.

She had pilfered an envelope from Keating's desk. Folding the letter into it, she addressed the note to Baker Street.
She'd take it to a post office—someplace busy where no one
would remember her—and have the clerk post it several
days after she was due to return home. If she was home, she
could intercept it. If she wasn't, her uncle would know
something was amiss. Evelina tucked the note into her
pocket, feeling exhausted already. The practical side of this
adventure was one thing, but the emotional load of it was
more than she'd expected.

And then she pushed the notebook back into her bag.
When she did, she felt something cold, metallic, and very
much alive. Alarm jolted her as she pulled Bird from the
bottom of her bag. "I thought I left you with Imogen!" In
fact, she had left Mouse and Bird on her friend's dressing
table. They must have crept back to Evelina's room and then
into her bag when she wasn't looking. "I need you to stay
with Imogen. She needs all the comfort you can give her,
and I can't take you with me."

Bird crawled up her arm, sharp nails digging into the fabric of her sleeve. *Why not?*

"I'm going on an adventure."

Mouse squirmed out of the bag and hopped, landing on
the worn fabric of the seat. *Why can't we go with you?*

"You would be too tempting if somebody saw you. You'd
end up in a pawn shop or sold for scrap in minutes. And
there's nobody else who can look after Im."

And how shall we defend maiden fair? demanded Mouse.
Shall I nibble at her persecutor's toes?

"You can go for help."

Bird gave an indignant cheep. *Last time we did that, I
ended up in pieces on a streetkeeper's workbench.*

"If something bad happens, find Uncle Sherlock. He'll
know what to do." Her uncle couldn't speak to the devas, but
he'd figure it out. Probably using something involving an
algorithm, semaphores, and cigar ashes. "Go to Hilliard
House and wait for Imogen to come home."

Mouse cleaned its whiskers. *This sounds like an ill-conceived plan. I don't see how you're going to manage without us.*

"I'll manage if I know Imogen isn't going to end up marched down the aisle into a marriage she doesn't want."

But we belong to you. Bird huddled in the hollow under her ear, leaning its cold body against her skin. Mouse scampered up her knee, rising on its haunches to peer up at her from its bright black eyes. A soft pain crawled up her chest, threatening to turn her resolve to jelly.

I'm so afraid, she thought, but kept the words in the most private place inside her that even the devas could not hear. *I'm so afraid I can't do this.*

But when the train stopped at Paddington Station, all Evelina took with her was the carpetbag. Two tiny figures left the platform the other way, keeping to the invisible places as only devas could.

Another murder of the foulest kind was committed in the neighborhood of Whitechapel in the early hours of yesterday morning, but by whom and with what motive is at present a complete mystery. At a quarter to 4 o'clock Police-constable Neill, when in Buck's-row, Whitechapel, came upon the body of a woman lying on a part of the footway, and on stooping to raise her up in the belief that she was drunk he discovered that her throat was cut almost from ear to ear. She was dead but still warm.

—*The London Prattler*
on the death of Mary Ann Nichols

CHAPTER THIRTEEN

August 30, 1888
MAGGOR'S CLOSE

3:30 a.m. Thursday

IMOGEN DREAMED, AND AGAIN THE DREAMS BEGAN WITH the nightmare of being suffocated. But this time that part passed quickly, and she was once again standing on a dirty street. It was dark, the air chill and clammy, and it smelled of horses and vaguely like rotting fish, as if the river might be nearby. The blue haze of a distant streetlight touched veils of moisture in the air—not quite fog, but working toward it.

Before her was a gate about ten feet high, and something was on the sidewalk before it, almost at her feet. Imogen could see the shape, but she didn't want to look closely. She concentrated instead on other things—the row housing to one side, the big building, maybe a school or a hospital, to the other. Some part of her knew with gut-churning urgency that looking would be bad. But this was a nightmare, and so her chin tilted down, her eyes refusing to squeeze shut.

I looked inside, said the presence, *and I couldn't find anything that answered my question.*

The thing on the ground was—had been—a woman, her skirts pulled up to show a savage wound to her belly. Imogen squinted, her mind not making sense of the shadowy ruin, and her gaze quickly skittered away to the woman's face. Like the woman from the other dream, this person wasn't young. Her black straw bonnet had rolled a little distance away, and Imogen could see gray in the woman's hair.

And she could see the seeping slash at the woman's throat. *She's still bleeding!* That meant there was a chance she was still alive.

Imogen knelt, bending over the woman's face. She heard a faint gasp of breath, and saw the glitter of her eyes. Imogen lifted her hand to cover the wound, maybe stop the bleeding, and saw that it was already covered in blood. The woman's eyes flared in panic, a horrible sound emerging from her ruined throat. Reflexively, Imogen looked down at her own body.

Her other hand held a knife.

Imogen sat straight up in bed, sucking in her breath. The sudden movement left her light-headed and she quickly sank back to her pillow, the tear-dampened linen already clammy and chill. She pulled the blanket up to her ears, eyes wide and staring into the dim light, afraid.

She'd hoped that Evelina's presence would stop the dreams, but her friend had barely arrived before she was gone again. And since that night—and Tobias's guilt and Evelina's tight-lipped grief—the dreams had come back worse than ever. *This time I killed someone.* She could still sense the stink of ripped bowels, the thick slickness of blood between her fingers. She poked a hand out from under the cover, examining the pale outline of her fingers in the glow of her guttering candle. There was nothing to see. *Am I going mad?*

She hadn't had a nightmare quite that bad since she'd been a little girl. That was when the dreams of the dark, suffocating place had started. The doctors said a violent shock could cause such things, and back then they had blamed it all on the death of her sister. Poor little Im, sick in bed and bereft of her double. No doubt she'd been stricken to the core of her soul.

Actually, she didn't remember Anna with any fondness. They'd been identical twins, but their similarity ended with their looks. Anna was vivacious, Imogen shy. Anna charmed the adults with her curtsies and pirouettes, but Imogen preferred a book and her puppy. Anna broke the china, and

Imogen took the blame. In truth, sweet Anna had been a little savage, as mean to her sister as only children could be. Everyone assumed she would grow out of her spiteful streak, but Imogen wasn't sure. There had been something out of tune in her sister, like a violin left too long in a damp attic.

However, since no one spoke ill of the dead, Imogen had kept that to herself once Anna had gone to ashes and dust. After all, she'd survived, and that should be victory enough. And yet the dreams hadn't gone away. They clutched at her like a tiny hand plucking her sleeve from the other side of the grave, a flickering, grasping shadow cast across her soul.

Imogen rolled over to face the candle. The flame shivered in the drafty room, undulating like a dancing imp. She had been able to live with the dreams when they were persistent but relatively mild. A sleepless night now and again could be overlooked. But something had changed, the wisp of malevolent shadow gathering into a storm.

One that she wasn't sure she was going to survive.

August 30, 1888

ABOARD THE RED JACK

1:30 p.m. Thursday

"THERE IS A SEA SERPENT IN THE LOCH, THEY SAY," SAID THE man who sat on the other side of the overturned barrel from Nick. They were using it as a chess table, a sturdy bench on either side. "I didn't see it, but that's not to say it wasn't there."

"Too bad I didn't know that sooner," Nick replied, surveying his black pieces carefully. So far he had lost three Steamers and a streetkeeper, but had taken Mycroft's white engine and one baron—though he had sweated for those pieces. "I could have flown over Loch Ness and had a look."

"I half expect it's one of the maker's creations meant to scare the council's army."

The rebels were secretive enough to try something like that. The Schoolmaster's real instructions, stuffed into Nick's pocket at the last moment, had only given coordinates. A casual observer would never have guessed the name of their destination in the misty Scottish wilds. Loch Ness, complete with sea serpent. Why was it that Nick never landed a simple job?

The *Red Jack* had dropped off the package, spent a few days at the new rebel headquarters, and then picked up the goods and passenger the Schoolmaster had asked they take to London. Half Nick's payment had been waiting for him. The other half would be at the drop-off point near London.

Casting a glance at his opponent, Nick wondered if he should have charged extra. He could hear the motors straining to keep the *Jack* aloft. Even with an air deva, there was only so much a ship could do.

Mycroft Holmes was not a small man. He was about forty, as tall as his brother but several Sherlocks wide, and with none of the younger man's mercurial energy. Instead, there was a patient stillness in the man's steel-gray gaze that Nick had seen in the best marksmen.

Nick moved one of his Steamers forward a square. "The loch seems like an awkward place to raise an army. Far away, bad supply lines, and the like."

"Who says that is what they are doing?" Mycroft replied, the merest suggestion of a smile lurking at the corner of his mouth. Nick studied him, looking for a family resemblance to Evie. There wasn't much beyond the dark hair, but he did have some of Sherlock's mannerisms—the way he held his glass between his thumb and middle finger and the way he waved away an argument that didn't please him. And beyond that, Nick felt a familiar and irritating sense of being in the presence of someone much smarter than he was. Mycroft slid his remaining baron a few squares, and Nick felt a tickle at the back of his neck that said he'd better look to his queen.

"I know a little about the rebels and what they are doing," Nick ventured. "They keep calling on me to run their missions."

"Is that a problem?"

"I didn't sign on with their cause." He moved his street-keeper into a defensive position.

"No?"

"The *Red Jack* is a pirate ship, plain and simple. Attack, plunder, burn, smuggle when it suits us." Over a tankard of beer, that always sounded easy. "Not that I mind giving the council a black eye now and again, but why me?"

"Sherlock recommended you."

Surprise brought Nick's gaze up from the board to the man's heavy-jowled face. "By the dark furies, why?"

"You stole Athena's Casket from Jasper Keating. You won the loyalty of his streetkeeper and together you killed the sorcerer Magnus. You put yourself in harm's way to keep our niece from danger. We want you on our side." And he promptly took another one of Nick's Steamers. "Check."

Bloody hell. Nick scowled at the board. "That's a leap of faith on your part."

Mycroft watched him carefully. "I understand our niece is very fond of you."

Nick couldn't tell if that was supposed to be a good thing or a bad one, but he doubted it was true anymore. Yes, they'd grown up together and been sweethearts, but as they'd got older the magic had become a problem. To put it simply, Nick and Evelina's powers were fine when apart, but together they were disastrous.

"Evelina is a fine lady," he said diplomatically.

"But you are still friendly?"

"Her life is very different from mine." *She's a lady. I'm a pirate. Sounds like a plot for a comic opera.*

Even Nick's magic was so different that no one had been able to train him to use it. Anything more than a casual touch—such as anything two young lovers might do behind the stables—had sparked a flood of raw, wild power. Gran Cooper—who knew what there was to know of such things—had called it wild magic. Devas flocked to it like butterflies to nectar, and the chaos caused by a swarm of inebriated devas was impossible to hide. In a world where magic carried a death sentence, such power could have cost the lives of every member of Ploughman's circus.

Nick had been desperate to find a solution, even if Gran Cooper denied one could be found. But right when things were at their worst, Evelina had left without a word. It had taken him years to find her again. But then she had sent him away.

Mycroft rested one elbow on the barrel, propping up his head. "Please take this the right way when I say that I approve of your keeping a distance from Evelina. She is wise beyond her years, but still of an impressionable age and headstrong disposition. My brother, Sherlock, is too prone to give her liberty. And while I applaud your enterprise and daring, I am cautious about encouraging her friendship with a, um—"

"Pirate?" Nick finished for him. *Pompous ass.* But he wasn't sure he'd want his daughter keeping company with some younger version of himself, either.

"'Scuse me, Captain," came a voice to Nick's right.

He looked up to see Digby standing there. "Yes?"

The helmsman looked exasperated to the point of tears. "I'm wondering if you could have a word with the ship, like. I'm trying to steer southwest and Athena keeps going the other way."

Nick felt the warm touch of the deva in his mind. Gran Cooper had been wrong about his magic being too wild to tame. Athena had taught him much, showing him things mind to mind in ways no human could. It was as if he were an orphan no longer, finally finding something to which he belonged. "Tell me, Athena."

But it wasn't the ship who answered. There was a sepulchral croak from the rigging above. Nick looked up to see Gwilliam land in the rigging.

"What the bloody hell is that?" Mycroft muttered.

"An informant," Nick replied. "And an ally. Fair winds, Gwilliam."

Fair greeting, but ill winds. The bird bobbed and gave another raucous croak. *The human is right, and your vessel steers to safety. More ships wait in the direction the steers-man tries to go. They have guns and flame. But no ships venture to the east.*

Nick put it together quickly, but not before a surge of anger brought him to his feet. "There's an ambush waiting. Athena is trying to avoid it."

Mycroft drew himself upright, casting the rook another curious glance. "No one knows where these supplies are bound."

"Obviously someone does." Nick's mind had raced on ahead. The Schoolmaster had said their next destination was Exeter, but his note had given coordinates just outside Salisbury. Either one was southwest of London. He turned to Mycroft. "Where is a viable drop-off for the crates where no one will expect to see us?"

"Hampstead," said Mycroft at once. "Or Harlow."

Both were north of London, but closer in than their original destinations. "Are you certain those skies are clear?"

"Perhaps you should ask your bird. Or your ship."

He felt Athena's disgust. *Must I do everything?*

You're the shining treasure of magic and wonder, Nick replied. Then he turned to Gwilliam. "Would you please scout for us until we land safely?"

Gwilliam made an odd sort of bow, and then flapped off with a sound like feathered thunder. Athena's voice was wry. *Keep in mind they're birds. If they spot a tasty bit of carrion, there's no keeping them on task.*

Now there was an image he could have lived without. He felt the ship changing direction and turned to Digby. "Double the watch. We're relying on feathered scouts."

"Aye, Captain." The tall man moved away.

Nick sat down, giving Mycroft a hard look. "Elias Jones said there was a traitor. He was right."

"It appears so. Tell me more about that bird."

"The ash rooks assist from time to time. They love metal and will trade their services for some bit of ornamentation. They don't share all their reasons for working with the *Red Jack,* but they like my ship and they don't like the steam barons digging mines everywhere. We started to see them when a forest was cut down near the Welsh border. I think they must have nested there."

Mycroft raised his eyebrows. "How useful they must be for carrying information."

Nick shrugged. "They talk to other birds, especially other crows and ravens, and so messages can be relayed easily over long distances. But they can't be relied on to remember details, or why timeliness matters. Birds have their own priorities and they aren't necessarily ours."

Mycroft's face fell. "Oh."

Nick almost laughed. *Thought you had stumbled onto something you could exploit, did you?* "So what's your role in all this? Why are you at Loch Ness?"

"I am a bureaucrat who is loyal to the Crown. An interesting enough job when the Steam Council has its own men in every position of influence. But as far as a revolutionary role goes, I'm afraid I merely push paper."

Nick was out of patience for chess games. "Don't play me for a fool. You're not merely anything."

Mycroft gave a dry chuckle. "Call me a repository, then. I absorb information like a sponge. I was with the rebels squeezing myself out to a handful of forward thinkers like myself."

"What do you mean?"

"The problem with most revolutions is follow-through. Once Rome burns, someone has to pick up the pieces. If we sweep away the council's supporters, who will take their place?"

A cold chill swept through Nick. "You're forming a shadow government for when the Steam Council falls. That explains the remote location. You're keeping your star players safe and secure, far away from the action." With a glance down at the chess board, he suddenly noticed patterns he hadn't seen before. His streetkeeper took Mycroft's baron.

"Very good, Captain Niccolo."

"And you trust me with that information?"

"I'm trusting you with my life as we speak. It's a long way to the ground."

"Why did you want Elias Jones so badly?"

Mycroft sucked his upper lip, moving one of his engines a few squares. "He believed he was part of a very deep game, playing one faction against another. We got that much out of him. He went to work for the Blue King, and ended up serving the Gold."

"He nearly blew up your brother and niece." Nick moved his king a square, making him a little safer.

"If that bomb failed, it was meant to."

"Then why—"

"An explosion was enough. The goal wasn't murder, but to kick over the rebel anthill and see who came running out." Mycroft moved the engine again. "Explosions cause confusion, consternation, chaos. No one pours tea and goes back to the newspaper like nothing happened. Not even my brother. Not even if he appears to do so. Someone meant to put our pieces in motion and it worked. It's up to us to double our vigilance. Your move, Captain."

Pieces. Sherlock. Evie. The Schoolmaster. The *Red Jack*. Nick looked down at the board. The pattern had become a lot less comforting, especially when he thought about the Blue King's weapons. It would have been easy—even sensible—to tell Mycroft Holmes what he'd seen, but instinct told him to keep his cards close to his vest. He didn't quite trust the man—at least not yet. "Who is the traitor who relayed my ship's position to council forces?"

"I don't know." The words sounded like they came at a cost. Ignorance was no doubt an unfamiliar experience. "I would like to say that it was Jasper Keating and his network of spies, or more of the Blue King's forces, but I cannot be sure. This matter is a little like those Russian dolls, where you pull one apart only to find another inside. There are plots within plots."

Nick reached for his streetkeeper.

"Think about that move, Captain," Mycroft chided. "You're about to put your queen in danger."

Nick withdrew his hand. "You're right."

"But then sometimes we have to sacrifice our queen for the greater good."

He thought of Evie, and the explosion, and the fact that

someone was pulling their strings. "There is no world where that kind of sacrifice is worth it." He moved his king another square.

"Perhaps, and perhaps not." Mycroft hopped his white streetkeeper over Nick's Steamer. "Checkmate."

CHAPTER FOURTEEN

London, September 15, 1888
WHITECHAPEL

10:45 a.m. Saturday

THE WOMAN ON THE BED WAS DYING—THERE WAS NO DOUBT about that. Someone had propped the single window open to relieve the stink, but it was a needless gesture. Half the panes were broken anyway, inviting the cold morning air to seep into the lodging house. The sun was a different matter. It wasn't a bright day outside to begin with, and the angle of the building seemed to shoulder away any stray light with an unsociable shrug. Evelina could barely make out the face of the sick woman until she was halfway across the tiny room.

"They want her to go," said the boy by the door, whose name she had learned was Gareth. His accent was pure gutter and he spoke quickly, so she had to pay attention if she wanted to catch the words. "Can't pay for the bed anymore."

What do you think I can do about it? Evelina wondered. She had rented a room on the floor below, and Gareth slept in one of the houses nearby. He'd noticed her because she'd finally scrounged a job fixing the illegal generator hidden behind the brothel next door. After ten minutes' conversation, Gareth had dragged her up here. Maybe he thought she could bring the woman back to life like a freshly oiled motor. *If only that were possible.*

Then again, anything Evelina could do had to be an improvement. She drew closer to the bed, giving in to the urge to press her hand over her nose and mouth. The only sign of life was the labored rise and fall of the woman's chest, each heave of the ribs accompanied by a wet rattle. It seemed a monstrous effort for so little air.

Evelina bent closer, her gorge threatening to rise at the stink of stale body fluids. She wrestled it back, searched for some sign of the woman's identity, and failed. The straggle of sweat-plastered hair might have been gray or blond, and her face was so pale that it washed into the mattress cover. There were no sheets. It looked like she had lain down in all her clothes beneath the thin blanket—not uncommon in a place where anything out of one's grasp was likely to disappear.

"I cleaned her up some," said Gareth.

A roughness in his voice made her turn to look at the boy. His face was almost expressionless, but she could sense turmoil. He'd taken care of this woman, so she meant something— but what? "How do you know her?"

He raised a thin shoulder. It was hard to guess his age— thirteen, perhaps, or an underfed fifteen, with soft dark hair and eyes the color of autumn heather. Too frail to go to work on the docks, and too pretty for his own good. "Lacey worked for Mrs. Loren, like I did, before Miss Hyacinth came along. I did odd jobs. She worked upstairs."

Evelina had never met either woman, but had heard Miss Hyacinth's name. She was the abbess of the pleasure house with the broken generator. That meant Lacey had been a whore.

"She's a friend, then," Evelina said evenly.

"A friend, yeah. The sickness went to her chest."

Consumption, she guessed. Her skin was gray and from the sound of it, Lacey's lungs were already gone. Life was a matter of days or hours. "How can I help?" Evelina asked, keeping her voice gentle.

"You know what to do, right?" He looked her up and down, almost accusing.

Evelina's insides clenched. She understood all too well what was going on. She was well fed—or had been up until a few weeks ago—her simple traveling clothes luxurious by the local standards. She sounded educated and had useful skills. That made her one of the blessed, and by rights she should possess almost mythic abilities to make things right.

But what magic powers she had were useless against disease this far gone. She had called wild magic—and half the devas in London—to heal Nick's ankle last spring, but simple injuries were another matter entirely. A raw sadness turned her cold, and she clutched her arms to keep in the heat. "I'll sit with her if you like."

"I can do that. I don't need you to do that." He sounded angry, like she was missing the obvious. "She needs medicine."

Evelina closed her eyes for a moment, fighting the claustrophobia that was as much a part of this place as its dirty walls and broken windows. There was no way to block out the sound of the woman's gurgling breath and the faint whimpers that spoke of a nightmare of pain. She longed for birdsong and the genteel clutter of Baker Street, or the high, airy chambers of her Grandmamma Holmes's house, or even a circus ring. Someplace where people didn't die abandoned like flies on a windowsill.

But Gareth wasn't leaving his friend; he was trying to get her help. That was probably why he'd attached himself to Evelina in the first place. She looked like the well-meaning, easy mark who could be talked out of a shilling or two. Still, decency demanded that Evelina do something. "Very well. You stay. I'll see if the apothecary has anything that might help her."

"Good. That's good." Gareth stood by the doorway, his fingers twisting the hem of his shirt.

Evelina's throat hurt with the sadness that clung to him. "You should know that there's a risk. She's very weak. Even the smallest amount of medicine might be too much."

He took a sudden interest in the view out the window, probably so that she couldn't see his face. "Not bad if she goes peaceful, is it?"

"No." Better than listening to those struggling breaths, each one a desperate battle for the fetid air. She picked up her carpetbag. It was heavy, but keeping it with her was safer than leaving it in her room. Anything that could be sold was fair game around there. "I'll be back as soon as I can."

He didn't thank her and she didn't expect it. That would have been too much for his young pride.

Outside the room, she let herself linger in the narrow corridor, sorting out her thoughts. It was dim here, too, the only light coming from tiny windows at either end of the long passage. The floors were bare of carpet, covered instead in a layer of grit and dust kittens that clung to the baseboards, the grimy drifts broken by the half-dozen identical doorways that opened into the hall. The place had been a fine house maybe a hundred years ago, but time had taken its dignity. None of the rooms were any larger than Lacey's— or her own—and many held entire families who paid five shillings a week to share a bed. Evelina shuddered. It was no good trying to think here. She started for the stairway, careful to avoid the mildew staining the walls on either side.

But the staircase was blocked by the substantial form of Mr. Earls, the caretaker. With twin white stripes in his bristling black hair, he looked like a badger in suspenders and a neckerchief. "What are you doing here? You're not on this floor."

"I was looking in on Lacey."

"You a friend of hers?"

"Not really. I was just concerned."

He scowled. "She's two weeks behind. She has to pay up or get out. That's why I'm here."

Evelina caught his arm. "Please don't."

"I have my orders. No charity."

No, places like this were run for profit by owners who never set foot in this part of town. And when these old places outlived their usefulness, they were knocked down and replaced with nicer housing for higher rents that the regulars could never afford. And so the rooming houses that remained would be that much more crowded—as would any doorway or alley that offered a bit of shelter from the rain. A lot could be ignored for a four percent profit margin.

Evelina increased the pressure of her fingers, dropping

her voice so low that it was almost a whisper. "She won't be a problem, I can promise you that."

"How?" he said roughly. "Are you going to pay her rent as well as your own?"

She wished she could, but it wouldn't be necessary. "I doubt she'll live to see tomorrow."

His face fell. "That bad, is she? That's a shame and all. She was a pretty thing in her day." He looked uncertainly at the door, as if remembering a time long ago. Of course, long ago in these parts could have been a couple of years. "I suppose morning won't make much difference."

Evelina let her fingers relax. "Thank you."

"Someone with her?"

"Her friend Gareth is there now."

"Friend? He's her boy." Nostalgia turned to disgust. "God only knows what he saw his mother do, night after night."

"Her son?" Evelina exclaimed in a low voice. "He never said."

Earls grunted. "Some won't admit to their brats in front of the clients. Makes them look old. Keeping quiet becomes a habit." He turned and trudged back down the stairs.

Her son. That explains so much. Feeling as if she'd intruded on their privacy, Evelina followed after. She wondered if the dying woman had the same remarkable, heather-colored eyes as her boy.

She left the building and walked down to Commercial Street just as the church bells struck two o'clock. Still lost in thought, she was vaguely aware of a mizzling rain and the hubbub of the streets around her. A stone's throw away were the worst places—doss-houses that made her cramped room seem palatial by comparison. Evelina always walked by with her knife or gun hidden in the folds of her skirt. She'd seen the men lounging out front of the crumbling facades. The lucky few got casual work on the docks. The rest lived by crime or starved, some selling even the clothes they stood in—too proud or afraid to go to the workhouses, where families were split asunder and not all lived to get out.

Keating's coin was both a lifeline and a source of guilt.

Playing at poverty when she wasn't truly poor felt disrespectful—and yet she didn't dare let her mask slip for an instant. She could be robbed and killed in a blink. Survival meant never dropping her guard, not even when she slept. Especially when she slept.

And yet, not far the other way, there was plenty of money to be had. Spitalfields Market sold fruits, vegetables, and almost anything else one could want, and the streets were jammed with a steady procession of handcarts, horse carts, and still more spewing steam. Business was excellent. That was the contradiction of these neighborhoods nestled at the base of the Tower of London—poverty and commerce existed side by side, layered like the leaves of a book.

Evelina's business lay down Fournier Street, past the fine Georgian townhouses where French silk weavers had worked until the Blue King's steam-powered mills had put them out of business. At the far end of the street was the apothecary she knew would sell her something at a good price because she'd fixed the device he used to press his powders into neat round pills.

She'd been in Whitechapel nearly three weeks—and there was just a week to go before Keating's deadline was up. The fact played like a refrain in her head, reminding her that if she didn't find the Blue King's maker, the life she had left behind would be a mangled ruin.

And yet her life in Whitechapel had proved far from an easy stroll, for all her ability to fit in. To learn what she could from the local makers, she'd picked up some jobs for herself, though not as many as she needed. She'd quickly learned that work was hard to get, and many didn't want a young woman when there were men about with the same skills. In fact, if she hadn't had Keating's coin, she'd be starving by now.

Nothing had been as simple as she had thought it would be. Her carpetbag held the train case with the equipment she used to repair clockwork. In the interests of blending in she'd bartered some of her other possessions—a shawl, a pair of stockings, and so on—for tools made for larger jobs, like fixing the brothel's generator. Paying that much cash up front would have attracted attention. And, in turn, no one had cash to pay her back. She'd done at least half her jobs for trade and, in a few cases, for nothing because she couldn't bear to take anything more from desperate people.

Yes, she remembered how to fit in, but she'd forgotten or never known many of the hardships the adults around her had sheltered her from. No matter what else happened, she'd realized how large a debt she owed their memory.

She neared the tiny shop with its narrow doorway and faded sign. A trio of children chased a spotted dog down the street, shrieking at the top of their lungs, nearly careening into a man selling hot pies. The pies smelled so good, Evelina started to drool.

The apothecary's was shut. "Gone to see his aunt, he did," said the pie man. "She's got a complaint with her belly. Like she ate bad fish, but it never stops."

Which was more than Evelina had wanted to know. "I'm sorry to hear that."

"Course everyone thinks it's that madman with a knife if someone don't show up where they're supposed to be."

"What madman?"

"Eh, you been hiding under the bed these last weeks? Every soul in the place is talking about what happened to those poor women. I knew Annie, I did!"

Evelina blinked. She had been so preoccupied finding a place to live and getting to know where the local makers congregated that she had spared no time for newspapers. "Is there another place to buy medicine?"

The pie man made a sale to a man in coveralls coated with brick dust, wrapping the pies in old newspaper. "They sell this and that round the corner at Mistress Skinner's, but I say you have to want it something bad to go there."

Evelina thanked the pie man and left. She found Skinner's Trusted Elixirs down an alley so narrow she could touch either side with her fingertips. In one of the rooms above, a baby was crying. A rusted water pump stood at the dead end, probably supplying all the buildings around it. Washing hung from the windows above, endangered by a flock of roosting pigeons. Skinner's was squashed between an old

clothes shop and a barber's, and none of the businesses inspired confidence. A rat the size of a terrier eyed Evelina
from a hole in the brickwork.

She opened the door to the shop cautiously, unsure what
she was about to find. It was gloomy and small, with a dark
wooden counter crowded with jars of every size and shape.
Shelving jammed with more containers lined the place,
leaving little room to actually get inside. The door set off a
bell that gave a muted tinkle.

Evelina waited. A curtain behind the counter parted and a
tall woman took her place behind the fortress of jars. "How
may I help you?"

Evelina blinked, every sense suddenly alert. The woman
was perhaps fifty, tall, black-haired and dressed entirely in
loose, gauzy black garments that looked like a combination
dressing gown and shroud. A necklace of pale, dangling objects rattled as she moved. Evelina shifted from foot to foot,
fascinated but not sure staying there was a wonderful idea.

"Mistress Skinner?" she asked politely.

"The same. And who are you, my dear?" The woman's
voice was husky and cracked.

"Evelina," she said, even though she hadn't meant to.
There was something about Mistress Skinner that was hard
to refuse.

"Ah, the girl who fixes things. I've heard about you." She
leaned forward, peering at her. "You don't look the part.
Where did you learn the art of gear and wheel?"

"My grandfather." He had fixed the mechanical wonders
at Ploughman's Paramount Circus—from the clockwork
fortune teller to the Swiss orchestrion with its dancing shep-
herdesses. "He let me help him from the time I was just old
enough to hold a pair of pliers."

"How charming," she said, her long-nailed fingers strok-
ing the counter with a whispery rasp. Silver rings coiled like
snakes over her knuckles, linked to each other with fine
loops of chain.

"If you need anything fixed . . ."

"No, I don't, but the puppet theater might. He has no end of
machinery, more than any one man could ever hope to fix.

But he must be clever, for King Coal brings him work to do, although his machines are of a different sort." She said the last with a curl of the lip. Evidently, Mistress Skinner didn't approve of the Blue King, and didn't care who knew it.

"A different sort?" Evelina prompted.

"King Coal likes what the puppeteer makes, although he doesn't understand the cost."

Evelina filed that tidbit away, cryptic though it was. Had she just stumbled on the Blue King's maker? With only a week left to find him, she wasn't turning away even the slimmest clue.

Mistress Skinner's nails tapped impatiently against the countertop. "But the clock is ticking. What may I do for you today?"

"There is a sick woman in my rooming house," Evelina said, and described what she knew of Lacey's condition.

The woman listened, her face impassive, then filled a tiny stoppered bottle with a liquid the color of dark whisky. "A few drops under the tongue. Any more and it will certainly kill her, but that much will ease her pain."

Evelina stepped forward. "Is it laudanum?"

"Yes, though it is stronger than some." She snatched the bottle off the counter, holding it out of reach. Her necklace, Evelina saw, was made of yellowing finger bones. "And it costs a bit more. I use nothing but the best Turkey opium."

Annoyed—and revolted by the necklace—Evelina lowered her hand. Laudanum was cheap, which was why so many used it for everything from chronic pain to quieting a fussing child. But in this case, strong was good. "How much?"

A look of satisfaction melted over Mistress Skinner's sharply boned face. "Your ailing friend will bless you, little Evelina."

Lacey would likely never know she existed, but in the end, Evelina left after parting with a threepenny bit. That was a quarter of a shilling and she paid four shillings a week for her room. A month ago it wouldn't have seemed like much, but now she was forcibly reminded of just how much every penny was worth. If she had been anyone else in this neighborhood, that small compassionate gesture would mean skimping on food for herself. And with work hard to get, it might mean the difference between a room and a doorway to sleep in.

Evelina walked slowly back toward Fournier Street. The baby in the rooms above was still mewling, hiccupping sobs that made her chest hurt. She stopped, unable to move until she heard a woman's voice hushing it. She still wasn't used to living in such close quarters again, where every drama felt like your own. Relieved, Evelina moved on.

Three pence. She didn't like to think that way, counting out every halfpenny like a miser, but a place like this made it impossible not to think of survival first. Now that Evelina had enjoyed a taste of champagne and ball gowns, she understood why her gently bred mother had wept every night. The harsh, spare life at Ploughman's must have seemed a prison sentence. Hardy as she was, Evelina couldn't wait to get back to clean sheets and a hot bath.

Even the thought of a steaming bathtub lifted her spirits— a bathtub, and Assam tea, and fresh fruit. No one here could afford oranges, so she had to walk by them as if they were beyond her reach.

She might be getting closer to those imagined luxuries. She was definitely going to investigate this puppeteer at her earliest opportunity. She turned onto Fournier Street, glad to be out of the narrow alley. The rain had stopped and the sun was trying to break through the clouds, turning the sky to polished silver.

"Did you find what you were looking for?" asked the pie man.

"Maybe." She spent another precious penny on two pies.

He wrapped the pies in old newsprint, one page around each to keep in the heat. "Eh, I always wear a rabbit's foot going past that shop. They say she has the evil eye."

Evelina wasn't going to argue. She walked back toward her rooming house, eating one of the greasy pies. The pastry was tough and salty, but the gravy inside was filled with onions and herbs. She gulped it down greedily as she mounted the steps to Lacey's room, reading the grease-splotched newspaper as she went. It was dated the first of the month.

> *Another murder of the foulest kind was committed in the neighborhood of Whitechapel in the early hours of yesterday morning, but by whom and with what motive is at present a complete mystery. At a quarter to 4 o'clock Police-constable Neill, when in Buck's-row, Whitechapel, came upon the body of a woman lying on a part of the footway, and on stooping to raise her up in the belief that she was drunk he discovered that her throat was cut almost from ear to ear. She was dead but still warm.*

Was this what the pie man had been talking about? Hadn't he said Annie? According to the rest of the article, this woman's name had been Nichols—Mary Ann or Polly, people seemed to call her both. Seeing it in print, though, triggered another memory, another newspaper article she'd read about a murder victim back at Baker Street. That crime had been only a stone's throw away from here. The Nichols murder was a few blocks away, but still too close for her liking. *Throat cut ear to ear.*

That made her shiver. She'd seen such a thing once, up close. A servant girl named Grace Child had died under Lord Bancroft's roof, her murder never solved. Reflexively, she skimmed through the pie crumbs again, finding out what she could about this new tragedy. Another prostitute. *Another woman whose choices ran out—and if I don't find what Keating wants in time, my own options are going to be precious few.*

Then she realized she'd stopped halfway up the staircase, the draft from the broken windows above eddying around her ankles. Feeling suddenly sick from the heavy meal, she mounted the rest of the steps to Lacey's room. Gareth had found a rickety chair from somewhere and sat beside the bed. He barely looked up when she walked in, his long, soft hair shadowing his face.

"I brought medicine," she said.

That made him look up, eyes wary. "You did?"

"I said I would." She handed him the pie, and he took it automatically.

"That's not for her," he said doubtfully.

"It's for you."

He tore open the paper and took an enormous bite, closing his eyes in bliss. In another time and place it wouldn't be right to eat with a loved one at death's door, but here one never turned down food. She took the medicine out of her carpetbag and pulled out the stopper.

"Let me," he said, finishing his meal in two huge bites.

She didn't argue, just gave him the directions Mistress Skinner had given her. The effect of the medicine was almost instant. Lacey grew quiet, her breathing shallower, but the restless movements and whimpering stopped.

"She didn't wake up," he said softly. He sat on the edge of the bed, one hand on his mother's hair. "She always looked out for me. I wish she knew I tried to do the same."

Evelina just took his free hand. There was nothing she could say that he didn't already know.

Gareth looked at their joined hands, but didn't pull away. Instead, a thoughtful look crossed his fine features. "Did you ever have someone who always looked out for you, no matter what?"

It was a more personal question than she liked. She didn't know the boy at all, and yet somehow they'd landed in a relationship that did away with formality. But when she went to answer, words failed.

"Once." That was all she could manage.

"We had our fights, but she was the one I could always count on when I needed her." He bit his lip.

"Keep that memory."

Something in her voice made him glance at her, but then all his attention was back on Lacey, where it had to be. That was fine with Evelina.

Once upon a time, there had been someone who was always there, no matter what. And now there wasn't. She never let herself think about Nick, because that heartbreak outstripped anything that Tobias Roth could ever do to her. And that one was her fault, too.

Lacey died a few minutes after the church bells struck midnight.

CHAPTER FIFTEEN

The police inspector entered the yard and found the victim, Annie Chapman, lying on her back. Her body was about two feet from the wall, parallel to the fence. Her face was turned to the right and her legs drawn up. On closer inspection, it could be seen that the throat had been deeply cut. The victim had been eviscerated, one bystander noted, as if someone had been searching for a lost shilling deep inside her gut. And yet there was precision enough to suggest an experienced butcher's hand.

—*The London Prattler*

London, September 16, 1888
WHITECHAPEL

2:05p.m. Sunday

EVELINA DIDN'T BOTHER GOING TO THE FRONT OF THE PUP-peteer's theater during the day. She'd been around such places often enough to know that if there was no matinee, one might as well be knocking at an empty building. No one would be in the front, unless they were sweeping up last night's playbills. Instead, she asked the flower seller on the corner for directions to the back door.

"You want the Magnetorium?" the old woman asked, gumming the words through a toothless face all but collapsed inward. Bent and bandy-legged, she looked barely able to stand, but she could count coppers faster than any bank clerk. Evelina had already been informed of the age, sex, and history of the old dame's six children and all their progeny, not to mention the career of her unlamented and thankfully late spouse. "What would a young thing like you want with a place like that?"

"I want to speak to the puppeteer," Evelina replied, admiring the pinks in the woman's basket. They made a bright, brave splash in the gray street. Their spicy scent tickled the nose, unaccountably conjuring thoughts of secrets and blushes.

"Are you sure, girl? He's a rum one, for all his fair words. And machines weren't meant to walk the earth with a human face. It's not proper." The old woman looked in her basket, knotted fingers fumbling at the blooms. "If I had some rowan I'd give it to you."

The words tugged at Evelina's heart, reminding her of Gran Cooper and her herb lore. Any country girl knew the devas of rowan were powerful protectors against dark magic. Where had the old lady come from? And where were all her children and grandchildren, that she still had to stand long hours on the street every day, in spite of the rain and the heat?

Evelina touched the woman's shoulder, feeling the bones beneath her shawl and putting a confidence into her words that she did not feel. "Don't you worry, I'll keep my eyes sharp and my ears pricked."

The flower seller studied her from beneath wispy brows. "You do that, girl. And remember what you're after once you get there. The man deals in illusions." And, reluctantly, the old woman gave her directions.

Evelina found the back entrance open and paused there, half in and half out the iron-studded door. It had the hushed presence of a crypt shortly after the local revenant had left for its night out. A shaft of afternoon sunlight spilled across the wide wooden floor, showing just how vast and deserted the back of the theater was.

The emptiness of it, and of the narrow alleyway behind it, sent gooseflesh crawling over her skin. She was growing to rapidly despise deserted places. Her conversation with the flower seller had strayed to the fate of poor Annie Chapman who had died just down the way only a week ago. That made a third victim in the area in the space of five weeks—and not just ordinary deaths. They were extravagantly gruesome to the point of sheer madness.

Every trick of the light, every bit of refuse tumbling in the breeze made Evelina skittish. She might be tempted to scamper home with her tail between her legs, except that she was running out of time to find the name of the Blue King's maker. And steady work with machines would usher her into the community of builders and makers more quickly than anything else she could think of. Whoever ran this forsaken place would simply *have* to give her employment.

"Hello?" she called into the vaulted space. The sound of her voice dissipated, no more than a puff of steam. "Is anyone here?"

Evelina creaked the door open another notch, letting in a bit more light. The sound of the rust-eaten hinges seemed enormously loud, but she welcomed the noise. It was the sign of something concrete in the land of the living. Something that needed fixing, and something she could effect with an oilcan and steel wool.

And she was ready for an easy success. She'd spent the morning helping Gareth deal with his mother's remains. It was Sunday, so Evelina had walked to Christ Church to fetch someone. Then the body was removed and questions answered, a pauper's grave arranged. Earls had put in an appearance to complain about the state of the mattress, but his protests had been halfhearted. In death, Lacey Cardew had been, if not beautiful, at least serene, and Evelina saw that had touched the caretaker. After everyone else had left, Evelina had helped Gareth take away Lacey's few possessions. Now the boy was sleeping off his grief, and she had to get back to business.

"Hello?" she said again, listening hard for movement anywhere in the building.

Like a hunter setting her snares, Evelina surveyed the terrain for clues that might help her get a permanent job in this place. The sunlight showed props and pieces of sets stacked against the far wall, a rack of ballet costumes and a workbench littered with clamps and a large drill hooked up to a

treadle. That caught her interest enough to draw her all the
way inside.

Trespassing? Perhaps, but Evelina wasn't getting anywhere
lingering on the threshold. She took one step, then another,
her gaze swiveling from side to side. The door swung closed,
shutting out the sunlight. A warning niggled at the edge of
her consciousness, as if a faint, bad smell hung in the air.
She'd come to count on Mouse and Bird to cross-check her
instincts, but they weren't there to give advice. So she put the
dark feeling to one side, not ignoring it but not letting it hold
her back.

Now that she was farther into the room, she could see that
there were more tables around the perimeter draped in white
sheets. They gave the place the appearance of a morgue.
Cautiously, she approached the nearest one and lifted a corner of the sheet.

Then she jumped back as a silky lock of hair brushed her
hand. Revulsion skittered up her spine, but she made herself
twitch the sheet fully aside. A porcelain face slept there, so
lifelike that Evelina blinked to make sure she wasn't seeing
flesh. Red hair cascaded over the doll's shoulders and down
onto a body sewn of velvety, flesh-colored silk. The eyelids
were closed and edged in tufts of perfect lashes. Even the
lips were astonishing in their detail, every angle sculpted to
give the impression of youthful softness. *Sleeping Beauty,*
she thought. Did her prince know she was nothing but a
fake?

So this must be one of the theater's puppets. Then the
other tables must hold more of the same. *Automatons, probably.* Ploughman's had never used such things and she had
no experience fixing them, but she'd read plenty about the
topic when Lord Bancroft's had been stolen. From what she
could tell, they were a finicky, complicated, and generally
useless breed of machine. *But good for me, if they need
someone to keep them running.*

"Do you like her?" came a horribly familiar voice. "Her
name is Serafina."

Evelina spun around, dropping her carpetbag to the floor.
It clattered as it struck the wood, the noise echoing in the

high rafters. *Where is he?* She looked about frantically, wishing the door hadn't blocked out that scrap of comforting sun. Shadows were everywhere, hiding the enemy from view. The smell was stronger now, the oily scent of a sorcerer's magic. A rum one, the flower seller had said. The old lady had no idea.

"My, my, if it isn't Miss Cooper. What are you doing in my lair?"

"Magnus!" she growled, pulling out the knife she kept in her boot. Nick had taught her a few things to do with a blade. She couldn't have lost all her skill. "You're dead."

But she was wrong and knew it. There had been a letter that had come just before she left London for her grandmother's house. The words welled up in her memory, turning her cold. *As I suspected, your natural talents are unsurpassed. There will come a time when you want answers, when the mysteries shall be mysteries no more. Then I shall find you and teach you the vast universe of what there is to do and know and imagine, my luminous Evelina.*

"Dead? I think not," the voice said dryly. "I've never been a beauty, but I do compare favorably to a walking corpse."

And then there he was, a dozen feet in front of her. Terror clawed up her throat, threatening to turn into a scream. She stumbled backward, her hands shaking too hard to do more than hang onto the knife.

"Good gracious, what *do* you think I'm going to do to you?" he mused, shifting his weight to one hip. The look in his eyes was a mix of surprise, concern, and something greedy. "Didn't you receive the letter I sent to you last April?"

"I hoped it was a hoax."

"But you knew it wasn't."

"No," she said weakly. It came out as little more than a croak.

"But I apologize for leaving things the way I did. I would have come to call sooner but I was indisposed for some time after my, um, accident."

"You threatened me," she retorted, but it came out in a strangled whisper. "You hurt Nick."

Magnus was tall and thin, his saturnine features from a country far from English shores. His eyes were dark and deep-set, his black hair swept back from a high forehead. A fine mustache and goatee framed a sensual mouth. It wasn't a pretty face, but it was strikingly male. He was a man one felt compelled to look at.

"Come now, Miss Cooper. I *threatened* to teach you to use your magic properly." His smile turned wry. "I can see how that horrifies you."

"Dark magic. Sorcery. Death spells."

He jerked his chin in, as if offended. "Magic has a full range of capabilities. You are free to choose where you specialize. I encourage you to explore it all before you limit your sights to sleep aids and recipes for superior scones."

"Succumb to temptation, you mean." Her heart was pounding fast.

"Always your choice, Miss Cooper. Always."

Her lips pulled back into a snarl. "That wasn't the tune the last time we did this dance."

"I admit to being overzealous."

"A nice way of putting it. I would have gone for barking mad."

"So judgmental."

"Ha!"

He'd paralyzed Nick with an agonizing spell and had tried to physically drag her from the house where she was staying. She'd fought him and she'd had him—Nick's knife poised to throw at Magnus's back as he disappeared down the stairs. There was no way she could have missed. And yet . . . she hadn't done it. She was no murderer, but there might have been something else that stayed her hand. Magnus was a practitioner of the darkest spells, but he was the only other magic user she knew—and he was right about her lack of a teacher. Her Gran Cooper had been gone from her life before she'd taught Evelina all she needed to learn.

But she couldn't let that blind her to the bare facts. "How come you're still alive?"

He chuckled—not an evil laugh, just rueful. "Because I

was never entirely dead. But I'll admit that healing such an injury took a lot out of me."

He leaned against the other end of the doll's table, keeping a respectful distance. Now that he was closer, Evelina could see he looked more worn than when she had last seen him. That evidence of vulnerability made her feel slightly better. Magnus gave a self-deprecating smile and spread his hands. "But enough about my adventures. What are you doing here?"

"It's a long story."

"But no doubt entertaining. You are not a dull girl, Miss Cooper."

Evelina wasn't sure how to answer. She was still struggling with Magnus's untimely resurrection. Where she and her Gran used the folkways, summoning devas and coaxing them to loan their magic, sorcerers used life force for their spells. Some used their own, never taking from others, but they tended to die young. Most thieved where they could, and the worst killed for it. She'd heard Magnus's heart had been blown clean through his chest. Only the blackest magic would be enough to get him up and walking around again.

And if he could do that, there was no point trying to lie to him. "Jasper Keating sent me here." She didn't, however, need to tell him why.

"To Whitechapel?" That seemed to take Magnus by surprise, even more than her sudden appearance. "I thought you were in his favor. Didn't you and your uncle find the merry band of thieves helping themselves to his ancient artifacts? Correct me if I'm wrong. I was indisposed when that all transpired."

Hanging upside down like a bat and licking your wounds? "That's true. But he recently caught me compromising the virtue of his future son-in-law."

"And who would that be? Young Mr. Roth? I remember how he gazed at you during the Duchess of Westlake's ball, as if you were a flame and he but a love-struck moth."

His words speared her. Evelina looked away, then realized that was a foolish thing to do. She should be watching his every move.

"Ah," said Magnus, with the lightest touch of sympathy. "You ran afoul of family politics. Keating wanted the boy's talent for his own uses."

"Exactly." And it made her so furious, she was glad to say so out loud—even if it was to a sorcerer. "And catching me in the wrong was an excuse to make me one of his minions. He threatened people I love unless I did his bidding. So I decided to play his game, at least for now."

Magnus folded his arms, looking thoughtful. "I'm sorry you were pushed so far. When Jasper Keating sent his assassins after me, I had provoked him. You merely kissed your beau."

She knew this reasonable fairness was just one of the sorcerer's many masks, but it still slipped under her guard. Grief welled up, making her throat close with a painful spasm. She sucked in a breath that turned to a cough. "I did what I had to." *Is this how Tobias feels?*

She slid the knife back into its sheath, tired of trying to keep up the offensive. Magnus obviously didn't mean to kill her that day. He watched her, looking no more nor less worried than he had been a moment before. A tingle of irritation bolstered her.

"Why are you here, in this theater?" she asked.

"Why are you?"

"I'm looking for the owner. I need work."

"This is Dr. Magnus's Magnetorium." He put a hand to his waistcoat with a sly smile. "I am the proprietor."

"You?" she asked, not managing to keep the horror from her voice. "You're the puppeteer?"

"Yes."

"Why?"

"Shifting circumstances. After my brush with an assassin's bullet, I have had a score to settle with Mr. Keating. To that end, I have been biding my time until things feel just right. Until Keating believes he's triumphed. I think that moment shall be soon."

Evelina's chest tightened, making it hard to breathe past her revulsion.

"Many of my resources were burned along with my house,

but I had enough put away to acquire this establishment and make a living." He gestured around the room. "My talents as a mesmerist have come in handy, as have my mechanical creations."

"So you're here to turn a coin."

"Just as you came looking for work." He nodded. "A place like this makes sense for you. I've seen your handiwork. Those tiny clockwork beasts."

"They're not here," Evelina said quickly. "So there's no chance for you to steal them this time." And there was no way she would work for Magnus, no matter how hungry she got.

"I never meant to keep your Mouse," he said gently. "But I don't ask you to believe that."

"I don't," she retorted, "but I still don't understand this place. You always had someone else do your mechanical work—Lord Bancroft or Tobias. You aren't a maker. What are you doing with a theater full of automatons?"

He flicked a hand. "Have you forgotten the tall case clock I made? The one that sits in Hilliard House?"

She had, but now its elegant form rose in her mind. It was a brilliant piece of machinery that not only told the time and weather, but also recorded whispers on the aether. "Of course."

"I am not incapable of winding a gear," he said grandly. "Some would account me a genius at it, but such nitpicking drudgery does not stir my blood. I am long past the apprenticeship of the workbench. I design. I envision. Others can do the humdrum work of calibrating bits of brass. And where I shine greatest is in that nexus between machine and something else, between the mystical and the mechanical. And I think that suits the stage admirably, don't you?"

Evelina listened with a mix of amusement, excitement, and dismay. One could never accuse Magnus of undervaluing his own talent. *But what if he is the Blue King's maker?* And what kind of an army could his talents build?

His mouth tilted in a smile. "Allow me to show you my prize creation."

Before Evelina could craft a scathing retort, he slipped the sheet from Serafina, revealing her entire body. She was wearing a shift of black lace topped with a set of low-cut stays covered in silk of brocaded scarlet. Evelina blinked, feeling heat climb up her face. There had never been lingerie like that in her wardrobe. It said a lot about the sorcerer, though—more than she wanted to know.

Magnus pulled a long pin from a slot in the table beside her and inserted it into Serafina's neck. "This activates her logic processor."

Evelina waited to be underwhelmed. Even the best processors couldn't handle a millionth part of the human capacity for reason—which was why automatons had never caught on for domestic use. They just weren't practical. When they weren't ironing holes in the shirts, they were putting the baby in the oven instead of the roast.

But then Serafina opened her eyes and sat up as gracefully as any human. For an instant, wonder blanked out every other thought. *The thing moves as naturally as a living woman. Where is the power source?* As little as she liked being near Magnus, anticipation honed Evelina's senses, keeping her riveted to see what the doll would do next.

It turned, swinging its feet over the side of the table. Its— her—toes were perfectly formed and flexible, overcoming a critical flaw in the early designs. No one appreciated the intricacies of balancing on two feet until designers tried to re-create the act of walking. Evelina ached to examine the joints more closely.

"Good afternoon, Serafina," Magnus said in a clear, firm voice.

"Good afternoon," the doll replied, the hinged jaw working in almost perfect synchronicity with a less convincing mechanical voice. It changed pitch in the right places, but the timber sounded wrong. "Do I dance tonight?" The doll turned to look at Magnus in an inquiring manner.

"No, it's Sunday. It's your night off from performing."

Serafina drooped, looking disappointed. The naturalness, the humanity of it was incredible—and a little unnerving. There was magic at work, Evelina was sure of it. She was equally certain there was no deva trapped inside. She'd never seen the likes of this before, and she was mesmerized.

She had long ached to study the intersection of magic and mechanics—that was what had driven her to make Mouse and Bird—but Magnus had done the same thing a completely different way.

"There is an entire troupe of these lovely creatures," Magnus explained, "but Serafina is the star. She is the most advanced of my creations, and her admirers are legion."

"How many puppets are there?" Evelina asked.

"Almost a dozen in my current show, but there are as many again in need of repair. I do not have enough time—or patience—to attend to all the fastidious work that needs doing. I need someone with your practical skill."

Serafina finally registered Evelina's presence and began tugging on Magnus's sleeve. "Who is that?"

"Not now, my dear," he said absently, patting her hand.

Evelina watched, sensing firmness but also an abstracted fondness in his reaction, as if Serafina was a favored pet. The doll was curious, which meant it was responding to its environment. *How did he do it?*

But she had to remember whom she was dealing with. "Didn't you try to recruit Tobias and his friends to help you with your mechanical work?" Tobias's fear of whatever Magnus had showed him had been profound.

"I put the young men to a test," Magnus replied with a shrug. "I had disassembled Serafina to fix her logic processor—she was malfunctioning on a grand scale—and I wanted someone to put her back together, which they did with admirable success. However, that was only part of the exercise. They were not ready for what else I wanted to show them."

"What was that?"

"That machines could live. Something you already knew."

There must have been more to it than that, but she had none of the facts and there was no point in debating it. Instead, she walked slowly toward the doll, every bit as drawn in as she was repelled. "What kind of a logic processor are you using? How does she work?"

Magnus made an inviting gesture. "Be my guest."

Serafina looked almost frightened. Since her face was immobile, it was hard to tell, but something tugged at Evelina's instincts. She stopped a few feet away. "My name is Evelina. May I touch you?"

"I'm pleased to meet you." Serafina held out a hand. Every joint was articulated so skillfully, it was almost impossible to see the workings. Evelina clasped the doll's hand to shake it. It was cool to the touch, but the pressure of her grip was perfectly regulated.

Evelina opened her senses, reaching with her magic to learn what she could. Instantly, she understood the doll was alive. She could feel Magnus's magic at work, dark and slippery, but Serafina was almost entirely her own self—barely formed, a little chaotic, but distinct. *A truly living machine.* Fascinating—and yet faintly repellent. "Dr. Magnus, you showed me a mechanical beetle once at Lady Bancroft's dinner party. It appeared to be alive."

"And you are wondering if Serafina works in a similar fashion? Not quite, but you are on the right track."

"What is her power source?"

"Now you want my instruction?" His words were thick with amusement. "Really, Evelina, make up your mind."

She shot him a hard look, and that made him laugh harder.

"Of course I will tell you," he said.

Excitement threaded through Evelina, but it was muted by anxiety. Magnus was clever and wouldn't give away something for nothing, no matter how small. Nevertheless, she gave the doll a reassuring smile. "Amazing. Serafina, you are a masterpiece."

"Thank you," the doll said politely.

"Don't praise her too much," Magnus said lightly. "Serafina is an addict for compliments, aren't you, my dear?"

The doll turned her face toward him. There was something behind the expressionless face, but Evelina couldn't read it. Was that confusion? Shame? Or was that a spark of temper?

"Every pretty young lady loves compliments," Evelina said, instinctively wanting to spare Serafina's feelings. "There is nothing amiss with that."

"You are the soul of diplomacy, Miss Cooper," Magnus

returned, his dark eyes fixed on the doll. "She is more than china and stuffing, that is certain, but do not forget that she is not fully human, either. She has half a soul, and that is an unpredictable thing. She has not always been kind to her makers, so treat her like the half-disciplined child that she is."

The doll stood, quiet and demure.

"Serafina," Magnus said in that firm tone he used with her, "would you please make us some refreshments? Perhaps some tea and sandwiches?"

"Of course," the doll replied, sliding down to the floor. Then she walked away, her step a little halting but perfectly steady.

Tea and sandwiches. Evelina's head swam with a sense of unreality. Magnus was being perfectly polite, but she remembered the terror she'd felt during their last encounter. She could still feel his bruising grip on her arm. "I can't stay."

"Don't be ridiculous. I'm not going to poison you."

"Is that what Hades said to Persephone when he offered her a dish of pomegranates?"

"That wasn't poison, that was his way of doing business. I know you don't want to work for me," he said easily, pulling himself up to sit on the edge of the table like a schoolboy. "But in my establishment, the hospitality comes for free. No strings attached."

"As long as that's understood." She sounded ungracious, but she wasn't going to lie awake worrying about a sorcerer's feelings.

"I could use you, though. What can I say that will change your mind?" And he gave her a disarming smile.

Confusion jammed her thoughts. "I don't know what there is to say. You're an insane practitioner of death magic who should be in his coffin by now. And you stole my Mouse."

"I apologize for the toy, but I had to lure you somehow."

"And look where it got you."

"Keating sent his streetkeeper to kill me. You can't take

credit for that." He gave a slight grimace. "At least we have the hatred of him in common."

"I'll give you that much, but it's not enough to make up for what you've done. If I've guessed correctly, you also stole Lord Bancroft's automatons."

Magnus chuckled. "You were the busy little detective, weren't you? They were mine as much as his, since we both had a hand in creating them. You might say I did him a favor. He was always terrified that his early experiments would become public knowledge. A touch of magic among all those logical gears? Tsk, tsk. His political career would be finished."

That sounded like Lord B, all right. "Do you still have them?"

"Alas, no, they burned in the fire that destroyed my house."

She fell silent. The matter of the automatons had been a convoluted mess. Two grooms had been killed during the theft, Lord Bancroft had offered a huge reward, and Magnus had used the automatons to blackmail Lord B. It was just another reason never to trust Magnus. But if the dolls were truly gone, there wasn't much she could do about them now.

"Consider this," said Magnus. "I can pay you decently. You do not need to hide around me. I know you are a magic user. There is no danger of being whisked off to prison for using magic under my roof. Here, you are entirely free and safe."

That was a strong seduction. Stronger than she had expected. *I could be myself without worry.* And Magnus, for all his evils, had always fascinated her. Just look at what he had accomplished here.

She jerked her thoughts back on track. She was forgetting why she was here. "What about the Blue King? Does he bother you? I thought the steam barons frowned on anyone tinkering without their approval."

"I may be down on my luck, but I can still protect my employees against the local ruffians. As for King Coal himself, he allows me to run my business and build my automatons despite the number of parts and other mechanical contraband it requires. I do him a favor now and again in return, mostly designing this and that."

"Like what?" All he needed to say was "an army of sentient automaton soldiers" and she could go home. But of course it wasn't that easy.

Magnus shrugged. "Men like him are forever in a race to destruction."

It was almost, but not quite, an answer. She had a week to find the information Keating wanted and if she failed, she was entirely at the Gold King's mercy. Her reputation and the safety of her family were at risk.

There was a good chance Magnus was the maker, but she also needed to know what weapons the Blue King possessed. *If I work for Magnus, I'll have plenty of excuses to go looking for parts and to mix with the other makers. And I'll be here, seeing everyone who comes and goes. Surely I'll find out something about what he's made.* And best of all, she could learn how Magnus had created his doll.

Serafina returned with a tray, setting it down on the workbench. Then she started to pour the tea with what appeared to be intense concentration. Evelina drew near, watching her work with renewed amazement.

Surely I can stand being near Magnus just long enough to find out what Keating needs to know. It couldn't possibly take longer than the week I have left. But she knew the drawback—Magnus was a sorcerer, and he was extremely clever. His goal had long been to enlist her as a student, and what he had to offer was in fact tempting. It would be too easy to grab that sorcerous knowledge and have her revenge on Keating for everything he'd done. Was she strong enough to resist touching it?

And Magnus was well aware of that struggle. Even if she decided to work for him now, she could not agree too easily. That would make him suspicious.

"If I agree to mend your automatons," she said slowly, still making up her mind even while she spoke, "there will be rules."

He spread his hands, all innocence. "I'm not asking you to

do anything but mend my automatons. I'll pay you a fair wage to do it. No further obligations on either side."

"No talk of turning me into your protégée in sorcery?"

"If that is what you want."

"It is."

When Serafina passed her a cup of tea, Evelina heard the cup rattle the moment she took it. The doll was steady; it was her own hands that shook. *Do I accept? Don't I?* What had her uncle said: *Difficult times do not last. Difficult, obstinate, and impertinent people do.* She had to take the risk.

She didn't want to. She didn't trust Dr. Magnus even enough to drink the tea, and she didn't trust herself. She set the cup down to hide the trembling in her hands. "I'll think about it."

Magnus just smiled. "You should come see a show."

CHAPTER SIXTEEN

THE FACADE OF THE MAGNETORIUM STOOD AT THE END OF A long, dark alleyway where the cloudy indigo gaslights of the Blue King barely reached. Evelina stood in the shadows to one side of the entrance, taking in her first impression of the place on a performance night.

The brick buildings that flanked the narrow alley were blackened by coal dust, the stony mud that passed for cobbles wet with that afternoon's rain shower. In stark contrast to the long, dark chute before it, the front of the Magnetorium was bathed in ghastly blue light, from the yawning, arched maw of the iron-banded doors to the vaguely steeple-like point of the roof. It gave the impression of a chapel of the damned.

And not a well-advertised one. Despite the size of the work area in the back, the entrance was narrow, the name of the place written above the door in neat black lettering. The playbills posted to the side of the entry were small and unremarkable. It clearly depended on word of mouth. But, judging by the steady stream of humanity approaching, that word was more than enough. If Ploughman's had done this kind of business when Evelina was a child, they'd all have been eating fresh meat twice a week and sleeping on feather mattresses. Already piqued, her curiosity about

Magnus and his enterprise strained like an overwound spring.

Only a day had passed since she'd found Magnus in the back of the theater, and she hadn't accepted his offer of work yet. Part of her reluctance was calculated, a necessary show of caution so she didn't appear to be too eager and give herself away as a spy. But the truth was that she simply hadn't had the courage—or perhaps desperation was the right word—to spend so much time in the company of a sorcerer.

But was Magnus more of a threat than the certain doom that awaited her if she failed Keating? She wasn't sure that watching the show would help her to a decision, but the doctor had given her a ticket, and it never took much prodding to get her to an entertainment.

Especially one that seemed to be so popular. The Magnetorium might have been located in the poor part of town, but the audience came from the fine houses farther west—a theory borne out by the price of the tickets. No doubt the trip to the East End was part of the excitement. Men and women—though mostly men—arrived in anonymous hansom cabs at the far end of the passageway and hurried toward the doors, anxious to get seats. Evelina smiled to herself, because she knew the names of a few of the fine gentlemen here and there. As for the ladies—well, many weren't.

She watched another moment, feeling the cold clamminess that promised fog later that night. And then she thought of all the people in the cramped, drafty buildings nearby who couldn't simply shrug on a thick coat and swagger out for an evening on the town. She desperately wanted to be back in the comfort of her old life, but at that moment she despised it.

Cross and tired of standing in the chilly darkness, she slid through the door between two young men she was certain she didn't know. Three of Magnus's other employees—a pretty girl in a low-cut dress, flanked by two burly bruisers prepared to keep order—were taking the ticket money. Another counter was set up to sell beer and wine—a better grade than could be got at the local taverns—salted nuts and paper-wrapped sweets. Evelina climbed to the farthest reaches of the seats, careful to sit in an empty row so far back that no one would look there. The last thing she needed was to be recognized by one of Imogen's gaggle of admirers, or a friend of Tobias.

The first thing she noticed was how intimate the place was. Despite the huge workshop in the back, the orchestra and boxes held only a few hundred seats. There were no bad views of the stage, and everyone was close enough to hear even the softest whisper. Whoever had designed the place had known his business—but it was no wonder the cost of a ticket was dear. One had to turn a profit, and fewer seats meant fewer pounds in the investor's pocket.

But then the lights dimmed to blackness, and Evelina's ruminations were cut short. An anticipatory whisper ran through the theater as a tiny flame appeared to hover in the dark. Then she understood the placement of the seats and the perfect sightlines. Every sense claimed that she was floating, the only point of reference that flickering light.

And then something passed before the light. Fingers, perhaps, teasing an audience suddenly dependent on that flame for an anchor in the limitless black.

"Welcome, sirs and ladies fine and fancy," purred Magnus. His voice seemed to come from everywhere—the stage below, the rafters above, the seat next to her. "Welcome to the Magnetorium, where wonders never cease."

Evelina sat poised at the edge of her seat, the hair on her neck already ruffling with the expectation of fear. But then something changed, the blackness becoming a little less suffocating. She couldn't tell if it was her eyes getting used to the lack of light, or if it was some trick of stagecraft, allowing just enough diffuse illumination to turn the atmosphere from midnight to the uneasy hours just before the dawn.

The stage was still a void of darkness, but then a gust of fog drifted across it, subtle as gossamer. As the trailing fingers of mist swept across the stage, tiny lamps were lit, one by one, by an unseen hand. The glimmering light turned the night to a cobalt blue, giving just enough illumination to see tombstones crumbling beneath a canopy of twisted trees. A graveyard, then—one of ancient vintage forgotten by any grieving heart.

The throb of a cello sounded from a tiny gallery high above—long, slow notes that ached under her ribs. Evelina searched the shadows above for the musician, but could only see the shapes of two carved angels, expressions of pity frozen on their wooden faces, fingers pointing to the stage. Inexorably, her gaze was drawn back to the stage below.

Dark figures stood or crouched, still and silent as the grave markers. As the music swelled, more lights glimmered to create an unearthly glow, not just along the ground but in the trees and spangling the sky. And it seemed to be the sky, for so beautiful and breathtaking was the set that Evelina forgot she was simply in a seat in the balcony. She was in that graveyard, beneath that star-strewn night, where the gusting breeze made the points of light glitter like diamonds spangling the fog's silken veil.

And then the dancers moved, their costumes as pale and insubstantial as the mist. And Evelina was stricken—not simply with the elegance of the choreography, or the perfection of their form, but that they existed at all. The automatons moved as one, every gesture smoothly executed, every step an exquisite achievement of the maker's art. She sat forward in her seat, forgetting to breathe. *I want to know how this was done. I need to know.* It was more than clockwork— there *had* to be magic involved. *And Magnus said he would teach me.*

And then Serafina entered from the wings, as light as if she had flown. She was clad in a gauzy white costume spangled with silver, as if a piece of the starlit mist had coalesced into female form. Her long, red hair was bound up in a glittering diadem, showing off the exquisite line of her bare shoulders and neck. In the strange cold light, nothing hinted that her bare arms and snowy bosom were anything but flesh.

A collective sigh rose from the audience, startling Evelina

because she'd forgotten they were there. The only sound had been the mourning of the cello, but now that was joined by another voice, the husky sweetness of a wooden flute. Like Serafina, it was made of something finer and brighter, dancing aloft like a creature made of aether.

Serafina floated across the stage *en pointe* to a melancholy tune. Steel-strong, immune to pain, completely obedient, and a machine of boundless energy, Serafina was the perfect ballerina, if one didn't mind a slight stiffness in the *port de bras*.

And then the ballet began in earnest, with the usual parade of set pieces in twos and threes. The company was small, and Evelina remembered what Magnus had said about some of his dancers requiring repair. Even at less than full strength, what she saw of the troupe enchanted her with their fluid precision. Yet as marvelous as they all were, Serafina was so much more. Evelina knew performance and performers, and while Serafina was more mechanically refined than the others, there was another reason for her superiority. All the dolls danced, but Serafina danced with joy.

But even as she performed, her companions twirling and weaving behind her, one corner of the stage grew dark, the lights winking out one by one to be replaced by an ominous red glow. When the light grew bright enough, Evelina could see Magnus. At first he was a silhouette in black, more a crow in his dark coat, his long hair trailing to his shoulders. Then, as he raised his bowed head, the crimson light grew bright enough that she saw he cupped the flame— without a candle—in his hands. *Magic*. Evelina knew it for what it was but others would not. This was the theater, the one place where true power was mistaken for a conjurer's illusion.

Serafina—ghostly sylph, vulnerable heroine—pirouetted across the stage, seeming as delicate as blown glass until . . . suddenly Magnus was there, dark and forbidding. He caught her in his arms, and she melted into a seeming faint, arms trailing as she drooped, captive to his brooding darkness. The cellist leaned into the dirgelike tune as Magnus bent over the doll. The corps de ballet swirled anxiously as Magnus swept up his captive, bearing her through the forest of tombstones as a red hue drenched the stage with an aura of blood.

The cello roared and wept. Blue lightning shot across the stage, dancing between coils like a demonic serpent. In the strange, horrible brightness, Magnus turned to glare at the audience, his eyes a glowing scarlet. Someone in the audience shrieked.

Sudden blackness swamped the Magnetorium once more, leaving nothing but the fearsome image imprinted on Evelina's brain. It lingered, refusing to fade. Suddenly ice-cold, she shook herself back to life, realizing that her breath was coming in short, sharp gasps. The performance had completely pulled her in, the terror of Serafina's abduction slipping past her guard. *Well played, Magnus.*

Time meant nothing in the blackness. A few seconds might have ticked by, or hours. But then someone started to clap. And another. And then the place was in an uproar of delight.

The house lights came up a notch to reveal a black curtain drawn across the proscenium arch. It was the first intermission. Evelina got out of her seat and hurried out the front door to gulp in fresh air. Even the brisk September night seemed warmer than her blood at first, but then her heart seemed to start again. A long shudder took her, as if to throw off the influence of what she'd seen.

"What do you think?" a voice said softly behind her.

It was Magnus, smoking a Turkish cigarette and looking pleased with himself. Other audience members stood mere feet away, but didn't seem to recognize him. That didn't surprise Evelina. It was an easy enough trick for a sorcerer.

"I'm impressed," she said, "but I have some ideas about the lighting. The red at the end is a touch obvious."

"Does the job tempt you, now you've seen the show?" One corner of his mouth curled up.

There wasn't much she could say. It did, very much. She wanted to look inside those automatons in the worst way.

And I'm running out of time to get Keating his information.

But her pride demanded something more than a straightforward yes. "The vampire, the maiden, and the horde of scary wraiths? I wouldn't miss it for the world. I loved reading old copies of *Varney the Vampire* as a girl."

Magnus made a face. "I was hoping for rather more gravitas than a penny dreadful."

"Come now, I can't wait to see what the villain does to our hapless maiden."

He tossed the stub of the cigarette aside, letting it sizzle on the wet stones. "I suppose I should go put my fangs in."

"You're aware of the concept of typecasting?"

He gave her a droll look. "So acidic for one so young."

Evelina lifted her chin, enjoying the banter despite herself. Truth be told, she was desperate for wit, beauty, and wonder, and this evening was giving her all three. "You said it yourself. Those that bite the hardest live to fight another day."

"Be careful who you nip, kitten." The words held just the suggestion of an edge.

"Always, nosferatu. There is every chance you might bite back."

"And yet I wager that you will stay on as long as there is a saucer of milk."

"How little you know me."

"We'll see, Miss Cooper. Milk is hard to give up."

"Then I immediately renounce all dairy products."

"That makes for a bitter cup of tea." He gave a slight shrug and disappeared in the direction of the stage door, whistling a dirge from the show.

CHAPTER SEVENTEEN

September 20, 1888

Dear Sir,

First, let me assure you that I have in no way forgotten the terms of our arrangement and that I have pursued, with all possible energy, the objectives upon which we agreed. However, the information that you seek is indeed well concealed and it has taken me until this date to find a strong lead. Accordingly, I have placed myself in a position to gain the confidence of the party involved. All I require is a little more time. I beg you to grant me until the end of the month to bring this matter to a satisfactory result.

Your obedient servant,
E.C.

PS—A response may be sent via The Ten Bells. It is a public drinking house, but the owner is trustworthy, for a price.

> —addressed to Keating care of the Oraculars' Club

London, September 21, 1888

DR. MAGNUS'S MAGNETORIUM THEATRE

11:30 a.m. Friday

THE MALE AUTOMATON LAY DISMEMBERED ON EVELINA'S worktable, the cover off his left thigh and a forest of tubes, pulleys, and gears scattered around him. Whoever had first assembled Casimir—obviously a connoisseur of male pulchritude—had chosen to make the doll as faithful to anatomy as possible. Feeling a little foolish, Evelina had ended up draping him in some attempt at modesty. She wasn't sure if it was because she cared, or if she thought Casimir might if he ever became as sentient as Serafina.

As far as she was able to determine, all the functioning automatons could understand and obey relatively complex commands. They had to, in order to carry out the intricate steps of the ballets. Most had logic processors that enabled speech, although their conversation was more of the "yes, ma'am" and "no, sir" variety. Only one or two, Casimir among them, had anything approaching the ability to reason at the most basic level, and none displayed what Evelina considered emotion or personality. Serafina was clearly where Magnus had focused his energies, exploring what he called the nexus between magic and machine.

The sorcerer was clearly curious about Evelina's abilities and asked if she had made any more creatures like Mouse and Bird. She knew from past encounters that he wanted to learn her methods, but this time around he was careful not to push. No doubt that would come eventually, but for now Magnus was paving the way by revealing his own process of discovery.

"Serafina was the recipient of my earliest experiments in mechanical emotion," he told her one afternoon as Evelina put away her tools for the day.

"It sounds as if you made several."

"I did. I was breaking new ground."

Evelina paused to wrap one of her cutting tools in cloth. "And you tried these all on the same subject? Is that good science?"

"I could argue that using one subject gave the process consistency."

"And your experiments did not conflict, one on top of the other?"

Magnus waved a hand. "Inconsistency is in itself a human trait. One might argue it is appropriate for a female." He winked as he pushed away from the workbench, drifting off to some other task.

Beyond irritated, Evelina had forced herself to pack the blade away. Like so many men—especially those doling out wages—he gave himself permission to make the occasional boneheaded comment.

Women may be fickle, but at least we work. There were three male dolls, and they were all out of order. Evelina had been working for Magnus for four days, and had spent that time—when she wasn't hunting for signs of the Blue King's weaponry—assessing what needed to be done with the automatons. A few needed minor repairs, but the others were a different story. Magnus had asked her to give priority to the male dolls because certain scenarios demanded masculine characters—the usual princes, huntsmen, and knights. Apparently Magnus had no ambition to strap on ballet shoes, so Casimir was the first onto the workbench.

But Evelina was quickly running out of supplies. Even with the Blue King's approval to use and repair machines, parts were hard to come by—especially the high-quality clockwork needed for the dolls.

The wire she was threading through a broken joint in hopes of holding two brittle pieces together snapped and rebounded into a curling tail, making a quivering, scraping sound almost like a snicker. Scalp prickling with irritation, she set her pliers down with an emphatic smack. The sound bounced through the cavernous space where she was working, emphasizing the fact that she was on her own with her problems.

Well, if Magnus wanted a dancing Casimir, he was going to have to get her parts. She flipped the sheet over the automaton and pulled off the apron she wore over her skirts to protect them from grease. She dropped the apron over the doll's feet and drew in her breath. She could hear the distant murmur of the street, her own breathing, and the rustle of a rat in the walls, but she could not hear Magnus.

The first two days, he'd barely let her out of his sight when she was at the theater, but yesterday he had gone out briefly once the other employees had arrived midafternoon. The rhythm of the Magnetorium was different from other theaters. They did put the dolls through their paces to make

sure everything ran smoothly, but those sessions were more
of a technical check than a traditional rehearsal and generally didn't take long. Consequently, the crew wasn't due to
arrive until well into the afternoon.

Did that mean she was the only one there? Evelina stood
quiet a little longer, listening, smelling the pungent mix of
grease, glue, and old wood, and tasting the air for any hint
of magic. There was sorcery there, but it was a lingering
memory, like the scent of coffee long after it was drunk. No
hint that Magnus was there. She'd been waiting for this opportunity for days.

It had felt like months. Tomorrow was Tobias's wedding.
Today was one day until Keating's deadline, and Evelina
hadn't yet received a reply to her note begging for more
time. Every few minutes, she had to force down her anxiety,
swallow back the rising panic that said everything was lost.
Tobias. Her reputation. Her uncle's safety. Her own future.
There was nothing she could do about the first, but she could
try to salvage the rest. All she had to do was be brave, brilliant, and extremely lucky.

Nothing to fret about, surely—if one was as stubborn as
Grandmamma Holmes and as sharp as her shrimp fork.

Evelina crossed to the door that led from the workshop to
the rest of the theater. It was unlocked, so she pushed it open
with a soft "hello?" The corridor was narrow and dark, but
nothing stirred. She walked quickly ahead, doing her best to
look confident just in case she was caught. She was just there
to ask for parts, after all.

The corridor led to the stage. Between the stage and
workroom were green rooms, storage, and the usual backstage paraphernalia. She'd already explored those areas, and
the ease with which Magnus had let her confirmed her
conclusion—there was nothing of interest in those rooms.
What she had yet to see was the upstairs.

About halfway along the corridor, a narrow staircase led
off to the right. There was no handrail, and the stairs were
thin pie-wedges that forced her to walk on tiptoe around the
narrow curve. Evelina's skin prickled at the notion that the
climb to Magnus's private domain was literally perilous.

When she came to the top, she paused to listen again. Nothing.

The upstairs was smaller than the lower floor, because the theater itself took up both stories. What she saw now sat above the workshop and storage areas. Two narrow hallways divided the space like a T.

Evelina walked forward very quietly, her chest tight with apprehension. A sign marked Private hung on the door to her right, indicating that was the entrance to Magnus's rooms. Her hand lingered above the knob a moment, then withdrew. There were other rooms behind her. Perhaps it was cowardice, but she decided to save the doctor's door for last.

She turned away, feeling instantly better as she moved away from Magnus's lair and toward the plain-looking doors ahead. There were two to either side. It took only a moment to determine that the ones on the right were dressing rooms. The largest was furnished in a fussy, feminine style, with a large wardrobe, vanity, and a dainty sofa in pale pink velvet. This, she surmised, was Serafina's. The automaton slept with the others, but she was dressed and prepared for the shows up here, almost as if she were a true prima ballerina. It was a clever bit of window dressing, for when the patrons of the theater begged to meet its shining star, they had to be shown something other than a machine lying inert on a cheap wooden table. At the Magnetorium, illusion was all.

The two doors on the left were locked. *Now this is more interesting.* She could try to pick the lock, but the rusted metal said it wouldn't be a silent procedure. Instead, she knelt, peering through the keyhole to see what she could. Quite a bit, it turned out, for there were no curtains on the window and the room was bright. Evelina bit her lip, angling herself to get the best view. Even though Magnus had said Lord Bancroft's automatons had been burned, she half expected to see the familiar stack of trunks, or a bizarre machine that the Blue King had commissioned—indeed some indication that the doctor was hard at work on villainy.

But disappointment flooded her, making her breath huff

out in defeat. The room was almost empty, the walls pa-
pered with outdated posters from the theater's previous
owners. A dressmaker's model stood forlornly in one corner, but that was all. Nothing the Gold King—or anyone
else—was going to care about. She got to her feet.

That left only one more room. Would it be another disappointment, or would it be the locked door that led to Blue-
beard's skeletal wives, or perhaps pentagrams painted on a
blood-caked floor? Then again, it might just be the doctor's
private collection of immoral publications.

She tried the handle, and as before it would not turn. Plus,
she felt the buzz of a spelled lock—a simple enough piece of
magic, but this was Magnus. Picking it would only end up
releasing who knew what magical attack. She knelt to peer
inside, but this keyhole had been blocked, perhaps hung
with a bit of dark cloth. Superstitious dread filled her, leaving her tingling from the nape of her neck down to the palms
of her hands. She got to her feet, pressing her fingers to the
door, and opening her magical senses.

All she felt was nothingness. Whatever was going on in
there, Magnus had shielded it thoroughly—and it was far
beyond Evelina's scope to pierce that veil. Now she knew
she had to get inside.

A chair scraped. Evelina gasped and started, her feet leaving the floor in a bound of fright. She clamped a hand over
her mouth, but it was too late. She'd made more noise than
she should have.

Why didn't I sense him before? The answer was simple. If
he could shield one room, he could shield another. She'd
been tricked.

"Who is there?" came Magnus's voice from the other side
of his door, and then his footfall.

Disgusted, Evelina stepped away from the door, shaking
the dust from her skirts where she had knelt on the floor.
There was nothing to do but act like she had legitimate business there. She cleared her throat, knocking on the door before nerves could overcome her. The experience was a bit
like putting her hand down a wild animal's burrow. No telling if she'd feel soft fur or something much less pleasant.

She was, after all, dealing with a man with a secret room, and one who ought to be dead.

The door swung open almost at the first rap of her knuckles. Magnus wore only his shirt and trousers, his jacket and waistcoat abandoned. The shirt was open at the throat, the sleeves rolled up over his forearms, the picture of casual comfort.

"Miss Cooper," he said with just a hint of a tease. "What might I do for you?"

"I need parts. Good ones."

"Parts?" he asked innocently.

"Mechanical parts."

With a sly smile, he stepped out of the doorway, gesturing her into the room. "Please, come in and tell me all about it."

She walked inside and caught her breath. In this bizarre theater, in this dingy building in the worst part of town, Magnus had a library. It was just three or four bookcases, and plain, practical ones at that, but they were crammed with ancient, crumbling volumes bound in gold and leather. Excitement flooded her with a mixture of greed and pure thirst, and a faint cry escaped her before she could hide her wonder.

"Lovely, aren't they?" Magnus strolled across the room to pat a fat tome. "And almost as necessary as food and drink to those who love them."

He was right, and she forgot everything for a moment: Keating and the Blue King's war, the locked room, her curiosity about the other rooms the doctor lived in—the ones beyond the connecting doors to her left and right. Nothing mattered but that she had stumbled upon a trove of written treasures.

Magnus pulled a volume off the shelf, the tan leather heavily tooled with swirling designs, and held it out to her. Evelina checked to make sure her hands were free of grease and then accepted the book, conscious that it had to be hundreds of years old. The title was in a language she didn't even recognize. Gingerly, she lifted the heavy cover. The binding creaked, releasing the scent of old paper and glue.

The smell brought back hours of pleasure she'd spent curled in her favorite chair, deep in study.

"The text is in English, though it's hard to read," she said.

"It was written by one of the alchemists of John Dee's time. That is his original hand."

Evelina glanced up, quickly reading the amusement on his face. It wasn't just a book, but a book about magic. She had been starved for this kind of information all her life. "And you're letting me look at it?"

"You're one of the few people I know who would even appreciate it. There is little joy in having such a thing if one can't share the experience. A book is so much more agreeable when it can be discussed over a glass of wine, don't you agree?"

She did wholeheartedly, but she could not help looking for the trap hidden beneath the offer. "Is this some kind of temptation?"

"I am the serpent and you little Eve? No. There is no moral edict here for you to transgress. I merely ask that you do not dog-ear the pages."

But she wasn't done groping for reasons. "You wanted me to be your student once. Your Helen, as you called it. Is that what is going on?"

He fell back into a large wing chair, steepling his fingers. "Ah, that was my error. Helen is the embodiment of eternal wisdom captured in feminine beauty. A pure being, as it were, and a creature that I have always pursued as my muse. I have oft thought a human soul in a body cleansed of fleshly desire could achieve that perfection. Something you have the technique to create."

"But last I checked, I was flesh. Don't mistake what I can do with who I am."

"And therein was my error." He gave a tiny smile and waved her to another chair. "I think, with your tendency to leave broken hearts in your wake, you are rather more Lilith than any other archetype of the female soul."

Lilith, seductress and mother of demons. Evelina didn't like the comparison, but refused to rise to the bait. "Where does Serafina fit into all this? Is she your new Helen?"

"She is hardly new, but you are correct in that she is the vehicle of my ambitions in that direction—one that I have had the leisure to improve upon of late."

Instinctively, she thought of the locked room, and wondered. "Was Serafina the doll that Tobias saw?"

"An earlier incarnation of her, yes. Since then, she has made significant leaps."

"How do you mean?"

"Ah, I can see the subject interests you. I would be more than happy to share what I've learned, colleague to colleague."

Evelina savored the offer a moment. How wonderful it would be to compare what he had done with Serafina with her work on Mouse and Bird, to have a meeting of minds with someone with different, and definitely more, experience. Yes, it was dangerous, but it was also intriguing. "You've never answered me about how the dancing automatons operate."

"I animate them magically. Surely you guessed that much."

"But how? What you do is sorcery. Death magic."

"Not at all. What I have achieved does not require death. Far from it."

"Not even Serafina? She is so much more alive than the others."

"And she needs to be, to serve me as I need her to. But truly, I have never put anyone to death so that Serafina could live. Does that satisfy you?"

Evelina nodded, though she knew very well the answer could be true and not true depending on a thousand things. Sophistry was second nature to practitioners of dark magic—at least, that was what her Gran Cooper had said.

"And why should it concern you?" Magnus went on. "You're not in danger of casting any dark rituals. Nothing but the crudest spell slinging is even possible until an acolyte has undergone the correct preparation."

It all sounded so reasonable. "But there is always the question of when studying a thing turns into condoning it."

He laughed, but she caught the flash of irritation in his eyes. "How puritanical of you. But like so many extreme views, it sees but a sliver of the truth. You believe I spend my nights drowning puppies in the service of the devil. In truth, I have never harmed the furred or feathered. I do not harm innocent things. Why bother? There are too many guilty ones ready to hand."

"So you only harm those you deem guilty?"

"You are so focused on harm. Have you ever thought that I can heal?" And he rose and grabbed her hand, pulling her to her feet. And then he dragged her close enough that the book was pressed against her bodice. She could feel his breath on her face, the smooth heat of his long fingers wrapped around hers.

And then his energy flooded her. She had always perceived his energy as dark and oily, and that was definitely there. And beneath that was an astringent bitterness, like the strongest of coffee without cream or sugar. But once the first bite of that had passed, a dark warmth welled up, flooding her like the heat of a hot, hot bath. It reached into every pore, through every branching vein and work-weary muscle. Strength followed, buoyant and bright, lifting her up as surely as if Magnus had pulled her to her feet. It seemed to start in her feet and crawl upward like flames licking up a tree, setting her alight with a fire she'd thought gone forever. For the first time in many, many days, she was not afraid.

"How does that feel?" he asked.

"Astounding!" she replied in an astonished whisper.

He released her hand, and she almost cried out. But unlike so many spells, it didn't fade when contact was broken. He left the vivid feeling of health behind.

She'd healed before, but it had been far less efficient. With a great deal of effort, one could summon enough devas to fix a sprain or a bruise. And the last time she and Nick had combined their power in a healing spell, they'd nearly wrecked one of the Hilliard House drawing rooms. Magnus's technique was like a thoroughbred compared to a pony.

"Imagine what that could do for the convalescent," he said. "And it is all power that already belongs to you as a birthright of the Blood."

She thought of Lacey. She'd told him the story of the dying woman, and knew he must be thinking of that, too. "What of the seriously ill? Can you heal them?"

His lower lip twitched in the suggestion of a smile. "Yes, but there is a difference between helping nature along and interfering with her plans. There is peril in being too good as much as there is in being a puppy-drowning madman."

But she could only see Gareth's grief and Lacey's suffering—that grief, swallowed down because there was no time to properly feel it, welled up raw as an open wound. And suddenly everything became clear.

To hell with Keating's reasons for sending her here to spy—all at once she had her own reasons for working with Magnus. She wanted to know what she could do with her magic. In fact, after that taste of power, she couldn't turn her back on her potential for one minute more. *Be careful. You know how using power gives a rush to the head.*

Evelina struggled to calm herself, gulped air to calm her speeding heart, but it was so hard. She'd experienced the freedom of holding a book of magic and openly discussing it. She was sick to death of hiding, denying what she was and covering up her power like it was a contagious rash. And now this—she could heal.

This was a miracle, and she could wield it like a sword against the suffering she saw on every street corner. She could cure Imogen, rid her of those nightmares about wandering away from her body. Best of all, she finally felt there was a means to take back control of her life from creatures like Jasper Keating—because anything that could heal was a two-edged blade. *Be careful. Don't even think that way. This is the kind of temptation Gran warned you about.*

Yes, this was the temptation she had feared, but perhaps it deserved a second look. There was definitely something here she could use. *Stop it!*

She looked up, catching Magnus's dark, dark gaze. "How did you do that?"

"Ah," he said with a mocking lift of his brows. "So *now* the little kitten wants lessons."

September 21, 1888
   To E.C., care of The Ten Bells. You have until the first of October. Do not abuse my patience.

Enclosed was a brown substance wrapped in a twist of paper. When Evelina unwrapped it, she recognized a pinch of her uncle's shag tobacco.

CHAPTER EIGHTEEN

London, September 22, 1888

PORTMORE HOTEL

4:05p.m. Saturday

WEDDINGS WERE NEVER THE SEAMLESS AFFAIRS ONE HOPED for, but Emerson Roth, Lord Bancroft, had never actually seen the walking dead intrude upon a celebration—until now.

He pressed against the wall, feeling the chill of marble against his back, and glared across the reception hall at the happy, noisy scene. The food had been eaten, the cake cut, and now the attendees were mixing and chatting, hoping to score a social point or two. In contrast, Bancroft's heart was pounding slightly, sweat breaking out beneath his immaculate shirt collar. He kept his face perfectly still since the father of the groom was not expected to run screaming through the champagne and truffles—at least not at this early hour. The clock had barely struck four in the afternoon.

He searched the crowd, trying to catch another glimpse of the one man alive or dead who could make his blood run cold. But the guests milled in thick crowds across the deep green and wine-colored carpet, obscuring his view. The social success of the event was going to be the bane of his hunt.

Above the throng, pale cream marble framed an airy space accented by extravagant crystal chandeliers. The Portmore Hotel, close to Hyde Park, captured all the elegance Mayfair had to offer. Keating had chosen it for the wedding breakfast—actually served after the eleven o'clock wedding—to show the power of his pocketbook. Although the bride's home was the traditional location for the meal, even the Gold King's elegant London abode could not accommodate the scale of the celebration. In Bancroft's opinion, the entire affair was splashy to the point of vulgarity.

Furthermore, for all its grandeur, the venue appeared to be haunted—at least, if the dead man walking from the stairway toward the exit was any indication. Bancroft was sure he'd seen a tall, thin form weaving through the crowd of guests. The silver-headed cane, the lean, dark face, and the insolent swagger had all been horribly familiar. *Magnus.*

But he's dead! Revulsion brought a fresh wave of sweat to his brow, and he pressed his hands against the marble wall to feel the chill of the stone through his gloves. Bancroft suddenly felt like a little boy again. Was it better to look under the bed and confront a monster, or simply ignore his terror in hopes the nightmare wasn't real? He felt the rich breakfast rolling uneasily in his stomach, and decided the dreadful uncertainty was worse than any disaster. He had to act.

He strode in the direction he'd seen the figure go, putting on the expression of a man hurrying to speak to a long-lost friend. Guests blocked his way, and he dodged around them with polite excuses. The endless blather of banal conversation irked him. Most of Keating's guest list was made up of the politically ambitious, to whom confidential information was more precious than gold, and everyone wanted to show they had learned important secrets before anyone else. After a lifetime of service to the Crown, Bancroft could play the game in his sleep. He had no time for hungry beginners.

He was after different stakes now—ones that counted. He *was* the secret. But if he actually had seen Magnus, that would complicate everything on a hundred different levels.

Bancroft reached the reception hall door without another glimpse of the phantom doctor. The afternoon outside was gray, the street slick with rain, and the cool, fresh air cleared his head. He looked around, wondering if anyone had noticed the father of the groom's rush to meet no one.

It didn't look like he'd been noticed. The roof of the narrow porch protected a gaggle of laughing guests while they awaited their carriages. A man put up his stark black umbrella to shield the ladies because their parasols were too delicate for such vile weather. Bancroft stood at the edge of the rain, not caring if he ruined his shoes. The shade of Magnus was nowhere in sight. Maybe now was the moment to return to the wedding and assume the monster under the bed had never been there.

The wedding. Bancroft felt a twist of pain in his chest. The only thing left to do on that front was to mourn the loss of his son to the enemy. *Poor bastard.* At least Bancroft had loved Adele when he'd married her. Tobias didn't even have that.

There! Bancroft started, drawing a look from the man with the umbrella. The ghost had stepped into view, lingering a moment in plain sight before turning the corner and slipping away. Bancroft launched himself down the hotel steps, the soles of his shoes sliding on the wet granite. His sudden departure drew exclamations from the guests, but to hell with dignity. Pushing himself hard, he raced down the road, hat under his arm, the tails of his coat sailing behind him. If Magnus was there in the flesh—rotting or otherwise—he wasn't getting away.

Bancroft dug his soft heels into the gritty paving stones and wheeled toward the narrow street where the apparition had disappeared. Then he stopped, panting, the heavy meal fighting his sudden exertion.

Nothing. The lane—little more than a passage—held only litter and pools of water. A steady *drip-drip* echoed through the miasma of wet refuse. Bancroft took a few hesitant steps forward, rain slipping under his collar with the chill of a kelpie's fingers. He shivered, half with cold and a little with sudden superstition. Where had Magnus gone?

Bloody hell. He'd given up drinking, true, but he'd thought the hallucinations would have stopped by now. Maybe it had been the strain of watching everyone raise a toast while all he had allowed himself was water. *Time to go back. Maybe you can say you saw someone who owed you money. Or a pickpocket who took your watch. Yes, that sounds plausible. The watch was a family heirloom.*

He turned and walked straight into Magnus. He jumped back, swearing.

"And here I thought you wanted to see me," said the doctor, his teeth very white against his swarthy face.

Bancroft had known the man well over twenty years. In their youth, he had even called Symeon Magnus a friend. In all that time, while Bancroft had aged to maturity, Magnus had looked the same—but now there were threads of gray at his temples, and more than the suggestion of lines in his face. Apparently death had taken something out of him. Bancroft felt a stab of petty satisfaction.

"How did you get here?" Bancroft demanded.

Magnus shrugged. "I took a hansom."

Bancroft fought the urge to bash his head on the brick walls hemming them in. Or throw up. The very unnaturalness of Magnus's presence made his flesh creep. "How did you get *here*? Alive? You were shot. Burned. The doctors had you on their slab."

A glitter of amusement showed in the ink-black eyes. "And yet I rise like the phoenix. I know. It is one of my more annoying talents."

"You're a bloody sorcerer!"

"It took you this long to figure that out?"

"Of course I knew. I just didn't understand the extent of your pact with the devil." Bancroft longed for a gun. Even if a bullet wouldn't kill Magnus, surely it would hurt like hell. That was worth something.

Magnus watched his face, tracking the play of his expressions. "Let's skip forward from the how to the why of my presence."

Bancroft's gut tightened, a part of him not wanting to know. "It's my son's wedding. Can't you respect even that?"

"I did. I drew you out here rather than marching in like Banquo's ghost, as amusing as that might have been. By the way, I thought for certain young Tobias would want Miss Cooper for his bride. Young men can be so fickle."

A foul taste filled Bancroft's mouth at the Cooper girl's name. "Good riddance to that bit of baggage."

Magnus leaned on his silver-headed cane, regarding Bancroft through heavy-lidded eyes. "Still annoyed that she played a role in exposing your ridiculous forgery plot? Or are you actually angry with your own stupidity?"

"Don't be ridiculous."

"That bit of folly put you in Keating's power, didn't it? It cost Tobias his future, since it was he who traded his considerable talents to Keating to spare your family's good name. How does it feel to have sold your only son to your enemy?"

How the blazes did he know any of this? "You go too far."

Magnus straightened, lightly tapping the cane's head against Bancroft's chest. "I merely correct your logic. It seems to me that poor Miss Cooper is merely a convenient target for your shame. You forget I know you far too well. And that is why I am here—to give you the chance to make things right. Maybe you will even save your son from a life of servitude to a man you both despise."

"Oh, really?" Bancroft's tone was skeptical.

"I'm more than a little annoyed with Mr. Keating for ordering my assassination. It was an incredibly inconvenient episode."

"No doubt."

"Scoff if you like, but I would not wish the tender mercies of a medical examiner on my direst foe."

Bancroft felt his meal shift dangerously in his gut. "Yes, yes, so you have a score to settle. What does that have to do with me?" *Dear God, I want a drink.* Abandoning his temperance vows couldn't be worse than seeing Magnus alive and well and critiquing his own autopsy.

Magnus paced to one side of the passage, flicking aside some damp papers with the point of his cane. "Events are finally turning my way. Those I had believed lost forever are suddenly walking through my door. Old projects are suddenly looking possible. Perhaps Mercury has gone retrograde."

He'd always hated it when Magnus stopped making sense. It usually meant trouble. "What are you babbling about?"

"Do you recall our last conversation, in which I asked you to help me steal Athena's Casket from Mr. Keating?"

"Yes, I remember." Magnus had cornered him at Hilliard House, where Bancroft had been throwing a dinner party. He'd called Magnus a vain tyrant. Magnus had prattled something about benevolence and world order.

Then Bancroft realized that it was no longer raining— except that it was, outside a circle that encompassed the two men. He could see the rain bouncing off the street, though he remained dry. He felt his cheek twitch with tension. *Magic.* And it was just like Magnus to remind him of what he could do in such a subtle way.

"I still want the casket. I know it was one of the artifacts that were melted down for gold during your forgery debacle, but I understand that the inner workings remained intact and have continued their adventures since. Are you aware of this?"

Since the entire world seemed to want the bloody casket, Bancroft had made it his business to learn what he could about the wretched thing. Accordingly, he'd paid handsomely for a look at Inspector Lestrade's files. "Yes. Holmes had the remnants brought to Keating's gallery, but then they disappeared."

"Stolen from Keating's gallery by a circus Gypsy named Niccolo, who later turned pirate. One of my would-be killers, as it turns out."

Bancroft had known some of this, but not all. "He's the one with the remarkable ship? The one everyone wants to catch?"

"Especially the Steam Council." Magnus's smile vanished, his expression closing down as if a door had slammed shut. "The casket is a highly sophisticated navigational device and allows for greater lift than mere science can offer. I don't need to explain to you, the former ambassador to Austria, what a leap in military technology could mean to a man like Keating."

"Wealth." Bancroft felt suddenly light-headed. The pic-

ture Magnus painted, of Keating and a fleet of magic war-
ships, threatened to give him nightmares to rival Imogen's.

The sorcerer nodded. "And territorial domination. I'm appealing to your experience and common sense, Bancroft.
Suffice to say that such a device falls more properly into my
domain than that of the Gold King."

That removed any doubt that magic was involved. Bancroft shuddered. "Keating burns witches. He doesn't play
with their toys."

Magnus gave a low laugh. "We're talking about imbuing
machines with life and intelligence. Keating would kill to
be the first to have that secret. To paraphrase the Darwin-
ists, it would make him the evolutionary survivor when all
his steam-powered rivals became extinct."

Bancroft swore. He'd had the device in his power, but let
it slip away out of ignorance.

"So you see why I must have it," Magnus declared. "I've
begun to set traps, but thus far the mouse Niccolo disdains
my bait."

Bancroft wondered what that bait was. Then he wondered
even harder what it had to do with him. He tried to avoid the
sorcerer's eyes, but in the end Magnus's dark gaze caught
him and pinned him motionless where he stood. They remained like that for a long moment, him frozen and Magnus
smirking, as the rain pattered down around their magic circle.

"What do you want?" Bancroft finally snapped.

"Many things," Magnus replied. "I will accept any one of
them from you."

"Such as?"

"What I want most is the casket, but I hold no real hope
that you can get it yourself."

Bancroft snorted. "Should I be offended or relieved?"

"Your choice. However, if Keating succeeds in obtaining
it, you're going to get it from him on my behalf."

"How?"

Magnus twirled the cane in his fingers. "The father of the
bride has just lavished a fortune on his daughter. I would say
she is the dearest object in his life."

Bancroft stared. He had done vile things in his career, murder included, but the notion of actually harming Alice chilled him. "She's barely a woman."

Magnus let the cane slip through his fingers until it met the ground with a sharp tap. "Don't play the sentimental card with me. I know you far better than that."

Bancroft let that slide. Some things didn't bear examination. "And if Keating doesn't get the casket?"

"Bring me his head. Let him experience the annoyance of assassination."

Shame bled into anger. Bancroft drew himself up, his chest burning with fury. "Blackmail? Ransom? Murder? What do you take me for?"

The man gave a thin smile. "A man who has made a career out of just such crimes. A man who literally put his own son on the altar to spare himself. A man who has no choice, because I still have something of yours."

The words struck like a fist. Air rushed from Bancroft's lungs in a wordless cry. *The automatons.* "You still have them?"

"Of course I do." Magnus took a step back. "I take care to guard my weapons well."

It was more than he could take. Grabbing for the sorcerer, Bancroft's fingers closed on thin air. He made a strangled sound, part rage, part terror, spinning around. Then he stopped, forcing himself to breathe. *Don't let him play with you. If you fall for his tricks, he'll win, every time.*

Then his voice was in Bancroft's ear. "I expect results quickly, old friend."

Bancroft lashed out, but his fist sailed through air. Then the rain came pounding down, drenching him to the bone.

CHAPTER NINETEEN

"DO YOU REALLY LIKE ALICE?" POPPY ASKED IMOGEN UNDER her breath.

Imogen looked down at her little sister—although "down" wasn't as far as it used to be. Poppy was fourteen and for once looked like a well-groomed young lady, her gloves clean and her hair combed and curled. They sat side by side at the edge of the reception room, ignored by the throng. Poppy was invisible because she was young. Despite her role as one of the bridesmaids, Imogen was hiding because there were far too many men present that her mother wanted her to meet. The odious Captain Smythe had stayed away, but the Scarlet King was there, and more than once he'd given her a ravenous smile. The sight of his strong, white teeth turned her skin to gooseflesh.

"Well, do you?" Poppy repeated.

Imogen had almost forgotten the question. "Of course I do."

"Truly?"

"Why shouldn't I?" *Except that she isn't Evelina.*

"Tobias doesn't love Alice."

Imogen barely resisted the urge to shove her sister behind a potted palm. "Hush."

"Don't hush me, Imogen Roth. You know exactly what I mean," Poppy said indignantly, tawny curls swinging.

She did. Sometimes Tobias looked at his bride with a vaguely confused expression, like he'd been caught napping and suddenly awakened at the altar. Other times it was barely banked fury. Imogen had known there was an attachment between her friend and Tobias, but since the kissing incident, a great many things made sense—such as the way her brother's gaze had so often followed Evelina in and out of the room. She'd put it down to the fact Evelina was pretty and Tobias was male, but apparently there was far more to it. *I wish she'd said how serious it was.* But Evelina had always been careful about presuming too much—until that awful scene at Maggor's Close.

Imogen felt bad about how horribly that had ended. And she'd felt terrible when she'd come home from Maggor's Close to find Evelina's clockwork creatures hiding beneath her armoire, looking dirty and sad. She'd taken them to her dressing table and polished them up, making them a nest among her scarves. She couldn't talk to them like Evelina, but it was plain that they'd been sent to keep her company while her friend could not.

But who was looking after Evelina? The official story was that she'd gone back to Devonshire three weeks ago, but Imogen knew that wasn't true and other people were starting to add two and two together. Somehow, word of The Kiss had slipped out and was spreading through the reception like a low-lying gas, poisonous and foul. Of course, Evelina—the dark-haired wench whose mother had eloped with a lowborn officer—had borne the brunt of everyone's wrath. Tobias, as usual, could do no wrong. Imogen heaved a sigh. Evelina was the most capable person Imogen knew, but she was starting to worry.

"Are you bored?" Poppy asked in a strained monotone.

"A little."

"Do you want to go exploring?"

Despite her better judgment, Imogen felt herself brighten. The Portmore Hotel was enormous, and the Gold King had rented most of it. And the Scarlet King was eyeing her again. "Let's go look at the wedding gifts one more time. Surely no one can object to that."

Poppy was on her feet in seconds and grabbed Imogen's hand. "Come on."

"Not so fast!" Imogen protested, feeling the hitch in her lungs that came whenever she moved too quickly in that particular set of stays. "I'm an old lady."

"You're nineteen. You need more exercise." Poppy half dragged her across the vast carpet and toward the stairs. "And you should be grateful I'm here to provide some excitement."

"Ugh!" Imogen protested. "The last time you were around I was abducted by a highwayman and Bucky nearly got himself shot in a duel."

"The duel was his stupid idea. You can't blame me for that."

"You were the one who played Cupid." Something for which Imogen adored her little sister, although the universal code of siblings forbade speaking any such sugary sentiments.

The grand staircase was so grand that Imogen had to stop and rest halfway up. She'd been weakened by a nervous ailment that had struck when she was five years old—the same one that had eventually claimed Anna.

"Come on," Poppy said impatiently.

"I told you, I'm old," Imogen said lightly, forcing her feet to continue. Since April she'd felt generally weak. Maybe it was simply that there had been too many shocks of late, and there seemed to be no indication that they would ever stop coming. She'd heard whispers that Evelina had never made it back to London, that she had run away from a broken heart. Imogen didn't believe it for a moment. Evelina certainly had been hurt, but she was tougher than that. Something else was going on, and no one would tell Imogen a thing.

"Here." Poppy hauled her up the last few steps, then waited while Imogen caught her breath. "You're not going to faint, are you?"

"No." But Imogen leaned against the wall just in case. She closed her eyes, but that was worse, so she focused on a flower in the wallpaper.

Poppy's brow furrowed. "Are you sure? I can call Mother if you want."

That was all she needed. "No, I'm fine. Let's go."

Just then a couple of men rounded the corner. Imogen knew in an instant they were Keating's men by the long black coats they wore. Strange-looking weapons hung from their shoulder belts. Unlike many of the steam barons, the Gold King didn't fill his domestic life with steam-powered toys, but he had access to almost infinite industrial power. Those rifles or guns or whatever they were reminded her Keating's genteel face was just a facade. The lion had claws and fangs, however fuzzy he appeared.

"Who are those men?" Poppy asked in a whisper.

Imogen pulled her back out of the way. The men started down the stairs without a word or a glance in her direction. Both were weather-beaten and rough beneath the neat uniforms. Not the toy soldiers who asked her to dance at every ball, but the real thing. One was missing an ear. "The one with the gold braid is Mr. Keating's new streetkeeper."

"How do you know that?"

"Alice told me she helped pick out the braid."

"And what do the streetkeepers do?"

"They run the security forces for their steam baron. All the members of the Steam Council have a streetkeeper." And a private army, if what she'd heard was true. Bucky had said it was only a matter of time before two of those armies had a problem with each other, and then things would get very interesting indeed.

"Why does he need security forces at a wedding?" Poppy wrinkled her brow. "Does he think someone's going to steal the cake?"

"Important men have enemies." Imogen watched from the top of the stairs as the two black-coated men crossed the floor of the reception hall. It was like watching sharks scare away all the other fish. The guests parted rapidly, leaving a wide path through the crowd.

"Is Tobias in danger?" Poppy asked.

"No. He's the Gold King's son-in-law now. We're all safe from harm." But she wasn't that naive. No one was safe in a world where armed men showed up at a wedding. Either Keating was showing off, which was horrible enough, or he was expecting trouble. But Poppy was too young to worry about that—or so Imogen hoped. "Let's look at those gifts."

The room with the gifts was shut, but not locked. Imogen

looked around for anyone guarding the room, but no one was in attendance. She wondered if it was worth mentioning.

Oblivious to something so mundane as security, Poppy pushed the door open, then ran forward with a squeal of glee. "Lucky Alice. People are so nice when your papa owns half of London."

Imogen winced, but it was true. A horseshoe of tables lined the room, draped with snowy damask cloths. A fortune in luxury covered them. There were elaborate clocks and steam-driven tea sets, silver trays and Chinese urns of tea, and a gas-fired cigar lighter shaped like an elephant raising its trunk. Someone had sent an entire bolt of Brussels lace picked out in gold thread, and another had offered a crate of very expensive Bordeaux. Most beautiful of all was a set of emeralds—a necklace, bracelet, and earrings—framed in gold and pearls. The case, while there was no name attached, bore the crest of the Palace. Imogen touched the velvet box with reverent fingers.

And then there were a thousand bizarre inventions no doubt aimed at Tobias—gauges and barometers and bizarre-looking eyepieces that magnified bugs to the size of dirigibles, tools and microscopes and a thing that measured how many pounds a spring could sprong. Imogen didn't know what half of them were for, but Tobias had said they were all of the finest workmanship. The spring-spronger seemed to excite him more than the wedding itself.

Imogen bit her lip. No, she didn't dislike Alice, but she loathed anything that felt like a cage, and she knew her brother was trapped. Her own illness was part of it. He'd given up Evelina in part because she was a survivor—circus bred and smart as her famous detective uncle. Imogen and her mother and even Poppy were far more vulnerable. More of a burden. *Damn it all, I don't want to be anyone's responsibility but my own.* But she didn't know how to be anything but Lord Bancroft's sickly daughter.

"Bucky Penner!" Poppy cried.

Imogen whirled around. She hadn't heard the door open or close, but Bucky was in the room holding a wrapped parcel. He looked like the boy caught stealing apples. The first thing she thought of was those armed men and her heart almost failed. She felt her face drain, as if she were about to faint.

"Miss Roth." He set the parcel down. "Imogen."

And then she was in his arms. His coat was damp with rain, but she didn't care. He was warm and solid and steady and she fit perfectly against his broad chest. "You aren't supposed to be here. It's too dangerous," she whispered. "But I'm so glad that you are."

Bucky was smart, rich, and good-hearted, and had been Tobias's friend from the first year of school. But in the eyes of her viscount father, he wasn't the right class to wed Imogen—and that had rapidly become a point of friction. After the duel, Bucky's ban from the Roth household had become official. But so had their secret engagement. When Bucky's lips gently touched hers, the kiss was as forbidden as it was sweet.

"I'll be outside on lookout," Poppy said mildly, slipping from the room.

Imogen heard the words without completely understanding them. All her attention was on Bucky, and he was certainly pleasant to look upon—especially his mischievous smile. He had brown hair, dark brown eyes, and a tan that said he'd spent much of the summer months out of doors. As always, he was neatly dressed, with excellent clothes tailored to his muscular frame. Even if his family owned lucrative weapons factories up north, he still had the physique of his blacksmith grandfather.

But what she loved about him most was his ability to surprise her in the nicest ways. "I didn't expect to see you."

"You didn't see me," he said in a quiet voice. "I am utterly invisible. But I did want to bring Tobias a gift, so I came through the back entrance."

"You brought him a gift? Even when he didn't ask you to the wedding?"

"I might be persona non grata at your dinner table, but he is my best friend."

"You're nicer than I am," she confessed.

"I'm trying to steal you away, and I'm nowhere near good enough for you." He gave her a wicked grin. "Peasant that I am."

"Weddings put me in a romantic mood," she said dreamily.

"Good." He kissed her forehead. "Do you want to share a secret?"

"Naturally." She loosened her grip so that she held him at arm's length.

"I've finally found a place to set up a toy factory." He looked a trifle apprehensive.

"You have?" she said excitedly.

His face cleared at once. "You approve?"

"Yes! You'll be brilliant. What does your father think?"

"That it's youthful folly, but he'd rather see me working at some kind of moneymaking venture than spending all day in a gambling den or drinking myself blind." Bucky shrugged. "He has a point."

"Not that you ever played the rogue."

Bucky made a contrite face. "I have spent a lot of time carousing with your brother. All in the interest of keeping him out of trouble, of course."

"Of course." She was delighted, because she could tell he was happy. Yet she couldn't contain one small protest. "I still think you should have been in the wedding party."

Bucky shook his head. "I don't think I could have borne it. Neither could Tobias. He knows that I know how miserable he is. That just makes him feel worse and probably jealous. It's better that he doesn't see me for a while."

That was the most ridiculous thing she'd ever heard. "He needs a friend right now."

"Only if he allows it."

Imogen shook her head. "Promise me you won't be an idiotic male any more than is absolutely necessary."

He took her hands in his, kissing her through her gloves. "But I'm your idiotic male. I'll never belong to anyone else." And then he gave her a smile that warmed her all the way to her core.

Imogen felt tears sting her eyes. "I'm so glad."

He looked up, startled by the catch in her voice. "What's wrong?"

"Nothing." It was the spark of happiness in her breast that threatened to shatter her. It was a glow as fragile as a dandelion fluff, and she wished she could encase it in steel to keep it from harm. But that wasn't how it worked. "I just feel so very lucky right now."

His smile quirked. "Why?"

She thought of Evelina alone, Tobias miserable, Alice stranded in a marriage that was doomed from the start. All she had to do was play a waiting game. She could do that.

"Because I have you."

"That you do," he whispered. And he kissed her again, this time on the lips. And this time it lasted a long time, with searching, aching heat.

CHAPTER TWENTY

"I'M NOT A FOOL. I KNOW YOU LOVE HER."

Rather than reply to his new bride, Tobias stared out the window of the hotel. They were supposed to have left for their Italian honeymoon hours ago, but word had come that the steamship had been rerouted for repairs and the next available passage wouldn't leave for at least three days. Tobias's new lodgings were not yet ready, so he had the choice of waiting at the hotel or taking Alice to Hilliard House. He had chosen the hotel. The Roth family home was inexorably linked with Evelina, and he couldn't bear to spend his wedding night there with anyone else. But Alice didn't need to hear that.

"Don't be ridiculous," he replied calmly. "I was the one who ended things. It's been over between us for months, and there wasn't much there to begin with."

Good God, I sound like my father. Chill and reasonable and a complete liar.

In the following pause, he could hear her breathing—the rasp of someone swallowing back disappointment. The thought of having to hear that sound for the rest of his life made him want to rage. Maybe break things. But instead, he schooled his face and slowly turned around to face her where she perched on the edge of the four-poster bed.

Her face was deathly pale, made whiter still by a layer of face powder she thought no one could see. Good girls weren't supposed to wear cosmetics, but they all did. Why Alice thought she required them was beyond him. With her deep blue eyes and copper-colored hair, she was a pretty girl—especially with her long locks unbound and falling around her like bits of stray fire. But that only made him think harder about Evelina's dark, lustrous curls.

"Why?" asked Alice.

"Why what?"

"Why everything?"

She looked so small and painfully young, stripped of her snowy wedding gown and now wrapped in a white robe of Chinese silk. She was the same age as Imogen, and she already had his child in her belly, though it was too soon to show yet.

"I don't know," he replied, bridging the awkward pause.

"I see." She touched her fingertips to her mouth. It was an odd gesture—he couldn't make out if she was kissing them or about to be sick—and then he saw it was to hide the trembling of her chin. But she dropped the hand a moment later, folding her fingers primly in her lap.

Silence dangled like a noose.

Blast and damn! Now there would be a good place to start the whys—why had he seduced her that rainy afternoon in her father's study? He'd taken her maidenhood on the big velvet chaise longue, the rain pounding on the windows in an endless, mindless patter. He'd been obsessed with having her at the time, maybe just to convince himself he might learn to love someone else besides Evelina. And so that study had become the scene of a dozen such stolen afternoons as he tried to erase the past from his senses. *Stupid, stupid, stupid.*

And now his ring was on her finger. He'd done his duty—no one could say otherwise, not even her bear of a father. "This is what you wanted, isn't it?" he replied.

Her gaze darted to the wide bed, the movement as quick and fearful as a wild animal. A fox, with all that red hair. And then she was looking at him again, confusion plain on her face. "Yes, I . . ." She trailed off helplessly.

He could read her thoughts—maybe her one flaw, because she was so transparent it drove people away. *You thought you would be marrying that lover, the one who caressed you like you were all the beautiful things the universe ever dreamed of. But instead, you got me.*

"I wanted this." Her brow was crunched into a disbeliev-
ing frown. She slid off the bed, rising to her full height—
which wasn't much. There was something else in her face
now, something like anger. "But you never did, did you?"

His tongue froze, unable to manufacture another lie.

Her voice rose—not much, but enough to show she had
backbone. "You should have said something long before
this. You had your chance to back away. Now you've trapped
me."

She was right, and that made things worse. He felt his lip
curl. "You like to think of yourself as smart."

"I am. I'm as good at the accounts as father."

"So what did you miss? What sign didn't you see? Is that
what you're wondering?"

She gave a single, jerky nod. She was so damned innocent. Tobias felt like the worst Lothario ever to grace the
London stews.

"Nothing. This is it. We're married. You won," he said
dispassionately, and knew it was cruel. But there was an
anger inside he couldn't rein in—it leapt from his belly, hot
and snarling, even while his words turned cold as frost.
"You have nothing to complain about."

The savagery in his tone made her flinch. "Tobias," she
said in a small voice, but then she swallowed whatever came
next, clearing her throat with a delicate cough.

He made a cutting gesture with his hand. "There's nothing more to say. Don't ever mention her name to me. The
subject is closed."

"If that's how you want it."

"I do."

She folded her arms, clutching the front of her robe closed.
They stood so close that he could have touched her cheek,
pulled her to him and reassured the poor girl that he would
keep her safe. But she represented everything that had snared
him—her father, his family obligations, his fear of throwing
everything away on a wild gamble with fate. Most of all, she
personified the destruction he'd caused—or would cause, if
he was anything less than the perfect son-in-law—and he

wasn't quite coldhearted enough not to care. And so no action was completely his own. He was damned.

This was her wedding night. He should have pretended some affection, but he couldn't stand to touch her right then. And from the look on her face, she knew it—almost. He took a step away, putting air between them. She followed the movement, her face turning up like a flower following the sun.

"You're going?" she asked, somehow knowing before he did.

Yes. His answer stuck in his throat, closing off the air before he could give it voice. And he barged from the room before he suffocated.

NOW DRY AND changed out of his formal suit, Bancroft prowled the hallway of the hotel, his head a squirming mass of thoughts. Setting aside the fact that a mad sorcerer he'd believed dead had popped from the grave demanding his personal services . . . well, there was no setting that aside, which was the problem. He was a busy man. The last thing he had time for was an episode from a Gothic potboiler—especially one that could actually explode his political career like a hot harpoon in a barrel of gunpowder.

The ironic thing was he wouldn't mind killing Jasper Keating. It just wasn't time yet. There were other things he had to get ready first, and he'd be damned if Magnus was going to come crashing in and making a mess of his meticulously laid plans.

He stopped outside of the room where the wedding gifts were laid out. The hotel, and not Keating's own guards, had been engaged to watch over it. Bancroft had learned who organized the security among the hotel staff, and had paid them to ignore the room for the next hour. Hence, the coast was clear. The door had been locked after the wedding guests had gone home, but Bancroft had learned early on in his diplomatic career how to coax open a door. The tumblers gave way with a quiet click, as hushed as a cough in a library.

Once the door was closed behind him, he reached inside

his jacket and pulled out a brass tube. He twisted the top half, then waited as chemicals mixed and a faint green glow began to radiate from its tiny glass window. The tables sprang into view, the white cloths reflecting back the green glow. A few carefully placed questions had told him Keating's servants would be arriving soon to inventory the gifts, then pack them away for storage until the couple set up their new house. He had to act quickly.

And yet he couldn't quite resist the pull of the scientific equipment. Bancroft lingered over the tension gauge, the leather case of calipers and fine-nosed pliers, the brass microscope with its perfect lenses. A rush of pleasure took him, pushing aside purpose for simple curiosity. He touched the cool metal of the gauge, loving the craftsmanship. He'd dabbled once with such things, but had no stomach for it anymore—not since the automatons. Not since Magnus. For a moment he envied his son the chance to use his talent, even if it was for the Gold King.

Then the tube light flickered, sending alarm through his thoughts. Time had slid past. He swept the light around, searching for what he wanted. Equipment was too large. Wine was useless. Lace was worse. But there—that was what he was looking for. He picked up the case with the emeralds. They slid chill and sinuous into his palm, and from there to the inside pocket of his jacket. He closed the velvet case and returned it to the table with a smirk of satisfaction. *A gift from the Crown, stolen so that I can save the Crown from monsters like Keating.* There was a poetical symmetry there. *And here's hoping this scheme works better than the forgery fiasco.* He'd used up at least five of his nine lives on that one. This time, he was far more careful about whom he was working with, and even more cautious about who knew he was involved.

Bancroft twisted the brass tube again to extinguish the light and drifted toward the door. He turned the handle slowly, careful not to make a sound, and peered outside. No one in the hall. He stepped quickly outside, pulling the door shut but not locking it. It was easiest to let the theft be blamed on careless staff.

He moved quickly down the corridor, not fully relaxing until he had descended the stairs to the main level below. Then he released the air from his lungs in a heady rush, barely able to contain an urge to strut. There was nothing more to do but go home.

Then he saw his son slouched in an overstuffed chair, alone in a darkened corner of the foyer. A pair of chairs and a low table had been placed there, near the windows, for visitors awaiting their carriage—not for young men poised at the brink of life.

Bancroft's steps slowed as irritation mounted, spoiling his mood. *The boy's supposed to be with his wife. What's he done now?* Tobias always managed to throw a spanner into the works, no matter what. And yet—Bancroft couldn't completely avoid a surge of concern as he crossed to survey the wreckage of his son and heir.

"What's the matter with you?" he demanded.

Tobias looked up wearily. "Why are you still here? Shouldn't you have gone home?"

Bancroft sunk into the chair next to him. "I had to meet someone."

"Who?" Tobias asked without much interest.

The meeting was a fabrication, but for an instant he considered telling his son about Magnus, then dismissed the idea. Tobias was in Keating's power now and by definition could not be trusted. Which meant Bancroft shouldn't be talking to him—but, well, there was only so much parenting even he could avoid. "That's not important. Why aren't you with your wife?"

Tobias gave him a hard look, filled with accusations left over from a hundred bitter conversations.

Bancroft waved the look away. "Oh, dear God, you still want the Cooper girl." It was a statement, not a question.

"She's gone." His son nearly choked on the words.

Bancroft shrugged. "You've always had the option to follow her."

For an instant, he thought Tobias would hit him. He had before. The moment had almost given Bancroft hope for his son.

"You're despicable," Tobias snarled.

"I've never laid claim to goodness."

"No, you haven't. Just expediency."

"Ambition," Bancroft corrected. "At least accuse me of the correct species of sin."

"You have no heart."

"Not really." And yet, that wasn't exactly true. There were things he cared about. The Steam Council was destroying the Empire he loved. They were destroying the villages, the countryside, the way of life he'd grown up with. If opportunism dovetailed with a just cause, he wasn't going to argue—so long as he was the one to hand Victoria back her England to the applause of a grateful multitude.

His son's silence reminded Bancroft that he was supposed to be dispensing fatherly advice. "Is that the problem then? Wrong woman?"

"What am I going to do?" Tobias said in a low, strained voice.

Stop whining. But that was hardly helpful. "Keating expects you to make his daughter happy, and you will regret the day he decides you've failed. At least pretend to be a good husband for a month or two. You liked her well enough for a summer's entertainment."

Tobias winced in a way that said he'd struck close to the bone. "She deserves better than a lie."

Ah, the drama of the forlorn yet noble heart. "I learned long ago that the one who fights the longest and hardest for truth does the most damage to everything he loves. Nothing withstands that kind of scrutiny."

Tobias narrowed his eyes. "I pray that I never turn into you."

"Give it time." Bancroft rose, suddenly weary of the conversation. "But I recommend vigorous protest instead of sulking. It has the advantage of healthful exercise."

He walked a few steps before taking a last look at his son slumped in the chair, exasperation overcoming his instinct for a clean exit. "Bloody hell, Tobias, if you're going to make a bonfire of your life, at least do it with gusto!"

CHAPTER TWENTY-ONE

London, September 22, 1888

THE TEN BELLS

8:15 p.m. Saturday

THE TEN BELLS SAT ON THE CORNER OF COMMERCIAL STREET, where some of Evelina's neighbors went in their off hours. The pub was angled across the corner of the block, two pillars framing a double door. She could hear the noisy crowd as she approached, an ebb and flow of merriment and alcoholic fumes. It was the kind of place people went to to forget their lives for as long as the liquor lasted—and right then that was the best use she could think of for a few of Jasper Keating's coins. *But if I miss another of his deadlines, I might be trying to lose myself here in earnest.* If she missed another deadline, that pinch of her uncle's tobacco said it all. The Gold King could destroy her in so many inventive ways.

She knew she was in very deep water. As welcome as Keating's terse reprieve had been, it had sent her scurrying to the distant post office where she had left her letter to Uncle Sherlock. When she'd first come to Whitechapel, she'd paid the proprietor with instructions to mail the letter a day after she was scheduled to return to Baker Street—if she didn't intercept it, her missive would serve as an alert to let Holmes know where she was and that she needed help.

Of course, the extended deadline changed the date the note would need to be sent. So, she went to ask for a delay—only to discover that the letter had been lost, leaving her utterly vulnerable without even knowing it. She'd left a replacement, praying it wouldn't suffer the same fate as the first. As safety nets went, it seemed a flimsy thing, but what else could she do?

Try to stay away from trouble. But sometimes one needed distraction. As Evelina opened the pub door, the din was a physical force that stopped her in her tracks. She wasn't much of a drinker, but she liked the noise and company—and tonight of all nights she needed it. It didn't matter that there were too many bodies smelling of not enough soap and water, or that the temperature inside was intense. This was Tobias and Alice's wedding day, and Evelina did not want to be alone.

She scanned the room, looking for a familiar face, and to her surprise saw Gareth waving her over. She hadn't seen him since the morning after Lacey's death. There were still traces of shock and grief in his eyes, but he hid them behind a broad smile.

"Over here, then," he called, then bellowed in a voice more robust than the rest of him, "Hey, Maggs, another glass, will you?"

She had a sudden moment of doubt, wondering what she was doing there. She'd worked so hard to learn to be a lady. She'd spent years at Wollaston Academy for Young Ladies and been presented to the queen. She was about to sit down in a public place with . . . well, it hardly mattered now, did it? She'd tried to be everything her Grandmamma Holmes wanted, and where had it got her? Alone, in an East End drinking hole, mourning the marriage of the man she wanted to someone else. And nobody here cared if she liked to work with her hands just as much as she liked dancing, or that she couldn't carry a tune in a hay wagon.

For an instant, she felt almost light-headed. The thought had taken her by surprise, dragging regret and resignation in its wake, but also a pinch of relief. There was something to be said for not having to try so hard—but it wasn't an unalloyed pleasure, either.

Evelina shoved her way through the throng, barely able to see what the place looked like beyond all the people. She caught an impression of blue and white tiled walls and a scatter of wooden tables, but everything else was just coats, hats, warm bodies, and bad breath she had to dive through. "Excuse me," she said. "Excuse me." But nobody heard her or cared.

By then Gareth had somehow found another chair and drawn it up to the table, holding the back for her like a footman. She'd barely sat down when he pressed a full glass of ale into her hand. "Here you go, then," he said, his soft, dark hair flopping in his eyes.

"Thank you," Evelina said, finally able to take a look at the other people at the table, all women. "Hello."

"This is Miss Cooper," Gareth said with as much pride as if he'd somehow invented her. That made one or two of the others raise their heads with interest. "She's the one who brought medicine."

"That was right kind of you, dear," said an older woman to Evelina's left, who reached over to pat her hand. Her accent sounded slightly foreign.

"This is Greta," Gareth said.

"Mrs. Horst to you, young man," Greta said reprovingly, exposing a mouthful of brown-stained teeth.

"Greta owns the tea shop down the way. And this is Miss Lucy Andrews," Gareth went on, indicating a brunette not much older than he was. "And the lovely Miss Mary Jane Kelly."

"A pleasure, miss," Mary Kelly said, her words softened by a Welsh lilt. She was pretty, about twenty-five, with blond hair and blue eyes.

Evelina nodded to both, trying to engrave the names on her brain so that she wouldn't forget them. The women were shabby and a little drunk, but she didn't particularly care.

"And this here is Miss Hyacinth."

She knew the woman ran the bawdy house where Gareth worked, but they had never met. Evelina did her best not to stare. Hyacinth had a luxurious head of hair tinted a pale crocus purple. Even her eyebrows were a darker version of the shade. But that wasn't what riveted Evelina's attention with mounting horror. She knew this young woman—who used to have locks the color of russet autumn leaves.

Hyacinth cocked one purple eyebrow. "Well, well, Cooper. Isn't this world a funny old place?"

Evelina had known her as the Honorable Violet Asterley-Henderson, the most proud, horrible girl at the Wollaston Academy for Young Ladies. Evelina had hated her all through school.

Unable to think what to say, Evelina took a swallow of beer, hoping the alcohol might spur inspiration. It was strong and bitter, clinging to the tongue. Actually, it was rather good. "Good heavens," was all she managed. "What do I call you?"

"Everyone calls me Miss Hyacinth. At least while they're being polite."

For a fleeting moment, Evelina contemplated making a lunge for the door. Those awful memories of school were still strong as ever.

"So what brings you to this fashionable neighborhood, Cooper?" Hyacinth planted an elbow on the table, leaning her head on her daintily gloved fist. She was still stylish, perfectly groomed and impeccably dressed despite the outlandish hair. And she still had that *something* lurking behind her eyes that said she would throw peasants into a pit of starving tigers just to see the show.

"Same thing as you, in a way," Evelina answered, all too aware of the others at the table. It was bad enough telling her tale to an old school nemesis, let alone perfect strangers. "An indiscretion."

"What kind?"

Evelina took another sip of beer, liking the buzz but telling herself to go slow. She was tired and not as used to drink as her companions. "There was a young man in the picture."

"Ah, the ruin of us all!" Mary Kelly laughed, a fat, merry sound that had them all going in an instant.

"You?" Hyacinth scoffed. "You always had your nose in a book. I never thought you knew what a boy was for."

Evelina flushed. She was an innocent compared to these women, but it would never do to let that show. "I suppose I figured it out." There was another volley of laughter from Mary.

"We all make mistakes," Hyacinth said with a shrug.

"Mine are just more extravagant. Everything about me is. You remember that, don't you, Cooper?"

Evelina winced. Her schoolmate had always been difficult, but had achieved new heights when, at the end of their last term, she'd tried her hand at black magic. As magic was illegal, the school was shut down, Violet—or Hyacinth, as she called herself now—had been expelled, and her family disgraced and imprisoned. No one had even known the Asterley-Hendersons had the Blood until Hyacinth had revealed it with all the discretion of a brass band in full blare.

"But you landed on your feet," Evelina ventured. It had been less than a year, too—not so much landing on her feet as locating a launch pad.

"Indeed I did," Hyacinth replied, lifting her chin. "The profession is a bit like absinthe. The first time I tried it— with my jailors, no less—I didn't like it. But it kept me alive. It's instructive what one will do to stay alive."

She gave Evelina a hard look, as if daring her to say something. "Eventually I got accustomed to the experience and began to see the financial potential. Like any other business, it's all about expansion and diversification. It just took some intelligent maneuvering. I never undertake anything unless I can rise to the top."

"And what a top she is," said Gareth with a grin.

There was an acquisitive flash in Hyacinth's eyes as she regarded the boy over the rim of her wineglass. "Now, now, my sweet," she chucked the boy under the chin, making him squirm. "I'm young and at the threshold of my career. There are plenty of peaks to climb yet."

The girl named Lucy groaned. Evelina was fairly sure she understood the joke, but wasn't going to open her mouth and make a mistake.

But Hyacinth was watching her. "And I think our young friend here should mind his manners, unless he wants to put his jests into action. Fine young men are always in demand."

Gareth sat back, his face an inscrutable mask. "Maybe I'd fancy working on the docks."

"Don't be empty-headed," the madam said kindly. "They'd

eat you alive. So, Evelina, what are you going to do, now that you and your fine mind are here with us?"

"I have work," Evelina said, thanking all the gods that she had skills to sell instead of her female charms. "I'm at the puppet theater."

"With Dr. Magnus?" Hyacinth said curiously. "He's never done us any favors. Weren't you dead set on college?"

Evelina shrugged, not knowing what to say. Keating had given her until October 1 to finish her business in Whitechapel, and then presumably she would go home. And there was no question that she wanted to see her uncle and Imogen and to walk in safe, clean streets. But the truth was—for the first time in longer than she could remember—she was oddly at peace. She was free to study magic, indulge in her love of clockwork, and she was not forced to be anyone she was not.

It was going to be devilishly hard to let go of that freedom. "Maybe I'll do better than college."

"I always liked the fact that you weren't a coward," Hyacinth said, almost sounding as if she meant it. "You stood up to me, after all. You have what it takes to make it—but you won't be happy sitting in taverns forever."

"I don't think I have much of a choice at the moment."

"A smart girl makes her own choices." Hyacinth sank back in her chair, picking up her glass of ruby red wine. "There isn't much a sound investment plan can't overcome."

It was hard not to marvel. Society had lost a force of nature when they tossed Miss Asterley-Henderson to the wolves. They were likely to find her banging at the castle gates with the wolves as her own private army.

"I'll take your advice under consideration." Then Evelina couldn't help smiling. "In the meantime, let us toast to Mr. Tobias Roth and his bride, the lovely Alice Keating. It is their wedding night."

Hyacinth's eyebrows rose. "Imogen's brother? The pretty boy?"

"The same," Evelina replied, and couldn't keep the regret out of her voice, the echo of all the things that might have been, but that would never happen now. They were not new thoughts—she'd already been over and over this ground as her Grandmamma dragged her through Devonshire drawing rooms—but that fatal kiss had breathed new life into her grief. She'd lost Tobias, and suspected that he'd lost himself. Truth be told, it was the thought of that future man—the one who would have been if he'd only been free—that made her eyes burn.

"Ah, I see." Understanding flickered across Hyacinth's face. She had been hard to live with, but never stupid. "Poor Evelina. Toby always did have that Byronic ennui down to a science."

Evelina nearly choked on her beer. Gareth pounded her on the back.

"Good health, Mr. Roth, from all the whores in Whitechapel." Hyacinth raised her glass. She took a sip and swallowed, the muscles working in her slender throat. "May your new bride bring you as much joy as you give her."

The others laughed, Mary loudest of all. Regret needled at Evelina. It had been petty to drag Tobias's name into the conversation—and yet she deserved some acknowledgment. She'd been disappointed. Maybe she could move on now that she'd had her tiny revenge.

Hyacinth turned to the others before Evelina could chase that idea any further. "And to Evelina."

"Evelina," the others repeated.

"Funny to think we came to say farewell to Annie. Who knew we'd be joined by a new old friend."

"To Evelina," said Mary Kelly, "and to Annie."

"Annie?" Evelina whispered to Gareth.

"Annie Chapman," he returned. "She used to drink here sometimes, too."

Evelina turned the name around in her mind, and then remembered where she'd heard it. Annie Chapman was the most recent murder victim, found just down on Hanbury Street.

"Damn my eyes, I miss decent wine," drawled Hyacinth, setting the glass down with a clunk.

Evelina ignored her, turning in her chair to scan the room. Somewhere in Whitechapel was a killer—a lunatic who was getting bolder and more violent with every kill. *And Annie Chapman drank in this place.* There was every chance he was sitting there with her in that room.

CHAPTER TWENTY-TWO

London, September 23, 1888
221B BAKER STREET

11:30 a.m. Sunday

THERE WAS LITTLE IN LIFE MORE DISTASTEFUL THAN ADMIT-ting one's parents were right. Nevertheless, Tobias decided he had to act, even if he had only the vaguest notion of what that would entail.

He had planned and executed plenty of pranks, but real-life plans had never come easily. They had consequences, and that made him freeze up like a piss puddle in January. But one didn't make a bonfire of one's life without burning a few bridges. With gusto.

At least that's what he told himself climbing into a hansom after sleeping in a hotel chair all night. Somewhere in the wee hours, while his bride moped upstairs, he'd had a flash of insight. But by the time he climbed down at Baker Street—at what was barely considered a civilized hour by Society—he wasn't so sure sharing that brainstorm was a brilliant idea. Still, he had to do something.

But it didn't look like it was going to be easy. There was a Yellowback on the porch of 221B Baker Street, and two more on the street, lounging against the posts of the gaslights. Tobias had known that the Gold King was keeping an eye on Holmes, but had no idea that was extending to an entire gang of thugs—because if he saw three, there were doubtless more.

"Mr. Roth?" said the one on the porch.

Tobias knew the face, but couldn't place the name. "Good morning," he replied, approaching the door and the Yellow-back with what he hoped was careless unconcern.

"You have business with Mr. Holmes?" The guard's eye-brows rose in inquiry. There were a thousand questions on his face, at least half of them along the lines of *What the bleeding hell is a bridegroom fresh from his wedding doing on a detective's doorstep?*

Tobias reached for the knocker. He'd be damned before he explained himself to one of Keating's Rottweilers.

The guard caught his wrist, the iron strength in his grip momentary, but a clear warning. "Don't do anything that might disappoint Mr. Keating."

"I wouldn't dream of it," Tobias ground out between clenched teeth, holding the Yellowback's gaze until the guard began to smirk.

"Allow me." The thug knocked, giving three sharp raps.

Tobias snatched his arm away, straightening his jacket. It was only then that he realized that he was still wearing his wedding clothes, a wine stain dribbling down his shirt-front. *Brilliant.*

A gray-haired woman answered the knock. She looked first at the Yellowback with fear and barely concealed dis-like. Then she turned to Tobias.

"May I help you, sir?" She looked him up and down with that disconcerting way women had of sizing one up and fil-ing one away. He guessed he'd landed under "I" for idiot.

"I'm here to see Mr. Holmes," he said in his most ingrati-ating manner.

Her eyebrows lifted a fraction. "Is he expecting you?"

"I was bound to turn up eventually."

She gave him a confused look.

"Just tell him it's Tobias Roth."

A few minutes later, he was ushered into the great man's domain. Holmes was sprawled lengthwise on the couch, ankles crossed, smoking a long-stemmed pipe. Despite his apparent idleness, his fingers twitched nervously. Tobias was reminded of a leopard he'd seen caged at a zoo, just the tip of its tail thrashing. Holmes was every bit as hemmed in.

Tobias stood marooned in the center of the bearskin rug, unsure whether to sit or remain standing where Holmes could view him from his prone position.

"Are you here to shoot me a second time?" Holmes said dryly.

Tobias wasn't surprised that Holmes knew he had been the one to pull the trigger. After all, Evelina had figured it out fast enough, despite his efforts at secrecy. *I can't do anything right.*

"Not today," he said lightly. "Forgot my revolver."

"Good. I do believe Mrs. Hudson might turn me out if there was another incident so soon after the bombing."

"Bombing?" Evelina had mentioned something about a bomb, but he'd never quite figured out what she'd meant. Had someone finally got annoyed enough with Holmes to blast him to smithereens?

"Yes. Didn't you notice the fine gentlemen outside? I'm told they're here for my safety. I can't stir a foot without one of them on my heels. I fear I have become the prize in a fearsome game of capture the flag."

"I don't understand."

"Blue and Gold are vying for the privilege of either blowing me up or owning my genius. Flattering, but annoying in the extreme."

A phrase nagged at Tobias's memory—something Keating had let slip about ensuring Evelina's good behavior. It was one of those sideways mutterings he'd chosen to ignore because there was so much else to worry about in the post-kiss debacle, but now he wondered if this was what his father-in-law had meant. Evelina behaved, or Holmes paid the price. *Why? That doesn't even make sense.* No, it was more likely a spat between Keating and King Coal.

Holmes swung his legs around, sitting up and waving a hand toward the basket chair. "Sit. Tell me why you braved your master's hounds to be in my study the morning after your wedding."

Tobias sat. "I'm sorry. About the shooting, I mean."

"And so you should be, but that is not why you are here."

"It's about Evelina."

"Of course it is." Holmes's voice was suddenly like ice.

The room temperature dropped to freezing, leaving Tobias longing for the door. "I'm sorry about that, too."

"It seems to me that you have a great many regrets for such a young man."

"I need to find Evelina."

"Why?" Holmes snapped. "So you can disappoint your wife as well as my niece?"

"I want her to be all right!" Tobias jumped out of the chair, unable to keep still a moment longer.

Holmes's expression chilled another degree. "And you think she is not?"

"I don't know. We all thought she'd gone to Devonshire after she left Maggor's Close. Keating told everyone that her grandmother was sick. I knew that wasn't true, but I still believed she'd returned to the country. But then my friend— well, not really a friend anymore—Smythe turned up and said no one had seen her in Devonshire, so I thought she must have come to you. But now I'm in London, and no one has seen her here, either. All through my own wedding reception, I kept hearing rumors that she's run away. What is the truth, Mr. Holmes?"

There was a moment of perfect silence. Tobias could hear the noise from the street, the clatter of pans downstairs. Finally, Holmes spoke. "I am no wiser than you."

"How is that possible? You're the Great Detective."

Holmes gave him a cold look. "I sent telegrams. Your friend is correct. Evelina did not go to my mother's house. I have inquiries with all the members of her father's family whom I can locate. She did not return to the vicinity of her old school, or show up on my brother Mycroft's doorstep."

Tobias curled his lip. "If I were you, I would be doing more than lying on the couch smoking a pipe."

"You have no notion of how I work."

Tobias scanned the room, counting the bottles of strange chemicals, the knives and pistols scattered among the clutter, even a spear with a tuft of feathers near the razor-sharp head. He had a pretty good idea of how Holmes worked once he put his mind to it. There had to be material his doctor friend never included in his stories. But then again, how effective could Holmes be with the Yellowbacks camped outside? And if they trailed after him like pet wolves, they'd no doubt frighten any witnesses into mute silence.

Tobias tempered his tone. "Did you check with that other friend of hers? The horseman?"

"The Indomitable Niccolo. Yes, I have set about getting word to him as well. Never fear, I have eyes in a great many places."

"So does my father-in-law."

"You saw them on the way in, did you? There are far fewer than there were. I can actually give them the slip now, if I put my mind to it."

"That's not what I meant."

His words finally caught the detective's attention. "Could it be that you have something useful to say?"

"The night Evelina arrived at Maggor's Close, there was an incident." Tobias felt his face heat, even while his heart seemed to shrivel in his chest. Something in him had died that night.

"Oh, I know all about that." Holmes leaned back against the sofa, but his eyes were completely alert. "I've heard the details. You were lucky to escape with your virtue intact."

Tobias clenched his jaw. "It wasn't like that."

"Be very glad I'm not the one holding the revolver right now."

Tobias swallowed. "We—"

"Does it really matter? Whatever happened, you should have known better. So get on with it."

Tobias clenched his fists, hating the man but needing him all the same. "What happened after matters. Keating was the one who walked in on us. There were heated words."

"Did he blame you?" Holmes pointed with the end of his pipe. "Or just her?"

"I heard from Keating, as you might expect. I wronged his daughter, and so on. Nothing I didn't deserve. But he had Evelina behind closed doors for a time as well. I don't know what he said, but she came out white as a ghost and then started to pack at once."

"You saw this?"

"Imogen, my sister, did."

Holmes mused a moment. "Interesting."

"You must find her!"

"How very astute of you, Mr. Roth."

Tobias blinked uneasily. "I'm sorry, I didn't—"

"Of course you didn't," Holmes sneered. "You're here to vindicate your conscience. I am entirely happy to oblige. Go home. You're forgiven for dishonoring my niece and chasing her into ruin and possible death."

Tobias scrambled for a comeback, but came up with nothing.

"You don't think I've already been looking for my own relation?" Holmes's voice sizzled with sarcasm. "She sent me a letter, you know. I just received it now, though it was written weeks ago, by the date. *Weeks* that I might have been looking for her, if someone at Maggor's Close had seen fit to warn me she had been sent away."

The jab was clearly directed at Tobias, but he let it fly past. "Where did she send it from?" Tobias demanded. "That's a clue, isn't it?"

Holmes gave a slow nod. "She sent it from a post office near the Exchange. It is run by a husband and wife, an elderly couple who luckily remembered this particular letter when I went to them for details."

Holmes paused, and Tobias shifted impatiently. "Yes?"

"The husband recalled something about a young woman asking him to mail the letter on a certain date—hardly an unusual practice in a district that specializes in business payments and the like. The only reason it stuck in his mind was that he was sure it had been lost."

"But you received it."

"Indeed I did. The letter was not lost at all, but gathered up with some others and sent on a day early by his wife."

"But why did Evelina ask them to hold it?"

"And why did she come back later, and ask to have the letter held another few days? Not realizing his wife had already sent the note, the proprietor told Evelina the first one was lost, and she left a replacement, which I also have now."

"What do they say?"

Tobias could see the tension in the corners of the detective's mouth, a slight pinching almost like pain. "She did her best to include hints in the message, though some are not as clear to me as she intended. No doubt she assumed someone would intercept it."

"Did they?" Tobias asked.

"Of course. The envelope of the original note had been tampered with. It is little surprise that rumors abound that my niece ran away, for that is what the letter states. What happened in that interview with the Gold King, Mr. Roth? Surely you know *something*."

Tobias's head pounded. "I can't answer that. But I do know Keating. He uses people. And I know Evelina—she protects those she loves. In all probability, he's coerced her into one of his unholy games."

Holmes sat up, his eyes glittering. "And what game is Keating playing this time?"

Tobias wished he'd paid more attention, but he spent much of his time trying to ignore the incessant intrigues. In truth, he'd been trying to pretend he wasn't living his current life at all. "He's been cozy with the Scarlet King these days. I think they are scheming against King Coal."

Holmes nodded. "This clarifies what she said in the letter."

"What do you mean?"

The detective narrowed his eyes. "Thank you for coming today, Mr. Roth."

Holmes's face said it all. Tobias was in a gray zone, halfway part of the enemy's camp—trusted a little, but not completely.

Tobias recognized the dismissal, felt it sting, but ultimately he didn't care. He'd been thinking about Evelina every second since the miserable affair with the kiss blew up in his face—but at least he'd finally shared his suspicions with someone who could do something. "I've said all I came to say. I need to go." Tobias picked up his hat.

"Mr. Roth," Holmes said in that deceptively pleasant way

he had, "once again, thank you for sharing this in such a timely manner."

This time, the barb struck home. As Holmes had said, it had been weeks. "I hope it helps."

He'd nearly reached the door when the detective spoke again. "One other thing."

Tobias stopped, feeling like a thief caught in the act of escape. He just wanted to be out of there, away from the cursed man and his cutting remarks. "What?"

"I respect the fact that you came here at all, given what my investigation did to your family. Let me repay that a little with a piece of information. While searching for my niece, I got wind of a very odd fact."

Tobias turned, a nauseous sense of anticipation crawling up his throat. "What?"

"Dr. Magnus is alive."

TOBIAS BOLTED UP the stairs of Hilliard House, bursting into his sister's bedroom. Imogen was huddled in a chair, her knees drawn up under her chin and a knitted blanket cocooned around her. He skidded to a stop, taking in the dark circles under her eyes and the hollows under her cheekbones. She was glued to a newspaper, a horrified expression on her face.

"What are you reading?" he asked.

"These murders in Whitechapel." Her voice was faint, as if she didn't have the strength to speak up.

"You shouldn't read that rubbish. It's vulgar."

She lifted her head, her eyes huge and dark. "You don't understand. I dreamed this. Every detail."

Tobias waved a hand. "If you insist on reading all that, of course it will make your nightmares worse."

"But this was before—oh, never mind." She let the paper drop to the floor, then blinked at him as if she suddenly realized who he was. "Tobias, what are you doing here?"

For an instant, he wished he could spare her everything he was about to say, but this was too important. "Magnus is back."

Imogen curled tighter under the blanket. "Bloody hell, you're still in your wedding suit. Where's Alice?"

He blinked, not sure he'd ever heard his sister curse before. "Still at the hotel, for all I know."

Imogen's eyes flared wide. "Tobias!"

"Listen to me. Dr. Magnus is back!" He articulated every syllable.

"Back how?" she finally said, looking at him as if he'd lost his wits.

"Alive! Holmes said so. I went to see him. I had to know if he'd heard anything about Evelina."

She shook her head, as if trying to clear it. "Had he?"

"No. But he'd got wind of Magnus." And while Holmes would almost certainly find Evelina, it was anybody's guess how the doctor could be brought down.

Imogen shifted uneasily. "Magnus wrote to Evelina months ago."

"She knew?" Tobias snapped, his temper slipping its leash. "Did you?"

Imogen licked her lips. "Father threw her out. Why would she say anything to our family? And why would I raise it with Father? You know what he's like."

Tobias did at that. Frustration bubbled in his gut, but he closed his eyes, breathing hard and ignoring the many, many questions that would only drag him down another dark hole. "Magnus was dabbling in magic. The dark kind."

"Everyone acted like he was a friend of the family," Imogen said doubtfully. "At least at first."

Tobias had believed that, too, until he'd seen the other side of the fiend. "He was friends with Father long ago, but they had a falling out. Something to do with those automatons that disappeared."

Imogen frowned. "I never quite followed that. What was so special about them?"

That was a good question. The maid servant, Grace Child, had died at almost the same time they were stolen, and he'd always wondered if there was a connection. Tobias rubbed his eyes, his sleepless night dragging on him. "Father told me a story once. He built the automatons, and Magnus made the dolls walk and talk. It was amusing at first, but eventually Father got nervous and told Magnus to stop. They argued and Magnus demanded to be paid a huge sum of money for the work he'd done, as if Father had hired him to do it."

"Did he?" Imogen prompted.

Tobias shrugged. "Who knows the truth? He said he threatened to destroy the dolls until Magnus claimed a curse would rebound on our family if they were so much as chipped. So the pater stored them in the attic and kept them a secret."

Imogen fiddled with the fringed end of the blanket. "But then Magnus turned up in London last spring, and father tried to move the trunks someplace else."

"And Magnus stole them anyhow." Two grooms had died during the theft.

"No clue as to where they went?"

"None. As long as we all thought Magnus was dead, I never gave them much thought. But if he's still alive, that means he's still holding them hostage. I think that's why Father was always polite to Magnus in public. There was some kind of blackmail going on."

"They were just dolls," Imogen protested. "Ugly ones, from what little I remember. Papa made them around the time Anna and I were sick. I think they were meant to cheer us up, but—ugh."

They were indeed hideous, but Tobias had seen less of them than his invalid sisters. "You would have been—what? About six?"

"Six or seven," Imogen said distantly. "Anna died after we'd just turned seven."

And Imogen's illness had dragged on for years after that. She still wasn't strong. Tobias rubbed the bridge of his nose, feeling a headache coming on. "Everything horrible that ever happened in this family dates from those automatons. And a dozen years later, Magnus is still using them as a weapon."

Imogen blinked at him. "What do you think that means?"

Finally, he could see a clear path to follow. "We have to find out the whole story. I remember seeing a folio of Father's notes in Magnus's things once. There was probably something there, but I never had time to read the whole thing. Maybe there are letters or diaries or—or maybe we'll just have to ask. But we need to know everything that happened. And then we have to get the wretched things back."

"No," Imogen said.

Tobias stared at her. "No?"

She shook her head, glaring at him. "You've just been married. Yesterday, in fact. You have more important things to do than to rake up the past."

His temper spiked. "Evelina is missing. Now Magnus is hanging over our heads."

"How do you know? You didn't even know he was alive until an hour ago."

"But he will be. I know him. And I can't go to Italy right now and stare at paintings just because custom requires a honeymoon."

"What about Alice?"

"What about her?"

"You're hurting her." Imogen slid down in her chair, a picture of misery. "At least try."

But Tobias was more worried about his sister right then. He put a hand on the blanket lump that was his sister's knee. "Im, what's wrong?"

"Everything." She swallowed, curling into a tighter ball. "The nightmares. And I'm worried about Evelina, too."

A wave of pain and guilt stole his voice for a moment. "Holmes will find her. You know he's the best." And now the detective had another clue, for what it was worth. Tobias hoped like hell it made a difference.

Imogen pushed her hair out of her eyes. "I know he is."

"Then cheer up, eh?" He wished he could take his own advice.

She gave him an owlish look. "I'll make you a bargain. I'll help you look for answers if you go spend some time with your wife."

Tobias rose, knowing she had a point. Sooner or later, he'd have to face Alice. "Allies?" he asked. It was a ritual from childhood, the relic of a thousand war games in the woods.

"Allies," she said with some resignation. "You're still my brother, after all."

CHAPTER TWENTY-THREE

London, September 23, 1888

SARACEN'S HEAD

7:45 p.m. Sunday

THE OLD NICHOL ROOKERY WAS ONE OF THE WORST CLUMPS of dense, run-down tenements anywhere in London. The Saracen's Head clung to the edge of the slum like something stuck to the sole of its shoe. A short, squat, whitewashed building, it had always been a place where the legally averse had congregated, and it continued that proud tradition even in the face of King Coal's Blue Boys.

Nick had to bow his head to get through the doorway without knocking himself silly, but he heard Digby's grunt behind him as the tall helmsman predictably forgot to duck. Striker followed up the rear, the metal bits on his coat jingling as he moved.

The place stank of the ashes and spilled beer that formed a greasy black slick under his boots. Mugs and cups belonging to the regulars hung on nails above the bar, but a shelf nearby held a stock of additional tankards. Old, cracked saucers sat on the bar filled with scrapings from the frying pans, a twist of cloth set alight as a wick for the improvised lamps. The Head wasn't one of the Blue King's places, and so it had no gas, coal, or steam. That suited everyone just fine, as long as one didn't mind carrying the stench of burning bacon in one's clothes.

"Well," said Black George, the barkeep, in his usual rumble. "If 'tisn't the scourge of the high aether come to drink our porter. Sing me a shanty, boys, and tell tall tales of the clouds." He rumbled a laugh, hawked, spat, and plucked three tankards down from their hooks. He was a big man, shaped like one of his own casks, with curly black hair that turned into a curly beard without interruption. He began filling the tankards with the Saracen's notoriously sour ale.

"There won't be any shanties tonight, my friend, though maybe Digby will play you a tune." Nick strolled toward the bar, noticing who immediately cleared the path, and who waited till the last moment to step away. There were always a few who wanted to inch up the pack order by taking on one of the pirates, but tonight there were no takers. Just as well. Enough heads would be broken as it was.

"Business?" Black George smacked three pewter tankards, rumpled with dents and dings and glistening with foam, upon the scarred counter. The other drinkers shuffled away from the tankards as if they might explode. "It's always business with you boys. Except you, Digby. You're a man who knows what makes a good time."

"Aye, George," the tall helmsman said, pulling a battered fiddle out from under his coat. "And it's a royal treat to come to a place where folk appreciate a good tune. Not like these airborne billy goats."

"The beer comes free as long as you play," George said. "Just take it to the back."

And Digby did, for once remembering to duck when he passed beneath the black wooden beam that stretched the length of the place to reach a circle of chairs. The seats were drawn around a smoky fire that smelled suspiciously of the stables. Nick guessed the fuel was picked up off the street once horses had gone by.

"We've had a good run," said Nick to George. "Took three of the Gold King's transports before the job you sent my way."

"Did it go well?"

Nick tried to decide if that was a polite question, or if George was fishing for information. "The customer is satisfied his deliveries were made in good order. And now I'm free to sell my merchandise."

"There are plenty hungry for whatever you have to sell."

Nick gestured, and Striker stepped forward, spiky hair standing out around his face like a hedgehog's quills. The flickering light danced over the metal on his coat. "Show him."

Striker turned around, displaying the back of the garment. Samples of the gears, wheels, plates, and every bolt and screw were stitched there in decorative array. Of course, there were plenty of items too large to include, but it worked well enough as a sales tool. Striker had always covered his coat, both for protection and as a means of carrying the valuable parts with him. It wasn't a fashion for everyone. Nick had tried the coat on once and felt like he could hardly move.

"Ah, some nice gears there for sure," said Black George, hooking a thumb into the bib of his apron. "I know just who might be looking for a few o' those."

Of course he did, for a percentage. Nick didn't begrudge him that—his complaint lay in other quarters. As if on cue, Digby struck up a slip jig, tapping his heel on the floor to keep time. A man with a wheezy concertina joined in. Striker turned around and put on his best thug-at-large expression. "I know you have buyers lining up at the door," Nick said in a hard voice. "My question is who else you've got hanging around the back alley."

"And what would you mean by that, Captain?" George said uneasily.

"The wrong kind of folks have known where to find me and my ship of late."

Striker leaned on the counter, an unfriendly smile on his swarthy face. "Folks with very bad manners. I was right testy by the time they shoved off."

Black George shook his round head, sweat running into his beard. "I'm a businessman, and I know that kind of nonsense does no purse any good."

Nick believed him—Black George liked his shillings, but he lived for his throne behind the bar and the thrill of striking a bargain. He wouldn't put all that at risk. But there were plenty of other eyes and ears in the Saracen's Head. As

much as Nick was glaring at George, he was watching the
bystanders from the edge of his vision.

He leaned close, his face inches from the gaping pores in
George's nose. "Then tell me how they found out where I
was to meet the Schoolmaster. You were the only one who
knew the place."

George recoiled, his eyes so wide the whites gleamed in
the murky light. "I said nothing!"

"Oy," said a thin man in a brown suit, grabbing Nick's
arm. "Leave him be."

Striker grabbed Brown Suit by the scruff and hauled him
away from the counter. He let the man dangle in one hand,
not quite letting his heels touch the floor. "Don't interrupt
the captain when he's talking."

The man spit in Striker's face, the foamy blob catching
him right between the eyes. Nick's stomach turned cold and
hollow. "Oh, bloody hell." A palpable sense of horror blan-
keted the room, and Digby's lazy slip jig suddenly somersaulted into a reel.

"Ha!" Striker tossed Brown Suit onto the bar one-handed.
The man skidded, the soft cloth of his coat sliding as slick as
a bar rag across the worn surface. Black George lurched out
of the way as the man went over the far side, dragging a
mess of dirty tankards and makeshift lamps with him. The
barkeep began stamping out the flames. A patron helpfully
pissed on a particularly obstinate fire.

Someone pushed Nick from behind, knocking him forward so that he stumbled into a stool and nearly went down.
He wheeled around, clinging to the stool, and raised a foot
just in time to catch a big man in the chest. The man staggered back, arms waving wildly to catch his balance. He
had the grin of a man who was fighting just for the joy of it.
Nick looked wildly around, seeing the same gleam in a
dozen pairs of eyes. *Bloody, bloody hell.* Nick's crew might
have had a reputation, but there were still only three of
them.

"Digby, get over here!" he roared.

"But I'm helping, Captain!" cried the helmsman, winding

around one more chorus. "I'm playing you some fine tunes for courage."

"I'll tune you, scrawny bastard!" Striker shot back. "I'll use your guts for your next set of strings."

"Sure you will, and I'll put you and your coat in a corn field to scare the crows." Digby countered by hopping onto a table and striking up "Rocky Road to Dublin." Nick had to admit it was a fine fighting song.

And a good thing, too, because the man who'd hit him in the back returned, this time with a chair. Nick ducked just as he swung it, coming up underneath and driving a fist into his gut with all his weight. The chair spun out of his hands, smashing into a pillar with a shower of kindling. Black George picked up a leg and thumped another brawler over the skull.

Nick drove his assailant backward into the wall, driving a fist into his jaw once, twice. The man's eyes rolled up in his head and he slid down the wall, a dribble of spit finding its way down his chin.

Hand stinging, Nick turned just in time to see Striker smash a tankard into someone's face, but another fighter was picking up a splintered piece of chair to use like a dagger. And then he recognized Brown Suit as the man with the aether gun from the *Leaping Hind*—the one Captain Hughes had named Bingham—no doubt looking for a chance to silence them for what they'd seen.

"Sweet Mother of Darkness!" Nick rushed forward to grab him, his skull pounding with the music just as the wooden weapon was raised to skewer Striker through the back. It might never have made it past the coat, but he wasn't taking any chances. He drove his shoulder into the man so hard they both flew into the rack of tankards, sending the whole mess crashing to the floor, tankards bouncing and spinning with a clatter. Nick's head hit the floor hard, stunning him.

"Enough!" bellowed George, bashing on the counter with his chair leg. *"Enough!"*

Digby lifted his bow from the strings. The sudden silence caught as much attention as Black George's roar. There were a few thumps and clatters as bodies came to rest, but no one landed another blow. Blinking hard to clear his vision, Nick sat up, disoriented. The motion made his stomach lurch as a blinding pain blotted out his vision. He took one slow breath, then two, waiting for the hurt to recede. Then he slowly glanced around the room, wondering where his opponent had gone. The man had vanished. *Bugger!* The *Leaping Hind* had disappeared, but if this man was alive, that meant it landed safely. But what had happened to the ship and crew?

He hadn't gone to anyone with information about the Blue King's weapons. For one thing, he'd been in mid-flight most of the time. For another, he wasn't sure whom to tell. And now it appeared the information was even more valuable—and dangerous—than he'd thought. He would have to be very, very careful where he placed his trust.

Nick sprang to his feet, wondering if he could still catch Bingham, but dizziness swamped him, along with a blinding pain in his head. *By the Black Mother of basilisks!*

Striker picked something up from the floor that looked to Nick like a metal croquet ball with legs. He was turning it over, his brows furrowed with curiosity, when Black George grasped Nick's sleeve and dragged him into the back room. Nick followed at a stagger.

"Are you trying to kill my customers?" the big man growled.

Nick straightened, doing his best not to wince. "I have knives. If I wanted them dead, they'd be bleeding by now."

"I've been your friend. This," George said, waving an arm toward the destruction, "is no way to repay me."

Nick's temper stirred. He hadn't started the actual fighting. But he was saved from the folly of explaining himself when Striker pushed through to the back.

"Yours?" he asked George, holding up the metal object.

"No," said the barkeep, unimpressed.

"It was above the shelf. Fell down when the captain knocked it over."

"What is it?" Nick asked.

Striker turned the thing over. Patches of grillwork showed here and there, revealing clockwork that moved when he spoke. "It's got a recording cylinder inside. It takes down everything we say."

George and Nick exchanged a stormy look. "That's not mine!" Black George boomed, sending the device into a flurry of whirring gears.

"I believe that," said Nick. He was pretty sure he did, anyway. Sophisticated devices just weren't part of George's world. *So whoever the traitor is, they have access to expensive toys.* That ruled out the local snitches, anyway, unless they were working with a steam baron or some other maker with an ax to grind with the rebels.

Nick turned to Striker. "Can you figure out who made it?"

The big man shrugged. "I'll strip it down. See what I can find."

Nick glared at the blob of dull metal. Had someone put it in the tavern near where George always stood? Did someone collect it from time to time to copy out the many conversations gathered in its clockwork brain? What had he said that could twist around to bite him? Nick had always been careful, but this was a hazard he hadn't foreseen.

The muscles up the back of Nick's neck screamed with tension. He hadn't signed on to fight a revolution, but the enemy was trying like hell to make the fight personal. *They've attacked me, my ship, and my men. Now they're targeting the people I deal with—the people I have a pint with. Does it get lower than that?*

"After my folk under my roof, are they?" George muttered. "I'll be taking some bones for the soup pot before this is done."

"Don't invite me to dinner that night," Striker said, trying to pry the device's case open with a knife. He'd be obsessed until he figured out exactly how each component worked.

Nick sat on a cask, gathering his scattered thoughts. A pounding headache was making it hard to reason. "George, you need to think about new faces around the Head. There was at least one man who made himself scarce once the shelf came down. He calls himself Bingham."

Striker muttered something foul.

"I don't know that name," George replied. "There are my

regulars, but always a few strangers passing through. I've had no reason to think ill of any of them, till this." George jammed his hands into his curly dark hair. "That's a fine thing, isn't it? I've run this place for a score of years, never had a problem. And now I don't know who to let through the door."

It was a miracle that the Blue King hadn't shut him down sooner, but whoever had found the Saracen's Head was fishing for a bigger catch. Yet saying so wouldn't help a thing. "We'll help you clean up."

Just then Digby stuck his head through the door and waggled his eyebrows. "There's a very pretty girl out here wanting to buy parts."

Nick gave him a withering look.

"I'm telling you the truth!" Digby insisted. "She said she's been told to ask for the captain and no one else."

Traitors, devices, rebels . . . Nick had had enough problems to deal with lately without adding the female variety, but he followed Digby out nonetheless. A captain's work was never done, and he was the deal-maker—but if this was no more than a crewman's prank, Digby would be scrubbing pots for a month.

The helmsman led him through the wreck of the Saracen and out into the street, where it was quieter. Dusk had fallen, and someone had set a row of the improvised lamps in the window, and writhing flames cast a weak pool of light into the muddy track of the street.

Then Nick saw her. An instant wave of heat surged from deep inside him, rushing through his brain like a quart of brandy drained in a single swallow. He curled his fingers into fists, as if to clutch whatever shreds of reason still remained. Anger and need curdled into a poisonous elixir, stinging wounds still bloody and raw.

"Go," he said to Digby, his voice little more than a rasp. Digby went.

Evelina was turned to the side, looking nervously toward a couple of drunkards laughing and pushing each other from one wall to the other. The sight of her made him forget the pain in his head, the fight, everything but the two of them. She looked thin, wearing what looked like a traveling dress that had seen happier days. Her wavy dark hair was pulled back in a simple knot. Nick was no expert in fashion, but he knew the difference between this outfit and the expensive gowns she'd been wearing last spring. Something had happened.

"Evelina." He managed to keep his voice steady. A point for him.

Her head snapped around at the sound of his voice. "Nick?"

"Yes." He folded his arms, reminding himself to keep his distance. Four strides of air between his hands and her flesh. Four strides between fury and forgiveness. There would be no crossing it.

On top of the desire of a man for a woman—which was sharp enough, thank you very much—his Blood chafed at the distance between them. But being close had always been a disaster. The silver fire that came whenever they were together drew every deva from miles around and sent the spirits into a drunken frenzy. Athena had taught him much, but he wasn't sure if his training could withstand the assault of Evelina's touch.

"I suppose I could ask what you're doing here. Out alone in the dark on these streets," he said. Angry as he was, he couldn't help wanting to know—and wanting to know what he could put right. He'd been her protector all through their childhood. Some habits were impossible to break.

"You stole the gold and the casket," she said, her voice low and tense. "Everyone is looking for it. The Steam Council . . ."

"I know."

That made her blink, as if she'd expected to warn him of something he hadn't already heard, but then she regrouped, squaring her shoulders. "You ran from everything. Why?"

"I needed a fresh start." And her detective uncle had all but handed him the fortune. He'd never known the reason, but it had been a godsend. "You said you needed a different life from the circus, and I thought maybe I did, too. After all, you landed in the lap of luxury. Why shouldn't I?"

"But what did you . . ." She trailed off, looking him up and down. Every line of her body spoke of bewilderment.

"You said you needed good quality parts." He smiled, though there was no joy in it. "Everyone has need of a pirate from time to time, even you."

"Nick!" she cried softly, her eyes wide with dismay that quickly slid into disappointment.

"My, my, so much judgment." He wanted to go on, to vent all the bitterness clawing up from the pit of his soul, but there was no point. "Yet you're quick enough to want what I have to sell."

"True enough," she said dully, lowering her gaze.

"How did you land here?" He took a step closer, risking that much. He was worried less about the magic than about his sanity. Half of him wanted to slap her, the rest to cradle her in his arms like a foundling child, promising her protection from the entire world. Neither impulse would do them any favors.

"Keating. I found myself on his bad side."

"What did you do to him?"

She covered her eyes, looking as if she might scream. "Tobias married his daughter yesterday."

The tone of her voice said everything. A jolt of fury sickened him, and he took another step forward, choking back jealousy. "You wanted the golden ponce for yourself."

She flinched. "I thought I did. I kissed him. But we were caught, and Keating used that against me. I had to go."

"To the bloody East End?" Nick demanded.

She lifted her face from her hands, blinking at him. "There were reasons."

"Surely Holmes didn't agree to this."

"It's not your business!" she said, suddenly angry. "I have work and a place to stay. I'm fine."

And she doesn't need me. Not even here, in this place. "You always like to make choices for other people. Have you thought what Holmes would say if he saw you here, like this?"

She swore under her breath. He knew she was fumbling, trying to deny that she'd made mistakes, to prove that she still had the wits to survive, despite all the time she'd spent in silks and lace. He knew her inside and out, but that just made things harder. "Evie, you pushed me away twice. Are you sure you want to do it again?"

But all he saw in her face was confusion. *She wanted Tobias Roth, but I don't see him here taking care of her. He threw her aside for the steam baron's girl.* And that was a travesty Nick couldn't fathom, adding another layer to the rage eating through his gut. *He's dead if he ever crosses my path.* And that was the last coherent thought he had.

His mouth found Evelina's—not angry and hard, like the last time they'd kissed, but simply like he meant business. He claimed her the way he took a merchant ship, swift and thorough—and no apologies. Her hands flew up, as if to strike him, but he caught her wrists, holding them until she surrendered.

Her lips were cool, her skin chilled by the night air. He let one of her hands go free, and it dug into the front of his coat, crushing the fabric in a fist. He cupped her cheek, warming her as he bid her to let him in, to let him taste her. She hesitated, checked by pride or fear or simple astonishment that this was happening at all—Nick couldn't tell. But then her lips parted, sighing into him as the tension went out of her frame. *Another point to me.*

Her soft weight pressed against him, fuel to his mounting desire. He felt the tug of his Blood wanting to run free, to call wild magic from the air, but he clamped down on it, forcing it to heel like a stubborn hound. He bargained, he promised, he wrestled it with sheer strength of will until he had forced it under his control.

The feel of her against him was worth all of that and more. As his tongue found the sweetness of hers, his pulse seemed to grow fast and slow at once, too thick for his veins. His hands slid down the curve of her back, the gentle swell of her hips, and he could not silence a low rumble of pleasure deep in his chest.

But then a tendril of reason slid through his triumph. *She walked away from you last time this happened. It doesn't mean a thing.* The same must have occurred to her, too, because they pushed each other away almost at the same moment.

"What happened?" she demanded in a low whisper. "There is no silver light, no devas, no magic."

"I told you I would find a way to control it. You never believed I could." He heard the sourness in the words, but he couldn't help it.

Astonishment flattened her expression. "How did you do it?"

"Does it matter? I wasn't the one you wanted anyway. At least, not until the golden boy threw you over. Welcome back to the gutter, Evie. I'm as low as it gets."

Evelina's breath hissed in, the same gasp of pain he'd heard from men he'd stabbed. "Are you done?"

He glared at her a moment, even angrier now because he'd hurt her. *This has to end. I keep making it worse, moment by moment.* Turning to the door, he squeezed his eyes shut a moment, praying they would stop stinging before he had to face his men. "Sorry I disappointed you, Evie, but I'm making my own choices now."

"Nick," she called softly. The plaintive note in her voice hinted at a longing he'd always wanted to hear. But wishing like that would only hurt them both. It always did, with them.

"I'll send Striker to talk about the parts." With that, he went inside to deal with an easier kind of betrayal.

EVELINA HUDDLED ON the bench outside the Saracen's Head, every muscle suddenly too weak to stand. The weakness might have been from shock or sadness, but it felt like she had simply broken like an overwound spring. She'd endured too much, and the encounter with Nick had been the last straw.

The fiddler inside struck up another tune. It was one she knew, but for the life of her she couldn't remember the words—a fact that suddenly seemed wildly important, because if she were singing the song, she couldn't be thinking about what had just taken place. *How did any of this happen?*

She'd asked for the captain. That was what Magnus had told her to do—he'd given her money to go buy what she needed, and suggested that she try the Saracen's Head because there was a ship in town that had parts to sell. The doctor hadn't named the ship, and he hadn't mentioned Nick. And if he'd said to ask for the captain, well, that was the done thing. That's how she would have played it anyway, had she learned of the ship on her own.

Had Magnus sent her on a fishing expedition, and was he waiting for her to come back and say she'd met an old friend that night? Or did he truly not know his would-be assassin— and Evelina's old sweetheart—was in the neighborhood? There was no way to tell.

And what would Nick say if he knew his little Evie was working not just for Keating, but for Magnus as well? And what right did he—a pirate, of all things—have to say anything about what she did?

She closed her eyes, emotion warring with facts. There was no time to dwell on her aching emotions, because the next decisions she made carried too much weight. But no sooner had she formed that thought then those feelings swamped her.

Grief clogged her chest, too thick for mere tears. She took a gulping swallow, forcing air into her lungs. *Damn you, Nick, why did you have to kiss me?* The touch had given her a glimpse of everything they'd—she'd—let slip away. Nick had tamed the wild magic, just as he'd said he would—but she had always doubted him.

And yes, she'd wanted the life that Tobias had represented— wealth, comfort, and safety. Little did she know how much danger could lurk in a drawing room, or how quickly Tobias would set aside his promises of love. *He is married!* She had no idea what to do next—none at all, and that left her helpless.

The phantom of Nick's touch still clung to her skin, taunting her. She sprang to her feet, as if moving would let her escape the ghosts of his caress . . . and she nearly walked straight into Striker. She'd only met him once before, but there was no chance of forgetting him. The man's blunt, dark face was rumpled with disbelief. "Miss Cooper? What the bloody hell are you doing here?"

"Mr. Striker."

He looked her up and down, taking in her clothes. "What's going on, miss?"

"I can't explain."

He folded his arms, his voice going gruff. "Well, you'd better. The captain's in a right mood."

She didn't want to answer his question, so she grabbed at one of the hundred questions swirling around her thoughts. "How did he get to be captain? He's no pirate!"

"He's Niccolo," Striker replied, as if that made everything clear.

And it did, in a way. Evelina sank back down on the bench, all the strength draining out of her again. "Yes, Nick is Nick."

"So?"

"I came here to buy parts," she said quietly. "But I don't think I should."

Striker's brow furrowed. "Eh?"

"There was a fight here. I was standing outside in this dark alley when I heard it," she said. "I think I was frightened away, and I never learned the identity of the people selling machine parts."

Striker slowly sat down on the other end of the bench, making it creak. "Who sent you?"

Evelina studied his face. It was hard and wary, but there wasn't any trickery there. And Striker was on Nick's side, and that's what mattered right then. "Nick says he knows people are after the casket, but I doubt he knows about everyone."

"Yeah?"

"Magnus is still alive."

She saw the flare of surprise that widened Striker's eyes, but he didn't seem the kind to waste words on emotions. "Yeah?"

"I don't know if he's aware that Nick is here tonight, but I don't want to take the risk."

For a long moment, Striker regarded her. "Why are you buying parts for Magnus?"

"He has information I need."

"Why can't he get them himself? He seems the type who could wave his hand and make them appear."

That was a good point. "I should go," she said.

"You hurt him," Striker said unexpectedly. "Last spring."

Of course he meant Nick. Her first instinct was to retort that it was none of the streetkeeper's business, but she was too tired. "I know, and I'm sorry, but it was the only answer I had then."

"Do you want him?" Striker asked bluntly.

"Why?"

"Finish it with him either way, but for feckin' sake stop going back and forth."

The statement should have made her angry, but instead Evelina looked down at her hands in her lap. "I don't have a right to him anymore."

"What does that matter?" He grimaced. "I don't want the answer. I just want peace and quiet. And until you've made up your mind, there'll be neither."

She rose, not sure what to say. A yearning filled her, not just for Nick but for the simple existence that had made their affection easy. Of course, she had been little more than a child, before the wild magic and still young enough to be awestruck by a lad who could ride like a centaur. Whatever their love would be now, it wouldn't be that easy.

Loneliness ached like a fever, making her hug herself against the cold. She turned to Striker, putting something like a smile on her face. "Good night, Mr. Striker. Tell Nick I'm sorry, and that I was never here."

And she went back to the Magnetorium empty-handed.

CHAPTER TWENTY-FOUR

WHAT SHOULD I DO?

It was a good question. An all-purpose one, really, because there wasn't a corner of Evelina's life where it couldn't apply. And the question brought with it a cottony despair that was oddly restful. She could sink into it as if it were a thick mattress and never get up.

She sat on a stool by her workbench, elbows on knees and chin in hand. If her Grandmamma Holmes saw her slouching like that, she would have delivered one sharp tap to Evelina's ear, the lace of her gloves raspy on the skin. A straight spine was a sign of good breeding. Good posture encouraged good thinking. A lazy body was the mark of a lazy character. The Holmes creed of discipline.

Evelina pulled herself up with a sigh. She wasn't able to honor her maternal grandmother in much else at the moment. The old woman would have fainted at the sight of Evelina's hands, work-roughened and creased with grime and machine oil—but Whitechapel was shockingly deficient in good-quality cosmetics, not to mention ladies' maids who knew how to give a good manicure. And there was a piece of Evelina's soul that wanted nothing more than to crawl back to a pleasant, quiet world where such things mattered and the worst that could happen was dancing the quadrille with a carrot-brained suitor.

In that world—before she had kissed Tobias—she didn't need to be a spy. She could sit with her books and tea and dream of college. She could toy with a thousand exciting futures, but she didn't really need to risk herself on any of them. It wasn't expected of her, and if she wanted to retreat there would always be a gentleman to hold the door.

But she had erred, and the Gold King was quite willing to turn her life into another Crowleyton. He had purposefully set no limits on what he might choose to do. And she had seven days to give him what he wanted, and no clue where to begin.

And he was only one corner of an unholy triangle of problems. There was also Nick—whose appearance had acted like a sudden blow, leaving her to slowly bleed inside. Every time she tried to think about their encounter last night, it felt like touching a throbbing bruise, and she'd shrink away, hot and sweating. His anger had left her sensitized, as if she could still feel it like a hot wind on her flesh.

And there was Magnus—whom she was sure knew every answer to her woes, but was as impenetrable as a Chinese puzzle box.

As if summoned, the sorcerer descended from his upstairs room and strolled into the workshop. It was still morning, so the others who came to prepare for the evening's performance had not yet arrived. She rose as he came in, wiping her thoughts from her face. He gave her an inquiring look, but said nothing.

"Good morning." Evelina picked up a tool at random and attempted to look busy. Casimir lay on the workbench before her, utterly inert.

"How is the work coming along?" Magnus asked. "Were you able to find what you needed last night?"

Evelina felt herself tense. "I found something that might serve with a little adjustment. I stopped at Brownlee's last night. He'll bring the assembly around this afternoon."

She felt Magnus's dark gaze slide over her. "You didn't try the Saracen's Head?"

"There was a fight going on. I didn't go in."

Magnus huffed with disgust. "I thought Black George

kept a better handle on his customers. I'm sorry I sent you there. How is the rest of the repair going?"

Evelina cast him a sidelong look. Had he known Nick—and by extension, the casket—was in town? Magnus had touched the subject so lightly, it was impossible to tell. But since he'd passed over it, she wasn't going to risk lingering there. "I'll show you."

Like Serafina, Casimir was brought to life by activating his logic processor. Evelina slid the long pin into his neck and it clicked into place with a slight rattle of metal on metal. The doll's long-lashed eyes immediately opened, the glass orbs so cunningly wrought that each brown iris had the same striated variation as a living man's. Slowly, Casimir sat up. But that was all he did. Unlike Serafina, he didn't look around to see who was there.

"How are you?" Magnus asked.

There was a slight pause, and the silence was filled by the sound of gears churning in Casimir's head. His face slowly turned toward Magnus's voice. "My left knee is still not functioning in an optimum manner." The oddly mechanical tone of his voice was not as pronounced as Serafina's, perhaps because it was deeper.

"Your knee will be fixed soon," Evelina promised.

The doll didn't respond.

"Does that make you happy?" she asked, curious to see how he would respond.

"He will only find it satisfactory," Magnus supplied. "He has no capacity to feel pleasure, for I have never imbued him with more than basic consciousness. There are many degrees of such things."

"Would it not improve his performance on the stage if he had more personality? Serafina is dazzling, and I am sure much of her talent has to do with the fact that she is more alive."

Magnus moved his hand in a seesaw gesture. "In principle, I agree. But I have found that there is a risk inherent in half-measures. Too little and, yes, one has an automaton that is nothing more than a sophisticated toy. But I have learned to my sorrow that a toy with a will of its own can be dangerous. I do not venture there lightly, and certainly not in a widespread fashion."

"Hence Serafina, and all your experiments on a single subject?"

"Some of the earliest results were, shall we say, slightly nerve-racking. You may note that I am still careful to pull her pin every night."

Casimir sat through the conversation like a statue. What would he be like, Evelina wondered, with a personality of his own? The doll's expression was strong, square-jawed. The very picture of masculinity—and yet utterly vacant. "How do you do it? How do you make them more than they are?"

"Ah," Magnus gave a quick smile. "That is a long and complex process, but the short answer is that there are two methods. One is what you have done with your creatures— taking an existing entity and housing it in the machine. That requires pure Blood talent, which you obviously possess in abundance. What I have done with my dancers is rather more straightforward. I gather enough of my own life force that I am able to split some of it off. A spark of life—me and not me—that then powers the automaton. As long as I live, they live. I am in no way aware of their consciousness, but there is a reason that the corps de ballet moves in perfect unison. On some level they are truly all of one mind."

Evelina listened, fascinated and bewildered. "But how do you do that without depleting yourself to nothing?"

Magnus gave a quick smile. "Did your Gran Cooper never tell you how to gather your power into a cohesive force? That is the first step."

Evelina bit her lip. "No."

"Do you want me to show you how?"

She did. Desperately. "How easily can I learn this?"

She meant *how quickly*. She only had a week before she was supposed to report to Keating and go home. There was no time to spend indulging her thirst for magic lessons, for she'd already extended her deadline once. *What sort of excuse could I give so that I could stay a little longer?* That would be pure folly.

Magnus folded his arms and leaned against the workbench, the picture of casual ease. "There is a simple way to discover that. Do you know how to call fire?"

"Yes." She could light a candle or kindling just by awakening the potential flame within it.

"From nothing?" He opened his hand, a ball of flame appeared, just as it had during the ballet.

Evelina flinched away. "Witchlight." A sign of sorcery, her Gran Cooper had said. A sign to be reviled and avoided, because such displays were typically powered through death magic.

"Always handy if you're caught without a candle," Magnus said, closing his palm to extinguish the flames. "It's the simple tricks that one ends up using the most."

Evelina floundered a moment, caught between his matter-of-fact tone and a mire of grandmotherly disapproval. "So how does that help you gather your power?"

"Unless you know how to pull it together, the light won't work. In ancient days, when I learned my craft, the technique was taught as an exercise."

"When was that?"

"A long, long time ago, little kitten." His voice was a gentle rebuff. "Now do you want to learn how to do this?"

For some reason, Evelina glanced at Casimir, but there was no advice from that quarter. The automaton sat expressionless and unmoving, a void waiting for orders. For a moment she envied him, not having to decide anything. Not caught between choices. She remembered the light-headed rush of power she'd felt when Magnus had shown her his healing trick, and she was more than a little scared of it.

"All you need to do is to imagine your power gathering into a tight, hard ball," Magnus said. "Then feed a tiny bit of it into the flame. Not on your hand—you'll burn yourself—but just over it."

He sounded reasonable, reassuring. The one person who understood the Blood could teach her to light up dark places—a symbolic gesture if there ever was one. Her Gran Cooper would tell her to back away, that no amount of knowledge was worth dealing with Magnus. And yet Gran wasn't there to teach her anything.

Nothing moved in the workshop but dust motes, swirling in the soft morning light that fell from the high transom windows. All of a sudden Evelina felt very small in the vast space. *Make a decision. Stay safe, or learn to use your power. Yes or no.*

It was just a light. On the other hand, she needed every tool she could get if she was going to defend herself and the people she loved from Jasper Keating. A bit of witchfire might be all she had.

"All right." Evelina held out her hand, palm upward, just like Magnus had done. "Teach me."

He gave a gentle smile. "Excellent."

"WHY ARE THERE no devas here?" Evelina asked Magnus the next day. She had been working on witchlight all night, and had rushed into the theater earlier that morning to show him the pale glimmer she'd finally managed to produce. And then—as seemed to happen with them—one bit of conversation had led to the next.

"Why do you think the devas have left these streets?" Magnus replied, lifting his cup of tea.

Evelina blinked, coming back to the present, and watched the sorcerer, trying to figure out what part he played in the complex game for power. Was he really the Blue King's maker? Or was he pursuing some gambit of his own? And why was he taking the time to teach her?

"I don't know why the devas are gone," she said. "You'd think something would thrive here. There's a river, and there are still gardens."

"Think harder."

It was late morning and they sat in his library, surrounded by all those wonderful books. He'd pointed some out to her and she'd spent blissful hours curled up in a large, comfortable chair poring through the writings of a mage from five centuries ago. It was a history book of sorts, but not the history of kings and queens and borders. It was the history of her people and their Bloodlines, and how they had come from the steppes thousands of years past, and from the Gardens of Babylon, and the deepest roots of the Niger. The words were like a voice whispering from somewhere deep inside her. On some primal level, she knew this story to be true, and that she had a right to hear it. As strange a turn of events as it seemed, Magnus was giving her the birthright of her Blood.

Not many months ago, she had refused him out of fear, and none of her reasons had gone away. And she wasn't sure what would happen once her deal with the Gold King was done. But until that moment for decision came, she would learn all she could.

"All right," she said. "The devas used to be everywhere. Every herbwife and hedge wizard left offerings to their favorites, asking them to help with their spells. Then the factories came along. No one liked them tearing up the woods and fields and driving the devas away."

"And so Church and State turned against magic," Magnus finished. "If no one had reverence for the woods, there would be no objection to tearing them down, putting up manufactories, and offering the people jobs instead. Quite the contrary, because in this new century fewer and fewer work their own land. They need employment, and will silence anyone who stands in the way of earning a living. The steam barons and their witch trials have taken this to new heights."

That was all very true, but nothing that Evelina didn't know already. "But there are still devas in parts of London. The garden at Hilliard House has some, and Regent's Park . . ."

Magnus's lip curled in a half smile that said he was about to come to the point. "Think about it. Devas do not go near human habitation without incentive. The residents of Hilliard House place a high value on the beauty of their gardens, and thus they attract the spirits. But if a relationship with devas is fostered by affection for the leafy wood and rippling stream, what drives them away?"

"A need for the engines of commerce, and a fear of whatever stands in their way," she said quietly. "Gardens and parks are exceptions."

"Every human needs nature to be whole, but how many of the wretches in the Old Nichol rookery have time and energy to spare for flower gardens? Their attention is on the business of filling their bellies."

She knew that all too well. "But with no spirits around to help, it's a wonder any magic gets done here."

"But it does." Magnus sat back, crossing his long legs. "It's a question of harnessing what is available."

She looked at him suspiciously. He waved a hand. "I'm not speaking of stealing life from living bodies other than your own. We've been through that. You can't even do it with your lack of training. But there are other sources of energy. The spirits of the dead is one, but I do not recommend it. They aren't pleasant company—all very full of their missed opportunities and the unfairness of it all. True necromancy is another, but even I hesitate to start casting circles without a very, very good reason."

"So far, you're not inspiring me. With this lack of life going around, how do you make your magic?"

Magnus flashed a smile. "Ah, that is simple. You remember once I showed you a toy beetle?"

He had let the wretched thing run all over the dinner table at Hilliard House. "Yes. But anything on a larger scale takes a great deal of power."

He nodded.

"So does Serafina work the same way?" She had approached the question several times but never got a satisfactory answer.

"In part," he said with a smile. "She is something of a trade secret. There are a few concepts you need to master before you would understand."

"Then teach me more. I've made the witchlight."

"Very well. Did you ever learn to work with wands?"

"No." She sat forward in her chair. "My Gran Cooper gave me some tools, but she never showed me how to use them. She said I didn't have enough training."

"You mean these." He reached into the pocket of his neat black jacket and pulled out a handful of objects. One looked like a bracelet of twisted copper, another a wand no bigger than a pencil, the third was a painted stone with a hole in it, and the last a triangle of silver etched with tiny runes.

Shot through with sudden panic, Evelina nearly jumped out of her chair. "You took those from my tool chest!"

"I did," he said calmly. "Pardon the invasion of your belongings, but I wanted to look them over before introducing them to our conversation today. They may not look like much, but they are good workmanship. I think it's time you learned how to use them."

She slowly sank back into the chair, nerves still tingling. A feeling of guilt nagged at her, as if she were betraying her Gran's memory by allowing a sorcerer to teach her to use her gifts. *But what harm can there be? These are Cooper family tools. I'm supposed to use them.*

Without waiting for an answer, Magnus handed her the tiny wand. It was made of smooth, plain wood with a pattern of vines burned into it. There were no gems or words of power. It looked as magical as a knitting needle. "So how does it work?" she asked.

"It's not a steam engine. It does not *work*. It is a receptor. You are right-handed, yes? Then hold it lightly in your left. We are not producing here; we are listening. Your left hand will do that better. Stand up."

Evelina did as she was told, standing in the center of the study, her hands at her sides and a little away from her body. She'd seen Gran do this much before.

He adjusted her arms slightly, his hands gentle but not too familiar. "Good. Now close your eyes and reach out through the wand. Move it about until you feel something."

"What? What am I supposed to feel?"

"I invoke the right to be irritating and say you'll know it when you feel it."

She didn't argue. Evelina had quickly realized most of Magnus's lessons consisted of him putting her in the best position to discover things for herself, and that suited her perfectly. Her talents wanted to grow almost of their own accord—all he needed to do was point them toward opportunity, and even the past few days of instruction had made a difference. She had to admit, however grudgingly, that he was a good teacher.

Evelina raised the wand, sending her consciousness down her arm and through the slim piece of wood. She instantly understood that someone had charmed it and used it many, many times. When her powers reached the wand, it was like sliding in stockings across a polished floor—she zipped forward, her energy faster, and launched outward into the world with her perceptions wide open. In fact, the wand must have enhanced her ability to read the energies in the air, because she got far more information than she ever had before.

She was aware of herself, and of the dark lodestone of Magnus's strong magic, but she was far more interested in the wider city. London was a seething mass of energy, surging and writhing like something coming to a boil. Each person walking the streets shed a little of his life force as he hurried from club to home, or factory to doss-house, or the nursery to the kitchen. Concern and laughter, love and anger all rose off them like steam from a kettle. The cloud of it hung over the city, thick as London's famous fogs. It was the city's collective, invisible life, huge and not a little daunting. Uncertain, she drew back.

"You will never learn unless you touch it," Magnus said. "Trust your strength."

So she plunged into it, and she recognized much. The gaiety of the theater district, the pride and strife of the Parliament, and the eager, forward energy of the counting houses and shipyards. And running through it all like a ribbon of rot was the despair of the poor. Evelina jerked away from that, afraid to let it touch her any more than it had. Then, for a moment, she let herself drift, experiencing the vibration of all the life. It seemed to fall in veils around her, and though it wasn't a visual thing, it felt like there were colors to the waves of life that came from here or there. It wasn't the same thing as a deva's energy—it was much more diffuse— but she wondered if it could be spooled up like honey or spun like fleece, somehow concentrating it into a form that a spellcaster could use.

And then she remembered that Magnus had told her to move the wand about. It took Evelina a moment to remember where her arm was, but then she began to inch it in a slow arc. The effect was like moving the lens of a spyglass. She could see the energy rising from a park, or the river, or a night market. And then there was something hideous. "What's that?" she whispered.

"A fire in a workhouse." Magnus's voice was utterly neutral, simply stating a fact.

But it was like nothing she had ever seen. Sheets of twisted energy leapt up, struggling in the jaws of a cleansing blast. Destruction was a palpable force, almost an entity with its own conscious will. It snapped over the scene like a flag in a gale, buffeting everything else away. There was death there, swarming over the scene. Lives sizzled to nothingness like rain on hot iron—but then those lives escaped, free and wild, floating into the void like mist.

Evelina was appalled, but fascinated. This was a view she'd never seen, and she felt herself drifting closer, wanting to witness just one more detail, then another, of the compelling play of forces. Part of her wanted to hang back, thinking she didn't belong there, thinking she might be hurt by those mad, snapping flames. But she was supposed to trust her strength, and this was as good a time as any to start.

"I will catch you if you fall," Magnus assured her.

And so she kept going, drawing closer and closer. She could feel the frantic energy of those trying to help, but the weight of destruction pushed down harder, an invisible force that crushed every stroke for good. Evelina could feel those many lost lives floating up like a vapor. If she had lungs on this plane, she might have simply breathed them in. Instead, she reached forward, feeling them spangle like stars against her soul. They slid around her, smooth and slippery, leaving trails of vibration that tickled. The touch of them was delicious, every nerve in her body electric as they brushed her. Each one left her a little more exhilarated, a little more alive herself for the time that they touched. And maybe she did somehow absorb them, because a wave of heady drunkenness made her swoon.

Magnus caught her as she began to swoon and eased her into the armchair. "Easy now," he said. "That's a lot of excitement for a first journey."

Evelina opened her eyes, staring up at him in stunned wonder that was followed quickly by a sense of having done something terribly wrong. "Blood and thunder," she muttered. She rarely used strong language, but nothing short of a curse would do. "You said I couldn't do that."

"Pardon me?"

"Those lives were at the point of dissolution, the very stuff of death magic."

"Indeed," said Magnus with an enigmatic smile. "Did you dislike the taste so very much?"

"No," she said, and burst into tears.

CHAPTER TWENTY-FIVE

London, September 26, 1888
THE DOCKS

2:45 p.m. Wednesday

COLD, WET RAIN HAD SOAKED THE DOCKS, LEAVING THE brickwork dark with moisture and the air heavy with moist, ripe smells. The warehouses facing the river seemed to squint under the arched brows of their windows, peering down at the unforgiving gray of the Thames. Ragged children watched the steam-driven vehicle as it chugged past, running alongside for a few steps, then giving up and gaping after it with eyes too old for their faces. Decrepit men drifted into doorways like yesterday's newspaper, some old, some injured, some simply at a loss. A handful of charity workers moved among them, bringing food enough to keep them alive for another day. A few hundred yards down the way, a ship was in and men swarmed over the gangplank, moving off crates and barrels with single-minded efficiency. Gulls swooped overhead, mewling as they scouted for opportunities.

Sherlock Holmes watched it all out the window of the Steamer, grateful that he'd finally given Keating's Yellowbacks the slip. They were good, but not as good as he was. He'd switched places with the man who'd come in to fix the plasterwork after the bomb, using his talent for disguise to slip out under their noses. Mrs. Hudson would keep the man fed until they could repeat the switch.

The freedom was almost intoxicating, and he drank in the

views of London, however squalid, with the thirst of someone wandering out of the desert. There were barrowmen
and ragpickers, whores and mummers. Ragged children
sang to heartbroken charity workers while accomplices cut
their purses. Holmes identified the thieves the way others
watched birds, cataloguing species and plumage. He'd left
anything of value back in Baker Street—that was merely
good sense. He was destined to pay a call on the Blue King
that afternoon, and would be lucky to leave with his internal
organs, to say nothing of his pocket change.

Unfortunately, the Tower Hamlets had already swallowed
up something far more important than anything he possessed. If Tobias Roth was correct, Evelina was here, caught
in one of Jasper Keating's games—and as anxious as he was
about the Blue King, he was far more concerned about his
niece. She was the only thing that guaranteed he would return to his cage in Baker Street—if he defied Keating too
openly, the cost to Evelina, once she was found, might be
too great.

He recalled the words of her note: *It is best that I go to
some place where I am unknown, and where my shame cannot follow me. Please, do not look for me, for this is the
bosom of your enemies. Know that I will do my best to earn
a blameless life in hopes of redemption in the eyes of the All
Powerful.* This was indeed the bosom of his enemies—or
one of his enemies, at any rate—and, if he was reading the
note correctly, she was here on Keating's orders for what
was probably a trifling transgression.

But why had she been gone so long? It had been nearly a
month since she had left Maggor's Close. He had been absorbed in Baskerville business and hadn't really noticed
anything was wrong until her letter had arrived—and then
nothing else mattered. *Why the devil didn't she come to me?
Surely she didn't think explaining why she left would stop
me from coming to find her?*

He braced himself on the seat as the vehicle jogged over a
pothole, the rough springs threatening to dislodge every
tooth in his head. The Schoolmaster, seated next to him in
the backseat, didn't seem to mind it. But then he never

seemed to mind anything, and had readily agreed to help locate Evelina.

Frustration burned in Holmes's chest—not an uncommon feeling when dealing with his niece. She was too much like him—proud, impatient, self-contained, and convinced she knew what was best for the people around her. There was a reason young ladies should be locked in towers until they were twenty-one. He'd thought she was sensible, but apparently his detective skills did not extend to predicting the whims of precocious nieces.

Frustration bled into fear, making Holmes tighten his grip on his sword cane. *And where do I begin to look for her? I solve insoluble problems, I piece together the most profound and complex puzzles, and this certainly qualifies to be among them. But do I have the time to sift through this ocean of people, looking for just one girl? Or will I be too late? Or when faced with the impossible, do I attempt the unthinkable?*

"I half expected a strike by now," the Schoolmaster said, breaking into Holmes's worries. His eyes were hard to read behind the green-tinted spectacles, but his mouth was a hard line. "There are radicals among the dockworkers. I wonder that they haven't taken a stand."

"I don't think that will happen until something changes," Holmes replied, keeping every trace of anxiety out of his voice. Much of his authority came from his impenetrable sangfroid, and he needed that power now more than ever.

"Not after the match girls, you mean," replied the Schoolmaster.

"Indeed." Almost seven hundred had gone on strike from the factory in July. Two hundred of those had vanished in the space of a week. The rest had gone back to work without further complaint.

"Is that what's going to happen?" the Schoolmaster asked, one corner of his mouth turning up. "We open the cage, let all the pigeons fly free, and they crap on our shoes?"

Holmes felt a twist of resignation. "If, by that tortured metaphor, you are asking if a populace liberated from the stranglehold of the Steam Council is going to be fractious, unmanageable, and appallingly ungrateful, then I would say yes. The point of a rebellion is that they are free to be that way."

"You're hardly a utopian."

The idiocy of the statement was like a slap. Helpless anger flashed up, hot as an exploding airship. Holmes smacked the tip of his cane on the floor of the Steamer. "My niece has been missing for weeks. In the past three days, I have questioned train officials, cab drivers, hoteliers, fellow passengers, and the agents of the Gold King lurking at my heels every moment of the day as to her whereabouts. The ignorance, indifference, and general stupidity of our fellow citizens are appalling beyond measure. Where in that is utopia?"

Another pothole jerked the vehicle so hard that their rumps left the seats. "Are we there yet?" snapped Holmes.

The Schoolmaster flashed him a grin. "Missing your horseflesh, are you?"

"I'm missing several vertebrae."

The Schoolmaster ordered the driver to stop and then paid the man after they got out. Holmes stood next to the Steamer's back wheel, which was a good five feet in diameter. The front wheels were slightly smaller, giving the appearance that the vehicle was crouching, its tall, crooked exhaust pipe reaching into the air like a squirrel's tail. The Steamer chugged away, belching gouts of coal dust and steam. "Mine's faster," the Schoolmaster said, adjusting his scarf. "Better pressure, better output."

"And I'm sure yours toasts tea buns as well," Holmes said icily. "Shall we get on with this?"

They started weaving their way through the mass of humanity clogging the dockside. The Schoolmaster shrugged his long coat tighter around him. With his low-crowned hat, muffler, and hair in need of a barber, he looked like one of the artists lurking in the local garrets. "Are you sure you want to do this? You know the Blue King tried to kill you. Elias Jones, the bomb, and all that. There is a reason Jasper Keating has you under lock and key. You're in danger."

"Jasper Keating never does anything for one reason. I may be in danger, but he wants something from me besides my well-being. As for Elias Jones, according to our friends at Loch Ness, he confessed to working for both the Blue and Gold Kings. We must split the credit between the two barons for that escapade."

"You're just as dead, whichever one pulls the trigger. Just because King Coal sends you a note to drop by, that doesn't mean you should answer."

"Ah, but I shall save him the trouble of sending another bomber if I answer his invitation. Mrs. Hudson at least will thank me."

"That note was more like a summons."

Holmes shrugged. "What it lacked in spelling it made up for in textbook civility. It's my brother they want. Mycroft is in London now, for all the good that will do the Blue Boys or the Yellowbacks. He's ensconced in his club as securely as a pearl in its oyster. It would take an army to reach him. The Diogenes Club has hired a private guard, and they take their lack of sociability seriously."

The Schoolmaster wrinkled his nose. "But walking into King Coal's lair? That's a boneheaded idea. He could take you captive and use you for bait."

Holmes had thought of that. It was a calculated risk, but there was nothing more he could do from Baker Street. He needed access to the East End, and only the Blue King could grant him free passage. "Is that why you volunteered to come along? To dissuade me from seizing this opportunity to find a young woman lost in all this romantic scenery?" Holmes swept an arm around the docks, neatly stepping around a mass of gulls fighting over something dead.

The Schoolmaster snorted, unperturbed. "I came to watch your back. Better me than the doctor on this one, I think. I'm not so likely to be tripped up by a sense of honor."

Holmes cleared his throat. "True." When they knew where to look, he'd take Watson to rescue Evelina, to be brave and kind and to say the right words. But not today, just in case they went the way of the match girls. Come to think of it, he should have left the Schoolmaster behind. The entire Baskerville affair depended on the young man, but he did more than his share of work without complaint. It was easy to forget he wasn't just another rebel soldier.

Holmes shoved down his misgivings, his guilt, and his grief, until they passed through his mind like strains of music from another room. There, but distant. They beckoned, they edged his way, but he did not let them close. At times like this, emotions were a drug to be carefully administered. Just enough gave strength. Too much rendered a person—most people—useless. And he had to ration just how much he cared if he wanted to keep a clear head.

"Where is this warehouse?" he asked. The Violet Queen had her headquarters in a bordello, the Gold King in a palatial suite of offices. The Blue King, in keeping with the neighborhood, had his in a dockyard.

"There," said the Schoolmaster, shouting a little to be heard over the racket of the dockworkers. He pointed ahead to where the river curved, giving a view of the buildings ahead. "Between the two taller buildings."

They carried on, getting closer. The Blue King's headquarters looked nondescript at first glance, a coffee wholesaler to the right, a chop house to the left. It was a main floor and two above, each with a row of eight windows with no blinds or curtains. It looked utilitarian to the point of seediness. Holmes wanted to ask if the Schoolmaster was sure, but then took another, more careful, look. There were large men standing outside, spaced neatly apart, most holding a stout club with an air that said they never so much as bathed without it close by. He saw a baker carrying a tray of bread to the side door. There was a dog digging in a scrap heap. The mutt carried off a bone most of the locals would have used for their own meal. *When is poverty not poverty?* Holmes asked himself. *When the Blue King lives there. And now it is time to set this comedy in motion.*

"You stay here," he said to the Schoolmaster. "If I don't emerge in a half hour, I urge you to contact Inspector Lestrade of Scotland Yard."

"Am I to believe you haven't already told him what you're up to, just in case?" The Schoolmaster lifted his green-tinted glasses to give him raised eyebrows.

"If I am incapacitated, he will have to take up the search for my niece."

"And you haven't got every plod in London on the lookout for Miss Cooper already?"

Holmes returned the look impassively. "Of course they are."

Lestrade had jumped to his aid at once, but Scotland Yard was already burdened with a series of murders—and the same interjurisdictional tension that plagued their work from time to time hampered Holmes's case. If Evelina had passed within the borders of the square mile surrounding Westminster—just a few streets away from Whitechapel—she would be in the territory of the City, and it had its own police. Depending on the detectives involved, each force could sit on its own files like broody hens.

But that was off topic. "I don't want the Blue Boys getting a good look at you."

"Robbing me of my hour in the footlights?"

Holmes ignored the sally. "You're more valuable than I am."

"Dunno about that. I just know people who make things."

"That's like saying the queen has a large chair. Nuance is everything." He turned and stopped, forcing the Schoolmaster to look him in the eye. People shoved by, unimpressed by two men blocking the path. "If they tortured you, what would they learn?"

The Schoolmaster's lips pressed together, forming a grim line.

"I thought so," said Holmes. *Fool. He's as bad as Watson, trying to throw himself in harm's way for the sake of the Great Detective.*

"Doesn't seem right, letting you go in alone. That's not what friends do."

Holmes couldn't stop the wrench of irritation that made him grip his sword cane until the wood creaked. "That's why I'm here. So someone isn't thinking sentimentally."

The Schoolmaster flushed. "Then if you must do this by yourself, for God's sake be careful."

"Always." Holmes touched the brim of his hat. "Wait here."

This time the Schoolmaster stayed put, drifting toward

the window of a down-at-heel bookshop. Holmes went on, much relieved. He had his niece on his conscience; that was quite enough for now.

The sign over the warehouse door read Old Blue Gas and Rail, Mr. Robert Blount, Esq., Prop. Holmes was just reaching the short walkway to the door when two of the large men with clubs converged. He nodded politely. "I am here to see Mr. Blount."

"Not at home," said the larger of the two. He was bald, with a soft cap on his bullet head and the loose, practical clothes of the dockworkers—except his were new and clean.

Another man was approaching, this one smaller, with a pencil shoved behind one ear. "What's all this?"

"Sherlock Holmes to see Mr. Blount," Holmes said with perfect politeness, handing the man his card. "I received a letter with his kind invitation to call."

"Holmes, eh? Like in the newspapers?" The man gave a gap-toothed grin.

And if I die, those wretched scribbles are all anyone will remember of me. "Yes, the same."

"Right-o, I'll see what the boss says." And the man darted off, his quick movements reminding Holmes of a bird. He came back no more than five minutes later. "He says come right in."

The warehouse was divided into a warren of tiny rooms and twisting corridors, a few of them painted, most just bare wood and plaster. Barrels and boxes filled some, others had mysterious shapes draped in dust covers. Holmes's escort, whose name was Benjamin, led him through at a quick pace. When they finally ran out of corridor and the space opened up to a large room, he ushered Holmes past with a flourish.

More large guards stood just within the door. Benjamin joined them, standing against the wall and all but saluting the figure who waited within. Holmes strolled past, carelessly passing the sword cane to the nearest muscle-bound hulk before he was searched for weapons.

Holmes had never seen King Coal in person, and he found himself momentarily stunned. There was something almost

mythical about the sight, as if he were regarding the per-
sonification of Gluttony in some absurd pageant. To say the
man was enormously fat fell short. He was a mountain of
suet draped for modesty and enthroned in a chair. The chair
itself was on wheels, powered by a steam engine because no
human alive could have pushed its weight. In fact, three
scruffy boys strained to merely steer it into place.

Holmes, whose relationship with food was cordial but at
times optional, was fascinated and appalled. His revulsion
was not due so much to the man's bulk, but to the contrast
between his excess and the ruinous poverty around him.
One might have fed half the district on what this one man
must consume at a meal—more, since the starving welcomed even scraps. That, if nothing else, made King Coal
less a monarch than a tyrant.

The room reeked of the Blue King's body, as if they were
breathing his effluvia. Sweat trickled in a steady stream
down the rolls and folds of the man's slug-pale flesh, the
heat of the chair's engine rendering him down to oil.

It took as much will to look away as if the man were a
railway accident, but Holmes did it, forcing his gaze about
the room. It was all but empty, a few maps pinned to the
walls, a jumble of what looked like empty crates and spare
parts filling one side. The floor was a slab without mat or
carpet, the walls painted but scuffed. Gaslight flickered
from plain brass brackets. It might have been a factory floor
just waiting for the machines and workbenches.

A score of men, women, and a few children stood in a
semicircle behind the man in the wheeled chair. Some held
glasses and goblets of drink, others plates of food both
sweet and savory. Obviously King Coal never suffered the
slightest pang of hunger or thirst. In this neighborhood, that
had prestige all its own. *His warehouse and his men match
these dismal streets, but this is a throne room. It doesn't
look like much, but does that matter when you have what
impresses these people the most?*

"Welcome, Mr. Holmes. I've wanted to meet you for a
very long time." The man's voice wheezed, high and thin
like a punctured bellows.

Holmes gave a nod. "Mr. Blount."

The fat man laughed, the jiggling of all that flesh shaking burning cinders loose from the chair's engine. They hit the concrete floor and smoked until they died. "Call me King Coal. Everyone does."

"Very well, Your Majesty," Holmes said with a pinch— but no more than a pinch—of irony. He wasn't there to mete out lessons in humility but to get the man's cooperation.

King Coal raised a pudgy hand to stroke his lip. "I wasn't sure you would come."

Holmes narrowed his eyes, watching every twitch in the man's puffy face. "I assume my refusal would do little good."

"You think me impolite."

"I do not hold up Mr. Jones as an example of courtesy."

"No," wheezed the man. "I take your point."

"How may I serve you, Your Majesty?"

"You get right to the point, Mr. Holmes."

"There is little benefit to doing anything else."

"Then down to business." Another cinder fell on the floor, smoking.

Holmes tensed, but made himself hide it. *First he makes his request, then I make mine.* "Go on."

"There's a hue and cry over some dead whores. A mad-man with a knife. The women are afraid to work. Bad for business."

"The one they're calling the Whitechapel Murderer?"

"The same. You must solve it."

Confusion scrambled his thoughts for a moment. *Why does a steam baron care about a handful of women? There's a loss of profit, yes, but enough to warrant calling me?* "I am always pleased to assist the police, if they permit it."

"They will allow it," the Blue King snapped.

Holmes wasn't so sure. Lestrade was already complaining about Warren, one of the officers in charge. "I will do what I can."

"Answers. An arrest. Peace and security. That's what I want from you, Mr. Holmes. A little fear is good to keep the streets in line, but too much makes 'em restless."

Understanding snapped into place. *Riots. That's his weak point. He pushed the limits silencing the match girls. The whole of Whitechapel is already on edge, and this madman might just push them over.* And once roused, the East End would be a powder keg. Despite the best efforts of his street-keepers, there were already reformers, radicals, and anarchists thick on the ground. The Whitechapel murderer was a match hovering over all that tinder.

How very entertaining. "In return, Your Majesty, I have a boon to ask."

"And what would that be?" The king's eyes shifted like suspicious raisins in a blob of undercooked dough. He waved one of the attendants closer, plucking a sugarplum from her plate and popping it into his mouth.

"I am searching for two individuals who may be in this part of London. If you know where they may be found, I ask that you tell me. If you do not, I seek your permission to carry out a search."

"Who is it you wish to find?"

"A young woman and a man. He is a sorcerer who may have taken up residence in your midst."

"Sorcerer?" the Blue King scoffed. "We've precious few of that kind around here."

"What of Symeon Magnus?" Holmes let the name roll out crisply, watching for a reaction. No one in the room shifted. They'd learned well how to hide what they knew.

"Him?" the Blue King's manner changed, growing curt. "You'll not go bothering him, Mr. Holmes."

"He's dangerous."

"Not to me, Mr. Holmes," the Blue King said in a warning tone. "I suggest you leave him be."

It was plain that King Coal had an interest in the sorcerer—enough to put him under his protection. Did he realize who—and what—he was dealing with? Magnus's presence made matters much more difficult—including the awkward question about what to do with a man who couldn't be killed. *And whether he still has an unhealthy interest in Evelina.* It had taken Holmes some time, but he'd put together a disturbing picture of what had gone on last April. *I wonder if he could survive a bath of acid?*

King Coal shifted impatiently. "You said there were two people you wanted to find."

"I am also looking for a young lady."

"Ha! We have lots of them." Suddenly restored to good humor, the Blue King pulled over a waif of no more than thirteen, holding her hand to his lips as if she were a countess. "Any color, size, or shape you like."

Holmes hesitated, weighing the risks of alerting the Blue King to Evelina's existence. "There is only one in particular that interests me. Her name is Evelina Cooper. I want her back, unharmed and untouched."

"And good luck to you, because I don't have her. But answer my two requests, and I'll have my men mount a search."

"Two?"

"Two." The fat man rubbed his palms together, and then beckoned for another sweet. He tossed it into his mouth and talked around it. "I can't stop at just one."

Holmes was in no mood to bargain, but he could see it was expected. "If Magnus is off limits, I only owe you one."

"No, this is your kin. Yes, Mr. Holmes, I've asked a few questions about your affairs. You're fond of this Evelina, so the price goes up if you want my help." Again, that ghastly split in the flesh that passed for a grin. "You can search all you like for free, but I don't guarantee the Blue Boys will mind their manners if they catch you."

Holmes felt his composure crack, fissures spreading through it like a piece of glass about to shatter. He took in a breath, long and steady, praying it would have some good effect before he grabbed his sword cane back from the guard and spitted the Blue King through.

He would die, of course. There were at least six guns pointed his way—two in the gallery, one behind the side door, and three in the hands of the lads in charge of pushing the Blue King's chair. No doubt they thought he hadn't noticed.

Fury seeped through the cracks, eating away his control another notch. He swallowed, now not daring to breathe. *If you die, who will look for her?* Not Mycroft, who was too deep into his politics. Not Tobias Roth, who was so confused it was a wonder he could dress himself.

"Then two," he grunted between clenched teeth. "But I need your help now."

"After." King Coal snapped his fingers, and one of the guards knelt on all fours. The king rested his heels on the man's back. He wore nothing but socks with a hole in one toe.

"One before and one after," Holmes finally said, light-headed from the heat and stink of the room. "I'll solve your murders, and you'll mount a search."

"Excellent."

"What is your other request?"

The raisin eyes shifted again. "Things have gone wrong. Orders changed. Confidences betrayed." The king's voice, already thin and wheezy, whistled like a broken flute. "I look around and wonder who did it."

As if to demonstrate, the eyes rolled toward his attendants, but he was too fat to properly turn his head. The atmosphere shifted, as if every stomach in the room clenched with trepidation. Holmes braced himself, planting his feet a hair wider. Few ringleaders ever admitted such weakness in front of their lackeys, and he wondered where the conversation was going. But he didn't have to wait to find out.

"I am thinking that I should kill everyone in this room, just to be safe," the Blue King said so quietly that the utterance was barely audible. The threat in his voice sent skitters down Holmes's spine.

It must have had a similar effect on the others. Three of the attendants rushed forward, offering food and drink. King Coal grabbed at it, weeping, touching each plate and cup as if to reassure himself that it was truly there. Two of the women leaned over the back of the chair, petting the Blue King's hair, smoothing the collar of his enormous checked jacket. "It's all right, Your Majesty," one murmured. "The Great Detective is here to find out who did it."

The melodrama of the scene was thick enough to slice. Affected by his fawning horde, the Blue King began to blubber, nose running with slime. Holmes gazed desperately at the door. *Dear God, he's barking mad.*

"Get away! Get away!" King Coal cried, waving his servants off, but not before stuffing a third sugarplum into his mouth. "Yes, Mr. Holmes will find him, and then we'll boil the flesh from his bones. We'll make a dinner out of him! I think with rosemary and a splash of Bordeaux and, oh, maybe a daub of quince jelly."

Holmes kept his face utterly still and vowed never to eat any dish prepared east of Blackfriar's. "Are you able to provide specific details? Of the treachery, I mean, not the culinary event."

"You and I will have a private conversation about that," said the king, settling back in his chair and planting his swollen ankles on his human footstool again, now perfectly calm. His upper lip still glistened with snot. "Best not to let on how much we already know."

"Your Majesty is quite correct." But of course, he suspected it was Jones. How many traitors could there be? "But I have a theory or two you might find interesting."

The Blue King studied Holmes for a long moment and then flicked his hand toward the door. "We're done here. You have your orders. Go, go. Bring me the Whitechapel Murderer and we will turn the town over looking for your girl."

Is it a jest, or do I really walk away? Holmes nodded his head, and edged toward the door, remembering never to turn his back to a king. Only at the last moment did he wheel and nearly sprint for freedom.

Benjamin darted after him, doing his best to catch up. "Mr. Holmes." He finally broke into a trot. "Your walking stick."

Holmes wheeled, walking backward as he accepted the cane, unable to make himself slow down. "My thanks."

"What the king was saying about a traitor," Benjamin said under his breath, jogging alongside.

"Yes?"

"I'd watch yourself. I heard about that bomb." He stopped, glancing over his shoulder.

Holmes frowned, his interest finally piqued. They were in the doorway to the street now, the gray afternoon so close he could taste the air. He sucked in a huge lungful, expelling the stink of the Blue King. "And?"

"One thing you should know right away. The king said nothing about blowing you up. Someone else gave Jones those orders." The little man leaned close. "Someone doesn't like you much, Mr. Holmes."

Only half of London. And he could only assume that was the criminal half. Holmes narrowed his eyes, remembering the kiss of the gun barrel against his skull. "Jones was looking for Mycroft, my brother."

"Was he?" Benjamin tipped his hat. "Have a good day, Mr. Holmes. An honor to meet you."

Holmes stared after him, suddenly realizing that he'd been a fool. Keating and the Blue King weren't running this show at all, and Jones could well be just a mask for the real traitor in King Coal's court. There weren't many men in London who could play a game with so many twists. *Dear God this Baskerville business goes deeper than I thought.*

CHAPTER TWENTY-SIX

ALICE YEARNED TO GO HOME. SHE COULD SNEAK OUT, SLIP back to her pretty bedroom in her father's house, and pretend that nothing had happened. In that dream place, she'd never met Tobias, never heard of Evelina Cooper, and would never have a baby. She could be innocent again.

But that wasn't going to happen.

Her tan leather suitcase yawned open on the bedspread, half filled with clothes. She'd left behind everything purchased for her trousseau, and just packed the things bought before she'd lost her mind and fallen in love. She would have preferred to leave the suitcase as well—she'd purchased it thinking she'd have a honeymoon in Italy—but there was nothing else to carry things in.

This was the second time she'd packed since her wedding, and it would be the second time she unpacked. Her father had made a deal, and he would keep his part of the bargain. She belonged to Tobias now and would not be going home. Her father had told her as much in no uncertain terms on her wedding night, when she'd wept so hard that Lady Bancroft had feared for the child.

The only thing that had changed in the last five days was that Tobias had finally tired of the hotel and moved her to Hilliard House. There would be no honeymoon, but she didn't mind. In truth, she had started to dread the idea of being alone with her husband.

Alice pulled a shawl out of the suitcase and wrapped it around her shoulders, snuggling into the fuzzy blue wool. She didn't feel well, the baby inside her objecting to anything approaching solid food. It was raining outside, the dripping of rain on the window echoed by the tick of the longcase clock on the landing. *Last year, I would have been at a tea, or a lecture, or a musical performance. I always had the best gowns, my choice of entertainments, and a steady stream of pretty young men with an eye on my father's gold.* She'd thought she'd found something more meaningful than an endless parade of expensive novelty, but she'd been wrong.

I started out this wedding with a husband, a honeymoon, and a set of emerald jewels. I must be a dolt to lose all three.

Something had to change, and soon, before she lost her mind—and before she became so bitter it poisoned her entire future. But today she couldn't think of a thing she could do.

Alice lay down on the bed, curling around the suitcase so her head reached the pillow. She could have moved the case, but that would have meant standing up and she didn't have the energy.

It was only when she rolled to face the door that she realized Tobias was there. The sight of him filled her with a profound dislike she'd felt for very few people—a far cry from the adoration that had once left her breathless every time he walked into the room. Or maybe a person needed one to really dig down to the other.

"Going somewhere?" he asked dryly.

"Daydreaming."

"Less than a week and you're already planning your escape." He closed the door to the hallway, crossing the room so that he stood where she could see him without moving her head. "I'm sorry about the trip. I have something to clear up. You understand, I hope."

"No," she said. Somewhere about Tuesday she'd exhausted the well of wifely understanding. She was just a beginner, after all.

"Oh." He stuffed his hands into his pockets and stared at

his toes, the angle of his face showing the dark circles under his eyes. "It's a family thing. Something I think I could clear up if I could just get to the bottom of it. Of course the pater will have his own ideas."

Alice tucked a bit more pillow under her head so she could see him better. It was the first time he'd actually talked to her since the wedding. *He looks awful.* "Your father really won't like—whatever it is?"

"No."

"Well, you can love your father without agreeing with him. I know that well enough."

He gave her a cautious look. "I suppose you do."

Great Scot, did we actually have a civil exchange? She gave him a faint smile. "Can I help?"

"No. It's family business."

And I'm not family. "Fine."

He gave the suitcase another look, as if it might snap shut around his ankle. "I must go."

She didn't bother to answer or even move until he had left the room.

TOBIAS STRODE DOWN the corridor, down the stairs, overshot the door to his mother's sitting room, and turned around. He could see her through the half-open door, the muted tones of her dress blending into the quiet shades of the walls and curtains, gray on gray. Outside the window, the deep green of the trees was flecked with the first gold leaves. It was as if life lay beyond the walls of the house, and only ghosts dwelt within.

The rot that was killing the family had its roots in the automatons and Magnus and whatever the bloody hell had gone on with his father when he and Im were children. Anna had died—sad, but children did die. No, something more than that had happened when his father and that mountebank had made those hideous mechanical dolls.

It was as if a curse had followed them, along with the trunks. His father had abandoned his love of creation. His mother had faded to nothing. Secrets and schemes had sprung up like weeds in an abandoned yard, choking out any room for an actual family life. And, horribly, those schemes resulted in the whole forgery escapade. That had finally landed them in Keating's trap, resulting in the ruin of his life and—yes, he had to face the fact—that of poor Alice. She, least of any of them, deserved what had happened.

The automatons had power, or Magnus would never have taken them. And it had to be more than what his father had said. A magical backlash if they were destroyed? The father Tobias had grown up with would have regarded that as a dare. No, something more profound was at work.

Tobias pushed through the door, then closed it behind him. His mother looked up, her face shadowed by the brighter light through the window. He saw Imogen curled up in the chair to the right, a blanket over her knees. She always seemed to be like that lately—curled into a ball as if she was trying to burrow into the furniture.

"Tobias," said his mother gently, her tone holding neither question nor reproof but somehow managing both.

"Mother. Imogen." He grabbed another chair and dragged it close, putting it where they couldn't fail to notice him, and sat in it. "I need to talk about something that happened when we were children."

Lady Bancroft blinked. "Shouldn't you be spending time with the mother of your future children?"

He was tired of that song. "I think I can move forward more easily when I have the past put to bed. In case you weren't aware, Mother, Dr. Magnus is still among the living. There is every chance he still has father's automatons and will use them for whatever purpose he originally intended."

"For blackmail?" Anything with a whiff of magic was forbidden. Even owning the dolls would be enough to land them in prison.

"Was there another option?"

She didn't answer that, but stared off into the distance, as if seeing something long ago. That irritated Tobias no end. "Mother, whatever happened, we need to settle it."

She rounded on him. "You have no idea what you're saying!"

"Then tell me."

"Imogen is having nightmares again."

Tobias sensed his sister tense at the words. He couldn't blame her, after he'd ridiculed her the last time she'd brought it up. She wasn't one to enjoy the drama of the sickbed, and that's what the nightmares meant to her.

They always came before a relapse of her illness. Evelina had been the one who had nursed her when the two of them were at school. Tobias didn't have a clue how to deal with it.

"I'm sorry to hear that, but I don't see what it has to do with the automatons."

"They're in it," Imogen said softly.

"Say that again?"

"Sometimes the automatons are in the nightmares. I think because Father made them to keep Anna and I happy when we were sick. They danced and brought food and made the beds, because everyone was afraid of contagion. And then when I got a little better and Anna didn't, they went with her to the tower."

The east tower in the castle they'd grown up in. Their father had been the Austrian ambassador, the castle a black-stoned edifice that looked over an alpine cliff. If one had vertigo, it was a bad place to live. "I can see having nightmares about the tower."

"It's more than that. It's . . . them." Imogen looked down, curling into a ball. "I've started to dream of other things, too, like I told you, Tobias." She cast a look at him, clearly hoping he said nothing about the fact that now she was dreaming about murder.

Guilt flooded him. He knew his sister had been having a rough time of things—her suitors going at each other with pistols, being separated from her best friend, and watching his carriage wreck of a marriage. She wasn't strong, and he was doing nothing to help her. Still, that wasn't why he was here.

He turned to his mother. "What happened with the automatons? Every thread of misfortune in this family leads back to that moment."

"That is none of your business, young man." It was both the answer he expected, and not.

"Tobias," Imogen protested softly, but he ignored her.

"Why not?" he demanded.

"My first care is for my children."

She'd taken that line with him before, and it had stopped him in his tracks. He wasn't about to let that happen this time. "I know. I know it wholeheartedly, and I honor you for it. But saying that doesn't answer a damned thing."

It didn't answer why, over the years, her personality was fading from view, the distinctness of her being seeming to blur until he wasn't sure where his mother began and ended. Was she part of their father, or a separate person? Was she part of the house perhaps? Or the ocean of social activity that seemed to swirl and eddy in and out of the drawing room, leaving a silt of calling cards and invitations? Where Adele Roth actually occurred was a mystery.

But now her look was steel. "Your father would be furious if he knew you were speaking to me like this."

"He's always furious."

Until the time he'd tried to kill himself, and Tobias had smashed him in the jaw for that. It was hard to respect a man who gave up and left his family adrift. And for a few minutes, Tobias had felt like a man, drunk on his own self-righteous superiority. Not that it lasted.

"Your father is furious for a reason."

"Why?"

Lady Bancroft reached for her book, and for a moment Tobias thought he was going to be read to—some homily on filial obedience or the virtue of discretion. But instead she pulled out a piece of paper and flung it at him.

Reflexively, Tobias caught it. It was thick, soft stationery. Someone's personal monogrammed stock. He exchanged a glance with Imogen, but she gave a slight shake of the head. She had no idea what the paper was about, either.

He unfolded it, turned it right side up, and read the date. The letter had been sent that morning.

My dear Lord Bancroft—or am I still permitted to call you Emerson? When last we spoke, I reminded you of something I had of yours, and detailed something I wanted of you. Time is a-wasting. S.M.

Symeon Magnus. The handwriting was all too familiar, bringing on a primal, gagging revulsion. His mind was sucked back to the workshop where he and his friends had cooked up their lunatic inventions. Where Magnus had come with his offers and his projects. He remembered digging in the trunk where the doctor had stored his damned doll, Serafina, and finding the crazed diary of the man who had built her. The dead man had been convinced she'd been sucking out his life. At the time, Tobias had been so drunk it had seemed real.

Tobias shuddered, nearly dropping the letter. He'd mercifully forgotten all that. So many horrible things had happened right after. But Magnus was real, and he was writing to his father.

"Where did you get this?" he demanded, handing the paper to Imogen.

"It came by courier this morning. I took it from your father's study." She gave him a look that defied him to say a thing. His mother had never been the kind to even set foot inside her husband's private rooms, but apparently that had changed. "I recognized the monogram on the envelope. I thought it was a mistake. Magnus was dead. But I was wrong. Everyone was—and your tirade announcing his resurrection is hardly news."

"He's talking about the automatons," Tobias said, ignoring her barb. "I'm sure of it. He's still using them as a weapon. Why?"

His mother looked like she was about to cry. "I don't know. I could never get him to tell me. It broke our marriage in two!"

Tobias felt her words like a blow to the chest. For the first time in his life, as a husband, he had an inkling of what that meant. *There were no more children after that time. I was sent away. Was everything more fractured than I even guessed? What the bloody hell happened?*

Imogen looked up from the paper. "What is Dr. Magnus asking Father to do?"

"Whatever it is," said Lady Bancroft, gripping Tobias's arm so hard he flinched, "don't let him do it."

CHAPTER TWENTY-SEVEN

NICK CLOSED HIS EYES, FEELING THE SUN ON HIS FACE. AU-
tumn was creeping nearer, but days like this made it easy to
forget. The Posy Street market was a perfect place to spend
such a stolen scrap of summer—all one needed was a few
shillings and a pretty girl, and it would be perfect. But that
just reminded him of Evelina, and his mood soured.

"Are you coming or what?" Striker asked.

Reluctantly, Nick trudged after Striker. The Schoolmaster
had called a tribunal of some kind, and asked Nick and
Striker to attend. Nick didn't know what the matter was
about and didn't much care, but it couldn't be good. He'd
rather be at the fair—with or without a girl.

There was a round tent in the corner of the marketplace,
striped with black and white like something belonging to a
circus. That thought made Nick smile as he ducked through
the flap, but his amusement was short-lived.

The inside of the tent was dim and stuffy, the heat of the
day magnified by the trapped air. There were half a dozen
men already there, including Black George. It was so unusual to see the barkeep outside the Saracen's Head that
Nick almost didn't recognize him. Next to Black George
stood the Schoolmaster, who nodded, and then a jeweler of
their acquaintance, and finally two men Nick didn't know.

"Captain Niccolo," the older one said, and then his features clicked into place.

"Captain Hughes!" Nick exclaimed. Then he looked at Hughes's companion and recognized the young officer with the sword. Both were wearing the garb of common laborers, the wind-roughened features of the airmen suiting the disguise.

"And my son," the captain said. "Lieutenant Arnold Hughes of the Merchant Brotherhood of the Air."

"I wondered what happened to the *Leaping Hind*," Nick said. "I'm very glad to see you alive."

"The ship was damaged in the landing," Hughes said with an unfriendly look. "No thanks to you."

Nick shrugged. "Count yourself lucky that I let you down in one piece."

"But we're all on the same side," the Schoolmaster put in hurriedly. "At least on this one matter."

"Oh?" Nick was ready to get down to business. The heat in the tent was stifling, and sweat trickled down his ribs.

The Schoolmaster gave his easy grin. "Some acquaintances of mine live near where the ship came down, and went out to help. When they heard the tale Captain Hughes spun about a pirate and aether guns and cannons on wheels, they thought of me."

That said more about the Schoolmaster than Nick wanted to know. "Of course they did."

"And I of you, Captain Niccolo, for you are part of this drama, and should hear the end of it. You should have a vote on the fate of the players."

"The *Hind*?" Nick asked in surprise.

"No, the *Hind* is in safekeeping for repair, the captain's crew is healing, and he has volunteered his assistance to our cause. They have a happy ending."

"Begging your pardon," said Striker, "but doesn't that seem a bit convenient? Captain Hughes was flying under the Blue King's colors when we last saw him."

Hughes bristled. "I saw what you saw in that work yard. A steam baron might hire me to fly to Bavaria and back again, and as a transport ship, I'll take his coin. But I don't hold with building an army inside the Empire. Not when everything says it's simply to go up against another baron or, worse yet, against the common people loyal to their queen."

"Is there proof of how the weapons are to be used?" Nick asked.

"Him," said Hughes, nodding to a figure bound and slumped in a chair. Then he grabbed the man by the collar and dragged him to his feet. It was Bingham, gagged, and with his wrists bound before him.

"We've heard what he had to say," the Schoolmaster said neutrally. "We caught Mr. Bingham trying to slip back into the Saracen's Head. He was looking for the device you found there, Mr. Striker—the device that no doubt gave away our rendezvous at the tannery and the location of the *Red Jack* that night. Apparently Mr. Bingham is a compatriot of Elias Jones, and we're here to decide his fate. Actually, the real question is whether we have any further use for him."

From the looks of him, Bingham hadn't been a willing talker, but Nick felt no pity. "He tried to kill Striker in a bar fight. Why?"

Striker stiffened at the mention of it, his eyes going ugly.

In turn, the Schoolmaster's pleasant face grew serious. "You saw the Blue King's devices. Bingham ran home in the confusion after the *Hind* foundered, but his next set of orders were to march right back and do away with everyone on that flight to keep word of the wheel guns from spreading."

That was as much as Nick suspected.

"Of course," the Schoolmaster added, "everyone in my network now knows the guns exist, thanks to Captain Hughes."

He caught Nick's eye, clearly wondering why he hadn't come forward with the information. The truth was, Nick was still playing his cards close to his chest. He was a pirate, not a political man, and he rather liked it that way.

"I have a question," said Striker, breaking the tension. "When I opened up the listening device, it didn't work like any I'd seen before. It doesn't write sounds down, like a wax cylinder device. It's all electric pulses, like a telegraph code. Damned clever, because someone gets that information the moment it's overheard by the device. The old way someone has to pick it up before they learn what's on it."

"The question?" the Schoolmaster asked, obviously fascinated by the news.

"Who made it?"

This had a galvanizing effect on Bingham. He tore himself out of Hughes's grip and lurched forward, diving for the entrance to the tent. Nick was closest, so he moved to intercept. The man was heavier, and he was desperate, smashing into Nick with a grunt. Nick felt his feet leave the ground and his hat fly off, but he dragged Bingham with him, using momentum to topple the running man. From there, it was no contest. The prisoner's hands were bound, and Nick rolled him facedown. Then he put a knee between Bingham's shoulders, applying just enough pressure to pin him without cutting off his air. Nick drew his knife and sliced the knot of the man's gag. Bingham stunk with the heat and lack of soap and water.

"You heard the question," Nick said in a hard voice. "Who made the device?"

The man spit out the cloth, but said nothing. Nick tickled the skin below his ear with the knife point. Bingham flinched.

"Speak up," Nick said, the words almost singsong.

The man cursed. Striker hovered at Nick's side, the others still in their places but watching intently. Tears of fright leaked from Bingham's tightly squeezed eyelids.

"What more can you tell us that you haven't already said?" Nick asked. "What can you have to gain by running now?"

"Bloody Baskervilles!" Bingham cursed.

Baskervilles? That was the code name the Schoolmaster had used. Was that what the Schoolmaster had meant by his network? *Now there's a fascinating tidbit.*

"I've told you everything!" The man's voice was little more than a croak.

Nick let the cold steel linger against Bingham's jaw, rasping a week's worth of beard. "Confess."

"It came from the Gold King."

Bloody hell. He remembered Mycroft Holmes's words about Elias Jones. *He went to work for the Blue King, and ended up serving the Gold.* This was the same. "And did you tell the Gold King all about the Blue King's army?"

"No!" Bingham squirmed despite Nick's blade.

"Keeping a bit of insurance?"

"God help me, I wanted to protect my skin. I needed to hold something back, something on both of them. Just like no one else knows about the device in the Saracen's Head."

Nick almost laughed. "So the Gold King knows nothing of the army, and King Coal has no idea you have clockwork spies in his backyard, and yet you work for both men?"

"I'm not the worst snake in either of their camps!"

"Such a false friend you are. It's enough to make a man pity those poor steam barons."

"Give me half a chance to prove myself. I'll work for you."

Nick craned his neck to look at the Schoolmaster. There was no surprise in the young man's eyes. "I think not, Mr. Bingham," said the Schoolmaster. "If you would let our guest up, Captain Niccolo, we can get on with our meeting. I don't think we'll have any trouble coming to a decision about this gentleman's fate."

Striker gave an unpleasant laugh.

"We could always return him to the Blue King. Or the Gold." The Schoolmaster gave one of his trademark grins. "I'm fond of making a neighborly gesture, and I understand Their Majesties have a wicked taste for traitors."

"HE WAS A nice enough gentleman," Gareth said, mangling the word to "genlmun." "A straightforward enough piece o' work to send him home happy, but no one ever wants him hanging about. He has this dog that looks like a hedgehog."

Evelina was striding briskly down Commercial Street, Gareth loping alongside. She gave him a sideways look. "Is that another one of those code phrases the girls at Miss Hya-cinth's use?"

"What?" He gave her a lopsided grin.

"The hedgehog thing," she answered, her cheeks heating. She knew a lot of slang, but sometimes Gareth came out with expressions that were as rude as they were perplexing.

"Ha! You're seeing corruption around every corner, you are. It was a dog. Some French thing with hair like a shoe shine brush, and he kept it on a long blue ribbon. It yapped the whole time he was with Miss Lucy. Until Mr. O'Neill sat on it, and it bit the old bugger in the arse."

A flower cart rumbled by, drowning out whatever punch line came next. The street was busy as usual, so crammed with vehicles and pedestrians Evelina had to work to stay at Gareth's side. She was getting good at jabbing people with her elbows.

A young man was rushing toward them, a bundle under one arm, his head down. Evelina stepped to the side just quickly enough to avoid a collision, but when she caught sight of his profile, she gasped.

Gareth looked from one to the other with lively interest in his violet eyes. "Who's this, then?"

Panic exploded in Evelina's chest, drying her mouth and sending her stomach plunging to her knees. *Dear God, I've been caught!* But she turned and walked quickly, doing her best to dissolve into the crowd.

Gareth trotted after her. "Who's that?"

"Mr. Penner," she said automatically. "Someone I used to know."

Gareth walked backward a few steps, looking curiously at Bucky. "You think he doesn't want to know you now? Or is it you who doesn't want to know him?"

"Maybe both," she said. "I'm sure there are a few people curious to know what I'm doing." Evelina cast a quick glance over her shoulder, trying to collect herself. Visions of Crowleyton snagged in her mind like burrs, making it hard to see the crowd around her. Four whole days had passed since she'd missed the Gold King's deadline of Tobias's wedding day. She had only four days counting today to find the name of the Blue King's maker, and she hadn't found anything new. There was a clock ticking inside her head, and every swing of the pendulum pronounced the consequences of failure: *safety, future, safety, future.* Her uncle's safety. Her reputation. Her safety. His future. And on through every combination of punishment Keating could devise.

Every instinct said her target was Magnus—the very fact of the Magnetorium, with its automatons and clever sets, proclaimed the maker's talents Magnus possessed but shrugged off. And yet, she had no proof—and she was getting desperate for any kind of a lead. So she was going to get out of the place for an afternoon and look for other makers. If King Coal had an army, surely someone had to know about it. After all, not even Magnus could build one single-handed.

"Are you all right?" Gareth asked.

"Yes, absolutely," she said, her voice awkward. Now that the first shock of seeing Bucky had faded, she allowed her pace to slacken back to normal.

"So why can't you go home?"

Home. The word conjured visions of sitting in her fine lawn morning dress, reading the paper and drinking tea. Not the thin stuff she got here, brewed thrice over from leaves already used and dried out for resale to the poor. But necessity had driven her here, and that hadn't changed. "I can't," she replied.

"Why not?"

She debated a moment wondering whether he'd give up sooner if she said nothing, or if she gave him a smidgen of information. One look at Gareth's face said he wasn't going to be easily brushed off. She glanced around, then leaned in to speak softly in his ear. "It's not safe for me, or for people I care about."

Gareth fidgeted, his face lined with concern. "What did you do, then?"

Plunged in thought, Evelina didn't answer. She was trying to think of the last time she'd felt truly safe. Perhaps in the instant before the bomb went off in her uncle's study? Or was it earlier than that, even, at Wollaston Academy? Or earlier yet, when she was that child with Nick holding her hand, sure no one was going to call her names or steal her things because he was there to take care of her? Or maybe it was much more recent, when Magnus had given her a taste of real power, and put it within her grasp. There was something to be said for controlling one's own destiny.

"Miss Cooper?" Gareth asked.

Evelina snapped out of her reverie. "No need to worry. I've landed on my feet, right?"

Gareth brightened, glad the cloud had passed. "Right. And I've got to get to Miss Hyacinth's."

He ran off with a wave. Evelina carried on in the direction where she thought Posy Street lay among a tangle of byways to the west. Her mission—should Magnus think to ask where she'd been—was that Casimir still needed some of those brass screws so tiny that she used tweezers to pick them up. She had counted on being able to buy them at the Saracen's Head but, of course, that sale had never happened. She'd meant to get some at Brownlee's on the way home that night, but she'd forgotten. Mind you, after seeing Nick, after kissing him, it was a wonder she'd remembered her own name.

"WHAT DO YOU make of all that?" Nick asked Striker an hour after the trial of Mr. Bingham.

"I don't see how they can send our prisoner back to the Blue King. He knows who we are."

They were walking toward the makers' booths, where a fortune in metals could be bought or traded if you knew whom to ask. Their boots moved almost in unison, kicking up tufts of dust. He caught a young girl looking, and she turned away with a blush. For an instant, he hated himself for being so unworthy of that innocence. But then Striker's question sunk home, and he forgot all about it.

"They already know most of us. But Hughes is going to take him to join Elias Jones anyway."

"How do you know that?"

"Hughes said. The Schoolmaster was just winding Bingham up."

"That's nasty," Striker said with approval.

"He's quite the bastard for such a pleasant fellow," Nick agreed. The Schoolmaster had gone up in his estimation that afternoon. He respected the fact that the young man had won the admiration of someone like Hughes and yet still had come down hard on a rat like Bingham. Fair but tough was good in a leader. Not that Nick was ready to follow, but he didn't mind working beside such a man.

"Should've been a pirate."

They stopped near the back of the market. Nick looked around for his men. Poole was somewhere at the fair, Digby probably back at the Saracen's Head. The others were with the *Red Jack,* idling while Nick struck bargains to sell their haul. There were one or two dealers Nick still wanted to see, and they would likely be at the market that day.

He saw one dark female head, then another. Then he realized he was looking for Evelina and frowned. Striker caught the look, and Nick did his best to wipe his face clear of expression. He didn't want to answer more questions about his history with Evie right now. Or ever.

To his right, there was a table under a makeshift awning, and three men sat under it. One was the jeweler who had been in the tent earlier. Another was a weasel-faced man Nick recognized as a pawnbroker who catered to the wealthy, the third a tall, lanky friend of the Schoolmaster named Michael Edgerton. They were near enough that Nick could hear their conversation.

"Bancroft?" Edgerton was saying in a low voice. "I don't believe it. I know the man."

That caught Nick's interest. Edgerton was a toff, well dressed and well spoken, but hated the steam barons who had put his father's foundries out of business over the last few months. He'd thrown in with the Schoolmaster and quickly become his right-hand man because he was a maker and as shrewd as they came. And if Nick had his facts straight, Edgerton had been friends with Tobias Roth—

though that friendship had ended when Roth went to work
for the Gold King.

"He did," said the weasel-faced man. "My lord has always
responded when he could. He knows very well that any enterprise costs money, especially one so far-reaching as this."

The man put a black velvet bag on the table, and the jeweler picked it up, opening the drawstring with the efficiency
of long practice. Nick watched without appearing to watch
as the man poured a river of emerald jewelry into his palm.
Nick was no expert, but the fire of quality stones was unmistakable. The sight only lasted an instant before the others huddled around, blocking all sight of the gems.

"Very nice," the jeweler commented, peering through an
eyepiece.

"A generous gift," Edgerton said a little breathlessly.
"That will keep our makers working for some time to come."

"All for the cause," said weasel-face unctuously.

The Baskerville cause? Nick wondered. He'd kept his
ears open since coming back to London, and he'd heard rumors that the rich were growing as unhappy with the Steam
Council as the poor. He understood why Edgerton was
involved—his family had lost everything to the barons—
but Bancroft?

"And what does your lord wish in return?" Edgerton
asked, echoing Nick's thoughts.

"He wishes to be remembered when the time is right,"
came the reply.

Striker had been listening, too, and leaned over. "Bancroft's betting on the dark horse, eh?"

Nick frowned. "But just who is our dark horse? Does anyone even know the Schoolmaster's real name?"

Striker shook his head. "He does seem to be the bloke in
charge, though. Quite a feat for a skinny little lad, so someone has to be backing him up." He jerked his head toward
the tent selling beer. "Come on."

Knowing better than to come between a man and his pint,
Nick followed. He waited while Striker bought two tankards
of ale, leaning up against a fence and listening to the spar-
rows chatter.

That was my crumb.

No it was mine.

No it was mine.

Oh, now look! Someone stepped on it! And he's been by the horses.

You can keep your stupid crumb.

Look, there's another one!

When Striker returned, Nick was more than ready for the beer. His second in command moved to lean next to him on the fence. Striker watched Nick with the same narrow-eyed consideration with which he regarded a malfunctioning engine. His dark-eyed gaze was a palpable weight that made Nick twitch. It reminded him of the stare Gran Cooper used to give him when she'd caught him in a lie—a probing combination of scientific curiosity and acute disappointment.

"What?" Nick finally asked, taking a slurp of the beer and frowning. It was on the sour side.

Striker put on an innocent face, and it wasn't a good fit. Somewhere he'd found a pair of green-lensed goggles and was wearing them perched on his head, the brass and leather contraption almost lost amid his spiky hedgehog hair.

"What?" Nick repeated, his temper starting to slip.

"I spoke to her, you know." No need to say who *she* was.

"I know. You told me about Magnus."

"We talked about you."

Nick straightened, ready to end this conversation before it began. "You don't talk about that kind of thing. You'd rather chew rusty springs."

"She was sad." The man's dark eyes flashed. "And we blew up a sorcerer for her sake."

"So we did. Too bad it didn't take."

Striker rolled his massive shoulders, making the folds of his coat scrape together, metal against metal. "Yeah, a lot of trouble for nothing all around."

He left the statement hanging there like bait. Nick ignored it, stomach churning while the blood mounted to his head.

"It was fun, though," Striker said philosophically. "I'd been wanting to test that weapon."

They lapsed into silence again, Nick clenching his jaw.

Striker heaved a sigh. "So what the fardlin' hell is she doing here? And why aren't you taking care of business?"

"My *business* isn't open for discussion. And she doesn't want to be taken care of."

"Oh, bollocks. You don't leave women like that roaming around, Gypsy boy. Not anywhere, but especially not here."

"It's my—"

Striker poked him in the chest so hard it hurt. "I'm your friend, so take this right. Get your house in order. You're the captain. Your business is ours if it puts you off your game."

Nick glared at him. "I'm not off my game."

Striker glowered back, his dark face hard. "Think a while about that one."

Nick's face heated. "What are you saying?"

Striker repeated his battering ram poke in the chest. "You're walking around like a man who's sunk his own ship. Same as when you two parted before. You've got some choices to make, so make them. But make them quick, because you need to be sharp or it's all of our necks in the noose."

Striker turned and walked back into the market day crowd, coat shining in dull flashes. It was probably the longest speech he'd ever made.

Nick watched until the man had disappeared from view, biting back the dozen retorts he longed to make. But you didn't mouth off to Striker unless you meant it. And the man wasn't wrong. What the hell was Nick going to do about Evie Cooper?

EVELINA TURNED A last corner and found what she was looking for. The Posy Street market occupied a small square from edge to edge, the outermost tables squashed up against the brick sides of the surrounding warehouses. The booths were ragged and nothing looked particularly well organized, but the place was thronged. She waded into the madness of the market with a will to buy everything on her list. The day was clear and the late September sun still warm. In the press of the market, it might have still been summer.

If she hadn't had to think about chatting up makers and spying on the Gold King, she would have been in heaven. Color and plenty was here in abundance. There were baskets of smooth apples, pears, and quince, bushels of nobbly squash, and nuts in the shell. The sweet smell of the fruit hung in the air, overpowering the rankness of the drainage gutter running through the middle of the square. Evelina stepped carefully, avoiding rotten fruit, children, dogs, and squishy piles she refused to contemplate. A herd of geese terrorized passersby, earning a vengeful glower from a man selling sausages. Evelina recognized her pie man, who had set up shop beside a woman selling bread and buns. But Evelina passed all the food vendors, thinking she would save those until last.

She was looking for craftsmen who sold supplies. Two of the dolls required a touch-up of paint, and Serafina's dancing shoes needed a layer of fresh stitching on the toes. Embroidery thread was easy enough to find, and pale pink was a common color. The paint was harder, mostly because Evelina wasn't sure what she needed. Art and music had always been more in Imogen's line. Still, she found something to try. The brass screws were another matter—they wouldn't be on display. If she wanted to find anything here, she would have to ask the right people.

And, of course, once she found them, she could steer the conversation toward the question of the Blue King's armaments. She knew from her grandfather how much shop talk these unassuming makers knew once you got them chatting.

A man was selling cheap jewelry, the shining treasure gleaming on what looked like the remains of a black velvet curtain. But what interested her more was the steam-powered press that formed the cheap metal into the shapes needed for the gaudy bracelets and chains. Along with a handful of other spectators, she watched it hiss and stamp, hiss and stamp, wondering what else it might make if she asked. What the maker might know if she asked.

"Let me guess. We've lost your custom already."

She looked up, startled. Nick stood across the table, his weight on one hip. She wouldn't have noticed him but for his voice. He'd pulled back his hair, showing the clean lines of his cheekbones, and was wearing a low-crowned hat with a tuft of hawks' feathers in the band. Her gaze traveled downward, taking in the waistcoat of figured black silk, the snow white shirt, and golden watch chain. She'd never seen him dressed in such finery, and it all looked new. He wore his pirate riches well.

Something low in her stomach fluttered. She ruthlessly smothered it, or tried to, as he circled the end of the table, every movement smooth and deliberate, his weight perfectly poised. She'd never known a man who moved the way Nick did, like he was about to take flight. Well, she supposed he finally had once he'd found his air deva.

"I wasn't sure whether to run away from you or toward you," he said teasingly, his showman's mask firmly in place. They'd caught each other by surprise the other night. Today, he was armed.

"Am I less fearsome in the light of day?"

"That depends on how badly you wish to decapitate me for behaving like an ass." He tilted his head, giving her the full force of his dark, liquid eyes. In the sunlight, she could see the thin white scar that tracked beneath one eye where a knife fight had gone wrong.

The fluttering in her stomach started up again. "Decapitation is always so messy. But you didn't say anything you didn't mean."

"No." He drew himself up. "But we never gave each other a fair chance."

"You look good, Nick," she said, conscious that she had given up her finery to come to the East End.

"You have the advantage of me. They say a fine tailor makes a gentleman, but a lady shines under any circumstances."

His accent lacked refinement and, now that she looked more closely, his boots were scuffed and his fine shirt soiled with dirt as if he'd been in a fight. She was suddenly more at ease. Nick was still Nick.

And he held out a hand. After a moment's hesitation, she took it. His fingers were rough and warm—far from a gentleman's soft skin, for all his new clothes. But she felt the strength there, and remembered how well he could handle a knife or gentle a horse. She wondered what else his hands could do.

Like an eager hound, her magic leaped for his, but she firmly jerked it back. A public market would be the worst place to call wild magic—and that always happened when they were like this, skin to skin and with the unspoken yearning that it would be more than just fingers that touched. It quivered now, rippling over her skin like a breeze over a lake, raising her awareness of Nick in a way that went beyond simple touch. And with that knowledge came magic, bone-deep, earth-deep as the stuff of life itself. His power brushed against hers, making her shiver like the wind through pines.

And then it stopped as if a door had closed. And then their touch was just a touch, warm and human and familiar as from the time they had been children. "I can't believe this," she whispered. "There's no silver light. No devas."

He gave a slow smile, using his flirtatious showman's persona the way some women used fans to coax and tease. "Would my lady care to walk awhile?"

She swallowed, her mouth terribly dry. "If you like."

"You say that like you're afraid."

She didn't know how to answer that. "I'm not sure what's happening here."

His eyes were serious. "We got off on the wrong foot, Evie—and have been so ever since I climbed through your bedroom window last spring. I wanted to see you, desperately so, but I didn't give you any warning, and that wasn't fair of me. So let's take this slowly, take the time to get to know each other again."

"Very well," she said in a tiny voice. She slid her arm through his, feeling his magic as a low and pleasant tingle, as welcome as the sun on her shoulders. They fell into step, walking toward the place that sold ale and cider by the glass. She noticed people moved out of Nick's way, and that he knew exactly where he wanted to go.

"I'm not sure how you do this in your expensive Mayfair

houses," he said, still mocking, but there was a thread of uncertainty beneath his words. She'd known him too long to miss it.

"Do what?"

"Court a girl," he said slyly. "Do I bring you sweetmeats and roses and take you to a show?"

She dropped her voice to a murmur. "Can you even walk the streets without fear of arrest?"

"Evie," he said, his voice holding emotions she couldn't name. "I'd walk through Newgate if I thought it would win you."

"That's not the point," she said sharply.

"Then what is?"

She stopped and the crowd eddied around them. He was taller, and she had to tilt her head to meet his eyes. "I'm afraid for you."

"And you think I don't worry about what you're up to?" His words matched hers, edge for edge. "What Keating has to do with your being here?"

There were so many dangers caught up in that question, her mind couldn't hold them all. She put her hand on his chest, spreading her fingers against the splendid waistcoat. "You said it yourself," she said in a softer tone. "We take this slowly. Get to know the people we've both become. Then we can deal with the difficult questions one at a time, without fighting. It's too easy for us to fight, because neither of us has an easy temper." She envied Imogen and Bucky right then—they were loving people who simply wanted peace and laughter. She and Nick were far more volatile. They had also damaged each other's trust, and that had to be repaired.

Nick released a sigh, putting a hand over hers, trapping her fingers against his chest. The cloth was warm, but the silver buttons cool in the September air. He lifted her hand and kissed her fingertips, sending a thrill down her arm. "Could it be that one of us has grown wise?"

Relief washed through her, the tension in her shoulders seeping away. "Only in that I've learned to hesitate before touching a flame. The day I learn to leave it alone altogether is the day I attain true wisdom."

He smiled, and it was his real smile, quick and wicked. "Then how do we do this, Evie?"

"Perhaps we should begin with light conversation."

"Such as?" They began walking again, arm in arm, stopping only to avoid a near miss with a rampaging goose.

"Captain Niccolo, do you enjoy your time aboard an airship?" Evelina put on her best Society manner, and realized how much she had grown used to leaving it off. All of a sudden it felt as false as Nick's showman's patter.

"Yes." His smile finally reached his eyes. "Although I do miss my horses very much. And you, Miss Cooper, how do you find your new situation?"

She could hear him burning to ask exactly what that situation was, but he held to their agreement. "Tolerable. It is harder in some ways, but far simpler in many. However, I confess that I miss good Assam tea and baths with lavender." And she was very, very conscious that her clothes were worn, the soft leather of her boots starting to split because they had never been made for such hard use. Nick didn't seem to notice, but she felt like a garden going to seed.

Another beat passed. Nick turned away from the stall selling ale, and aimed for a shadier part of the market. The shadows were cool, filled with the dusty scent of the fading summer.

"Since you are buying parts for machinery, does that mean you're making your living with the skill at clockwork that Grandfather Cooper taught you?" he asked, the words painfully polite.

"Yes."

He digested that a moment. "Are you happy?"

She was suddenly taken aback. The question was so like the other time he had found her, back at Hilliard House. Just as he said, he'd climbed through her window then, wanting to know if she was all right after so many years apart—it had caught her utterly off guard. "I like the work," she said. "That part of it suits me."

He cast her a sidelong look. "Striker says there are lots of new inventions. Ways to signal without wires."

He caught her off guard, and she slipped. "They used that on the Baker Street bomb." Perhaps there was no harm in telling Nick that detail, but she hadn't had time to consider it, either.

"Who made it?" His words were sharp, and suddenly the fiction of polite conversation was gone.

Evelina quailed a moment, but her words came out hot. "Keating Industries. Jasper Keating tried to blow up my uncle, and Tobias Roth designed the remote detonator. Was that what you wanted to hear?"

Something flickered over his features, as if he'd figured something out. "I'd like to wring their necks for putting you in danger."

Without her realizing it, he'd somehow steered her into the shadows behind one of the roofed stalls. On the other side of them was a warehouse wall, giving them almost complete privacy. He plucked the string bag with her shopping from her wrist, setting it down at the foot of the wall, before taking her hand again. Despite the heat in their words, they couldn't seem to stop touching one another.

"What are you doing?" she asked, feeling a flutter of nerves.

"I can't go on without setting a few things straight."

"Such as?" Evelina was breathless, but whether it was from fear or eagerness, she couldn't tell.

"I'm going to ask you this only once," he said.

She could feel his tension through his grip and it made her stomach clench in response. "What?"

"Are you still in love with Roth?" The words sounded sharp, as if they'd hurt coming out.

He was searching her face. She wanted to hide. *I wanted Tobias. Did I love him?* She had, and she'd meant every soft word they'd spoken, and some piece of that affection would never die. But so much had happened in the last weeks, it felt like something she'd read in a book.

Nick stood there, his face utterly neutral, and waited for her answer.

Evelina swallowed, her throat raw with pain. "I loved who I thought he was, and who he wanted to be, but that person is gone. He wasn't strong enough. Keating killed him." The honesty of the answer surprised her. Some part of her had obviously been figuring things out.

"Then it's over?" Nick asked. "I don't think I would survive a third blow from you."

She closed her eyes. "I'm sorry, Nick. About the past. But there was always the matter of our Bloodlines. They never mixed." But now they were holding hands, and there were no excuses to hide. And part of her was terrified.

"That's not a problem anymore," he said, sounding almost amused. "Athena has taught me much about my Blood."

"So that's how . . ."

Before she could finish, he pulled her to him, warm and strong. A rush of sudden shyness took her, making her drop her eyes and turn her face away. This was the same old Nick, and yet he was utterly new. Her cheek brushed the soft fabric of his shirt. He smelled of soap and healthy male, and the flutter in her stomach turned to a delicious warmth. He tipped her face up, cradling her to his chest as if she were a wounded thing. And then his lips found hers, both gentle and bold, kissing one corner of her mouth, then the other, nipping her bottom lip, then the top. Evelina kissed him back, opening her lips to catch the maddening, biting teeth, and then finding herself lost in a deep, hot kiss. Then all sensation fell away but the taste of him, the heat, and the hunger.

"I thought we were taking things slowly," she protested.

"I don't know how to go slow."

His hands found the buttons of her jacket, slipped one, then the next free to loosen the collar. She'd worn ball gowns that had dipped almost indecently low, but Nick's lips on the sliver of throat he uncovered made her feel infinitely more daring. His heart pounded beneath the silk of his waistcoat, hard and quick against the palm of her hand. As she slid her hand down his chest, muscles jumped, live and electric, beneath her touch. A rumble came from deep inside him, vibrating through her. She sucked in a gulp of air, suddenly giddy with the contrast of the heat where they touched and the coolness of the September world around her.

His hands ran down her shoulders until he found the line where her stays cupped her breasts, then he let his fingers stray across the curve of it, his touch as light as a bird's wing. His breath released, a shuddering sigh, and fanned hot across her cheek.

Desire foundered her, filling her senses and leaving reason shattered beneath their feet. She could feel his magic now—bright as a sword in the sun, as a dawn on Midsummer Day. It was like nothing she'd ever known, and she realized that he'd been hiding the strength of his Blood since they'd met last night. It had an attraction all its own, the way the loudest roar or the longest mane called to the lioness.

"You have changed," she murmured.

He didn't need to ask what she meant. "I've learned control over my power."

"If not over some other impulses."

Evelina pulled away, needing to clear her head. Athena's Casket had taught him more than control; the deva had shown him how to marshal his strength, the way Magnus had been teaching her. She could feel it hard and hot inside him.

He studied her face. "You've changed, too. There is a new darkness in your power."

"Things have happened."

"Be careful," he murmured, running his thumb along the curve of her cheek. "I've always thought of you as my dark goddess. Don't take that too literally."

Evelina smiled, but was already wondering how she was going to keep Nick from finding out she was learning her magic from the very sorcerer Nick and Striker had done their best to kill.

CHAPTER TWENTY-EIGHT

EVELINA RETURNED TO THE MAGNETORIUM MUCH LATER that afternoon. She'd taken a long route home to clear her head, but she had promised to meet Nick again later that night. After so long apart—and now that so many barriers were gone—they both felt an urgency to make up for lost time.

Yet still more obstacles awaited. In three and a half days, she would deliver the Gold King's answers, and then— what? Go home? Have tea? Go walking with her pirate through Hyde Park on a fine day? Where did Nick fit with her life?

Evelina pushed through the back door to the theater and set her purchases down on the workbench. Her trip to the market had taken far longer than intended and the other employees had arrived. She hadn't mixed with them much, but she'd learned their names.

The ones that worked with the dolls were Franco and Vitale, and at the moment they were getting the automatons into their costumes. The two assistants didn't speak English—or pretended not to—and her Italian was limited to opera lyrics. And since she didn't want to serenade them, seduce them— they were both far too old—or swear vengeance, she was reduced to sign language.

"Serafina," Franco said, pointing at the ceiling the moment Evelina had set down her things. Then he wiggled two fingers, mimicking someone walking up stairs and then down again.

"She's gone upstairs?" Evelina asked. "You want me to go find her?"

"Up." He pointed, and then did the finger stairs again.

Evelina complied, mounting the narrow staircase. It was the same path she took to Magnus's rooms for her morning magic lessons, and it already felt familiar, the particular creaks of the old wooden steps a worn-out song.

Whether she liked it or not, Magnus had opened her eyes to the possibilities of her magic. Not just knowing how to use it, but how to enjoy it—and to enjoy the freedom of talking about it. And yet, while she wanted more, and yet more, the experiment with the wand had terrified her. It had reminded her that the road Magnus showed her would eventually go places she didn't want to travel. He was, and always would be, a sorcerer.

Still, she would learn what magic she could while she worked under his roof. Nick might have his air deva to learn from, but Evelina was of the earth. She had never been able to speak to Athena the whole time the cube had been in her possession, so there was no hope of honing her craft alongside Nick. Their Bloodlines might be able to coexist now, but they still weren't the same.

Unfortunately, if she wanted Nick, she would have to give up Magnus—and that meant no more lessons. *Three and a half more days.* And yet, there was no way she could let Nick go. Not again. She would have to make hard choices, and she was in no rush to do it. *Keating has to let me stay a little longer.*

She reached the top of the stairs, looking for Serafina. She found her standing outside the locked room, except that it was no longer locked. It stood open, curtains drawn, the floor dusty around the edges.

Curious, Evelina looked inside. There was a clean square in the middle, as if a carpet had been removed. And then shock ran through her, the jolt like a spell gone wild—followed by a tight, hard anger.

Open crates of mechanical supplies ringed the room—enough to repair a small village of automatons. *So why was I running all over Whitechapel looking for parts, if these were up here?* She bent to take a closer look. These weren't dusty, so they had recently arrived. *And if Magnus is in fact the Blue King's maker, he would have access to whatever he needed, wouldn't he? He simply brought these from wherever the Blue King has his stores. So why send me to Nick, unless . . .*

"Damn and blast," she muttered. So Magnus *had* sent her to the Saracen's Head to lure Nick. Magnus had always wanted Athena's Casket, and no doubt he had a bone to pick with the men who had tried to kill him. She'd suspected it before, but this was as close to proof—or a warning—as she was likely to get. Was he presenting a choice—her magic or Nick? Giving her an opportunity to betray her friend and prove her loyalty to her teacher?

Suddenly, in a simple, quiet way, everything became clear. On some level, Magnus was using her as bait. And if that was the case, she didn't want his instruction as badly as all that. She had to get the information she needed and get out—especially if Nick was in danger.

Evelina started as something touched her shoulder. She whirled to find Serafina standing there, head tilted slightly to the side. She'd forgotten the doll was there.

"Are you well?" Serafina asked in her strange, metallic voice.

"Yes," Evelina answered, a little unnerved that her distress would be evident to something that wasn't even human. Then she noticed the doll was staring into the recently unlocked room. "Why are you here?"

"I am trying to remember this place," answered the doll. "I remember waking up in there, and I was very afraid. But I can't remember why."

Evelina stared, forcibly struck by how different she was from Casimir. "What do you think happened?"

Serafina blinked her blue glass eyes. "Dr. Magnus repaired me and made me superior to what I was before."

"Is that what he said?" The words sounded like something she'd learned by rote.

"Yes. And I daresay it is true, but I do not remember everything from before."

So it had been Serafina's hospital room behind that locked

door. Another of Magnus's experiments. Why there, and not in the workshop below?

"I wish I remembered. There are times that I do not understand myself. My logic processor does not always seem to be properly assembled. And I am not like the others, and yet I am not like you. Is there something amiss with me?" The automaton walked to the window and looked out, every line of her body poised in longing. She reminded Evelina of a caged bird, too rare for its keeper to let fly.

"No." Mechanically, Serafina was perfect. "I think we all have days when we feel like we don't fit. And we all have days when our logic processors seem faulty."

Serafina turned her pure blue eyes on Evelina. "Is that really true?"

Caught between her uncle's rational universe and her innate magic, between the affluent world of the gentry and her childhood in the circus, Evelina's world was full of contradictions. "I am still trying to figure out who I am and where I belong."

Evelina studied the doll, the late-afternoon light slanting through the window to set her auburn hair on fire. It was almost the same color as Alice Keating's, and the blue of their eyes was the same, too—but there the similarities ended. Where Alice had a fully formed personality, there was still something unfinished about Serafina. *Just how sentient is she?*

"It's time for you to dress," Evelina said brightly. "You are to be the Beauty in the Sleeping Wood tonight."

The doll seemed to draw herself up. "I do enjoy that role."

"Your dress for it is beautiful," Evelina said, folding the doll's arm over hers in the same way she would Imogen's. Maybe it was because she missed her friend so much, and maybe because Serafina seemed to need someone to protect her.

"Am I beautiful?" Serafina wondered.

"Of course," Evelina said automatically. Serafina was the most exquisite automaton she'd ever seen.

The doll tilted its head again. That seemed to be its indication of curiosity. "Is that why people applaud when I dance?"

There were so many questions that it was like dealing with a child. Did Magnus never talk to her? "In part. But you dance very well. You must not forget that."

"I like dancing."

"It shows."

"Good. I feel when I dance. Just like when I'm with people who like me. Some of the people who come to see me dance like me a great deal. They make me feel, too."

They started for the stairs, Evelina pondering that last statement. "What do you feel?"

"Like I'm more than I am the rest of the time. Like I'm at peace."

"Peace," Evelina repeated, wondering what that meant for a doll.

IT WAS LONG after dark when Evelina finished her work at the Magnetorium and started toward her rendezvous with Nick. She had taken time to comb her hair carefully, doing her best to tame it without the scented oils she used at home. And she'd done what she could with her clothes, using the brushes from the dolls' costume trunk to make sure her hem and cuffs were free of spots and lint.

But those were not her only preparations. With all the talk about the death of Annie Chapman and the other murders, she'd strapped the Webley revolver beneath her skirt, making sure it was easy to reach through a slit in her pocket. Nick had said he'd be waiting inside the Ten Bells, but she found him slouching against the wall of the tavern instead, scanning the street with an air of intense concentration. He stood up as he saw her approach, tugging his jacket straight and touching the brim of his hat.

"Taking the air, Captain?" Evelina asked. In the blue-tinted haze of the gaslight, he looked older than his years, sleek and worldly. Her heart gave an extra beat as he began walking to meet her.

"Too many people inside," he said, one corner of his mouth turning up. "I wouldn't want to miss you."

Evelina was lost for a moment, not quite believing he was there. Joy stole up on her, making her smile before she knew it was happening. "I can't fault your caution. There are a few of the local beauties who'd tie you to a chair the moment they saw you. You're such a likely-looking lad, and they're not the type to share."

He raised an eyebrow. "I've seen the women in there. I'm not a paying customer."

Evelina bit her lip, trying not to laugh at his skeptical expression. "I think they would count themselves at the better end of the bargain nonetheless."

He drew himself up in mock affront. "Is my virtue at risk?"

"Oh, no, I'm not about to speculate on that mythical beast!"

"Evie Cooper, for shame. You have no faith in me." He grinned a moment, and then jerked his head toward the door of the Ten Bells. "Is this the best place for a private conversation, given the rampaging locals?"

"Probably not, especially if we run into Mary or Gareth. They'd want every detail and then some before they'd leave us alone."

That made him furrow his brow. "I know a better place. Do you mind?"

It was on the tip of her tongue to say she'd follow him anywhere, but she simply shook her head. Despite their kisses, they had agreed to take things slowly and already she was racing ahead.

He took her arm and began leading her away. She saw he had taken care with his appearance, although the waistcoat he wore tonight looked as if it was made of leather heavy enough to deflect a blade, and when she took his arm she felt the unmistakable shape of a sheath beneath his sleeve. Obviously, he wasn't as comfortable wandering the streets as he had been swanning about the market.

He walked confidently down the street, but his gaze never stopped scanning every doorway. His watchfulness made

Evelina uneasy, and she tightened her grip on his arm. He was warm and the night chill, and she found herself walking as close to him as she possibly could. She'd missed having the company of someone who might protect her.

"What do you do when you're not scouring the clouds for prey?" she asked.

"Buying and selling," he said. "Mostly around here."

"You already told me what you sell. What do you buy?"

"Supplies. A lot of food. You'd be astonished at how much Striker eats."

They laughed at that and turned the corner, and then turned another. The cats in these alleys were large and well fed, which said something about the rat population.

"Where are we going?" she asked, a little cautiously.

"Definitely not my lady's drawing room," he said dryly. "Are you up for a bit of adventure?"

She gave him a hard look. "Are you playing a prank on me?"

"No." His face was so close to hers, she felt his breath. "I'm not sure what you're used to anymore." He said it like a dare—almost like they were children again.

"I've not grown so fainthearted as all that," she said tartly.

He flashed a grin. "Then don't say I didn't warn you." He unwound her arm from his, but gave her fingers a kiss before he released her.

They had stopped in a narrow street between two rows of brick warehouses. Nick approached the back of one building and knocked on a low, narrow door. A metal panel slid open, showing an eye and cheek, and then slid shut again. A moment later a latch rattled and the door swung open, revealing a short stairway down into what must have once been a cellar.

Nick turned, holding out his hand. "It makes up in personality what it lacks in decor."

Evelina stepped forward to see a smoky room stained with yellow light. She took a deep breath before stepping down the stairs to the stone floor of an underground tavern. The door closed above with a bang and the clatter of locks.

"Welcome to the Indifference Device," Nick said, raising

his voice to be heard over the babble of conversation. "I think you'll agree that it's an excellent name for a tavern."

"I had no idea this was here," Evelina replied.

"It's off the steam barons' grid."

Which meant it was unlicensed, either supplying its own power or doing without—mostly the latter, from what she could see. The ceiling was barely taller than the patrons, heavy beams crisscrossing the room and adding to the oppressive feel of the place. The atmosphere was so thick with smoke, one might have been looking through a tobacco-brown sea. She had an impression of top-hatted silhouettes, straggling curls, and women stripped down to their stays and petticoats. Liquor flowed, and yet the atmosphere was more flirtatious than predatory. Here and there, she heard the sound of heated debate, but tempers were calm.

"Who are these people?" she asked.

"Students, anarchists, the odd rebel," he said wryly. "Once in a while, a pirate."

"I've heard a lot about the rebels since I got here," Evelina said. "Just casual chat in the Ten Bells." The East End was rife with anarchists, socialists, and suffragists, though few made any headway against the Blue King. Evelina surveyed the crowd. "I don't recognize anyone here. Am I looking at soldiers or students of philosophy?"

"These are talkers," Nick said, his lips close to her ear. "This is too open for the real ringleaders."

The cramped hole in the ground didn't feel public to her, but she obediently followed when he led her to a small, greasy table by the wall. He held her chair as she sat. "Notice how I take you to the best places."

"The singing's not as good as the opera, but the company is better."

He gave her a quizzical look. "You have left the ballroom behind. The last time I spoke to you, I never thought to find you in a place like this."

Evelina looked around pointedly. "You were the one who brought me here."

He gave her a pained look and was about to retort when the barmaid approached.

"Old Nick," she said, her voice teasing. She gave Evelina a look that catalogued every detail with frank curiosity.

"Tess," he said, a hint of steel in his tone.

But her smile was irrepressible. She was no more than sixteen, her skin still rosy with extreme youth. "What will it be?" she asked, tossing her head.

"Your best."

"Coming up." She flounced away.

Nick leaned across the table, catching Evelina's hand. "I need to ask you a question. One of the hard ones."

All at once, the familiar grin was gone. His face was stern, his eyes direct. This was a side of him she didn't know. Apprehension flooded her. Her fingers twitched under his hand, but he only clasped them tighter. "All right," she said. It was little more than a whisper.

He didn't waver. "You said you were here because Keating sent you. That you got on his bad side."

"Correct."

"What happened?"

She didn't want to answer, and he saw it.

"Evelina?"

"I don't want to drag you into my problems."

His gaze softened. "If they're yours, they're mine. That's how it's always been."

She looked away, suddenly suffocating in the smoky room. She'd managed everything so far, but it had been bravado carrying her forward. Like a rope dancer, if she stopped moving, she might fall. She was suddenly afraid to reach out to Nick. His dark gaze was enough to make her stumble as it was.

"Don't you trust me anymore?" he asked, voice flat.

"It's not that."

"Then why did you agree to come here?"

She took a deep breath, and then blurted it out. "As I said last night, Keating threatened Uncle Sherlock."

Nick's forehead wrinkled. "That's why you're in the Blue King's territory?"

"Yes."

"You don't think Holmes could look after himself?"

"He's not invincible. He was nearly killed in a bombing. A man had him at gunpoint."

Nick leaned an inch closer, worried now. "At gunpoint? What happened?"

"I hit the gunman with a broom."

Nick burst into laughter. Tess came back at that moment, clattering a pair of glasses and a jug of wine. She set them down without ceremony and left again, every line in her body etched with curiosity.

Nick was still chuckling.

"It's not funny!" Evelina snapped.

"Yes, it is." He sobered, the change almost instant. "But that can't be the whole story. What does Keating want?"

"He wanted me to convince Uncle Sherlock to disguise himself and blend into the Blue King's district. I said I would do it instead. That I could do a better job, given my background—which he knew about somehow. And then Keating said he'd let the next assassin who tried for my uncle have him if I didn't do what he asked. He'll ruin me, my family, whatever suits him to get what he wants."

Nick's brows furrowed, a mix of anger and sympathy. "What is Keating looking for?"

She hesitated, but Nick gave her another pointed look. She gave in. "The Blue King's maker and his army. Imogen overheard Keating and the Scarlet King. It sounds like there's going to be a war between the barons."

Nick sat back, clearly thinking that over. She felt his attention turn inward, and it felt like a warm blanket being drawn away. She shivered, and that brought his focus back to her in an instant. He poured out the wine, pushing a glass her way. "Do you care which baron wins?"

She hadn't expected that question. "No. I wish the whole Steam Council would melt in their own boilers, but most of all I want Keating to leave us alone."

Nick's dark eyes studied her over the rim of his glass. "Us?"

Her stomach fluttered. "Me. My uncle. Imogen's family. Keating's even using his own daughter as a pawn in his games."

"Tobias Roth?"

She refused to flinch. "Him as well."

"Have you found anything out about the Blue King's forces?"

Evelina took a sip of the harsh wine, stalling. "I have seen no evidence of his army, but I might have found his maker."

That made him lean forward again, reclaiming her hand. "Oh?"

She studied Nick's face, dread flooding her. The trust between them had been battered so many times, keeping secrets now would crush it forever—but telling the truth might be almost as bad. Evelina closed her eyes as if dodging a blow. "Didn't Striker tell you who sent me to the Saracen's Head?"

Nick's voice was tight. "Symeon Magnus. He was going to be my next hard question."

She opened her eyes slowly, tears already prickling in her throat. "I've gone to work for him. It seemed the best way to learn what he did, where he went, that sort of thing." Her voice was small and filled with apology.

Nick's face tightened. "You know what he is."

"He hasn't changed. He'd use me to get to you and the casket if he could."

"I'm sure he would." Nick released a huge breath. "I could shake you silly for taking such a risk." The words were mild, but the anger in his voice was like hot coals. They made her skin twitch and she shrank back in her chair.

"But I have to prove whether or not he's the maker, and not just for my uncle's sake."

"Why?"

"Think about it." Regaining her equilibrium, she picked up her glass. Confidence was easier with Nick and all the rebels around her. "Think about who the doctor is and what he can do, and then imagine that in the hands of a baron."

Nick's expression changed as that soaked in. "Death magic."

Evelina leaned forward. "He's quite capable of creating intricate clockwork—that longcase clock in Hilliard House is his work—but it's not his prime area of interest. He likes making machines work through sorcery. Right now he has a troupe of dancing automatons. And one is sentient."

"Then what the bloody hell is he building for the Blue King?"

"I don't know," she said. "And I have no idea where to look."

Nick picked up his own glass and clinked it against hers. "But I do."

Evelina nearly spluttered wine. That was Nick, always catching her off guard. "You do?"

"But if I tell you, are you going to run off and tell the Gold King?" She felt him tense, as if the knot was in her own gut. "Will it make you any safer than you are now?"

"The only thing that will make me truly safe is if I find a secret to hold over Keating's head."

"And then what will you do?"

It was the question she'd most wanted to avoid—not because Nick asked it but because she could not bear to ask herself. "This is the first time I've been my own person. Here, in Whitechapel. And yet . . ." She looked away, afraid to meet his eyes. "If I'm brutally honest, I don't belong here. The only reason I survived until Magnus offered me work was because I have money from Keating. I'm not really poor, and yet I still miss so many comforts. I miss my books, and my uncle, and I would miss the opportunity to go to college. I want all the freedom this life has to offer, and all the beauty of what I left behind." She finished on a weak little laugh. "That's hardly noble, is it?"

"I wouldn't want to be scraping by again, either. I've done all right, and I'll be the first to say there's nothing wrong with wanting a full stomach and a clean bed."

She bowed her head, grateful for his words. "I just wish I could have all that and be myself as well."

His face was a mask. "So what will you do?"

"Will you be here?"

"I'm a leaf in the wind, Evie. But if you want me, I'll be wherever you like as much as I can. I've never had a reason to stay anywhere before, but if anyone can bind me to a place, it would be you."

Is that what either of us truly wants? It was too soon to know. In truth, they hadn't spent any time together since she had left Ploughman's to become a lady, but she wasn't going to gainsay his words. Instead, she leaned across the table and brushed her lips against his cheek. "Thank you for still wanting me."

For the briefest instant, Nick actually looked flustered, but he regained his poise before she'd settled back into her chair, the taste of him still on her lips.

"I've kissed you," he said slowly, "but you've never kissed me."

"Perhaps you're an acquired taste," she said lightly, although her insides were quaking. She was not shy, but she knew she'd erased a line between them, and had no idea what she had invited across that protective boundary.

Losing Tobias had wounded her heart. With Nick, everything was more fundamental than that. He was a reference point, a touchstone for every instinct she possessed. They had been made from the same clay. She suddenly understood that if she lost him again—finally, irrevocably this time—she would lose a good part of herself.

"I've always wanted to be compared to Roquefort cheese." He turned the glass slowly where it sat, the foot of it scraping against the pitted tabletop. It was a nervous habit she knew of old, and it meant that he was searching for words. "I've done a lot of traveling lately," he said in a low voice. "One thing about being in my line of work, you do get out and about and meet a lot of interesting people. In a few short months, I've talked to lascars and scholars, nobles and beggars, all wanting what I have to sell. And you know, Evie, you're the only person I know who sees the world the same way as I do."

Even though she had been thinking in the same vein, the intensity of his tone made her skittish. "We grew up together, but we've been apart for a long time. There is a lot about me you don't know."

The glass stilled, the corners of his mouth twitching down. "There are some things that don't change just because you eat with four different forks at a meal. It's in our blood." Quick as a cat, he had her chin in his hand, his fingers rough on her skin. Inexorably, he turned her face to look across the tavern.

"Watch that man in the caped coat. The one with the silver watch chain." Nick's voice was furred with a pained blend of command and entreaty. "There is a world only we see, things only you and I experience. One that binds us together in ways we don't understand."

She wanted to argue, but couldn't—because what she saw was all the evidence he needed. The man in the caped coat was sitting alone, his head bent to his task. As Nick spoke, he poured a small measure of bright green liquid into a glass. It sparkled like emeralds—full of fire and shimmer, even in the murky yellow light. The man balanced a cube of sugar on a slotted spoon and placed it across the lip of the glass.

"He's drinking absinthe," she said.

"Have you seen it before?"

"No. But what else is that color?"

"There are other drinks, but you wouldn't find them here. Now watch." He let his hand slip away, the grip of his fingers turning into a caress.

The man lifted a pitcher and began dribbling water through the sugar into the glass. The liquid below churned with the drops, turning a milky shade. But that was not all that happened. As the bright color disappeared from the liquor, it seeped into the air around the glass, forming an unearthly nimbus of green light.

Evelina gasped. "The drink has a deva!" she whispered.

The glow swelled, surrounding the man. As he lifted the glass to his lips, it pulsed around him like a swirling cloak. Evelina watched with fascination.

"They call absinthe the green fairy," Nick said. "They have no idea. Once it's swallowed, the deva stays with the one who drank it for a while."

The implications boggled Evelina, but her thoughts snagged on something far more basic. "Why does that happen?"

"I think it's the wormwood in it. Your Gran always said it

was a tricky plant. The spirits that tend it refuse to let it go. And that's why poets love the drink so much. They see things not meant for mortals through the deva's eyes."

She reluctantly tore her gaze from the green-shrouded man and scanned the other tables. No one was paying the slightest heed. She and Nick were the only ones in the Indifference Device remotely aware of what was going on in their midst, and they saw because they both had the Blood.

And while others might belong to the Bloodlines, the gift had thinned and weakened over time, rarely reaching its full expression. As with Hyacinth's family, too many had gone to their death with their lands and fortunes forfeit. Even in Gran's generation, few could see devas, much less speak to them. What Evelina and Nick had was rare.

She turned to study Nick's dark face. His air was challenging, daring her to refute his proof. She couldn't. She and Nick shared a hidden and very dangerous world, and he'd just shown her how it bound them together. It was an obvious fact, but she wasn't used to thinking of it that way. She'd always thought of their magic keeping them apart.

"We see alike," she conceded.

His lips curled into a rueful smile. "Did I just score a point?"

She was trying to frame a reply when a boom resounded through the tavern. All conversation died in an instant, the patrons freezing to utter stillness. The only motion came from the flames of the tallow candles, dancing in the stifling air of the cavelike room. Evelina didn't know what the sound meant, but fear slid through her, leaving a coppery taste on her tongue. Moving on instinct, she gathered her skirts and slowly rose from her chair. "What is it?" she whispered.

"By the Dark Mother," Nick muttered. "It has to be the Blue Boys."

They were the Blue King's foot soldiers, barely more than street rats but as ruthless as fire. And if the Indifference Device was off the grid that meant it was fair game for their sport. The sound came again, and this time she recognized it as something heavy banging against the locked door. She saw one or two men tossing back drinks as if they might be their last. She turned to Nick, who was already on his feet beside her, settling his hat back on his straight dark hair.

"How do we get out of here?" she asked, incredibly grateful that he was there.

He grabbed her hand, his face grim. "This way."

He wound his way between the tables, working his way toward the bar. Casks of wine and ale were stacked to the ceiling behind it, and for a crazed moment Evelina wondered if he intended to hide her in a barrel, but he began veering to the right. By now the other patrons were stirring, more or less urgently depending on how much they'd drunk. The one constant was that they all tried to move as silently as they could, all too aware that there were predators outside.

Nick had just steered her around the long bar when the door gave way with a resounding crack. Splinters of wood flew down the stairs, then there was another boom as the door left its hinges. And then came the sound of running feet and the bellows and whoops of the intruders.

Evelina caught a glimpse of them—big men, some in cloth caps, others in the hard-topped hats worn by the fishmongers on the docks. Their only uniform was the long blue scarf slung over the shoulder like a baldric—and their many-barreled weapons.

The first two down the stairs fired into the crowd, clusters of bullets tearing through flesh. Nick dragged Evelina behind the bar, sheltering her with his own body from the explosion of glass, lead, and spilling wine. Bullets flew over their heads, crashing into the casks against the wall behind them. Ale fountained out in a torrent. There was a momentary silence, broken only by a wail. Whether it was a man or a woman, Evelina could not tell. With a trembling hand, she reached into her pocket, through the slash she had opened in the seam, and drew the Webley from the makeshift holster she had strapped to her thigh. Nick gave a quick nod of approval, drawing his own revolver and looking around. She could feel the heat of his body as they crouched together, her breathing quick and light, his barely faster than it had been when they'd been sitting drinking wine. She felt tears on her cheeks, though she bit her lips together to keep from making a sound.

Then shots fired again, and it was pandemonium—shrieks and the sound of rending wood as furniture shattered on the other side of the bar. Evelina peeked over the edge to see patrons flying up the stairs, their panicked numbers making up for the fact that most weren't armed. Nick nudged her and pointed to a narrow path between the barrels. Then he rose up and fired a volley of shots, hitting one of the invaders. He pulled Evelina down again, ducking a thunder of gunfire. Nick repeated his pointing gesture, more urgently this time. Her gun in one hand, her skirts in the other, Evelina darted forward in a crouch, turning sideways to wriggle through the gap between the stacks of casks, her scalp prickling as she imagined bullets flying at her back.

Nick was right behind her, catching up as she squeezed through the narrow passage and into a small room lined with crates of empty bottles. "There's a door at the back," he said.

It was dark, lit only by light leaking from the other room, but Evelina could see enough. A black ring of cast iron served as the door handle, but it was no higher than her knee. She lifted it and tugged, but the door barely budged. She cursed, too scared to act the lady. Then Nick shouldered her out of the way, pulling hard. It opened with a groan of old wood, opening a space only a few feet high and stinking with mold. There wasn't much to see in the square of darkness, but there was a ladder leading downward.

Nick flashed a grin. "You don't think I'd go anywhere without a secret escape route do you?"

She wanted to make a clever retort, but her mind was frozen. She just turned to start backing down the ladder. A raucous laugh sounded far too close, and she jerked with fear. Nick put a gentle hand to her cheek, the brush of his thumb a quick, silent comfort.

Evelina started at a motion behind him. Reflexively, she raised her gun. Nick spun, firing before Evelina had even figured out what she was looking at.

She made a terrified moan as the man who had been about

to shoot Nick dropped his own weapon, his legs gradually buckling. He hit the floor twitching, the top of his skull shot off. Face grim, Nick fired again, this time into the chest, and the man was still. It was over in a matter of seconds. Evelina stared in shock.

He shoved her toward the door. "Go!"

The single word snapped her back into the moment. Evelina dove for the opening, relieved to find that the ladder dropped only about twenty feet before reaching the ground. It was dark as only a place with no access to the sky can be. Nick pulled the door shut behind them, plunging them into utter dark. She heard him start to climb, following the sounds until he let go, jumping the rest of the way. His boots hit the earth with a soft thud.

"Wait," said Evelina in a shaky voice. "What about the others upstairs? Why isn't anyone else coming?"

"All the regulars know about the door. They'll come if they can."

Now that they were out of the worst of it, her head swam with a rush of spent terror. She gripped the ladder, grateful for the cold metal against her palm. The darkness pressed down as she took in a long breath, the musty air choking her. She tried not to think of that man's head flying to pieces, or that there were still people dying. She thought of Tess, the saucy girl who'd brought their wine. For a moment, her chest ached so hard she thought she couldn't stand. She wanted to have helped the others—the absinthe drinker, the barkeep, Tess—but there had been no chance. It had just been good luck that had seen them through.

She felt Nick's hand on her arm, steadying her. "We have to move."

Evelina wiped away the perspiration that ran into her eyes, then gave a single nod. And then she realized he couldn't see her. "Do you have any matches?"

She heard the rustle of clothing and the scrape of something on brick. A match flared, a firefly of light. Nick pointed to a dark tunnel ahead. "If we follow this, we'll come out almost by Commercial Street."

They hurried forward, covering as much distance as they

could before that match went out, too. Evelina had a brief impression of arching brickwork as the area beneath the tavern narrowed into a tight passage. "What is this tunnel for?"

"It was part of a sewer once, before someone dug so deep the waterways changed," Nick said. "Now it's a way to move things without being seen." He took her hand, finding it at once despite the dark. "We should save the matches."

"Won't we get lost?"

"Don't worry," he squeezed her hand. "I'm used to this."

He pulled her close, slipping an arm around her waist. It reminded her of when they had been children together, him helping her learn to ride a horse, or to walk the tight rope they strung for children but a few feet from the ground. She had trusted him utterly.

But now it was so dark, and they were underground without even the faded light of stars. She held out her hand, summoning a faint glow of witchlight into her palm. It cast a weak light, barely enough to see their feet, but at least they could move with more confidence.

"Evelina," Nick said in a tight voice, "that's not a deva."

"It's witchlight. I know Gran wouldn't approve, but I'm being practical."

After a beat, Nick gave a quick nod. "You're right, but be ready to put that out in an instant. There's no telling what that light might attract."

They moved forward, Nick keeping her within the circle of his arm. Evelina closed her eyes, her ears gathering information her sight could not. Small creatures moved in the dark, scurrying away as they approached. Voices carried from somewhere, sometimes laughing, more often murmuring low. Once, she heard an out-of-tune piano. There had to be other tunnels, because occasionally she felt a cross draft and sudden space around her, but Nick kept walking in a straight line, silent as a shadow. He held her close, never letting her stumble, but she could feel the tension in his muscles. They might have escaped the deadly raid, but his body told her that they were far from safe in that strange underground world.

All at once, he stopped. It only took her a moment to

guess why. The ground had been rising, and a few yards ahead was a short stairway leading to an ironwork gate. Beyond the gate was open air—and more Blue Boys. Evelina was snug in the crook of Nick's arm, pressed close enough that she could feel the throb of his heart quicken when he saw them.

She dulled the witchlight until there was just enough to see Nick's face. He jerked his chin in the direction they had come from. Wordlessly, Evelina complied, doing her best to move as quietly as he did. They retraced their steps about forty paces, and she felt the currents of air change.

Suddenly, he pushed her deep into the shadows, blocking her with his body until she could just see over his shoulder into the tunnel beyond. "Put out the light," he mouthed, his lips so close to her ear it was barely a whisper.

She did and saw at once there was another light ahead. Shadows crawled over the brickwork, flickering in a way that suggested flame. Nick saw it, too—she could tell by the way his muscles tensed. Then, some distance down the tunnel, a torch appeared, the light throwing all else into darkness. Evelina strained to see who bore it. Fear kept her alert, but even so burning the witchlight had tired her, and her eyes blurred with the effort of peering through the thick shadows.

The torch was coming their way, and soon she saw it was held by one of four figures in ragged dark clothing. She thought they were all men, but it was impossible to be certain, for they all wore something—a hat or a hood—that obscured their face.

They carried with them an aura of something fearful, a sensation that hovered between the physical and emotional. It reminded Evelina of the aftermath of a horrifying tale, or the moment one is sure to receive devastating news. It surrounded the figures like a fog. Distress bubbled inside her, pushing up her throat like an irresistible pressure. Her breathing quickened with the urge to whimper or cry out. Nick shifted, holding her closer. She was about to bury her face in his sleeve, hiding her eyes like a child, but then the group with the torch turned away, taking another tunnel, and leaving them alone in the dark.

"Wraiths," Nick said. "They don't usually come this close to the surface. I wonder what they're doing here?"

The Wraiths were like the Blue Boys or the Yellowbacks, but they belonged to the Black Kingdom, the member of the Steam Council who ran all things underground.

"I wasn't sure they were anything but a myth," Evelina confessed.

"They're real enough, Dark Mother forgive us."

"Maybe they're pulled into the Steam Council's squabble as well."

"Maybe," he said in a tight voice. "But they probably smelled your magic, so it's past time to leave."

Nick tugged her to the right, navigating fallen rubble by touch to find a crack in the brickwork. Nick wriggled through, then pulled her after. Evelina winced as she heard her hem tear. When they came out the other side, they were in an abandoned patch of dirt between buildings. Evelina shook out her skirts while Nick dusted the grime from his hat. She looked around, taking stock.

"I know where we are," said Evelina, keeping her voice low. "My room isn't far away."

"I'll see you home," said Nick.

A strange light-headedness took over. She shouldn't be talking about going home—it was too ordinary, too plain. Something dreadful had happened, but she was having trouble thinking. "What about the others in the Indifference Device?"

She could see in his face that he didn't hold out much hope for any who hadn't already escaped. "I won't trust your safety to the streets, not tonight. Someone—perhaps me, perhaps another—will spread the news of what just happened, and then the rebels will strike back. It will be a bloody night tonight, with the Blue Boys roaming their patch."

"Like Crowleyton," she murmured.

He gave her a puzzled look, but didn't press. Suddenly she didn't want him anywhere but at her side, because he was too precious to risk in a hopeless fight. "Then take me home," she said, her fingers brushing dust from the front of his jacket. "And be careful."

He smiled, but it faded almost at once. "Come on."

They slipped onto the road. It was far from empty, but there was a strange, jittery atmosphere that said people knew trouble was coming. She saw faces from the tavern— clumps of people on the street corners arguing, and she was relieved to recognize Tess. But Nick avoided them, herding her away from the thick of the crowd.

By now both of them were alert to danger, keeping well away from any but the broadest streets. Nick slid a knife from his boot, holding it loose in his hand. But when a pair of Blue Boys sauntered past them, he gave way, not meeting their eyes. Evelina knew he wouldn't risk a fight with her there.

They slowed as they came to the door of her building. There was no streetlight, but Nick drew her close to the wall, gaining the privacy of the shadows. "Do you go back to working for Magnus tomorrow?" he asked.

"Most likely." She was exhausted, and tomorrow seemed years away. "I don't have Keating's answers yet."

"I'll show you what I saw." He took her hands in his. "Then you won't need to go back. Please, Evie."

"Once I have what I was asked to find out," she said softly, "then I can leave."

"Where is your obligation to stay with a sorcerer?"

"I will have fulfilled the letter of Keating's agreement. Then he'll have to leave me alone, at least for a little while. That will buy me some time to think of what to do." Though she had no idea what that might be yet. She wanted vengeance. She wished she had enjoyed the opportunity to learn more magic. *Three days left.*

"You don't believe he will play fair." It was a statement rather than a question.

"Would you?" she asked bitterly. "Steam barons aren't known for their sense of honor."

"You have the makings of a rebel." His tone was teasing, but there was uncertainty in it, too. He was probing.

His eyes were dark pools, lost in the shadows. She wished

for more light so she could read his features. "What about you?"

"I've had dealings with them." He took her hands in his. "Nights like tonight draw me closer to their cause."

She understood, and that terrified her. She had grown up with the Steam Council, and they had always been the unbeatable villain, a dragon that devoured any foolish enough to challenge their strength. She shuddered at the thought of fighting them. Nick felt her fear and pulled her close, finding the darkest part of the shadows.

"We're together in this," he said, voice rich with emotion. "Neither of us leaves the other behind. Never again."

CHAPTER TWENTY-NINE

Mr. Baxter, coroner for the South-Eastern Division of Middlesex, has adjourned the inquiry into the murder of Annie Chapman, a widow aged 47. Her body was found on the eighth of this month at 29 Hanbury Street, Whitechapel, in the early morning. The jury returned a verdict of willful murder by person or persons unknown. The Whitechapel Vigilance Committee is questioning why the Home Secretary refuses to issue a reward for the apprehension of the violent lunatic, for surely such an individual cannot possibly pass unnoticed, even in the worst London stews.

—*The London Prattler*

London, September 28, 1888

HILLIARD HOUSE

1:15 p.m. Friday

IMOGEN SAT IN THE GARDEN BEHIND HILLIARD HOUSE, HER needlework idle in her lap. The bench was next to the wall and warmed by the late September sun. Some of the leaves had been touched by frost, the wind combing through the trees bringing a dry rustle rather than the gentle susurrus of spring. Her gaze was unfocused, not really taking in the cascade of pleated pink fabric that formed the skirts of her dress, or the last of the hollyhocks huddling in the shelter of the wall.

It didn't seem that long ago that she had sat there with Evelina, sharing secrets and planning for their first Season.

It would have been easy to wish that she could unwind the clock and go back to that moment, but what would she change? So many threads had woven the pattern they now lived, some of them from before she had even been born. And instinct said that those threads were headed for a fearsome snarl. She wasn't clever—not like Evelina or Tobias—but she had her fair share of good sense. And she had to believe that she was stubborn enough to get through whatever was coming.

But, oh, she was so tired. She had been sick again, and the familiar lassitude of her illness dragged at her limbs. If she could just stay strong, if she could just endure the nightmares, she would get through it all, but she missed Evelina. For so many years, her friend had given her the courage to keep fighting—but now no one had the time to sit by her bedside. They all had problems of their own—and a grown woman should be able to face bad dreams, shouldn't she?

She heard a patter of velvet-tipped paws, and blinked the world back into focus. Mouse was skittering across the newspaper folded on the bench beside her, whiskers quivering. Indoors, the creature's coat of etched steel was the gray of any mouse, but here the sun glinted on its hide and the finely articulated steel of its tail. It sat up, front paws tucked to its chest and a tiny sprig of heather in its jaw.

Bird was somewhere in the trees, enjoying the freedom to fly. Imogen knew her friend had sent the creatures for comfort, but the gesture had reminded her of the fact that Evelina had once again been exiled. And now she knew it was more than that—her friend had disappeared from sight. Only her adorable familiars were left behind.

"Thank you so much," she said softly. Mouse dropped the heather into her hand and she tucked it into her waistband. As she did so, Mouse clambered into her lap, wallowing in the mounds of pink fabric and soft petticoats beneath. The creature rapidly became lost at sea, sinking utterly from view. That was just as well, since Tobias was coming toward them. He wore a look Imogen knew well—something was on his mind, but he didn't want to admit to it quite yet. She wondered if it had to do with Alice or the automatons. To-

bias had been in and out of the house the last few days, dealing with the upheaval of a canceled honeymoon and his
move back into Hilliard House.

"Im," he said, settling at the other end of the bench. "It's
good to see you up and out of the house. Are you sleeping
any better?"

"Of course." She pulled her embroidery closer, covering
the sinkhole in her skirts where Mouse had gone down beneath the pink waves.

He studied her, gray eyes solemn. "You're lying."

"I'm telling you no more than you wish to hear."

He leaned against the back of the bench, angling so that
he faced her. "Someday you're going to stop being what everyone wishes you to be. We'll all be shocked, but you'll be
the stronger for it."

She returned his smile, but left it at that. Tobias meant
well, but he had no idea what it was to be a woman, or their
father's daughter. "Have you heard any news of Evelina?"

"No." Tobias looked away. "And you should stop fretting
over it."

She felt Mouse squirming. The creature had responded to
its mistress's name. "How can I *not* worry?"

"Because you're fading in front of my eyes." His brows
drew together, a note of frustration creeping into his tone.
"You've worried yourself sick."

"I'm her friend. You said Mr. Holmes is looking, but he's
not had any luck, has he?"

"Not that I've heard." Tobias flushed. "I blame myself. I
should have stayed away from her."

"Don't."

"Why not?" He swallowed hard. "Wasn't I at fault?"

"Blame isn't going to help anyone," she said, and her
voice sounded as tired as she felt. "We need to fix what we
can and move on."

But of course her words slid off unheeded. Tobias wasn't
done flagellating himself for what had happened at Maggor's Close—and right or wrong, it solved nothing.

"You need to get well." With a determined set to his jaw,

he picked up the newspaper. "You're still reading this non-sense."

"How can it be nonsense if it's real?"

Tobias made a huffing sound that was disturbingly like their father. "They embellish to sell papers."

"No," she said quietly, "this is how it was."

"How could you possibly know?"

"I'm still dreaming every detail before it appears in print." She took the paper from him, stabbing her finger at the headline. "This one—this Annie Chapman. I saw the tip of the knife sink into her flesh."

He started, his eyes growing wide. "Pardon?"

"I told you. I've told you a dozen times. I dream every-thing the same night it happens." Despair dragged at her shoulders, making her sag forward until her elbows rested on her knees. Her stays bit into her flesh, but she almost welcomed the pain. At least she knew it was real.

"You've gone pale," Tobias said, touching her shoulder.

The nightmares rose in Imogen's memory like bile, sick-ening and vile. Her skin felt suddenly hot and sticky despite the cool air. Her hands were shaking as she threw the *Prat-tler* to the ground with a sound of disgust. "I must be losing my mind. The only comfort is that we were in Scotland when they first happened. At least I couldn't have done the deeds myself."

"Dear God, Imogen." Tobias was clearly stunned. He had finally absorbed what she'd been telling him.

"The dreams keep repeating over and over, but there haven't been any new ones since we came back to town. That's some mercy."

"Im," he said, sliding closer to put an arm about her shoul-ders. She leaned into him, grateful for her older brother.

"I'm sorry to be such a bore," she murmured.

He stroked her back as if she were a child. "You need rest. I know how fatigued you get when you're unwell, and that makes the imagination play tricks."

Sorrow drained the last of her strength. "You don't be-lieve me," she whispered.

"Maybe. I don't know. I don't want to believe it."

It sounded like magic, and Tobias was like their father—terrified of such things. He would rather believe her mad than cursed with the Sight. Imogen pushed away from him, giving up hope of real help. "Maybe you're right. Maybe it is my imagination."

Tobias didn't quite relax, but he unwound a fraction. "You're doing the right thing, getting fresh air and sun. Would you prefer to go to the country for a while? Poppy could go with you. I know you seemed much happier there."

His sincere kindness made her want to weep, even if it was uninformed. The reason she'd loved the country was Bucky's presence—but now that Lord Bancroft had forbidden her to speak to him, even in a public place, it wouldn't be the same. At least in London, there was a greater chance of seeing him across a ballroom or salon, so she shook her head. "No. I love you for asking, but no."

"Is there another doctor we could call?"

"Please no, Tobias, not another one. All they want to do is give me laudanum."

He squeezed her hand, sounding urgent now. "Listen, Dr. Anderson is all very good for routine calls, but surely there are new men with fresh ideas. When did the nightmares start up again?"

She tried to remember. The illness had come and gone all her life, flaring up and then laying quiescent, sometimes for years. There had been a bad spell when the family had moved from Austria to England, and then again when they had first bought Hilliard House. Then again last April. "I suppose it's been stressful times that trigger it. The dreams of murder started when we were in Scotland, but before that they always seemed to coincide with times when we moved house."

Tobias gave her a quizzical look. "When you did, or when Father did? You were away at school the last few times you were sick."

Imogen blinked. He was right. "Maybe it's just the thought of change for the family that did it. All our things being packed and carried away. You know how I hate that sort of thing."

"We didn't move last April. You started dreaming then."

"But we had a murder in the house! It was a horrible time and more than enough to give anyone nightmares."

He gave her a significant look. "But that time's done and they're only getting worse."

She lifted her hands and then let them fall in a gesture of defeat. "I don't think another doctor is going to fix me."

With a look of defeat, Tobias rose. "Mr. Reading has come to call on you, but I'll send him away. He's speaking with Father at the moment. I'll tell them you're still ill."

Imogen gasped. "The Scarlet King?" So that was what he hadn't wanted to tell her. She'd seen something on his face, but she would never have guessed this.

Something like a smile crossed his features. "You shouldn't be surprised that he's fallen at your feet."

"I thought that was just his attempt to polka."

"He sent flowers twice."

He had, dozens at a time. They'd been scarlet roses, a bloody red that reminded her unpleasantly of her dreams. "I'd hoped he'd given up when he heard that I was ill."

"You underestimate your charms."

And yet she couldn't help thinking about what Evelina had told her about the Scarlet King's interest in poisons. She hadn't heard that detail from anyone else, which meant her friend might have learned it from her detective uncle—he would likely be privy to things no one else would know. And assuming the information was true, her first instinct was to protest. How could she be expected to entertain the attentions of a criminal? And yet—would that make a difference to her father, if he thought the Scarlet King could help his career? Lord Bancroft might not force her to the altar, but he'd play his advantage for all it was worth.

Imogen's mouth went sour as she realized that she wasn't sure how far her father would go. And she was even less sure that there was any point in mentioning an unsubstantiated rumor to Tobias, who had already sacrificed himself to the Gold King. Accepting a few flowers would be nothing compared to what he had already done for the family.

She began organizing her things, scooping up Mouse along

with her embroidery and packing everything into her work-basket. "I believe I should lie down for a while. It will make you seem less the liar."

They rose and Tobias led her inside, happy to do something concrete to help her. And all would have been well if they hadn't passed the door of the small drawing room just as Lord Bancroft had stepped out of it. "Imogen, there you are. Mr. Reading is here. It's time you thanked him for those bouquets."

"Imogen isn't well, Father," Tobias said. "I was just taking her back to her room."

"Nonsense, she looks well enough to me."

And she was swept inside the room along with Tobias, who shot her an apologetic look. Her mother was seated on the divan, looking slightly awed by the wondrous fact that a second steam baron had entered the family orbit. Resplendent in yet another red waistcoat, Reading rose to make a polite bow.

"Miss Roth," he began, giving her a confidential smirk. "I greatly missed your radiance once the shooting party dispersed. I had no idea until that moment that my heart had fared the same fate as so many grouse, shot down whilst on the wing."

Imogen curtsied. "Mr. Reading, you are quite the poet." *And how sad that you were not also plucked and baked into a game pie.*

"I know what ladies like," he said, the smirk turning into a full-grown leer.

He took her hand and bent over it. As she had been doing embroidery, she wasn't wearing gloves, and she had to endure the wet heat of his lips against her fingers. Inwardly, she writhed, and the bloody shadow of her dreams fell across her mind—not the images, but the dark, fevered atmosphere of the chase: running, hiding, cowering before the knife.

Reading straightened, keeping her hand longer than politeness dictated, but no doubt knowing that no one would correct him. Imogen felt his unwelcome interest like a wave of heat, but a smile curved her lips nonetheless. She was well trained, a good girl taught never to be rude to guests.

And yet she recognized the look in his eyes, and she stepped back with a rush of blood to her cheeks. That predatory look reminded her too much of the confused, angry hunger of the presence. It wasn't exactly the same—William Reading wasn't an overt lunatic—but it was a member of the same tribe. And it was similar enough that Imogen wanted to bolt for the door.

Tobias was at her side. "Are you all right?"

"Don't be concerned for your sister, Mr. Roth," Reading said with a chuckle. "Young maids are always skittish. They have the strangest fancies."

Imogen's breath caught at the edge of a hysterical laugh. *He has no idea.*

"Please, sit down," said Lady Bancroft from the divan. "I'll ring for more refreshments. This is a lovely opportunity to get to know each other better. We have so much to talk about."

They were treating him like they had her other suitors—the tea, the chat, the enthusiastic family intimacy. She could almost hear the unspoken lines of the parental script: *If only they could get their sickly daughter off their hands at a good price before the bloom was off the rose.*

Half in a daze, Imogen settled as far away from their guest as she could. Her mind clenched around a single idea, holding it with as much trepidation as if it had been a loaded revolver: *How do I escape this man? What do I do if I can't?*

CHAPTER THIRTY

A LITTLE OVER AN HOUR LATER, BIRD CHIRPED TWICE FROM the tree outside Imogen's window. They'd worked it out as an "all clear" signal, and Imogen pushed up the sash of her window as the clock on the landing struck half past two.

One positive thing about social protocol was that callers didn't linger long, even ones as persistent as the Scarlet King. By quarter past, the family had been able to scatter, Imogen supposedly retiring to her sickbed. The afternoon was sunny, so there would be no skulking in shadows. Either Imogen escaped quickly, or she didn't go at all.

"Are you ready?" she asked Mouse. The little creature sat up on its hind legs and she lifted it onto the brim of her hat. She felt it shift and hang on, digging its paws into the gros-grain ribbon of the band. Making a fashion statement was the best way to carry the little creatures, and fortunately no one recognized Mouse as the creature they'd seen scampering along the baseboards. In fact, Imogen had received so many compliments on her unusual ornaments that she half expected replicas to start appearing in the fashion papers.

She opened the trunk with her old schoolbooks—the one place she knew her maid, parents, and especially Poppy would not think to pry—and pulled out the ladder Bucky had made. Folded up, it looked like a fat dictionary with a heavily embossed paper cover. When she opened it, two hooks sprang out. She clamped them over the windowsill, pressed a button, and a metal staircase unfolded all the way to the ground in a cascade of wafer-thin metal. Bucky had tried to explain the details, but she'd only followed every third word. What she had remembered was that only one small person at a time could climb the stairs without breaking them. It wasn't perfect—the pitch was terribly steep and the whole thing felt wobbly—but she was on the ground in a minute, breathing hard but nothing like what she'd feel if she'd climbed down a regular ladder.

Another press of a button, and the whole thing folded right back up, disappearing into her bedroom and disguising itself as a book once more. Bird flew in the open window and then out again with an affirmative chirp that said everything was going according to plan. It bounced on the window to activate the button that slid the window closed, and then flew to join Mouse on her hat. Bucky had designed the staircase for purely human operation, but it worked much better with Bird's help. The two little creatures had certainly made her life easier the past few weeks.

Imogen put up her parasol and set off, leaving the garden by the side gate and working her way toward the main street. She had dressed plainly, though not so as to startle anyone who might recognize her. Nevertheless, she was out of the house without a chaperone, so she was careful to avoid the places friends of her parents would frequent. Plus, she was very adept at using the parasol to hide her face when needed. She'd had plenty of practice avoiding unwanted suitors over the past six months. At the thought of the Scarlet King, Imogen shuddered as if a cloud had passed over the sun.

She walked a good distance before she caught a steam tram and got off near the Royal Exchange. From there, she walked down Threadneedle Street. Here the lines between Gold and Green and Blue territories blurred, each holding a building here and a square there, all wanting a foothold in the business district. It was the farthest she'd ever been without someone with her. She felt curiously adrift, as if some leash might snap and she'd go spinning into the cosmos with no way to stop. The sensation was oddly appealing.

Penner Toy and Games stood halfway down the block. Imogen stood across the street for a while, just looking at the smart red and green sign. A warmth grew under her ribs. Bucky had wanted this factory and now he'd created it entirely on his own, with his own money, and exactly how he wanted it. She was so proud of him, it was all she could do not to point the place out to each and every passerby. *Bucky Penner, the man I love, made this place from nothing.*

She crossed the street and mounted the three steps to the door. They were painted in a checkerboard pattern of red and green. The knocker was a large brass lion holding a ring in its mouth, but when she lifted it, the thing gave a startled mew. Bird chirped in alarm.

She knocked, and the door swung open all on its own. "Hello?" she said, starting to feel just slightly nervous.

A toy train came whizzing around the top of the wainscoting. It came to a stop, a bell rang, and a tiny toy monkey popped out the top of the engine. "Card please." It held up a paw.

Imogen felt her hat shift as Mouse leaned forward for a better look. "It's nowhere near as wonderful as you two," she said, wedging her calling card in the monkey's paw. The train rattled off, leaving her alone in the tiny reception room.

She had little experience with factories, but she would have expected a place of business to have a desk and chairs for visitors to wait. Instead, there was a fleet of tiny dirigibles whirring gently near the ceiling, bright-colored propellers stirring the air. An elephant drank tea, sucking liquid up in its trunk and then blowing a cloud of bubbles that gently bounced off Imogen's coat. There was a unicorn on springs and a caterpillar in boots and—best of all, in her opinion—a bear that danced when you touched its nose.

"Imogen," Bucky said, emerging in a haze of sawdust and paint fumes. "What are you doing here?"

"I had to see this place," she said, reluctantly abandoning the bear. "I wanted to be able to picture it in my imagination, and you in it, doing what you love." She heard the brittleness in her voice and cleared her throat.

"Imogen?" Bucky dusted off his clothes and put his arm around her. "Why don't you come sit down?"

He took her into the back. It was much cooler there, and the huge space echoed with the sound of a half dozen men sawing and pounding, machines buzzing, and the hiss of an engine letting off steam.

"This way." They turned to the left, where a smaller room had been closed in, putting walls between them and the sound.

The room was plain, with a table and chairs and a mangy-looking sofa. Bucky looked doubtfully at the cushions, but Imogen sat on it before he could start fussing. She wasn't that delicate.

Bucky sat next to her. "What's wrong?"

Imogen looked down at her hands, which were clasped on her knees. "I don't think I'd be exaggerating if I said everything. I needed to see something happy for an hour."

Bucky gave her a lopsided smile. "I'm glad you thought I could provide it. But you know it's not safe to be walking about the city on your own. Yes," he bulled on when she opened her mouth to object, "there's the whole consideration of a lady's reputation, but we're not half a mile from where one of those poor women was killed by the Whitechapel Murderer."

That made her gulp. "I didn't think of that."

He lifted her hand and kissed her gloved fingers. "I don't mean to frighten you, but I won't sleep at night if I believe you might wander alone in this part of town when I'm not there to keep you safe."

She couldn't hold his gaze. "I'm barely sleeping at all. I keep having nightmares about . . . everything, including those murders. I don't know what's the matter with me. Perhaps my family has finally driven me mad."

Bucky touched her cheek. "You're worried about everything."

Imogen leaned into his hand, needing the solid strength of him. "Something is going on. I'm sure my father is plotting again. Alice is miserable. Keating won't look her in the eye right now. I think he knows she wants to go home." And all that unhappiness—the downright bitterness—was like a contact poison. She felt sick to her stomach at the thought of getting out of bed, and even worse when she wondered what other calamity her father, or Jasper Keating, or even her mother's relentless matchmaking was going to bring down on her head. Without Bucky or Evelina to turn to, nothing felt safe.

"To top everything off," she added, "Tobias won't even leave for his honeymoon with Alice."

Bucky made an irritated sound. "Tobias is an ass. And as a good friend of his, I mean that constructively."

Imogen couldn't stop a smile, but she couldn't stop the next words, either. "I don't think I can wait. The Scarlet King is paying me court and . . . and those dreams. They've changed."

Bucky frowned. "How?"

"The Whitechapel murders. I dream about them the night they happen. I'm terrified to go to sleep, because the next morning a woman might be dead." She bit her lip, afraid he would turn away, or change the subject like Tobias. She fought back tears. Worse than anything else would be pity.

Instead, Bucky pulled her closer, holding both her hands in his. She could see him thinking her words over, dark brows furrowed. "I'm the last person to understand such things, but to me it sounds like magic at work." He looked up. "Whatever else happens, you need to be protected. Maybe you need to leave London for a while."

She had her answer ready for that. "I want to get married now. I want to elope."

Bucky drew in his breath, his fingers suddenly stiff with tension. She didn't care anymore about what happened to her, but an elopement would cause him no end of problems, especially if he crossed a steam baron. Both the toy factory and his father's gun factories needed Jasper Keating's goodwill to stay in business.

"Say no if you can't," she whispered. "You've got the most to lose. I don't know what will happen to this place if we go away for a while."

He kissed her on the forehead. "I'll make it work. It might take some time, but I'll figure it out. I'm going to make you happy."

*   *   *

IT WAS MIDAFTERNOON, and Evelina sat on the steps of the Magnetorium. She was in a state of exhilarated exhaustion, still buzzing with the energy left over from that morning's magic lesson. It had been a grueling one, another session with the wand, and Magnus had told her to rest on the morrow. His advice had just made her impatient. She didn't have many chances left to learn. Magnus was a conniving schemer, essentially evil, and everything she'd been raised to loathe, but he was a good teacher and she was hungry to learn more. If it wasn't for the threat Magnus posed toward Nick, she might have invented an excuse to stay longer.

But her deadline was just about up again. She was already composing her next letter to the Gold King in her mind. *Dear Mr. Keating, I found a handsome pirate who will sneak me behind enemy lines, so please be patient while I determine whether your enemy's maker is an evil sorcerer who, by the way, is also my mentor in the ways of forbidden magic.* Best to avoid sending that note until she absolutely had to. She hoped she'd hear from Nick again soon.

She bit her nail, watching a rat scamper eagerly across the alley, skinny tail whipping behind it. She didn't want to know what it found so exciting. Then a moment later, the rat went bolting the other way, barely sliding through the claws of a one-eared tabby. *Even rats have their worries.*

"What are you watching?"

Evelina bounded to her feet, startled by the voice behind her. "Serafina."

She'd replaced part of the automaton's metal voice box with a piece of a violin's soundboard that she'd found at the market. It hadn't been an easy job, because there had been a metal housing in the doll's chest that she couldn't unlock, but persistence and long tweezers had eventually won out. Her voice still sounded odd, but it was less tinny than before, as if the wood had given it some warmth. Serafina touched her throat. "Thank you."

"My pleasure," Evelina replied. She was still mulling over what Serafina actually was—an independent being? Or just a piece of Magnus's magic? He had never really answered her question about what made the prima ballerina different from the other automatons. "What are you doing up and about? Who put in your pin?"

"I wished to speak to you," Serafina said. "Shall we walk?"

She saw that the automaton had dressed herself from the costume rack, including dainty boots and a long cape. It was a bit warm for the cape, but she doubted the doll could tell. And hadn't Magnus mentioned on more than one occasion that he had forbidden his puppets to leave the theater? But then she remembered the doll staring out the window with—what?—longing? And if Evelina was with her, she would not be unescorted. Surely there could be no harm in that?

"All right," Evelina said. "I'd put your hood up, though."

"Why?" Serafina asked.

Because you're not human and you'll scare everyone half to death. "You're the star of the show. You're supposed to be mysterious. It wouldn't do to have folk see you walking around like everyone else."

Serafina nodded. "If that's what people expect of me."

For some reason, her unresisting acceptance bothered Evelina, but then the doll was only doing what she'd asked. Evelina prodded at her misgivings, but couldn't fathom why she was uneasy. *Nothing is simple.*

They walked for a long time, Evelina content to wait and watch what the doll would do. Serafina examined the crowd and the goods in the shop windows with a keen curiosity that was more than a little charming. Passersby never looked past the hooded cloak.

"We spoke about what I remembered before I woke up in the room upstairs," Serafina said. "I do remember something."

"What?"

"I remember walking with Dr. Magnus at night, admiring beautiful houses. I remember waiting for him while he went inside and wondering if he had forgotten me. And I remember horses." She pointed to a cart hauling a load of barrels. "They were very large up close."

"What else?"

"I did not dance then. I don't think that mattered to me at the time. The dancing came after I woke up in the room. I think the ability to remember things was part of what I gained there, because I began to wonder about so much."

Evelina was fascinated. They walked slowly now, heads bent together like two friends gossiping. "What do you wonder about?"

"About myself. About people made of flesh. I know that I think here," she pointed to her head. "I am told that is also where you think."

"Yes." Evelina found the doll's expressionless face disconcerting. And yet there was something in the way she spoke—an unusual quickness, or maybe it was in the motion of her hands—that spoke of agitation.

"You have cables that move your frame, just as I do."

"More or less," Evelina agreed.

Serafina stopped in her tracks, head tilting. "But when you love, or you are afraid, or you are angry, where do you do that?"

A strange feeling of alarm seized Evelina, although again she wasn't sure why—outside of the fact that she was no longer sure if Serafina was dead or alive. *And that is quite disturbing enough, thank you.* "I don't know. We like to say it's in our hearts, but that's not really true. There's not a particular organ that gives us our emotions."

"Then where are mine?" Serafina touched her stomach. "I feel"—she seemed to search for a word—"*good* when I perform. I feel bad when Dr. Magnus is unhappy. But I feel very, very good when people from the audience see me. That is when I feel the best."

Evelina remembered their earlier conversation. "You are at peace."

"Until Dr. Magnus takes it from me."

"He takes it?"

"And I have to give it to him, or he becomes angry. And I can only take it when he tells me to, otherwise he becomes *very* angry. He made me. He can unmake me."

Evelina floundered, utterly lost. "I'm not sure what you mean." She was suddenly grateful that none of the clocks she'd repaired had ever discussed how they felt about their chimes.

"Look at the flowers, Miss Cooper." Serafina paused, turning her steps toward a window box filled with red geraniums, the fat globes nodding in the sun. "How lovely those are."

Evelina was fascinated by the fact that a piece of machinery saw beauty. "Do those give you peace?" she asked.

The doll turned her head sharply. "Do you mock me? That is not pleasant."

Was that anger? Despite the flatness of Serafina's voice, there was a note in it that was almost shrill. "No," Evelina replied softly. "I'm just trying to understand."

Serafina reached up and took one of the geranium blooms in her hand. Evelina caught her breath, wondering if she was going to crush it or pull the plant up by the roots. But that was clearly a ridiculous notion, for the doll touched it gently, setting the red globe to nodding. "Flowers look different in the sun."

Evelina let the air out of her lungs slowly. "They do." She thought of the hours she'd spent sitting in the garden at Hilliard House with Imogen, and a surge of nostalgia made her eyes prickle. Suddenly, the crowded street full of strangers and this strange doll was too much. "It's time to go back to the theater."

"I do not wish to."

"Why not?"

"There is more to see out here."

"We can walk again another day," Evelina promised.

"No, I want to be out here today." It was almost a child's words.

Evelina bit her lip. "Dr. Magnus is expecting us."

Now Serafina crushed the flower, sending a flutter of petals to the pavement. Wordlessly, she turned, her lovely face utterly blank. "Then we must go."

Evelina stood staring at the red scatter at Serafina's feet, not sure how to react. If the doll was a child, she would have called that a tantrum, or at least a rebellion. Serafina had mentioned Magnus growing angry with her. Did Magnus take her peace—whatever that meant—because he was a disciplinarian? Did he need to be, to keep control of her? She recalled his vague warnings about Serafina's moods the very first afternoon she had come to the theater. Evelina looked around nervously. They had gone a long way down Bishopsgate and the Magnetorium suddenly felt very far away.

And then she spotted a familiar figure across the street. It was so unexpected, she jumped in alarm, her first instinct to hide until she realized there was no reason that anyone would recognize her in her rumpled traveling clothes and in a neighborhood where the Evelina Cooper of old did not belong.

As her thoughts settled, she recognized Bucky Penner, with someone at his side. With a leap of joy, she saw it was Imogen. They were arm in arm, Imogen's face turned up to his. *They look so happy.*

"You are distracted," said Serafina. "Why?"

"If you want to understand peace, look at that couple there." Evelina pointed toward them. "You see how she leans toward him, as if he is her support, and he has his hand on hers as if he will never let go. That is what two people in love look like."

Serafina stared, her fingers flying to her face. "She is beautiful."

"Yes."

Evelina watched curiously as Serafina tracked the couple, her entire body engaged in the act of observation. "Who is she?"

Something in Evelina balked. She couldn't place what, but she chose to listen to the inner warning. "I don't know. Just a woman."

"I feel that I should know her." Serafina's hands dropped from her cheeks as Bucky and Imogen became lost in the crowd. "Why does she lean on him so?"

Evelina thought about that, trying to put it in terms an automaton would understand. "Because he makes her feel as if she is entirely perfect, and there is no component she lacks. He makes her feel that she fulfills every function that he will ever desire."

"Ah, that is peace. I want to feel that, too."

So peace means love to her? Happiness? "We all do," said Evelina. "Trust me on that."

CHAPTER THIRTY-ONE

LATE SEPTEMBER BROUGHT WITH IT MORNINGS CRISP AND sweet as apples, the heavy dew sparkling as it clung to railing and iron grills like ephemeral jewels. The golden light, angled lower in the sky than it had been only weeks ago, seemed as thick as honey as it gilded even the weariest of the Whitechapel buildings.

Evelina arrived early at the theater after a restless night. Somewhere in the jumbled images of her dreams, Magnus had handed her the train case with her clock-making tools and told her the Blue King's army was inside. She'd opened it only to discover the case was actually Pandora's box, and she had just unleashed evil on the world. Another time, she might have dismissed the dream as silly, but today it weighed on her mood. She put it down to the fact that she still hadn't heard from Nick.

Magnus had given her a key to the workshop door, and she let herself in, running through the list of tasks for the day. They had already decided there would be no lesson, but she had plenty to fill the void. Foremost was taking advantage of her early arrival to have a second look at the upstairs rooms. She'd exhausted every ledger, cupboard, and cranny downstairs, having searched them twice over. If there was anything to learn at the Magnetorium, it was upstairs and probably in Magnus's private rooms.

She wondered if he was there or—as seemed to happen on Tuesday and Friday nights—he'd gone out after the show and would not return until the early afternoon. It had not been easy to learn the doctor's schedule from the other employees—not without arousing suspicion. It had taken days of a question here, a comment there, but eventually Evelina had guessed the pattern of his movements. If Magnus had another workshop, these late-night jaunts had to be when he went there. The others assumed he had a mistress—true, she'd seen him flirt with the female patrons often enough—but she was willing to bet his assignations were of a very different kind.

This all passed through Evelina's mind in the time it took to shed her wrap and chafe her hands against the cold of the workshop. She began mounting the stairs, the old wood creaking as she went. Sunlight shone through the dirty glass of the windows, giving the upstairs an almost cheerful glow. Light made all things seem possible, even finding proof that Magnus was the name Jasper Keating wanted.

But Serafina was there, and the automaton looked up, registering Evelina's presence the moment she reached the upper floor. Evelina froze, inwardly cursing. Her first thought was that it would be next to impossible to search now, with the doll looking on—and possibly reporting any such activity to Magnus. Her second thought was that Serafina was precisely where she'd found her before, staring into the room where she had awakened after Magnus had worked on her last.

"What are you doing up?" Evelina asked. *And what happened in that room that you keep coming back here?*

The doll inclined its head. "Is it wrong for me to be awake?"

"Someone forgot to take out your pin so that you could rest." She would have a word with Magnus about his Italian puppeteers.

"Do I need to rest?"

"Everyone needs to rest," Evelina said brightly. As far as she knew, the automatons needed no such thing, but it seemed kinder than saying it was better to have their stars dead and out of the way when they weren't actually making money. Serafina's sentience raised a host of philosophical questions Evelina couldn't even begin to solve.

"I am glad you are here," said the automaton. "It is pleasant to have someone else about." Serafina walked toward the window. She was wearing a simple day dress and from behind looked like a human woman, her fiery hair caught up in ivory combs. "Do you ever watch out the window?"

"Sometimes." Curious now, Evelina moved to join her. The scene below was unremarkable, with barrowmen and delivery carts drawn by big-boned horses. Some folk hurried to their work and others idled on the corners with nothing to do. "What interests you?"

"The people. I watch what they do. There are a lot of women who come and go, many of them very late at night. Look at that one—the one with fair hair. I've seen her often."

Evelina looked and saw Mary Jane Kelly, looking a bit disheveled this early in the day. She was talking with a man Evelina hadn't seen before. The two seemed to know each other well, because Mary gave him a familiar bump with her shoulder, half a chastisement, half a caress. "She seems happy," said Evelina, hearing Mary's fat laugh all the way to where she stood.

"She was with someone else yesterday. She has many men."

"That she does," Evelina agreed.

"That must be why she is so happy," Serafina said.

Evelina decided to leave that one alone.

"And do you see that man?" Serafina pointed to a fellow in baggy tweeds. "He stops to purchase flowers from the old woman on the corner every day. He says a few words, the woman laughs, and then he walks away."

Evelina considered the young man, who had heavy side whiskers and the build of a prize fighter in the prime of his career. "I would say that he gives them to a lady, and the flower seller is encouraging him."

"He wants to kiss someone," Serafina said, her fingertips

touching the glass. The gesture tugged at Evelina's insides. There was something wistful in it.

"He wants to make this lady like him."

Serafina tilted her head. "Men bring me flowers, but I do not like them. But I do like to kiss them."

"They kiss you?" Evelina asked in surprise.

"Of course. They think I'm beautiful." Serafina touched her hair in a purely feminine gesture.

Evelina stared, something ruffling the back of her neck. Foolish clients kissing a mechanical dancer was more silly than sinister, but Serafina's preening disturbed her—just like her sudden fit of temper on the walk. A memory knocked relentlessly at the door of her mind: Tobias had been afraid of the automaton. What had she done?

But all that had happened before Magnus came to Whitechapel, before the locked room, before the doll was born anew in the doctor's latest experiment. How different was she than before?

"I know you don't remember much about your past, but do you remember what you did before you danced for Magnus?"

Serafina hesitated before answering. "I went with him places. I did as he asked. I made sure things were done. That is all I remember."

"And do you do these things for Dr. Magnus now?"

Serafina gave a slow blink. It clicked slightly. "I please the patrons. That is why I was remade. So that they could kiss me. So that they could give me peace."

And Magnus takes it away again. A chill crawled over Evelina's skin. She had to talk to Magnus about this. Or not. She didn't know what to do. There were too many questions— was Serafina a slave? Was she actually alive? How much responsibility did Evelina have toward someone who was technically a machine and someone else's property to boot? She had to make her way through this one step at a time— and she still had to search the upstairs for clues as to what Magnus was actually up to.

"Come," she said with her kindest smile, even though she itched with guilt. Suddenly tricking the doll felt wrong, but it had to be done. "Come downstairs, Serafina. You need your beauty sleep."

WITHIN MINUTES, EVELINA had settled Serafina on her table, removed the pin that activated her logic processor, and covered her with a sheet. She had just finished adjusting the folds of the white shroud, feeling oddly maternal, when she heard the door of the workshop open. She turned to see Nick standing on the threshold.

Alarm made her stiffen. "What are you doing here?" she whispered, her words little more than a hiss. "It's not safe. You know *he* wants the device." And Magnus wouldn't hesitate to hurt them both if that would put Athena in his power.

"I came for you," Nick said, as if that explained everything.

All of a sudden it felt as if she hadn't seen him for months. At the sound of his voice, the tight-wound worry she'd been holding let go. In a heartbeat, she was across the room and flinging herself into his arms. He caught her, falling back a step but taking her weight with ease. She breathed in his scent—wool and shaving soap and man—and closed her eyes, grateful that he was there and safe.

"Where were you?" she demanded once her heart stopped racing.

He chuckled. "Taking care of some things. Come with me."

"Where?" She'd been going to search the upstairs.

His dark eyes held a thread of mischief. "I said I'd help you find your answers. If you want them, come with me now."

This was even better, and Evelina didn't need to be asked twice. She grabbed her shawl and left the theater, locking the door behind them. The street was busier than it had been when she'd arrived barely an hour before. She looked over her shoulder, afraid that Magnus would be mere yards away, returning home after a night of evil-doing. Then she looked up, half expecting to see him peering down from some window above. She could see Nick take note of her apprehension and tried to shake off her unease.

He cast her a sidelong look. "I suppose you are aching to ask what exactly I was taking care of."

"Perhaps." She had to trot to keep up with him.

"I had to make arrangements for this morning," he said. "And I was due to go back to the ship today. I had to explain to my crew that plans had changed. And then there was the Indifference Device. The Blue Boys left the dead where they fell. Something had to be done, and I helped the Schoolmaster do it."

"The Schoolmaster?" Evelina mused. "How do you know him?"

She'd mentioned the name in connection with the Baker Street bombing, but Nick had given no indication that it was familiar to him. She suddenly realized that he'd been playing at least a few cards close to his chest, waiting until he'd learned a bit more of her story. There had been trust to rebuild between them, but this clear evidence of it brought heat to her face.

He gave her an apologetic half smile. "I've had a few dealings with him. As to who he is, I don't know his real name. No one I know does. The man represents the face of the rebellion, but whether he is the true power behind it—probably not, but who knows. Maybe your uncles have a name, but I certainly don't."

"Uncle Sherlock?" *And maybe that's why there was a bomb on Baker Street? Uncle Sherlock knows something he shouldn't?* She'd had the same thought herself, but was it true?

"Maybe. And I've met Mycroft Holmes in my travels. They both think like knotted balls of string. I could be from now till Christmas untangling their logic and I still wouldn't be at the end of it."

She couldn't disagree, but wondered where Nick would have run into her reclusive Uncle Mycroft. For some reason, an encounter with him never brought good news—but there were other things to worry about at the moment.

They'd come to the side of an old church, and Nick opened

the oak and black iron door for her. "Welcome to Saint Winifred's. I hope you don't mind a bit of a climb."

"Why are we here?"

"Patience. I know you don't have any, but pretend for a while."

Evelina looked up, too close to the building to see much more than a lot of old stone and a few pointed arches. She wanted to press Nick further, but the look on his face was firm. Obediently, she stepped inside and blinked in the gloom. The door creaked shut behind them, the sound echoing through the vaulted space, and the place grew even darker.

"A climb?" she asked.

"This way," he said, leading her toward the right.

As her eyes adjusted, Evelina saw the church itself was a shell of graceful arches, a row of windows high up in the walls admitting shafts of sunlight. A rose window glowed over the main doors, seeming to float in the hushed atmosphere. There was little other ornamentation in the place, but the austerity made what was there that much more potent.

At the far side of the nave there was a small door, and behind that was a winding stone staircase. Evelina paused, tired of following without explanation. "What's up there?"

"The roof."

"Why are we climbing all the way to the roof?"

He gave a wicked grin. "You haven't grown soft lounging about in your silk gowns, have you?"

"But why are we going up there?"

"Trust me."

She released an exasperated breath. "Nick?"

He sprang lightly past her and took the stairs two at a time. With an irritated noise, she trudged up the worn stairs after him. It wasn't a particularly interesting task. Rough beige stone hemmed her in on every side and she lost count of the steps after 127. Just when her legs burned with the effort of climbing, Nick opened another door, and they were outside.

They weren't at the top of the square tower, but at a lower

part of the roof where flying buttresses arched overhead. Gargoyles, so weather-worn it was hard to tell what sort of beast they were meant to be, crouched at the roof's edge and scowled down at the maze of narrow alleys below. Evelina forgot the fatigue of the climb, distracted by the view. Beyond the tangle of streets was the steel gray of the Thames and its parade of boats, large and small, swarming toward the docks.

Nick moved to her side. She could feel the heat of his body, warm with exertion, even though they did not touch. "If you think this is impressive, you should see the world from the *Red Jack*." He took her hand, kissing it. His lips were soft and warm and the best advertisement for air travel that Evelina could imagine.

"Can we see your ship from here?" she asked.

"No. She's safely away right now, out of the reach of the guards that patrol the skies over the city."

That made no sense to her. "If she's not here, how would you get away in a hurry?"

He smiled, but it wasn't a happy expression. "However I could."

Her stomach fell away, as if a trap door had opened. She reached for him, her fingers gripping the hard muscle of his arm. "Nick." It was all she could think of to say.

He waved to a stone ledge. "Before we carry on, shall we sit for a moment?"

She wanted to ask why, but didn't. If they sat, she could keep him right beside her, and time with Nick in that sunny, sheltered spot safe above the city seemed a stolen moment of peace. "Very well."

Nick settled beside her, his face serious. "We won't be found here. Dr. Amiel and the others who work here are friendly, and I for one could use a few minutes to think through what we know before we make our next move."

"What about finding the Blue King's army?"

A hint of humor crossed his face. "We don't know so much that this is going to cause much of a delay. Let me talk this through with you."

"All right."

Nick nodded. "First, there was the bomb and Elias Jones. Blue King initiated the event, but Gold King turned it to his own purposes. Why? And don't rely on anything Jasper Keating told you."

"They all want a war," Evelina said. "Obviously the Blue King made the first move, but Keating blunted it."

"Why not stop it?"

It was a good question. She was slower to answer this time. "He didn't want Blue to know he had done it. I think Keating wants to know just how strong Blue is before he openly opposes him. He's stringing him along until he can strike a definitive blow." Evelina laced her fingers together, resting her elbows on her knees. "That's why he sent me here, so he knows exactly what he's up against." And she only had another day before her extension ran out. Nick had turned up just in time.

"He's trying very hard to find out," Nick added. "He has devices that transcribe conversations and transmit the information over a distance. I found that out from Bingham, another of the Blue King's men that he turned."

"If the Gold King had access to the Blue King's men, why didn't he simply ask them what weapons Blue has? He said they didn't know, but is that really true?"

"Maybe they don't know the information he needs. Jones was no more than a foot soldier. Bingham might have known more—he was on the craft that was carrying supplies back from Bohemia—but he might not have known everything. The Blue King is known for being a suspicious man, and he's been far more secretive about his strengths than any of the other steam barons. No one knew about the army I saw—it's in a place I doubt anyone goes by accident. It was news even to the Schoolmaster."

Evelina bit her thumbnail, deep in thought. "And every baron has a maker. Their names are all known, except who works for Blue."

She didn't utter Tobias's name, but it hung between them like a moment, until Nick made a gesture that swept it away. "Exactly."

"Am I right?" she asked quietly. "Is Magnus the one?"

Nick lifted a shoulder. "I wondered, so I asked a few questions about our sorcerer. The Magnetorium might be the toast of the town right now, but it's brand-new. Even if people connect Magnus the showman to the Magnus who came to town last April, almost no one knows that he has any interest in mechanics, much less enough knowledge to act as a steam baron's inventor. If the Blue King likes secrecy, he's the perfect choice."

Evelina blew out her breath. "But why would Magnus do it? I know it buys him protection to run his theater, but is that enough of an incentive? I thought he despised the barons."

"Unless he intends to rule through the Blue King," Nick said flatly. "I can see him using one of the steam barons as a puppet, first to defeat the others and then as a mouthpiece."

She buried her face in her hands. "That's brilliant. Of course that's why he's doing it!"

"You forget," said Nick. "I worked for him, too. I've heard him ramble on about the barons. He thinks he's smarter, and maybe he is."

Evelina, growing excited, began ticking points off on her fingers. "So we have the barons all fighting each other so that only one will rule the roost, we have Magnus waging his own war for supremacy through the Blue King, and then we have the rebels trying to get rid of the lot of them."

"Yes," said Nick. "And we're not sure who precisely is behind the rebels, besides your Uncle Mycroft. That's why the barons fear them. They're an unknown quantity."

"That gives the rebellion an edge, doesn't it?" she asked, her mind racing. Jones had mentioned Mycroft's name, and Nick had casually mentioned her uncle earlier, too. "What do you know about Uncle Mycroft's involvement with the rebels?"

"Not a lot." Nick was suddenly cautious. "I thought you knew."

"No." She sighed, a shiver running down her arms—though she wasn't sure if it was excitement or anger. "I'm not sure Uncle Sherlock even knows half of what Mycroft does. But if there's a game to be played, I'm sure he's in it."

"Is that lucky for the rebels?"

"Depends on where he places his bets. I hope he's for them."

Nick's face grew solemn. "Do you?"

"I've lived in Mayfair and I've lived here. It doesn't matter where you are, the barons make life hard." She didn't say more. She didn't need to.

They fell silent, thinking their separate thoughts until he leaned down and kissed her gently, a touch of affirmation rather than arousal. "Now I'm going to show you what I saw, and then you will report to Keating and never go back to the Magnetorium again."

"You're telling me what to do," she pointed out.

"This once, yes," he said in a tone that brooked no argument. "Your life is in danger. Now, come on so I can show you that army."

She wanted to protest, but held her tongue for the moment. Nick meant only the best for her. "There's something I don't understand," she said as he pulled her to her feet again. The touch of his hand was distracting, and she lost the thread of her thoughts for a moment. "If this army place is supposed to be secret, how come you could see it from the air? Why haven't others seen the same thing?"

"Most everything is kept in sheds, and the day I saw it there was very low cloud cover. Maybe they only bring the machines out when the conditions favor secrecy."

"So how come you were so lucky?"

Nick coughed slightly. "I was, uh, engaged with a ship at the time. One bound to make a delivery to that very place. In other words, it was pure chance. An associate has done some reconnaissance since then. Gwilliam reports that the toys rarely come out of the sheds."

"Is Gwilliam another airman?"

He paused. "Sort of. He was with the *Red Jack* when we saw the army."

He was leading her around the corner of the roof when she realized that Saint Winifred's had a peculiarity that was impossible to see from the street. The arch set high at the back of the church tower, rather than being filled with stone tracery and stained glass, was empty. In fact, the space extended under the roof like a giant barn, leaving a perfect landing bay for the tiniest dirigible that Evelina had ever seen.

It looked like a giant dragonfly, with a long tail and backswept fins with propellers either side. The balloon was a slender oval of sky blue, the gondola a pale gray. It fit inside the arch of the church tower as if one had been designed for the other. Nick craned his neck to give the craft a fond look. "She runs on aether distillate, but she has two small engines for speed."

Evelina watched him regard the machine with the same admiration he'd once shown for his horses. Nick had always loved to fly—he'd just found a more literal way to do it. "Whose craft is this?"

"The Schoolmaster's." He shot her an amused glance. "I owe him a favor. There's no piracy involved."

"We're going to fly in that?" Her stomach churned with jubilation and horror combined into one heady mix. Then she surged forward, itching to look inside the engine. This was better than fifty new dresses. But when she touched the housing, it was warm. She drew back with a pang of disappointment. "The boilers are already hot."

"Digby?" Nick called.

High above, a hatch opened in the side of the gondola and a head emerged. Evelina couldn't see the face well—the man was wearing elaborate goggles—but she got the impression of red hair and an enormous grin. "At your service, Captain, ma'am."

Nick looked smug, regarding her with his arms folded. "I told you to trust me. We'll go find proof and take care of your Jasper Keating problem."

CHAPTER THIRTY-TWO

NOT LONG AFTER, THE *WREN* SLIPPED OUT OF THE CHURCH
tower and flew southeast. It was a credit to Digby's skill that
Evelina barely felt the wind catch the ship as they circled the
tower and joined the handful of dirigibles flying over the
city. She learned that the church was only one of several
landing sites for the craft, which changed frequently since
the ship was too valuable to risk falling into the hands of the
Blue Boys. And, typically, the *Wren* came and went at dusk
or dawn when she was harder to see. The Schoolmaster had
made an exception for this mission—whatever favor Nick
owed him, it would be a large one.

She only gave half an ear to Nick's explanation. She had
never been in a flying machine before, and there was too
much to take in. There was the constant vibration of the motors, and the eerie sensation of drifting aloft—like being on
a trapeze but not quite. Like Nick, she had trained young as
an acrobat and heights did not frighten her, but here her
safety was not reliant on her agility or sense of timing. She
was entrusting her life to an engine that she hadn't inspected
herself, and she did her very best not to think about that.

The gondola of the *Wren* was closed in, with the pilot up
front and passengers on a long seat behind him. Evelina remained glued to the large window beside her. The ground
below was a map that had suddenly come alive, with all the
people and boats and houses in miniature. Her sense of space
and distance, of the shapes in a landscape she thought she
knew, was utterly reborn. It was like developing a sense
she hadn't known she'd missed—and she wanted more. As
the shadow of clouds moved below, she felt it a crime that the

small craft would not fly high enough to sport in the billows of mist.

And although he had his own window, Nick seemed to delight in sitting close behind her and peering over her shoulder, his breath hot on her cheek. She knew it for the flirtation that it was. She also knew she would never be able to separate his closeness from her first memories of flight any more than she could take Nick out of learning to ride, walk a tight rope, or throw a knife. Time had taken them on different paths, but some patterns remained. He was still showing her the world, and he was irrevocably entwined with discovery.

But as they neared their destination, Nick grew still. Evelina began to make out the white roofs of enormous sheds, each as large as a hangar for a dirigible. They were a little distance away yet, in a fenced field that had watchtowers at each corner. There was no flag or other marking visible that set this large industrial compound apart from any other that dotted the countryside. Since the advent of the Merchant Brotherhood of the Air, shipyards, while not common, were certainly not rare. The only clue that something was different was a brick tower that arched over a wide stream of water to the west.

"What's that?" she asked, raising her voice to be heard over the chugging of the engines.

"Water power," Nick replied. "If I'm right, they run a wheel or turbine of some kind. That kind of power is less conspicuous than if load after load of coal was being delivered, or if an entire power station was dedicated to this yard."

Evelina frowned out the window, wondering about the water source. London had many tributaries that joined the Thames, and this was probably one of them.

Then the world tilted as the *Wren* began a gentle, circling dive. Evelina braced herself on the window frame. "What's happening?"

"We're going to stay far enough away that they don't suspect the *Wren* of spying on them." Nick narrowed his eyes, suddenly all business. "Now that we've had a better look at the layout of the place, we'll go in on foot."

"Over the fence?" she asked incredulously. She'd seen the watchtowers.

"Through the river gate. It's the one break in the perimeter we can use. And I'll need your help," Nick said. "You know Magnus's magic best. I've no doubt the place is guarded with more than weapons."

His words caught her off guard. She'd expected to have to fight to go with him into the compound, and now his confidence unnerved her a little. She nodded, not able to trust her voice. If she had wanted proof that Nick trusted her again, this was it. They would rely on each other to make it back safely.

The dirigible hovered close to the ground and Nick tossed the ladder out the hatch. Digby was to stay with the *Wren* and keep her safe, and he would be the one to get help if they didn't come back. As Evelina climbed to the ground, she realized that she was, as Nick said, very close to completing the mission that had brought her to the East End. Joy and anxiety both made her knees weak. Giving Keating his answers would keep her uncle out of harm's way for the moment and buy her time to plan for the long term—and whatever Keating thought, that future would be the result of her choices, not his. Unfortunately, none of them would be easy.

They set off along the path of the river, about half a mile away from their goal. Partway along, she noticed a flock of birds circling in the sky. They were ravens, but bigger than any she'd ever seen.

"They're the ash rooks," Nick said with a sly smile. "They can fly where we can't."

Two landed in the grass ahead of them. Evelina saw one was wearing a helmet and neck chain. "Are they trained?"

Nick laughed. "They won't thank you for saying that. The big one is Gwilliam."

Evelina recognized the name of the associate who had scouted the Blue King's compound. She was about to ask for an explanation when Nick crouched close to the birds. Instinctively, she hung back and a heartbeat later his magic prickled against her skin. With a touch of awe, she understood that she was witnessing some of Nick's newfound powers.

The larger bird gave a rattling croak and the smaller one, who wore no metal, bobbed and spread his wings in an enthusiastic gesture. Nick spoke softly to them, too low for her to hear. Evelina felt a sense of wonder—this was a kind of magic that she'd never seen. *But it makes sense. He is a creature of air and so are they.*

Not long after, the larger bird flew away in a thunder of wings. The smaller one fluttered onto Nick's shoulder. He rose and walked toward her. "This is Talfryn," he said. "He is ready to earn his first piece of metal."

"Hello," she said to the bird, who gave her a look that was too shrewd by half. In fact, the creature kind of reminded her of Nick, its shining black feathers mingling with his straight black hair. "Is he part of the plan to get through the gate?"

"Not entirely. His part comes later. For now, we're going to have to leave the path."

So they did, detouring over the rolling ground to come at the gate at a less visible angle. As they approached the brick structure, the ash rooks made a clamor over the south tower, distracting the watchmen as Nick and Evelina crossed the one patch of ground that had no real cover. Once they were in the shadow of the fence, it was a matter of creeping up to the mouth of the passage where the river flowed under an iron grill.

Whoever had designed the gate had never envisioned these particular visitors. Glad she had eaten little breakfast, Evelina wriggled through the gap between the brick wall and the gate. For a moment she dangled over the running water, but her toes quickly found solid ground. With the help of a rope and a grappling hook, Nick squeezed between the iron gate and the brick archway, walking along the top of the gate to drop down safely onto the dry walkway. Talfryn simply flew past unremarked.

On the other side of the gate, a narrow brick ledge ran on either side of the river, but a dozen yards along was the waterwheel, a good thirty feet in height with angled blades that made the most of the river's steady flow. An enormous shaft ran through it, the ends disappearing into the brickwork on either side. But the wheel wasn't just driven by the paddles striking the river. A separate channel of water was directed to the top of the tower and dropped from above, driving the wheel with greater force. It made the space inside the brick tower very noisy and very wet.

Nick and Evelina exchanged a glance. The shaft of the wheel was enormous—too high to jump over—and the waterway was too dangerous to swim. Evelina eyed the space under the shaft, wondering if she could squeeze beneath it. It might have been possible if she were Mouse.

Then Nick threw his grappling hook at the brickwork above. It took three tries, but eventually it found solid purchase. He climbed partway up the wall, digging fingers and toes into cracks in the mortar. Then he held out a hand for Evelina.

She balked for a moment, knowing what he intended to do—but the roar of the water drowned out any protest she might have made. Nick was drawing on a game they'd played in childhood, a way to cross a stream from bank to bank without a bridge, or a way to dangle over the largest mud puddle they could find, daring each other to fall. It was a game of agility, but mostly it was a game of trust.

It was insanity, but she didn't have a better idea. Gamely, Evelina crawled up the bricks just ahead of him, scraping knuckles and scuffing the last shreds of leather on her boots. She could taste brick dust and mold, and the stink of rotting vegetation clinging to the walls. Then Nick's arm gripped her hard around the waist, she clung to him, and they swung over the turning shaft.

Evelina's stomach swooped a beat behind the rest of her, and she was suddenly ten years old again, free as only a child can be. She remembered to tuck her feet up, but she forgot about her trailing skirts. She felt something snag, and the surreal strength of the machine jerked her. She grabbed her skirt, relying on Nick's strength to hold her as she ripped it free. But his one-handed grasp wasn't secure enough and as hard as he tried to hold her, she began to slide. She reached for him, but it was too late and she slithered from his arms.

Mercifully, they cleared the shaft before she fell. Childhood training made her try to roll as she landed, but she dropped onto her hip and shoulder, smacking hard against the bricks. She began to tumble toward the water, but Nick was there. He caught her just as her feet went over and hauled her back to safety.

"I'm sorry," he said, his voice urgent. "I'm so sorry."

She lay gasping in his arms a moment, stunned, aching, and gasping for breath. The fall had knocked the wind out of her.

"Are you all right?" he demanded, brows drawn down into a frown. He was feeling for broken bones, but she swatted him way. "Hold still!" he said crossly. "You're always the worst patient."

She made an inarticulate noise, trying not to cry but feeling her nose start to run anyhow. She hurt, but the shock of falling was worse. "Just get me on my feet."

He complied, saying nothing as she drew in her breath with a hiss and sagged against him. "Did you twist your ankle?" he asked.

"Girls only do that in books," she snapped, then felt awful for being cross. Never mind that it felt like her leg might fall off at any moment, and she wasn't likely to sit down comfortably for a month. She lifted her chin and forced a smile. "I'm perfectly fine."

"I'm sure you are," he said, sounding utterly unconvinced. "I'm sorry."

She squeezed his arm. "It's not your fault. We made it over, didn't we?" She was still leaning into him, not sure she could carry on without the feel of his warm strength against her. Reluctantly, she swayed away, putting her weight on both feet. A pain shot up her right side, but she didn't topple over. That would have to be good enough, because there was no way she would slow him down. "Lead on."

"Are you sure? I can get your proof for you. You don't need to do this." His eyes were dark with concern.

She ached with the sweetness of that look. "Nick, you were smart enough to invite me on this adventure. You know who I am and what I'm capable of, and that means more to me than I can say."

"I knew you wouldn't thank me for leaving you behind. You never did." He pulled her close, wrapping his arms tight around her. She heard his heart beat, quick and strong with emotion. "It drives me to madness some days. Just don't be too proud to tell me if you're hurt."

"I'm not," she said, lying only a little. "I'm with you all the way."

The words carried a subtle weight, as if they meant more than she'd thought when she let them go. They both heard it, bodies tensing. Then softly, he kissed her forehead. They stood like that for a dozen heartbeats, the rush of the water surrounding them in a glistening mist. To Evelina, it felt like a blessing.

Talfryn found them on the other side of the waterwheel, settling to ride on Nick's shoulder. It was now close to midday, but there were few people outside the sheds. The buildings were a mix of tin and wooden structures, painted white and set close to the high fence. There was a path a few feet wide behind the buildings, hard to see unless one was at the perfect angle. That's where they went first. Although the narrow passage was sheltered from view, they moved quickly, afraid to linger. Evelina did her utmost not to limp.

They were there to find evidence, but she wasn't sure what that would be. What they wanted was a workshop or an office—something with papers to look at, perhaps incriminating letters or a blueprint for one of the rolling cannons Nick had seen. Most of all, they wanted someplace easy to get in and out of unseen.

They paused behind each of the enormous sheds, listening. Some were filled with the sounds of labor—banging and sawing—and others were perfectly quiet. The tin buildings had shoddy seams with gaps wide enough to peer through. The first was uninteresting, but the second had a machine that made them stare. It looked like a great steel carriage, high wheels looming at the back, with three thick steel fingers protruding from the front. They might have been tentacles, but they looked more suited for stomping than for grasping. The next shed turned Evelina's stomach. It was filled with some kind of mechanical serpents, large and small, that draped over every available surface, trailing like vines or coiled in heaps like animate ropes. Here she felt the first whiff of dark magic and knew that her guess about Magnus was correct. He was the one designing these things—but her word would not be proof enough.

Nick felt the magic, too, and his uneasiness made Talfryn shift nervously. They moved on quickly, coming next to a wooden building that looked more like a small house with a porch and windows. Here, too, she felt the buzz of magic, but it was the warning prickle of a threshold ward. Only the authorized could enter.

Too bad. Evelina could smell the spicy scent of a curry and her mouth began to water, the fresh air and physical activity making her stomach feel hollow. As they looked through the window, they could see it was occupied. Evelina ducked below the sill, then cautiously peered over the edge. A man sat at a wooden table, writing. A half-eaten dish of curry sat pushed to the corner of the table. Evelina fought an impulse to bang on the window and ask him if he meant to finish it.

But he didn't look like the type to share. Everything about the man was precise, the visage pale, smooth, and cold. He looked about thirty, his neatly trimmed mustache and hair nutmeg brown. He wore a dove gray suit of the latest cut, for all the world as if he meant to attend an afternoon social at the Duchess of Westlake's country manor. And yet nothing about that face was kind.

"I know him," said Nick, murmuring low in Evelina's ear. "His name is Arnold Juniper. He's the Blue King's man of business."

Evelina chewed her lip. Judging by Juniper's clothes, running London's poorest quarter must have been remarkably profitable. She saw him pick up a page of sketches, and she longed for a better look at them. Then he put the page on the stack of papers he was reading and squared the edges of the pile, his fingers fussing until it was perfectly neat. Juniper picked up a pair of gloves, the kid so soft they draped like satin in his grip, and slid them on carefully, smoothing the fingers until each was free of wrinkles. Then came a dove gray top hat and a Malacca walking stick. Finally, he picked up the papers and strode toward the door. Nick and Evelina ducked out of sight.

"I think those papers might be what we need," she said softly.

Immediately, Talfryn launched himself from Nick's shoulder, croaking like the herald of the apocalypse. Nick and Evelina scuttled to the corner of the house, peering after the bird. Before Evelina caught a glimpse of the action, an explosion of curses filled the air. She jerked away from her vantage point, pressing her back against the side of the house, and watched in horrified fascination as a snowstorm of paper began tumbling her way. Nick gave her a wide-eyed look and she bit her lip, flirting dangerously with laughter.

And then the page of sketches fluttered by. She dove for it, ignoring Nick's mime of protest, and caught it just as it reached the fence. Amusement died as Juniper rounded the corner of the building, picking up papers one by one from the grass.

"Damned bloody bird," he growled, snatching up another sheet.

She dove for the shadows close to the house, but they wouldn't be any protection if Juniper looked up. The quick movement ignited the fire in her hip and shoulder, robbing her of breath for a moment. Sweat prickled her skin, and she realized with horror that she couldn't run if she had to.

As if he read her thoughts, Nick raised his gun. The blast would give them away, but Juniper might make a useful hostage. Evelina's pulse pounded, her lips going numb with fear.

But then Nick gave a flick of his wrist, and Talfryn snatched Juniper's hat right off his head. Juniper wheeled with a cry of horror, while the rook gripped the costly topper in his claws, flapping madly to stay aloft with that much weight. Juniper

dropped the papers and ran after the ash rook, long legs pumping and bellowing a litany of invective. The rook bobbed,
seeming destined for a crash landing, but then redoubled his
efforts, gaining altitude. Juniper leaped, snatching at the hat
brim, but Talfryn veered away, croaking what sounded suspiciously like a laugh.

Evelina reeled inside, limbs numb with relief. And then
Nick and Evelina darted forward, grabbing all the pages
they could.

Their retreat was slow but without incident. Evelina felt
the world leach of color as the pain from her fall gradually
took hold. It hadn't seemed bad at first, but now it grew like
the roots of a plant, sending shoots that branched and
branched again until every inch of her flesh was pierced
with it. She prayed Juniper would assume that the wind had
snatched his papers, because she couldn't afford pursuit,
and the long trek back to the landing site would have been
her undoing if they had been forced to detour. Pride alone
kept her going, and Nick had to help her up the ladder to
crawl inside the *Wren*.

Evelina collapsed onto the seat and then yelped as her
bruises felt her weight. Nick curled his arm around her, pulling her close against his chest as the craft took off. "You
were magnificent," he said. "Strong and brave."

She gave him a droll look. "Don't flatter me. I fell on my
backside and now it hurts."

He smiled slowly. "You're a work of art, Evie Cooper."

She blushed, half ashamed that she was so susceptible to
his praise. It would have been easy to fall asleep right there,
curled up against the strong chest of her pirate captain, but
there was still work to do. Summoning strength from some
remote corner of her being, she forced herself to sit up.
"What's in those papers?"

Nick pulled them out from under his jacket, turning them
right side up and smoothing the pages. "Letters. Invoices."
He got to the page of sketches and stopped. "There it is. This
handwriting belongs to Magnus."

"How do you know?"

"Do you remember those plans for a ship that I took when his house burned down?"

Nick had shown them to her and Uncle Sherlock. "Yes."

"The handwriting is the same."

"You remember it that well?"

"I've stared at those plans for ages." He gave a slight smile. "I'm building that steamspinner with Lord Bancroft's gold, plus some that I've won for myself with the *Red Jack*. Or rather, I'm having it built. She's going to be an amazing ship with Athena on board."

His words pulled her mind away from the problem of collecting evidence. He studied her reaction, but she kept her face carefully schooled. "Truly, what made you think of turning pirate?"

Nick busied himself with the papers. "There was an air deva who wanted a ship, and I wanted a life that would make me rich so that I could come home a gentleman with fine clothes and a full purse."

She was about to ask why, but then guessed the answer. He had wanted to be a gentleman for her. She said nothing.

He gave a low laugh. "I found out I had a talent for this life and made the best of it."

Evelina was suddenly heartsore, aching with the disappointment she heard beneath his words. She'd pushed him away for good reasons at the time, but she wasn't going to do that again. She leaned into him once more, resting her head on his chest, and he slid his arms around her. "I'm so sorry," she said, wishing she could give in to sleep.

"Why? You didn't make me do anything. I chose this life."

"It only takes a pebble to begin an avalanche. Sometimes that pebble is another person. They act, you react, and suddenly everything changes."

Nick was silent a long moment. "Is that how Keating came to turn on you? I know you're protecting your uncle, but there's more to the story than that."

Evelina closed her eyes, hating the conversation. "In his own way, Keating was protecting his daughter. Tobias was marrying Alice. Keating caught me with him."

Nick stiffened. "*With* him?"

She turned her face to look up at Nick. His face was tense, waiting to be hurt. "I kissed him, that was all."

"I thought you said it was over between you."

"It is now, but I was still hurting then. And he had to marry someone he didn't love." Evelina shifted. "He isn't the type to turn the world upside down to get what he wants."

"To get you?" Nick's gaze went dark with a possessiveness that brought heat to her skin.

"He'll never fight for me." She settled back into the comfortable spot on Nick's shoulder. "And maybe that's for the best, because I'm not the woman he needs." It didn't feel good to say it, but she knew now that was the truth.

"Why not?"

She lifted a hand to stroke Nick's cheek, feeling the clean line of bone and the roughness of stubble. She didn't want to talk about Tobias anymore. "Because he doesn't know who I truly am. He only knows one part of me, and I would have had to hide the rest. I'm happier right now than I have been in years."

A long silence lapsed. She could almost hear Nick thinking. Finally, he made a sound, a slight throat-clearing. When he spoke, his voice had gone flat. "I have to take these papers to the Schoolmaster, and you have to take them to Keating. And then you have to go home to your uncle."

"What?" she sat up, twisting to look him in the face. Pain shot through her at the sudden movement, but she ignored it. "You're telling me what to do again. What if I want to stay with you?"

His lips thinned to a line. "What about all the things you want—college, a future? You told me how much that meant to you. And what about your uncle?"

She saw what he was doing—trying to save her from making a mistake—and she loved him the more for it. "We'll figure it out. You said it yourself: We see a world that no one else understands. You know who I am no matter what I've become, and you've put yourself in harm's way for my sake." She swallowed hard, realizing that she was making the difficult choice, here and now, between Society and

Nick, between the knowledge Magnus offered and the man she had always loved. "You're the thread running through everything I've ever done."

"Ah." Nick's voice cracked on the sound. It wasn't a word, but it held everything he might have said more eloquently than an entire library of verse. Nick reached out, fingertips grazing her cheek. She could feel his magic yearning to escape like a warm fur of power brushing her skin. Emotions were high, and that made control hard. She folded her fingers over his, and the silver fire of wild magic crept over and around their clasped hands. Then he leaned in and kissed her, his hunger all too plain.

Digby coughed, and they jumped like guilty schoolchildren. "I know half a dozen good hotels in the area, if you would like some privacy."

Nick flushed, but grinned. "Pillaging isn't all about the loot."

Evelina's jaw dropped. "I beg your pardon?"

He took her face in both his hands, his eyes brimming with life. "Come with me. Now. Today."

She put a finger over his lips. "No. That would tip our hand. If I run without explanation, with no warning, Magnus will be on the alert. That might undo everything we've accomplished."

She could tell by Nick's expression he didn't like the idea, but he sat back with a sigh. "You're right, of course. But that causes more problems. I need to tell the Schoolmaster about Magnus, but I can't risk his men making a move as long as you're at the theater—and I hate the fact that you'll be in his company one second more."

"And I don't want to stay any longer. Take the papers to the Schoolmaster today, and then bring them to my rooms tomorrow morning. We can proceed from there."

Nick's brows furrowed. "What do you plan to do?"

"Settle with Keating, then it will be time for my uncle to find me. There is nothing in Uncle Sherlock's discovery of his long-lost niece that Magnus would find strange, especially when the Great Detective drags me back home by the ears."

"And then?" Nick said uneasily.

She took his hands. "Then we unfold our future."

"No regrets? You know who and what I am."

There were things she'd wished for but hadn't got. She wished she had found something to hold over Jasper Keating's head, and if she were leaving the Magnetorium, there would be no chance to learn more about her magic. But she couldn't have everything, and it was Nick she wanted most. "No regrets."

One corner of his mouth turned up. "You're sure you want to be a pirate queen?"

Evelina glanced toward the back of Digby's head. "If the pirates will have me. You're my port, Nick. Any other place is exile."

Finally, he truly smiled, and he looked just as he had as a boy. "Welcome home, Evie."

CHAPTER THIRTY-THREE

London, September 29, 1888

SCOTLAND YARD

2:20p.m. Saturday

"I APPRECIATE YOUR EAGERNESS TO ASSIST US IN CATCHING the Whitechapel Murderer, Mr. Holmes, but I'm not certain what you can do that we cannot." Inspector Frederick George Abberline reclined in his desk chair, fingering his dark brown mustache. "Many good men are on this case already."

From the other side of the cluttered desk, Holmes regarded the drifts of correspondence, reports, and forms that silted every flat surface. One might have thought the inspector was some woodland creature lining his burrow—but with public pressure about the case mounting the way it was, he might just as well have been digging his grave.

"Oh, but I might be of some small assistance," Holmes replied, pushing his annoyance behind the steel door he kept between Holmes the detective and Uncle Sherlock.

"With all due respect, Mr. Holmes, this is a grave case. It's more a matter for professionals."

Holmes bit back a sour remark trying to make its way past his mental divide. Striking out at the inspector wouldn't help matters. More to the point, it wouldn't help Evelina. If the Blue King wanted Holmes on the case, that was fine with him. After all, what better excuse to walk unhindered through King Coal's streets than a hunt for the very killer he was required to find?

Even better, he'd discovered that the Yellowbacks loathed police stations the way vampires feared sunlight. Keating's Rottweilers would stay on the opposite side of the street from Scotland Yard, keeping out of sight of the coppers. No doubt Keating would keep his thugs out of jail, but old reflexes died hard and not every charge could be swept away. Today's guard dog had been so distracted that he hadn't even asked for details of Holmes's errand. No doubt he would assume it was all about Evelina, which was the truth—in a roundabout way.

Privacy, freedom, and a case to work. It was enough to make Holmes covet a bunk in one of the cells. He couldn't survive much longer as Keating's caged lion.

But first he needed an invitation to join the chase, and Abberline was the obvious way in. Of the three officers Scotland Yard had sent to assist with the Whitechapel Murders, Abberline was the one Lestrade recommended that Holmes approach. Apparently the man was smarter than most.

If only this had been Lestrade's case, everything would have been so much simpler. A surge of irritation rasped Holmes's nerves like coarse wool, making him fidget. He was put out whenever one of his rare instances of civility wasn't immediately rewarded.

Time for a new tack. "I understand you're relatively new to Scotland Yard, Inspector," Holmes said smoothly.

"That's right."

"But you've been requested to assist the H Division because of your superior knowledge of the area and its criminal population."

"I know my way around."

"You were promoted to first class just this year. You'll be a chief inspector before long."

Holmes had heard all this from Lestrade, although he could have told as much from the detritus in the room. The thick files on the desk were the most telling. Capable men were the ones who got buried beneath the most problematic tasks.

"Well, you've proven that you can research a man's career and flatter his pride," Abberline replied with a hint of amusement in his soft voice. "And I'll return the compliment by saying that I've heard my lads say how much they enjoy reading about your escapades in the papers. But as I said, we do have a full task force of talented men on the case."

And if you can't differentiate between them and me, you are—whatever Lestrade's opinion—an ass. "What have you found out so far?" Holmes asked, crossing his legs and leaning back in the uncomfortable chair.

Abberline grimaced. He was in his midforties, portly, and balding, as if all his hair had migrated to his luxuriant side whiskers. It should have been a friendly face, but he had the sharp eyes of a seasoned officer, and he was turning them on Holmes now. "I'll be honest with you, Mr. Holmes. It's been strongly suggested that I open my casebook to you. I don't appreciate interference, no matter from how high up it comes. So I mean it when I ask what you can do to justify that I take the time from all this," he smacked a hand on a stack of files, "to cater to a gentleman dilettante?"

Holmes's mouth went sour. Ah, so the Blue King had made his wishes known, and destroyed all the goodwill the world's only consulting detective might have brought to the table. Help like that was worse than a fatal pox. And Abberline's reluctance to knuckle under meant that he valued the integrity of his investigation. That should have been a good thing, but right now it just made Holmes's job harder.

"Give me five minutes to convince you of my worth. Perhaps that will erase the ill effects of my endorsements."

Abberline narrowed his eyes. "You're going to solve the case in five minutes?"

He had no idea what he could accomplish in five minutes, but he knew that he'd put on a good show. "Let us review the facts. First, there have been three victims, all unfortunates selling their bodies. The murder scenes are reasonably close together, one in George Yard Buildings, one in Buck's Row, and one on Hanbury Street. Each attack was more savage than the last. The last two were certainly carried out with a long-bladed knife." He had already bribed his way to the postmortem reports, which had been fascinating reading.

"Agreed," said Abberline. "But I knew all that."

"Have you found any connection among the victims besides occupation and area of residence?" Holmes prompted. "Who are these women?"

"Nobody," said Abberline with a huff of frustration. "They were all middle aged, none of them beauties, and all of them poor. Dark Annie lived more or less honestly until her husband died and his ten shillings a week dried up. In the end, all got their living in the back alleys."

"Regrettable, but not helpful. Did they know each other? Common acquaintances?"

Abberline's mouth twitched, but whether in sympathy with the directness of the questions or disapproval of them, Holmes could not tell. "Not that I'm aware of, but it's possible."

Holmes was warming to the task. "Have you interviewed the other women on the street?"

"Of course. That's when we started hearing about this Leather Apron character extorting money from the working women."

"I read about that in the *Star.* You made an arrest but the suspect had an alibi."

Abberline sank back in his chair with a sigh. "And since then we've had to suffer the assistance of George Lusk and his Vigilance Committee. The current suspects are anarchists, butchers, doctors, and sailors, and there are a great many of all of those in the East End. Interviews proceed apace."

"Description of the perpetrator?" Holmes asked.

"Nothing consistent." The inspector tugged on his whiskers, clearly being drawn into the conversation. The stiffness had left his shoulders.

"Physical evidence? Murder weapon? A dropped button?"

"None."

"I begin to see the difficulties with this case. On one hand, you have too much data. On the other, almost nothing at all."

"Not to mention a number of key officials on leave, a hysterical press, the Blue King, and now bloody nonsense like this." Abberline rustled in the piles of paper, pulled out an envelope, and tossed it across the desk. "What do you make of that, Mr. Holmes?"

He picked it up, giving it a cursory look. "It's postmarked the twenty-seventh."

"It was forwarded on to us today."

The envelope itself was unremarkable, but the ink was not. The scrawl was red, addressing the missive to *The Boss, Central News Office, London City.* A cold feeling crawled down Holmes's neck as he pulled out the paper folded inside, a fresh gout of red words spilling to both sides of the page.

Dear Boss,

I keep on hearing the police have caught me but they wont fix me just yet. I have laughed when they look so clever and talk about being on the <u>right</u> track. That joke about Leather Apron gave me real fits. I am down on whores and I shant quit ripping them till I do get buckled. Grand work the last job was. I gave the lady no time to squeal. How can they catch me now. I love my work and want to start again. You will soon hear of me with my funny little games. I saved some of the proper <u>red</u> stuff in a ginger beer bottle over the last job to write with but it went thick like glue and I cant use it. Red ink is fit enough I hope <u>ha. ha.</u> The next job I do I shall clip the ladys ears off and send to the police officers just for jolly wouldn't you. Keep this letter back till I do a bit more work, then give it out straight. My knife's so nice and sharp I want to get to work right away if I get a chance.

Good Luck.

Yours truly
Jack the Ripper

Dont mind me giving the trade name

PS Wasnt good enough to post this before I got all the red ink off my hands curse it No luck yet. They say I'm a doctor now. <u>ha ha</u>

Holmes read the letter, then reread it, taking in the missed punctuation and awkward grammar, the postscript written crosswise at the bottom of the page. An amateur might be fooled, but this was someone trying to appear illiterate rather than a man truly struggling with words. Then Holmes pulled out his magnifying glass, peering at the writing more closely, examining every stroke.

Again, disguised, but not to him. A peculiar feeling crept over him, half triumph and half horror. *Got you.* He sucked in his breath, forcing back a wave of dismay that threatened to derail his train of logic altogether.

"You recognize the writer?" Abberline said, a little mockingly.

"If I did, I would have more than earned my place on this case, Inspector," he said in his coolest tones. "But there are a few details of interest."

"Such as?" asked Abberline, leaning forward in his chair with eyebrows raised.

Holmes cursed his obligation to interact with the man. He wanted to take the letter away and study it in peace and quiet. "Your killer did not write this letter. It is decidedly a hoax."

"I might have guessed that much, Mr. Holmes."

Holmes lowered his glass, feeling as if all the strength was ebbing out his toes. Strange as it seemed, there were things he truly didn't want to know.

But he refused to show it. "I'm sorry, Inspector, all I can say is that the individual who wrote this is a well-educated man of about forty to forty-five, unmarried, with a sedentary lifestyle. He smokes, but not excessively, and has recently traveled to the north of the country. By occupation I would assume he is required to exhibit a degree of necessary creativity. Perhaps a journalist." *Or a bureaucrat.*

"Impressive," said Abberline. "Perhaps I can use you, if your powers of deduction are that acute."

Holmes managed a smile. *They are, but my ability to lie is even sharper.*

* * *

BONG! BONG! BONG!

Poppy sat with her back to the longcase clock that sat on the second-floor landing. If she touched it at the precise moment the chimes rang, a weird magnetic thrill rattled her teeth. No other clock did that, but this one was special. The doctor friend that Papa had known in Austria had made it, presumably when they were still friends. They weren't now, and that was about all Poppy had been able to determine on that subject.

She rose, turning to admire the thing. The wood was a rich brown that gleamed in the sunlight. The top was arched with pointy bits at the corners like little towers. There were seven moving dials besides the actual clock, telling about things like whether the sun would shine that day—but that dial was usually wrong. The top part of the arch showed the scales at the apex of the sky, followed close behind by the scorpion. Below that were the painted faces of the moon, which currently appeared to be falling asleep. The most bizarre feature was the slot that shot out punch cards from time to time. Only Papa knew what they meant, and they usually made him curse and stomp off to his study.

When she was little, Poppy used to make up games about the clock, but since she'd reached the threshold of womanhood—as her mother never tired of reminding her—such things were beneath her. So she slumped to the floor in a sulk and stared moodily down the corridor of bedroom doors. *Bored, bored, bored.*

Something darted across her field of vision. She blinked, not quite sure she'd really seen it. And then it moved again. She sat up very slowly, peering down the carpet. It was a little gray mouse! And Poppy liked nothing more than animals.

A shiver of potential fun tickled through her. Silently, Poppy eased forward until she was balanced on her toes. The creature was standing on its hind legs, pushing on Imogen's door as if it were trying to get inside. Since it was about the size of an eggcup, that obviously wasn't working.

"Hey!" Poppy said in a stage whisper. "What do you think you're doing?"

The mouse gave a startled squeak and dropped to all fours. They stared at each other for a long moment. There was something oddly shiny about the creature, and the thing turned tail and scampered off faster than any mouse had a right to. Poppy launched after it, having her first good time in what felt like weeks.

The thing slipped through the crack in Alice's half-open door. Poppy lunged after it, tripped on the rug, and landed sprawling across the foot of the bed. Unfortunately, Alice was in it. She sat up with a squeak that sounded a lot like the mouse. "What are you doing?"

Poppy bit her lip, wondering what she should admit to. Alice glared, but still had that look like she was about to cry any moment. *Oh, bother, it's not like I can make things any worse.*

"I'm chasing a mouse!" Poppy announced, maybe a little too loudly.

"What!" Alice snatched at the covers, her red hair tumbling around her like one of those paintings by Burne-Jones. Poppy so wanted Alice's hair.

"It's only a little one." Poppy measured with her thumb and forefinger.

"Ah!" Alice squeaked again, pointing at the floor.

The mouse was making its escape in a gray blur. Poppy heard Imogen's door open and her sister exclaim, "Oh, there you are!"

Poppy had always been convinced that her sister was odd, but that confirmed it. She heaved a sigh, having lost her quarry, and looked around the room. Then she noticed the suitcase on the bed. "Why are you sleeping with your suitcase?"

Alice made a face. "I'm dreaming about traveling to exotic lands."

Poppy shrugged. "I'd pack the Worth gowns, if I were you. If you're going to dream, you may as well look your best."

A tear slid down Alice's cheek. "I suppose I could dream those emeralds back, then." She didn't sound like she much cared.

"Unless you wanted something else. Like a camel."

Alice looked up glumly. "Why a camel?"

"If you're going to an exotic land, shouldn't you pack a camel?"

It was a silly statement, and something like a smile hovered around Alice's lips. That was good, Poppy thought. She'd begun to worry that Alice might never smile again. "Do you want to do something? I'm bored."

Alice looked shocked, but then shrugged. "I don't know."

Poppy leaned forward, giving her best conspiratorial whisper. "We could make an alliance, like two prisoners in a tower."

Alice's eyes went wide. "We could?"

It made perfect sense to Poppy. She and Alice were the ones always left out, but Poppy guessed that Alice was pretty smart. Together they'd make a crack team of spies. "Tobias is tearing up the attic. Let's find out what he's looking for."

"Oh, I wouldn't do that. It's something of your father's, I think. He wouldn't really say. Some old family business."

Poppy rolled her eyes. "They keep whispering about those silly mechanical dolls. I bet that's what it's all about."

Alice had the look of someone translating from another language. "Automatons?"

"We used to have some, up in the attic. They're gone now. Tobias wants them back and Papa doesn't want to talk about it. There's some big secret about them."

Alice look confused. Poppy knew exactly how she felt. "Listen, there's a bundle of old letters in the steel box under the floor in Papa's study. I bet whatever Tobias is looking for is in there."

Alice blinked. "How do you even know that?"

Poppy felt a slight swell of pride. "I found out where he hides the key. It rained a lot last Christmas and I didn't have much to do."

"Do you know what those papers say?" Alice asked, shaking her head as if to clear it.

"No, they're in German. I don't read German. But I heard Tobias say that everything going wrong around here would be cleared up if he could just find out why the automatons are such a big secret."

Alice looked sideways, obviously thinking. Hoping. She sat with her arms wrapped around her shins, her chin propped on one knee. "If it's causing everything that's gone wrong, it must be a huge secret."

"The biggest." A surge of anticipation made Poppy's scalp prickle.

Alice raised one eyebrow. "You may not read German, but I do."

CHAPTER THIRTY-FOUR

BREAKING INTO LORD BANCROFT'S STUDY WAS NOT AS EASY as it sounded. The brass handle had an impressive lock, and despite Poppy's claim that she could pick any lock ever made, the thing refused to budge.

Alice felt like an idiot standing at the end of the corridor, listening for approaching footsteps. What she was doing was wrong, foolish, and potentially dangerous. She'd been led into a complete breach of everything sensible and right by a fourteen-year-old hoyden, and in her soul Alice knew she was going to pay.

But at least she was doing something besides moping, and even burglary was preferable to being trapped in misery for another afternoon. Her eyes were sandy from weeping, her limbs rubbery from lying down too much. Worst, her emotions still smarted, as if she'd been physically beaten but the bruises had sunk deep into her soul. Now this brainless escapade seemed rather fun—and after so much unhappiness, she planned to grab it with both hands and morals be damned.

She edged another inch toward the corner of the wall, straining her ears for any sound of movement, and felt something tickle her foot. She jumped, flicked her skirts, and saw something gray streak across the carpet.

"I think I just saw that wretched mouse again," she hissed.

"We should go fetch the cook's cat," Poppy replied, rummaging in the keyhole with a pair of slim tools.

Alice felt her whole body wince at the thought of mouse bits all over. "Can't we just catch it and put it outdoors?"

"Spies can't afford to be tenderhearted."

"You're a bloodthirsty girl."

Poppy made a comic face, about to respond—and then the lock clicked open. They scurried inside, closing the door behind them. The room was masculine, paneled in dark wood and smelling of Turkish tobacco. A desk sat crosswise in the corner opposite the door, a tiger's head hanging above it. The tiger must have had a rough time of it, because it was missing one fang.

Alice walked farther into the room, wondering what she could find out about her new father-in-law by looking at his private space. There was a fancy spirit lighter as tall as she was, shaped like a silver phoenix. Books lined every wall, interrupted only by the windows and a huge wardrobe in the corner. Above the mantel, a clock ticked disapprovingly.

"The box is under the carpet," Poppy said, pointing to the floor. "You lift that up while I get the key."

Alice saw the corner of the carpet was beneath a fern stand. She moved the china pot with its luxurious occupant to the corner of the desk, then moved the wooden stand and peeled back the fine Turkish carpet. She saw at once that there was a slight gap in the floorboards. Alice got to her knees and began poking with her fingernails while Poppy was sticking her head up the chimney and feeling around for the secret hidey-hole. It was a good thing no one had decided to light a fire, or their plans would have been utterly ruined.

"Here it is," Poppy announced, emerging with a sooty smudge on her forehead.

Alice couldn't help wondering what had possessed the girl to go looking up the chimneys in the first place. Too many adventure stories? Then again, what was she doing scrabbling at the floor? Finally, a short section of floorboard lifted up. Once that one came up, the next two were easy. And sure enough, a steel box sat nestled in a dusty hole.

"Here." Poppy handed her the key.

Alice inserted the key into the lock. It turned with a metallic clang, and the lid lifted smoothly. The box was crammed with coins, papers, medals, small gold bars, bank notes, and a lot of odds and ends she didn't have time to take in.

"You want the bundle with the yellow envelope on top," Poppy said.

Quickly, Alice rustled through the box until she found what she wanted. She'd just pulled it out when she heard Lord Bancroft's voice in the corridor. They froze. There were footsteps coming their way.

"Balls!" Poppy hissed. "Cover it up! We can hide in the wardrobe."

There was no time to think. Alice closed the lid and locked it in one motion, shoving the letters and the key down the front of her stays. Poppy was already replacing the floorboards. Then the carpet went back, and then the plant stand, as silently as they could manage it.

"This way!" Poppy whispered. She grabbed Alice's wrist, hauling her toward the wardrobe.

"Wait!" Alice pulled free, dived for the fern on the desk, and replaced it on the stand. There was a scatter of dirt left behind, but she didn't have time to clean it up. She darted after Poppy, climbing into the wardrobe and pulling the door shut just as the brass knob rattled and swung open.

The wardrobe had been filled with coats, ready to hand if Bancroft decided to leave the house in a hurry. Alice and Poppy were squashed together in a sea of itchy wools reeking of tobacco smoke. It wasn't quite tall enough to stand up straight, and within a minute Alice was feeling a cramp in her legs. She could also smell the perfume Poppy was wearing, which was suspiciously similar to Imogen's scent.

It would have been tempting to scratch or sneeze, but fear kept her still. Her eye was right by the crack between the double doors. She could see Lord Bancroft unconsciously flick away the crumbs of dirt the fern had left on his desk. Her heart climbed into her mouth, waiting for him to react, but instead he picked up the carved cigarette box that sat on the desk, opened it, and turned to offer it to whoever had come in with him.

Alice felt Poppy pushing against her side, trying to see through the crack as well. But Alice couldn't move, utterly transfixed by curiosity. But then she saw a hand reach forward to take a cigarette, and she knew the ring on the fourth finger—a jet stone set with a diamond—mourning jewelry worn since her mother's death. It was the only outcome worse than Lord Bancroft himself ripping open the wardrobe doors.

A tiny mewl rose up her throat, barely stifled by Poppy's warning glare. *Oh, dear God, it's my father!*

BANCROFT CLOSED THE lid on his cigarette box slowly, resisting the urge to snap it shut on his visitor's fingers. Keating strolled over to the phoenix statue, stepped on its claw, and lit his cigarette at the flame that sprang to life in its beak.

"How goes Reading's suit of your fair daughter?" Keating asked.

"Imogen will come around," Bancroft answered, wishing he had more faith in the statement. She watched the Scarlet King as if he were a monster crawling out of the compost pile at the bottom of the garden. "She always does what she's told in the end."

Bancroft watched his guest, wondering. He'd noticed the unlocked door, the crumbs of soil on his desk. The intruder had probably been a servant going about household business—the butler, Bigelow, had one of the few keys to the room—but he never ruled out intrusion of a different kind. These days, spies were everywhere, and he was careful to the point of paranoia.

One of the Gold King's companies was undertaking the repairs on the unhappy couple's future home, and the work was taking an unnaturally long time. Bancroft half suspected that was a ploy to force Alice and Tobias into Hilliard House. What better way to insert spies than to do it in the character of your own son and daughter-in-law? But of course, he could prove nothing.

Keating made himself at home in one of the brass-studded leather chairs. Bancroft lit his own cigarette and settled into the other. He let the smoke bite his tongue and throat, then he exhaled in a pungent, heavy cloud.

"Did you hear something coming from the wardrobe?" Keating asked.

"Probably mice," Bancroft said, wishing for a whisky to go with the cigarette. "We've seen a little gray devil running the halls. Bigelow has ordered traps to be set."

"Hm." Keating resettled into the oxblood leather. "So back to the matter of Alice's emeralds. The police found them during a raid at a less-than-reputable establishment in Bethnal Green. It appeared that they were on the verge of being dismantled and the stones reset."

"Thank heavens they were found." And, fortunately, after the jeweler had already secured a buyer and a tidy sum was in the hands of the Schoolmaster's men. For once, the gods were smiling on his efforts. Bancroft tipped his ash into a silver ashtray that wheeled about on clockwork feet. A tiny brush swept out, flicking the ash into a reservoir hidden beneath the tray.

"Indeed." Keating picked a crumb of tobacco from his lip. "My question is, who would have access to a private affair in Mayfair and yet have connections in a place like that?"

"Hotel employees?" It was a safe suggestion. Bancroft had paid a staff member of the Portmore Hotel to leave the door to the display of wedding gifts unguarded, but he'd also arranged for the man to take a long vacation to America.

"We've had them questioned already—the ones we could find. We got confessions of all manner of things, but not the theft of my daughter's jewels."

Bancroft recalled the men in black coats patrolling the wedding breakfast. A sick feeling fluttered through his stomach, almost like remorse. But he hadn't felt that for so long, he couldn't be sure. "It has to be one of them, or a thief who looks sufficiently like one of us that he would not be remarked among the other guests."

"I imagine he might look like a gentleman," Keating said evenly.

Bancroft didn't like his tone at all, and aimed for a fork in the conversational road. "The stones might have passed through several hands."

"And probably did. The current theory is that they were

sold to fund rebel activities. The shop where they were found has known connections to a network of rogue makers."

A seeping, anxious nausea raised a prickling sweat between Bancroft's shoulder blades. "Did they question the jeweler?"

Keating narrowed his eyes, regarding Bancroft speculatively. "He did not survive the experience long enough to name names. A damned inconvenience."

Bancroft ground out his cigarette, giving up on the idea of a relaxing smoke. *Magnus was right about one thing. Keating must die.* "The rebels must be desperate if they are reduced to robbing brides."

"They are desperate enough to have hired on pirates. They seem to stop at nothing."

"Pirates?"

"A vessel called the *Red Jack*. The wretch who commands her is one Captain Niccolo, who by all reports is the same piece of trash who stole the remains of Athena's Casket."

Bancroft crossed his legs, wondering if the conversation was about to turn in his favor. A week had passed since Magnus had blighted the wedding, and the man had written nearly every day demanding either the casket or Keating's head. Bancroft, however, wasn't about to spoil his shot by rushing in too soon. "What makes you think there is a connection?"

A pinched look came over the Gold King's face. "The ship flies higher and faster than it has a right to. Its navigational capabilities are unsurpassed."

Bancroft put on his best musing expression. "All this from an ancient lump of melted metal? It still seems strange to me."

"The ancients knew some secrets that we have forgotten." Keating ground out his cigarette. "And now the rebels have that knowledge, and we do not."

Bully for us? But Bancroft was dubious about the value of those secrets. No one with any wits messed with magic, and sailors—even pirates—had to be practical men. Still, he wasn't going to argue.

Instead he put on a comforting smile and spun what he

fervently hoped was a lie. "Perhaps if they've lost the emeralds, they will not be able to pay the pirates, and they will be right back to where they began—a handful of disgruntled makers and political rabble-rousers."

Keating gave him that searching look again. "An interesting theory."

"A realistic one."

"Aren't you forgetting that the highest ranks of society are infected with the blight of these malcontents? The so-called Baskerville connection?"

Bancroft spread his hands in a gesture of surrender. "There are always romantics, but are these high-society poets going to thrive if the insurgents are dug out? A vine won't flower without roots, no matter how high it climbs."

"We'll see," said Keating. "Some prefer a snake metaphor, and speak of lopping off its head. The Steam Council has dealt the serpent a blow. This morning Mycroft Holmes was taken into custody."

The news raised the hairs up the back of Bancroft's neck. He reeled, but tried to cover his look of shock with a laugh. It didn't sound convincing, even in his own ears. "You got into the Diogenes Club? With all those guards?"

"A warrant against treason is an effective passport."

Smug bastard. And the reason Keating brought it up was obvious. He suspected Bancroft of rebel sympathies just like Bancroft suspected Keating of spying on his every move. The conversation was a warning.

Feeling his face heat, Bancroft rose from his chair and plucked another cigarette from the box, needing something for his nerves. He wanted a drink so badly his bones hurt. He turned to the phoenix, forcing himself to stall as he lit the cigarette. He needed a moment to gather his wits.

Mycroft Holmes, taken. Others had ignited the fires of rebellion—when it came to objecting to the Steam Council, those fires rather lit themselves—but the elder Holmes brother had emerged as their guiding intelligence. Bancroft had no idea if those sympathies extended to Sherlock. The two brothers were not close, so there was no reason to assume, and Bancroft was too recently admitted to the inner circle to know. He had only become aware of Mycroft's involvement in July, when the man had invited him to attend the Stranger's Room at the Diogenes Club. Bancroft's steady financial support of the rebel makers—often at the cost of his own family—had at last paid off.

Bancroft admired few men, but he respected Mycroft Holmes. He had turned unfocused anger into measurable gains. He had crafted the shadow government that would step in to rebuild after the rebellion was done. He had vision and organizational acumen. Best of all, Mycroft Holmes wanted no power for himself. Too much work, he said. He just wanted the fun of redesigning the Empire.

The invasion of the Diogenes Club was a wholesale disaster. Bancroft dragged smoke into his lungs, trying to wipe the dismay from his features before he turned back to his accursed guest.

"So that is one fire halfway to put out," Keating said speculatively. "Not a bad week all told. My daughter's emeralds recovered, a rebel leader taken. There's the pirate ship to capture, but we came close. We'll do better next time. There only remains the situation in the Blue King's domain."

"What's that?" Keating asked, but he already knew.

"The Whitechapel Murderer. The rebels are using terror and police incompetence to whip up a riot. I can feel it in my belly."

"But isn't that your colleague's problem?" Normally, one steam baron seemed to enjoy the discomfort of another. They were like a savage species of fish, each prone to eating its fellows.

"It's a big enough threat that the entire council has taken an interest. Must protect innocent citizens, you know." Keating gave a cynical smile. "We didn't start the murders, but I almost wish we had. Money can't buy the kind of goodwill catching the killer will provide."

"Isn't that the job of the police?"

"The Yellowbacks and Blue Boys are at their disposal. King Coal has hired the other Holmes. He's my man, though. If he cracks the case, I'm not letting the Blue King take all the credit."

"Sherlock Holmes?" Bancroft spat, the name like dirt on his tongue.

"His niece is missing." Keating frowned, but to Bancroft's trained eye something was off. "Apparently he thinks she's in the Blue Territories and he wants King Coal's help to find her. He's offering his detective skills in trade for their goodwill."

"Really?" This was news to Bancroft. "I'd heard rumors that the girl had run off, but I assumed it would be someplace more pleasant. Why Whitechapel?"

"To be honest, I've expected the girl to come crawling home by now, but she's either truly lost or has more fortitude than I expected."

Once, Bancroft had underestimated Evelina Cooper. That wouldn't happen again. "I would think you'd be helping Holmes to look for her. I thought you rather valued their services."

"The girl overstepped her welcome at my country house. I pointed that out to her, and she chose to run rather than repair the wrong."

So that was why Keating looked so shifty. Bancroft's gut grew cold. *The little foolish chit.* He didn't like the girl, but he knew Evelina's loyalty to the family, and to Imogen in particular. Keating used that kind of love like a weapon, and her fall from favor meant nothing good for Bancroft's children, whatever other alliances they might make.

But realistically, if Evelina Cooper had lost herself in Whitechapel, she was gone forever, a lost cause. Bancroft knew grown men who wouldn't set foot in certain streets there. And even if she survived, her reputation was dust. *Keating has to go.*

It seemed the man read his thoughts, as he was getting to his feet with the air of one who had stayed long enough. He pulled a black velvet case from his pocket and set it on Keating's desk. "The emeralds are in there. See to it that they're safely returned to Alice, will you? I don't have time to visit with her today. I've work to do."

You don't have the stomach to look at her unhappy face,

you mean. Bancroft knew Keating loved his daughter, but not as much as he loved owning Tobias's genius. His idiot son had already introduced efficiencies to the Gold King's steam-generating plants that doubled their profitability. Who could have guessed the boy had it in him? And that poor Alice's happiness was expendable in the face of so much earnings potential? Bancroft was actually starting to feel protective of the girl.

"I'll see to it she gets her jewels," he said. "I'm sure having them back will brighten her day."

"I'm sure it will," Keating said with yet another of those narrow-eyed looks. The man was going to develop a squint.

Bancroft ushered him out of the study, then closed and locked the door behind him. Then he was finally free to do what he'd been aching to for the last half hour. He all but ran to the fireplace and reached inside. The key was gone. Without that, he couldn't even see what was missing from his box under the floor.

Fury crawled over his skin, down his throat, through his belly. *Who took it?* He backed out of the chimney, breathing hard, his vision blurred with panic. *Try again.* He reached inside and up, feeling for the chink in the stone where he kept the key. The hole was there, but nothing else. Thinking it might have dropped, he scanned the grate, but it had been recently swept. No key there, either.

He stood, breathing hard and working his hands as if to grab control of his racing heart. But all his fists clenched was thin air. *So either someone swept it up and put it out in the ash bin, or someone stole it.*

But when had he seen it last? Bancroft tried to tame his thoughts. Just last night, he'd gone into the box to dip into his secret supply of gold. With Magnus in town, he'd wanted to enhance his collection of specialty weapons. Protecting himself from the unkillable would take more than a common revolver—but a purchase like that was best kept untraceable, so he'd bypassed his usual man of business.

But that narrowed the range of possibilities. The thief had to have broken in between last night and now. He needed to find out who'd been in there that day. *Could it have been Magnus?*

Bancroft ran for the door, rattled his way through it, and bolted down the hall bellowing for the butler. Someone in the house had to know who'd been there. He'd find out if he had to hire some inquisitors of his own.

Chapter Thirty-five

BY THE TIME THE SUN WAS FADING, ALICE WISHED WITH ALL
her heart that she'd never agreed to snoop in Lord Bancroft's
study. After they'd fled the wardrobe and made it safely to
the corridor, they'd split up, retreating to their own rooms
like shamefaced children. Unnerved, Alice couldn't shake
the conversation she'd overheard. She'd understood little of
it, but echoes of it went around and around in her mind,
ominous as the great black rooks that had clustered around
Maggor's Close. She'd always known her father's business
had tendrils in much more than gas and coal. She knew he
was ruthless. But this had hinted at so much more darkness
that she barely recognized the man who had cared for her all
her life.

Cared for, until he'd traded her happiness for a son he
wanted more. In the end, diving into the German letters was
an act of self-preservation. Anything to focus her reeling
mind.

And then, with a rising nausea born of horror, she wished
she hadn't done that, either. She read them through, pacing
back and forth across the bedchamber, as if walking would
help her concentrate. At first, she thought her German was
at fault, that she didn't understand what she read. But when
she finally accepted the words on the page, she wasn't sure
what to do.

She had to tell Tobias. It wasn't so easy when they barely
spoke and when he would all but run from the room when
she appeared. But after what she'd read, Alice was in no
mood for any more games. Her best option was to ambush
him in his own chamber. So she was sitting on the edge of

Tobias's bed when he came into his room that evening, the papers spread out on her knees.

"What are you doing here?" he asked, a look almost like fear on his face.

"I'm not here to take advantage of you," she snapped, and then regretted it. "I have something you're going to want to see."

His gaze fell on the stack of correspondence. "That's in High German."

"It is. You've been looking for the history of your father's automatons," she began.

"How do you know that?" he asked, his voice growing hard. "I didn't ask you to involve yourself."

"One would have to be deaf, the way you're carrying on about it."

He had that expression again, that deliberate absence of emotion that said exactly how afraid and angry he was. It gave his handsome face the look of a petulant Apollo about to turn her into a less troublesome object—a lampshade, perhaps, or a potted geranium.

"It's none of your business!" he growled.

"But this is." She waved the papers. "I think this is what you want to know. Read the top page." She thrust them into his hand before he could back away. "These were in your father's safe under the floor in his office. I broke in and took them."

He gave her a dumbfounded look that had just a hint of admiration. "You did?"

"I got bored." But she could see the questions coming. She waved her fingers at the papers. "Just read these before you worry about how I got them. There will be time enough for conversation afterward."

He stared at her another long moment, then turned his attention to the page. Then—as she'd hoped—her petty crimes didn't seem to matter anymore. "Dear God, these are from Magnus."

There were so many questions she wanted to ask, the words cramming into her throat with choking intensity, but she let him read. As she watched, the wall he'd pulled around him-

self faded, a crease forming between his brows. She saw his
shoulders sag, and then he sat on the stool at the end of the
bed, turning the paper over with trembling fingers.

Alice wanted to reach out and touch his shoulder, but she
couldn't summon the courage to offer sympathy. And he read
the next letter, and the next, his face growing paler with every
page. There was nothing she could say that would blunt the
shock.

When he finally finished, he sat motionless, his head bent.
"Now I know why he's such a miserable bastard. He can
never make up for what he did."

"Imogen needs to know," Alice said quietly.

"Fetch her," he said dully. "Father is in his study. Meet me
there."

Alice went without argument.

TOBIAS TOOK THE time to read the letters through again before he rose from the stool and went down the stairs to his
father's study. The clock on the landing spit out a card as he
walked past, but he left it lying on the floor. Evelina had
broken the code to the cipher, but he couldn't afford to think
about her, and he didn't want to hear anything one of Magnus's creations might have to say.

He pushed the door open to find his father sitting behind
his desk, his hands jammed into his thick, iron-gray hair.
Tobias strode across the room and slapped the letters down
before Lord Bancroft had more than lifted his head. "You're
going to explain all this to Imogen because *she* of all people
shouldn't have to learn the truth from Dr. Magnus. What did
you do? Keep these as proof he is a sorcerer? Or as a reminder of how low you sank?"

"Always be thrifty with evidence, even if you can't use it
right away." Bancroft's hand slid over the letters, his eyes
icy slits. "What in all the black hells gives you the right to
steal from me and then demand I explain myself? You've
surrendered the moral high ground these days."

"I might begin to understand you, but I don't forgive you,"

Tobias said, his jaw so tight it was hard to push out the words.

"I didn't ask for absolution."

"You will, now or later."

"Are you a prophet now, boy?"

Tobias heard movement behind him, and he stepped back from the desk. Alice was walking toward them, a resolute set to her face, as if she meant to kick them both in the shins. Imogen trailed after, an uncertain frown clouding her eyes.

Alice stopped at the edge of Lord Bancroft's desk and set the key on his blotter. "I believe this is yours."

"You took it?" her father-in-law asked incredulously.

She hesitated for a heartbeat and then lifted her chin. "Guilty as charged."

"You little snake!" Bancroft leaned across the desk, as if he meant to leap over it. Tobias grabbed his wife's arm, pulling her back. Alice stiffened. And then he realized it was the first time he'd touched her since their wedding. He dropped his hand as if she'd burned him.

"What's going on?" Imogen asked nervously.

Bancroft's face was growing red, the veins in his neck bulging at the collar. "How dare you creep into my study and put your thieving fingers all over my things? Are you spying for your father, little girl?"

Tobias could not stop himself from turning to face her. He'd been wondering the same thing. "Alice?"

"No!" she snapped. "This is your family's affair. And I know what my father would do with what's written there. I'm married to your son, Lord Bancroft, and what happens to him happens to me. There is no good ending for any of us if I open my mouth."

"What are you talking about?" Imogen cried, her voice shrill with frustration. "Will someone please tell me what is going on?"

"Will you?" Tobias demanded of his father. "She's the one who needs to know."

Bancroft fell back into his chair. "And if I don't? Are you going to pick up a gun like you did the last time I failed to live up to your ideals?" He sounded nonchalant, but his eyes were haunted.

Tobias's jaw ached with tension. "For God's sake, just do the right thing for once."

Alice sat down in one of the chairs and crossed her arms, as if she planned to wait out Bancroft's stubbornness. Imogen followed suit, though she looked like she'd prefer to bolt for the door. Tobias remained standing. A silence fell, as if no one wanted to be the first to start the avalanche that would bury whatever remained of their family bond.

"Who was this Dr. Magnus?" Alice demanded. "I know Father despised the man, but little else."

Bancroft sat perfectly still, as if weighing the situation and calculating odds. Tobias could almost hear his brain whirring like the longcase clock, checking barometric pressure and the phases of the moon to see which way his advantage lay. But there was no way out—Tobias and Alice already knew the truth. The only thing that was left was to give his version of events.

For once, Tobias had his father cold. And, true to form, Bancroft settled back, looking as if he'd meant to play raconteur all along.

"Magnus was my friend when I was young. We met in Austria," Bancroft began conversationally. "I was very interested in mechanics, and so was he, although it might be said that I was the technician and he was the theorist."

His father sounded distant, almost as if he were talking of strangers. "Magnus was capable enough with tools—he built that longcase clock on the second-floor landing—but didn't have the patience to undertake the detailed project he wanted most to explore. He wished to create life-size automatons that went far beyond anything created before. This was the project that drew us together, for I relished such mechanical work."

And then his expression sagged, the urbane mask slipping an inch. "What I did not know at the time was that he was also an accomplished sorcerer."

"Sorcerer?" Alice exclaimed, her voice a squeak.

"A sorcerer," Tobias repeated, remembering all too well

the horrors of the doctor's project. *Serafina*. She still haunted his nightmares.

Bancroft gave his son an ironic nod. "At this time, we were a young family. Poppy was a baby, Imogen and Anna were about five, and you, Tobias, were ten. I was happy, a man with a healthy career and many friends. But then the twins fell ill."

Tobias could sense his father slipping into memories. At once, he seemed both more guarded and less, keeping his face turned from all three of them. He picked up a pen from his desk, turning it over and over in his hands.

"I remember the automatons," Imogen offered, her voice cracking with apprehension. "You made them to keep Anna and I amused when we were sick. They walked and danced and one could sweep with a broom."

"They were crude by today's standards, but I was proud of them back then," Bancroft admitted. "And Magnus kept making them do more and more. At first I found it amusing, but your mother became frightened. Magic is not illegal in Austria, but even so the living dolls made her uncomfortable."

"So you tried to put them away but then Magnus asked for money," Imogen offered. "Tobias told me that much."

"But there's a part in between," Tobias said grimly, putting his hand on his sister's shoulder for reassurance. It was the only thing he could do, letting her know she wasn't alone.

Bancroft's face went utterly blank, as if he had suddenly left his body. "There *is* more."

The words held more menace than all of Bancroft's bluster. The room seemed to grow cold with it, the wind rattling the windows drowning out any familiar noises from the street. It felt like the room, with them in it, was the whole world.

Imogen slid down in her chair, shuddering. Tobias looked around, but of course there were no wraps or blankets in the study. Comfort wasn't his father's way. Alice caught his eye. She took off her own shawl and held it out. With a nod of thanks, he draped it around Imogen's shoulders.

"You were ill, Imogen," Bancroft said slowly, "but Anna

was far sicker. The doctors never knew the name of the disease, but it affected the two of you differently. While you grew thin and wan, your sister's limbs began to twist, as if the bones themselves were writhing in pain. Soon, she could not walk, or even lift a spoon. My beautiful, vibrant little girl, who once loved to dance. And then came a time when Anna never stopped wailing in pain."

"I remember," Imogen whispered, clutching at the edge of the shawl. She looked as if she were about to cry.

Tobias remembered, too, with the sharp edges that only childhood horrors could hold. But what he remembered even more than his little sister's agony was his mother's fear and his father's desperation. That was how he'd known the earth was crumbling beneath their feet.

Bancroft's voice became hard, as if that were the only way to marshal the words. "In the end, I could barely recognize her as human, much less my own daughter. Your mother became hysterical. The physicians feared that she would waste away with the same fever. To make matters worse, none of the servants would come near Anna. They were all terrified of her. So I did the only thing I could think of."

He paused and swallowed convulsively, as if he were choking. "I hid my daughter away in the highest room of the east tower and prayed for a miracle. As a final act of folly, I asked Magnus to make the automatons her nursemaids."

Bancroft drifted to silence, as if he, too, were clockwork and the spring had wound down. Anger crawled through Tobias, but this time it wasn't on his own behalf. The little girl who'd been Imogen's twin—his sister—had been abandoned, alone and in pain with nothing but inhuman servants to watch over her. And the man on the other side of the desk had done it.

He knew what came next, and he didn't want to hear it out loud. Alice pressed her hands to her face, as if she wished she could block it out, too.

"And then," Bancroft said so softly that Tobias barely heard him, "Magnus made me an offer. He said he could end Anna's suffering."

"How?" Imogen said. It came out almost as a whimper.

"He said he could put her soul into one of the automatons. Let her live in a whole body, without pain. I begged him to do it. I offered him money." Bancroft had his elbow on his desk, one hand over his eyes.

"What?" Imogen stumbled to her feet. "Dr. Magnus killed Anna?"

Bancroft didn't budge. He didn't even speak at first, just worked his lips as if in prayer—but to what deity, Tobias refused to even guess. "Her body died. I came to his chambers after it was all over. The scene was like some trope from a Gothic novel, a stone room in a tower marked with chalk circles and guttered candles. But something had happened. I felt it like foul offal running down the walls, down my own soul . . ." His voice trailed off to a harsh rasp. "It was then I knew how evil he truly was."

Horror swarmed over Tobias's skin, kicking his heart into a shallow, quick gallop. This part hadn't been in the letters. He had to summon enough spit to wet his tongue before words would come out. "What about the doll?"

"Magnus said Anna was inside, but trapped. The spell had been imperfect."

Imogen sat down again, her mouth agape.

Bancroft took his hand from his eyes. They were bloodshot, his expression more naked than Tobias had ever seen it. "That was why I could never destroy the automatons. I believed just enough to wonder if that would be infanticide. It sounds like madness, but I couldn't accept that risk."

"She was my twin," Imogen whispered. "You paid Dr. Magnus to lock her soul forever in a prison of sawdust and cracked porcelain. A prison she could never escape."

Bancroft cleared his throat, the accusation seeming to steady him. The horror on his face faded to something bitter. "And, according to Magnus, that made destroying them doubly dangerous for you."

Imogen made a sound that raised the hair along Tobias's arms. It wasn't quite a scream, but a bleat of pain from somewhere deep inside her. "You put her in a dark, terrible prison for the last dozen years!"

Something stirred in the back of Tobias's mind, but Imogen spoke again before it was fully formed. "She would be mad by now. A little child, alone with no love and no light."

"We don't know if that's true!" Bancroft snapped.

"I do. I dream of it. Her soul is lost and can't get back to where it belongs."

Twins share a soul, Tobias thought, his insides bleak with cold. *At least in fairy tales. If it's true, no wonder she has nightmares.* Then he looked at his father, who seemed to be hiding his shock beneath a mask of contempt. *This is even worse than he knew.* For an instant, he almost felt sorry for his father.

Until the foggy idea at the back of his mind coalesced. "You put them both at risk, because every time the automatons are moved, Imogen falls ill."

Both Imogen and Alice stared at him, eyes huge. He saw the realization click into place for his sister, followed by helpless fury.

"I tried to save my daughter," Bancroft said coldly. "Wait until you hold your own child in your arms before you judge. There is no folly you will not commit."

Tobias took out the letter his mother had given him, and set it down on top of the others. "And that's how Magnus is still blackmailing you? He still has the automatons, doesn't he?"

His father made an exasperated grimace. "My, my, is nothing in my private study actually private anymore?"

"Dr. Magnus is alive?" Alice asked softly. "He has these automatons?"

"He reminds me of my situation almost daily," Bancroft said icily. "But before you run and tell the Gold King, madam, that I'm in the clutches of a madman, consider what Magnus might do."

"As I said, this is none of my father's business," Alice said defiantly.

"I'm glad you understand that so well," Bancroft said in a tone Tobias couldn't decipher.

"Does Mother know any of this?" Imogen asked suddenly.

"No," Bancroft said harshly. "I spared her that much. You may loathe me. You may never forgive me, but know that I desperately wanted to give her back her child."

But you failed, and that is why you are the way you are—lost in your own twisted games, because there you can fool yourself into believing that you might still win. But nothing will ever make up for consigning your own ailing child to a solitary prison, and then to murder by an agent of evil.

Imogen had gone entirely white. She slowly slipped off Alice's shawl and handed it back to her. "Well, Tobias, now that you have found the hidden wound in our family history, are we on the road to healing?" Her voice was thin and high with strain. In the uncertain light, her pale gray eyes were translucent, almost as if there were no color at all.

He couldn't answer. There had been no plan beyond finding the truth.

Imogen hovered a moment, her presence seeming to shrink until she was no more than a flickering ghost. Tobias took a step forward, instinctively wanting to wrap her in human warmth. But Imogen made a gesture, her palm turned to the lot of them, and stalked out of the room. It said more than any speech that she'd closed a door between her world and theirs.

After a hesitant look at Tobias, Alice followed. That left Tobias alone with his father.

"You know, I spent hours bullying the servants, but no one could say who took the key. And here it was your little wife." His father's voice smoked with angry sarcasm. "You should keep your eye on that one. She's going to give you trouble."

Tobias rounded on his father. "Don't."

"No? I thought you hated her."

"Don't," he repeated. "You don't have the right."

"Not after this confession, you mean?" His father's mask was back in place, the vulnerability Tobias had glimpsed banished from view. "Tell me, *did* you learn the secret that will stitch us all back into one big, happy family? Imogen has a point. There had better be some benefit to making us live through that misery again."

Tobias glared at him. "I hope you rot in hell."

Bancroft shrugged, plucking a cigarette out of the box on his desk. "Oh, no worries on that score. I'm halfway there already. However, you've left me with quite the little problem on my hands. You see, some secrets are better off buried."

Tobias turned his back on his father and stormed out, slamming the door behind him. Childish, but it released a tiny part of the pent-up tension twisting his guts. *Was that a threat?* Probably, but then his father threatened someone at least once a day. Maybe more. But it was high time he and Alice left, whether or not his own townhouse was ready. *There is still that honeymoon trip.*

He turned his feet toward the stairs, mounting them two at a time. Would Alice really keep all this from her father? He didn't know her well enough to tell. What he did know was that she'd come to him with the letters, even after he'd treated her abominably. That said something about her will to make things work.

He stopped in front of her door and knocked, but there was no answer. He turned the knob and slipped in anyway, turning up the key on the lamp enough to see. His father never did have gas laid in on the upper floors—something a steam baron's daughter must have found odd.

Tobias made a circuit of the room, suddenly curious about her in a way he'd never been during their supposed courtship. The maids hadn't been through since Alice had left her bedroom. The suitcase was gone from the bed and sat closed and accusing by the wall. The wardrobe door was half open, a dress draped over the mirror and another dangling off the knob. The dressing table was a mess, lids off the jars, nothing arranged with even minimal care. *Not a natural housekeeper, then.* But there was a stack of unfamiliar books on the bedside table. Alice was a reader. And the box with the emeralds teetered carelessly on top of those. *She likes pretty things, but doesn't treasure them the way some women do.*

He'd made her so unhappy. He'd *been* so unhappy, but like some broken sewer pipe, he'd made sure everyone had the benefit of his mood. Remorse hunched his shoulders.

His father wasn't the only one tearing the house apart at the foundation.

The bed was littered with clothes. He picked up one of the finely knitted stockings and it draped over his hand, clinging softly. He recalled peeling just such an item from her calf last summer, the silky smoothness of her inner thigh damp under his hand.

"Tobias?" Alice said from the doorway.

He dropped the stocking as if it were a serpent. "Are you all right? After all that?"

"I think so." She went to the dressing table, pushing a few objects aimlessly around, but not bothering to screw the lids back on any of the jars. "I gave Imogen a sleeping draft and put her to bed. I don't know how well she's going to take this."

"She's tougher than she looks," he said, but knew Alice was right. They would have to take extra care with his sister for a while. "Speaking of sisters, was Poppy in any way involved with this escapade?"

"Whatever makes you think that?" Alice said, meeting his eyes in the mirror. She wasn't a very good liar.

"Thank you for protecting her." And he put his hands on his wife's shoulders, hardly adding any weight at all. He'd forgotten how small she actually was, barely coming up to his chin.

And then she put her hand on his, brushing his fingers with the tips of hers. "I'm sorry. None of this can have been easy for you." And then she laughed nervously. "How is that for understatement?"

He just gave a slight squeeze by way of reply. They could have talked about the horrors of what they'd learned, but he didn't want to right then. It was like a monster waiting outside the door, bloody ax in hand. There was every chance that fighting it would tear him limb from limb. Was it any wonder he didn't rush to invite it in? Especially now, when he'd found some little crumb of peace between him and Alice.

"I can't begin to make sense of what your father said," she

murmured. "It's going to take days to even believe I heard that story."

"I can't believe that you actually broke into my father's study."

"I'm sorry."

"No, you're not." He put a touch of levity into his voice.

The slightest smile touched her face. He turned her around to face him and cupped her cheek with his hand. Her blue eyes were open wide, reminding him of a startled bird. A messy, brave, capable little bird. "I'm an ass, you know."

"Mm-hm," she said, nodding.

He stroked her cheek with his thumb, tangling himself in a few strands of her coppery hair. In the warm glow of the flame, her skin looked ivory, the line of her jaw limned by lamplight. *Beautiful.*

And then, finally, Tobias kissed his wife—gently, sweetly, and with as much apology as he could put into it. The taste of her tugged deep inside him, calling up memories of lust. Her lips were warm, and not just in the usual way. There was something spicy about her, a bite that called to him in a way that sweetness wouldn't.

The first kiss done, he paused, waiting for her to pull back. As their breath mingled, a little quicker than usual, he waited for the slap across his face, or the shove to his chest. After all, he deserved all that and more. He deserved a kick to the head. But Alice hooked her finger into his collar button, pulling his head down, and kissed him back.

CHAPTER THIRTY-SIX

September 29, 1888

Dear Sir,

I have found the information you require and will be in receipt of proof first thing on the morrow. It is my intention to deliver this to you as soon as possible. Rest assured that you will be satisfied, and I humbly beg that you continue to regard me and my family as your most obedient servants. E.C.

—addressed to Keating care of the Oraculars' Club

London, September 29, 1888
DR. MAGNUS'S MAGNETORIUM THEATRE

11:50p.m. Saturday

EVELINA PICKED UP HER KNIFE, RUNNING IT THROUGH THE flame of the candle at her worktable, first one side of the glistening edge, then the other. The blade gleamed in the theater's cavernous work space, a scrap of lightning in the late-night dark. The evening show was done, all her repairs complete. The only doll missing was Serafina, who was in the private rooms with Magnus. Evelina had the place to herself.

She should go home, go to sleep, and in the morning Nick would fetch her. Her body ached from her tumble from the waterwheel, and she was as tired as she could be without falling over. And yet she felt a marked reluctance to leave the Magnetorium. The sorcerer was everything she loathed, but he held the secrets to her magical heritage—and so she lingered, tools packed, coat by the door. She would take her knowledge with her, but like a student proud of her perfect copy book, she attempted the very last spell Magnus had shown her. The theater was the safest place to do so, and she wanted to master everything before she left the place behind. It should take no more than a moment.

She lifted the blade from the flame, blowing on it to cool the metal. Then she pressed the honed, perfect edge to the base of her left thumb, where her hand had the most meat, and pressed it deep. She couldn't stop a ragged gasp of pain as fire lanced up her nerves and she dropped the knife to the worktable. *This had better work.*

For the span of a few breaths, she couldn't do anything. Blood welled from the wound, a glorious ruby in the candlelight. It spilled out the gap in her flesh, running into the lines of her palm like water finding dry streambeds, then dribbling onto the scarred wood of the workbench. But then Evelina let her mind fall into the void that Magnus had shown her the day they'd used her Gran Cooper's wand. Without the wand, it wasn't quite the same, but it was enough to remember the taste of the lives from the workhouse fire. And from that taste she could find the tiny bit of those lives she'd licked up and stored somewhere deep inside herself. She unspooled it from inside the way one unfurled a length of bandage from a roll, binding herself up in her imagination. It was impossible to say how it all worked, exactly, but as she pressed that bit of life to the cut on her hand, the slash grew back together, knitting as neatly as if the steel had never touched her. In a moment, all that was left was caked, flaking crumbs of blood and a terrible thirst.

It worked. A grin split her face as she crossed to the washbasin and scrubbed off the blood. All that was left was a thin pink line. Magnus had taught her well.

She picked up the water pitcher, found a tin mug, and drank her fill. Using magic like that always left her dry— and tired. Her limbs felt weak as rubber, and yet she couldn't control the gallop of her heartbeat. With this spell, she could heal so much better than she ever could before—faster, better, more completely. And if she could heal herself, there was no reason she couldn't heal someone else.

A flush of excitement heated her cheeks. She pressed the cool metal of the mug to her face, taking a deep lungful of air to calm herself. *And if I can do this, what else can I do?* Her mind shied away from the question, not wanting to know. This was sorcery, plain and simple. But not so simple. It seemed to have too many ambiguous faces to call it good or evil.

She hadn't forgotten her desire—no, her *need*—for something to protect herself from Jasper Keating. If a spell could heal, could it not also harm? She recalled that conversation in his study at Maggor's Close, the way he made it clear that she would cooperate, or he would leave her uncle vulnerable to the Blue King's assassins. All she would have to do is put a question to Magnus, and she would know exactly how to deal with the Gold King once and for all.

And that chilled her to the marrow. Before she had come here, such a thing would never have crossed her mind. *But I've made my choice. I will go with Nick and leave Magnus and his sorcery behind.* She rehearsed the words like a prayer, smoothing the trouble in her soul as if petting a bristling cat. She had skirted a dangerous mire, but she had not sunk in it. She would walk away before some will-o'-the-wisp lured her in.

Calmer now, she set the mug down, suddenly feeling as if she were not alone. Her gaze slid over the basin, then the table where it sat. The light was coming from the worktable behind her, falling on the rough wood in a yellow pool. She kept her gaze within the circumference of the light, not wanting to see beyond it.

They only came after she'd done one of Magnus's spells. Ghosts, she supposed, and yet they didn't look like any spirits she'd ever seen. They squatted in the corners, resembling the shadows of the furniture and tools—but if one looked closely, it was obvious that their awkward limbs didn't mimic any familiar shape. And it was best not to try to count those limbs, because they never added up to four—just a lot of claws and a head like melted wax. One of them hunched by the door to the alley, crossing and uncrossing its many arms as if it couldn't get comfortable. Another stretched out on a vacant table, watching her with the empty sockets where eyes should have been.

Go, please, go, she thought, praying all the while that they would never answer. With a quick, sideways step, she crossed the divide between the washbasin and the worktable. She picked up the candlestick, clutching the light like a shield. They never moved, never tried to grow closer, just watched. If she found a bright place and waited a half hour, they would be gone again. If magic drew them, they went home once the show was over. Or maybe she just stopped seeing them, and they were in truth always there. Now that was a disturbing thought.

She edged toward the stairway that led to Magnus's rooms. Light poured down the steps, banishing the shadowy figures wherever the bright beams touched. The creatures seemed as allergic to illumination as they were addicted to sorcery. What clearer sign did she need that what Magnus was teaching her wasn't wholesome?

Tonight, Evelina wasn't brave enough to wait them out— she wanted light, and lots of it. She picked up the candle and walked carefully to the stairway that led upstairs, anxious lest the flame blow out and leave her alone in the dark with the apparitions. They might not hurt her, but the idea was more than she could bear. Evelina mounted the winding steps, glad of the pool of light falling from above.

She reached the top only to encounter a man outside Serafina's dressing-room door, buttoning his jacket. Serafina stood by the window, beautiful and blank as ever although she seemed poised, as if she were about to break into another dance. The man was one of the patrons, dressed in evening clothes, but not his best set, she guessed. They had the look of clothes one might use for an illicit night out rather than dinner at the Lord Mayor's. Evelina stopped in her tracks, recognizing Mr. Jeremy, the odious man on the train that she'd met on the way to Maggor's Close. *What the blazes is he doing here?*

"Hullo there, do I know you?" he said, confusion plain on

his face. He looked sweaty and pale, as if he had just been ill, but that didn't stop him from ogling the neckline of her dress.

"No, sir," she said, as meekly as she could manage, and bobbed a curtsey.

"It's about time Magnus got some servants. Never anyone to fetch a brandy for a generous admirer." He reached forward, perhaps to give her cheek a pinch.

Evelina raised the candle to intercept his fingers with the flame. He jerked back with a curse. "I'm sure I don't know what you mean, sir."

He cursed again, flicking his hand in the air and sucking his forefinger. He gave Evelina a filthy look and stalked toward the stairs. Evelina stared after him, wondering what that was all about.

Now very curious, Evelina turned to the dressing room. The door was open, light spilling out into the hall. It was precisely as she had seen it before, fussy and feminine, but now lamps of delicate blown glass burned low, the soft light mingling with the smoke of burning resins.

A bundle of lilies and roses spilled over the dressing table, a white ribbon tying them together. A long velvet box sat beside them, open to reveal a single perfect pearl pendant from a golden chain. With a prickle of suspicion, Evelina struggled to understand what was going on. "Serafina?"

"Yes, Miss Cooper?" The doll replied. Her voice seemed to thrum, suddenly sounding far more human.

A prickling ran up the back of Evelina's arms. "What was Mr. Jeremy doing here?"

"He is an admirer. He came to kiss me."

I'll bet he did. Evelina bristled. "And he brings you gifts?"

"Yes. And he tells me that I am lovely." She stroked the front of her dress, her cleverly articulated fingers fondling the row of buttons between her breasts.

Evelina rounded on the doll, her protective instincts gathering steam. "Is that all he does? There is nothing more than kisses?"

She heard movement behind her. Magnus, and he gripped Evelina's hand with inarguable firmness and swung her around. "You should have gone home by now, my little kitten. And yet it seems you desire another lesson."

"What are you doing to her?" Evelina demanded, as the doctor pulled her into his study and closed the door, leaving Serafina outside.

"It is the perfect arrangement," he said quietly. "Men everywhere worship ideal beauty. Serafina provides all that and more. It is a guiltless encounter with the virtue of novelty."

"Guiltless?" Evelina protested, sinking into a chair because she wasn't sure she could stand. "Is that all they do then, bring flowers and baubles and sing her praises?"

Magnus shrugged. "Sirens the world over know how much favor to grant without giving away too much. I might encourage her to allow a little fawning from time to time."

Evelina said nothing, outrage mounting. Serafina was childlike, and children should never be subjected to Mr. Jeremy.

"You are censorious," Magnus said, amused.

"Serafina may not be human, but she's not without *something* inside."

He smiled, his dark eyes black in the half-light. "Such a soft-hearted thing you are. I made Serafina for this— fashioned her from a scrap of my own soul. She was made to serve."

"Serve what? Who? Men?" Evelina shuddered at the memory of Mr. Jeremy's knuckles casually grazing her skirts, trying to get what he could without being caught.

"Me." The word was cold.

"How? I don't understand. What is it you want from all this?" Evelina made a gesture that encompassed the room. "How can her degradation serve it?"

"Degradation. My, my." Magnus walked to a table that stood against the wall. It held a decanter of wine and a cluster of glasses. He poured himself a measure and drank it, but pointedly offered her nothing—a signal that he was displeased. "My interest is in survival. I want to recover my power. Coming back from the dead is not precisely child's play, no matter how well prepared one might be. And I would like revenge on those that put me on the cold marble slab of the police physician."

Nick. Evelina felt the blood drain from her face. She pushed the image of him out of her thoughts, just in case Magnus could read her mind. She wasn't fast enough—or maybe he just guessed by the sudden pallor in her cheeks. "Ah, yes, Nick with no surname, keeper of Athena's Casket. You know I still want the device, do you not?"

Evelina forced herself not to fidget, to stay focused on Magnus as if he were all that mattered—and most of all, to deflect the sorcerer from talk of Nick himself. She grabbed at a question to keep Magnus talking. "And what would you do with a deva? That isn't your kind of magic."

"The casket is a tool and a magnificent specimen worthy of study. I want to mix my kind of magic and yours and make something stronger than either."

"You want to enslave devas?" And no doubt that was one reason why he wanted her as his pupil. She knew how to command them.

"Enslave is a harsh word. Utilize has softer edges." He sipped his wine. "I want a means to an end. I'm tired of playing mountebank on the edges of true power, and I want a role at center stage. Most of all, I want an end to this ridiculous Steam Council, however cordial my relations with the Blue King might appear. At the moment it is convenient that King Coal and I both want Keating's liver baked in a tart. It makes for a convincing alliance, but let me say that Blue is more a puppet than my dancers will ever be. The man is utterly ensnared by his appetites."

Nick had been right about Magnus's plans. Curiosity rippled through her, quickly followed by dismay. What if Magnus did achieve a steam baron's position and influence? She had only seen a flicker of the doctor's darker side, but that was enough to know he should never be given that much leash.

He fingered his elegantly pointed beard. "I'm fighting to operate with complete freedom, without having to hide who and what I am. I'm sure you can appreciate my position?"

Her skin felt cold, robbed of all comforting warmth, but

she kept her face placid. Or she hoped she did. Her cheeks felt stiff with dismay. "I do."

"Excellent," he said, refilling his glass and this time pouring one for her. "And now that you have a glimpse of my motives—for they are relevant to the conversation—let us speak a little of Serafina. I understand that you took her for a walk yesterday afternoon. That was not wise."

"I will not repeat that mistake," Evelina said, sipping the wine to soothe her dry throat. "Although I am curious as to why she is . . ." She trailed off, not sure how to phrase what she meant.

"Volatile?" Magnus asked. "As I said, there have been incidents in the past, some more recent than I would like." For a moment, he appeared almost chagrined. "I am sure some is the effect of continued experiments on one physical vessel. One can never quite scrub away the residue of what came before. And then there is the shortage of quality materials. In the old days a sorcerer could simply get what he wanted. Now it is all torches and pitchforks if one steps over the line. Have you heard of this Vigilance Committee in Whitechapel? Where is their vigilance when their own people are starving in the streets?"

Evelina gripped the wineglass more tightly, her fingers growing slippery with cold sweat. "What does the Vigilance Committee have to do with Serafina?"

"Nothing, at the moment." Magnus's smile grew tight. "But I need to be careful living in a crowded neighborhood. Things would not go well if wind of a misbehaving automaton got out. I was forced to chastise her most severely."

"You were?" Evelina's muscles were so tense they throbbed. "So what is this peace she keeps talking about?"

"Ah, we come quickly to the heart of the matter, and your next lesson. You will understand all." He crossed to the door, turning the handle and letting it drift ajar. "Serafina, my lamb?"

The door creaked open, and Serafina appeared on the threshold.

"Come in," Magnus said gently, holding out his hand.

The automaton entered, her face almost animated. "That was the last man," she announced. "Shall I retire now?"

"You did well." Magnus patted her hand, steering her to a chair. "Sit."

Serafina sat. But the energetic grace of her movements bothered Evelina. Something was different. So she set down her wineglass and rose, crossing the room to put a hand on Serafina's shoulder. "Are you all right?"

But when Evelina's hand touched the automaton, it was like plunging her hand into a lake of living power. Her magic leapt for it, a beast suddenly desperate to feed.

With a start, the doll turned to her. "What are you doing?"

Evelina sprang back as if scorched, struggling against the urge to lap it up as a cat laps cream. "What is that?"

"You're stealing from me!" Serafina cried.

Magnus's laugh came soft and low. "Life. There's no going back after you've had a taste of it. Or don't you remember the burning workhouse?"

She stiffened, fear turning her muscles to rigid cords. "Those were dead souls." Or almost dead. Revulsion and hunger crashed inside her, tension aching up her spine.

Magnus lifted his wineglass. "This is nearly as good."

"You're like *him*!" The doll rose, inching toward the door.

Evelina rounded on Magnus. "What is she talking about?"

He shrugged. "Serafina is an amalgamation of things, but she does not have a complete soul. So, while a sorcerer may hunger for power to work magic, she hungers for her own reasons. She needs extra life to feel completely whole. That is what she calls being at peace."

Evelina stared at the doll. "Then she must almost always be hungry."

"That is how I made her. It guarantees that she is a good little hunter, although it is necessary to keep her on a short leash. No afternoon walks."

Serafina's hands closed slowly into fists. "But I am the one who dances. I bring them here. I do the taking."

"Yes, you do, my pretty lamb," said Magnus. "Serafina takes a bit from every one of her gentleman callers. They hardly even notice, unless they come back night after night."

"She takes their lives?" Evelina murmured. Shock had turned her mind hard and slippery, the words sliding across it without quite sinking in.

Magnus waved his hand in an exasperated gesture. "I take in a whiff of life every night—or don't you feel the emotion floating over the audience at each show? Haven't you heard of the energy of live performance? I didn't choose life in the theater for its financial reward."

"But this?" She pointed at Serafina.

"Is a slightly stronger brew, I admit, for all sides concerned. But then, she is the star of the show, is she not? Do they not give and take the most, after all?"

"The admirers give more than jewels, then," Evelina said, her voice sunk to a whisper.

"But they get what they want. When energy is harvested in this way, the giver of life swoons in the first embrace. He believes he has had a night of shattering pleasure, and yet rarely remains conscious long enough to unbutton his britches. It's very tidy, you have to admit. Our swain believes he has been to paradise, and yet our darling remains pure as the day she was stuffed. If he's a bit low on vital energy for a day or two, who is to complain?"

"It's unconscionable." Not that she had any great love for such men, but they were being cheated and drained, and Serafina—hungry and confused—dangled as bait.

"Why is it unconscionable?" asked Serafina, cutting across their argument.

Evelina couldn't think how to answer. Where to begin?

Magnus filled the gap. "I made her for this. She gathers the power I need to restore myself without the necessity of sacrificing a life. Or at least without more than what the French so poetically term the *little death*."

"Why?" Serafina asked again. "Why is it wrong?"

"Indeed," said Magnus. "None have come back demanding their trinkets."

Evelina swallowed hard. "No wonder Miss Hyacinth said that you didn't do the whores of Whitechapel any favors. How can they compete with this?"

A thunderous look crossed Magnus's face. For a fleeting

moment, he looked like a man who had been found out, and then his mocking mask fell back into place. "Enough," Magnus said, pulling Serafina to her feet. "This squeamishness ill becomes you, Miss Cooper, if you are to learn any more lessons from me."

More? The very thought made her stomach roil. "The shadows are already filled with monsters. I don't need to see more."

He gave her a searching look. "You can see them? Then you have progressed faster than I thought."

As much as she wanted to run from the room that instant, there was no way she could not ask. "What are they?"

His lip twitched, as if her question amused him. "They have no name. But where there is light, there is always a corresponding dark. Here the devas have fled, and these have grown bold, like any fungus when there is no light and fresh air. Only the Wraiths have ever harnessed them."

"The Wraiths?" Those were the creatures of the Black Kingdom's court that wore an aura of terror like a cloak.

"Indeed. They are to the Black Kingdom as the Blue Boys are to this slice of London. Once upon a time, I dwelled there and came to know the Black King and his subjects. The shadow creatures you saw are fearsome, but the Wraiths are worse. Some monsters cannot help what they are, but the Wraiths choose their lot out of a taste for inflicting horror. You do well to fear them, but that is not your only option. I can teach you to grind the Dark Kingdom's minions beneath your heel. If you let yourself, my girl, you might almost be my equal."

Evelina forgot to breathe. The room grew deathly still. *His equal?* The notion felt ridiculous, so far-fetched that he might have said she'd grow wings and fly to Venus. And horrible, because he was Magnus.

And yet, it stirred her curiosity. What might she be able to do? What would it feel like? Would it be the heady, cathartic rush she'd felt when she'd used her grandmother's wand? The memory of that experience quickened her pulse, awakening her appetite so acutely that her mouth filled with water. But it wasn't hunger for food. It was for the life buzzing around Serafina. "By the Dark Mother," she whispered in terror. "What have you done to me?"

"Nothing you did not ask for," he said smoothly. "I have forced nothing upon you."

He was right. She shrank back, as if mere proximity might grant him permission to do something else. "I'm leaving."

"Then go. Run back to your Nick. He loves you still, I think. Little does he know what a dark cat you truly are, my kitten."

"What are you saying?" she spat.

"Go, truly. I want you to. Then you'll bring me your pirate and the casket, surely you know that." He laughed at the expression on her face. "Do you think these lessons are free, dear Miss Cooper? The only question is when your thirst for knowledge—and your hunger for everything else—is going to outstrip your infatuation with a pirate and you'll drop him on my doorstep like a cat offers a bird. Sooner or later, that will happen. I play a long game and the seeds are sown. I can let you wander the world without a leash or collar, but you'll come around before the end. That clawing need inside you will become too great."

"Not bloody likely." She swallowed, though her throat was bone dry. *He's utterly mad!*

"Suit yourself," he said, and he held his hand just over Serafina's breast. "But the game is not over yet."

Then he peeled down the soft, silken fabric that covered the doll's throat, exposing a steel housing wired shut by intricate cables. Magnus took a key from a chain at his wrist and unlocked the metal case, and a moment later there was nothing where the delicate wings of her collarbone should have been. Inside was a spinning swirl of blue-black light, dizzying to the eye and crackling with energy.

Magnus raised his other hand, reaching for the humming energy. Evelina saw a dark shimmer appear between his fingers and the whirling ball. It seemed to rush upward, folding around and inside the sorcerer's hand as he savored all that delicious life. Evelina could taste it from across the room, could almost roll it around her tongue like champagne and feel it sparkling in her veins.

She scrambled from the room, her stomach trying to turn itself inside out. The only thing she could think of was how she was going to cleanse her soul. She had barely made it down the stairs before the urge to vomit overtook her.

A QUARTER OF an hour later, Evelina sat in the corner of the workshop, hidden from view behind a rack of costumes. She ached all over, stomach sore and bruises tender to the touch. Shock had left her shivering and sweating by turns, as if she'd fallen ill with a fever. Evelina had come to the end of her reserves, both in body and in spirit.

The revolver was slippery in her hands, there more for comfort than deadly intent. A bullet wouldn't kill Magnus, though it might buy her time if she needed it. She had to act, to somehow put an end to Magnus and his creation, but she wasn't sure how. Surely a plan would come to her before . . . well, before it was too late. Magnus's last words were burrowing into her like a parasite.

She couldn't see the things with the melted heads anymore, but her skin twitched and quivered as if they tickled her with their claws, plucking at her hair and clothes. She had always been content in the dark before this, but never, ever would be again.

She heard footfalls on the stairs and tensed, ready to flee or fight. But if Magnus knew she was there, he paid no attention. He led Serafina into the workshop, her hand on his arm as if they were strolling through the park. She walked mechanically again, the extra vitality in her step completely gone. He'd taken what she'd gathered from Mr. Jeremy and the rest.

They paused at Serafina's table, and he lifted back the sheet. "Good night, my sweet," he said.

She mounted the table, swung her feet up, and lay back. "Good night."

He carefully slid the pin out of her neck and put it in the slot at the side of the table. Then he covered her up and retreated through the door. In a moment, his footfalls faded and there was silence. Someone hooted in the streets outside, but the raucous sound seemed to belong to a distant, irrelevant world. Evelina shifted, her legs cramping.

Do I destroy her now? Evelina asked herself. It felt like murder, but what else could she do? *Can I leave even a clockwork doll at his mercy?* Serafina was more than just a machine, that was certain. But what other options were there? Helping her run away? What sort of a life could such a creature ever have?

Her debate was cut short when Serafina's hand slid out from under the sheet and felt around for the pin. Astonishment numbed Evelina, freezing her in place. *She's conscious even without her logic processors at work!* And Magnus didn't know. Serafina was enough her own creature that she'd learned to lie to her creator. Instinctively, Evelina shrank down into her hiding place.

Evelina heard the pin click into place. The sheet rustled, and a moment later Evelina heard the tap-tap of dainty boot soles on the floor, the swish of a cloak being donned. Then Serafina opened the door to the alley and crept out, closing it softly behind her. *Not only a liar, but a sneaky one. What is she up to?*

Slowly, Evelina rose, deeply curious. She took a few steps into the room. The candle was guttering on the workbench, throwing crazy sputters of light over her tools. But there was enough light to see the knife she had bloodied earlier that night was gone. It had been there only minutes before.

"What the fardling hell?" Evelina snatched her own coat and hurried into the alley, only to come to a halt, her breath puffing in clouds of mist around her. Serafina was nowhere in sight.

CHAPTER THIRTY-SEVEN

London, September 30, 1888

221B BAKER STREET

2:05 a.m. Sunday

Dear Mr. Holmes,
  Please be advised that your package has arrived
safely. We thank you so much for thinking of us.
Unfortunately, we have not been able to find the exact
key to wind it up and make it perform its intended
function. If you learn of anything useful to assist in
our efforts, please advise.

The note was penned on the stationery of Ness and Sons, Horologists. It had already been thumbed by the Yellow-backs, but they had obviously missed the code.

Holmes crumpled the letter, lit it from his pipe, and tossed it into the cold fire grate. One edge, and then another turned black, then orange, and then the ball of paper collapsed into a brief flare of light. He missed the drama of tossing bad news into an actual fire, but all that had been sacrificed to the steam barons and their hot water heating.

He fell back into his chair. So Elias Jones, after giving up his association with the Gold King, had nothing more to say. The rebels weren't the thumbscrew and iron-maiden types, but they still had a way of making men spill secrets. The local cuisine and a dip in the loch to meet the monster did for most. That meant Jones was unusually brave or unusually afraid of someone—or he simply didn't know any more. Holmes was betting on the latter.

That wasn't the only piece of bad luck that day. Late that afternoon, word about the morning's raid at the Diogenes Club had caught fire and flared through town. By the time he had finished his dinner, Sherlock Holmes had learned of his brother's abduction from three different people. It led to one overwhelming question: What the bloody hell was going on?

First, there had been Elias Jones and the bomb. Then there were the automatic recorders found at that favored rebel alehouse, the Saracen's Head. News of those had come his way from the Schoolmaster, who had already regaled him with the tale of the ambush in the tannery and the *Red Jack*'s narrow escape from Steam Council forces. And then there was this letter from Jack the Ripper, written in Mycroft's hand. How the blazes did any of it fit together?

He'd found out Magnus was running a theater and had arranged through the Schoolmaster to put a spy on the place in hopes of finding out something about Evelina, but in a final twist of bad luck, he'd heard that afternoon his man had been killed in a raid in some underground tavern called the Indifference Device. If only Holmes could have shaken Keating's hounds for a solid day, but they had only been thicker around Baker Street since his trip to Scotland Yard. Keating must have learned of his excursion and tightened his net.

It would have been so much better if he could ask his own questions about Magnus, but if the Diogenes Club had been breached, he was going to have to tread carefully. He *could* turn the lead over to Lestrade and see if Scotland Yard could ask the good doctor a few questions. Unfortunately, he was fairly sure Magnus could run circles around the coppers.

The only advantage he had was that Keating was in favor of his work on the Whitechapel murders. That had bought him at least a little freedom.

Holmes realized his pipe had gone out. He got up, made it halfway to the mantel where he had set his matches, then paused, lost in thought. It was very late, the streets sunk in that still, velvety blackness that said it was past midnight. It was almost too dark outside the window to see beyond the forlorn puddles of gaslight. He heard, rather than saw, the carriage pull up.

A rapping came at the downstairs door. He heard Mrs. Hudson's voice, then Abberline's. A moment later, there was a quick tread on the stairs. Holmes had his coat on before the inspector reached the top.

"There's been another one," Abberline said, breathing hard from the climb.

"Where?" asked Holmes, the detective in him eager for new data, the man inside terrified for Evelina.

"Berner Street, off Commercial Street."

"In the same general area as the others," Holmes noted. They were already hurrying back down the stairs.

"Yes, Whitechapel. A man named Diemshutz found her at one o'clock. He's the steward of a local workingmans' club. He was driving his cart into the yard adjacent to the club when the horse shied. That's how he found her. They think she's a whore, like the rest. That's all I have from the constable."

They swept past the Yellowbacks, who swore under their breath. Keating might approve of Holmes working the murder case, but they didn't like letting go of their charge. Abberline looked around, but Holmes ignored them, exultant. "Time of death?" he asked.

"She was still bleeding from the throat when she was found."

Holmes jumped into the carriage with the air of a fox escaping the hounds. The Yellowbacks might follow, but there was little chance of them crossing the boundary into the Blue Boys' patch. As long as he was with Abberline, Holmes was free.

They were in the vehicle and moving at a smart pace through the empty streets. Abberline looked rumpled, as if the news of the murder had got him out of bed, but he looked entirely alert. He'd been as good as his word—he'd promised to fetch Holmes if the so-called Ripper struck again. There were men under him who would be more likely to take the call, but he'd made the commitment to accompany the detective to make sure he had all the access required.

"Anything besides the throat wound?"

"No." Abberline tugged at his side whiskers. "If it's the same murderer, he might have been interrupted."

Holmes was almost grateful to hear it. He settled back, prepared to hold any other questions until they were at the scene.

"We've managed to keep the Dear Boss letter out of the papers," Abberline said, his face all but invisible in the darkness.

"So I noticed."

"That was a nasty piece of mischief all on its own."

Holmes didn't reply. Abberline was right. And it fit the pattern he could see emerging.

Before his visit from Jones, the rebels and the Steam Council had been in balance. The battle lines were drawn, the sides chosen, but no one had been willing to make the first move toward outright war—but the Ripper could change all that. The Blue King's territory had been a bubbling volcano for years—but giving the random madman a voice in the press would focus public rage in a way a political orator could only dream of. And Mycroft would think of that—and that was probably why he had written the letter Abberline had shown Holmes. Mycroft left nothing to chance, and putting a mocking face on the murderer was a stroke of genius.

Could this have anything to do with the Gold King seizing Mycroft at his club? To be honest, Holmes was more than a little worried about his brother. Mycroft was resourceful, but hardly a man of action. Unfortunately—and as usual— Holmes knew so little about Mycroft's plans, there was no way to help.

A sick fury chased through his stomach, but Holmes slammed the door on it. He clenched his jaw until his teeth ached. Tensions between him and his brother went back to the nursery, and it was nearly impossible to think clearly when it came to Mycroft. He didn't need that distraction now.

The carriage was drawing to a halt, and it was time to

focus on a different crime. They got out, and Holmes saw at once the crowd illuminated by the constables' lanterns. Abberline went first, pushing his way through.

Gates opened onto a passage to a yard. As Holmes drew closer, he could see a woman lying in a pool of blood to the right. Someone was introducing people to Abberline. "Constable Lamb. Constable Collins. Dr. Blackwell."

"I've brought Mr. Holmes along with me to have a look," Abberline said.

But he was too interested in one fact to bother to even look up. The woman was too tall to be Evelina. Holmes felt an ache in his throat—relief to be spared from something he hadn't even admitted as a possibility.

She was lying on her left side, face to the wall and with her feet drawn up. One arm was lying away from her body, clutching a tissue packet of candies scented to sweeten the breath. The other was bent against her chest, the hand red with the blood it had tried to stanch. Her bonnet lay to the side. Holmes crouched to get a better look at the wound to the throat.

"Someone says that's Long Liz Stride."

As he looked at the wound, something tugged at the back of Holmes's memory. Another unsolved case—the servants at Hilliard House. He'd read the autopsies of those killings as well as the Whitechapel crimes, and all but one were all killed with a cut to the throat just like this, a wound about six inches long, angling downward as it tailed off to the right. And they had all had similar bruises around the throat, as if someone with incredibly strong fingers had choked them. Could this be the same killer?

Every one of the Whitechapel murders showed some sign that the victims were overpowered, probably by strangulation. And killers perfected their technique, grew bold, and eventually indulged the demons that drove them. Every one of the murderer's victims—with the exception of the one he was looking at now—had been more violently slain than the last.

Only Martha Tabram had been stabbed around the neck instead of slashed—perhaps just an instance of having the wrong tool at hand—but otherwise, the hallmark cut to the throat had remained as individual as a signature.

A cold that had nothing to do with the chill, damp night puckered his skin—but a new excitement came with it. If he was right, his pool of suspects had just shrunk dramatically— Lord Bancroft, Magnus, and Jasper Keating were at the top of his list. *Whoever you are, I've picked up your scent at long last.*

THERE WAS NO point in Evelina blundering around White- chapel and asking if anyone had seen a sentient automaton carrying a bloody knife. For one thing, her body ached too badly to go one step farther than she had to. For another, the locals might be used to the drunk and deranged, but they were notorious for not getting involved—and Evelina didn't really want them involved until she understood what was happening. Instead, she inquired after a friend in a hurry wearing a hooded cape. That at least got her a few helpful tips and at least one offer of a glass of mother's ruin—the cheap gin that tasted like solvent.

The first person she met that she knew was Mary Kelly, who was on her way to the Ten Bells. "Come with us," she laughed. She had the bright eyes and lisp of someone who had already been drinking, and not a little.

Evelina wished she could. Mary had a sharp temper when drunk, but otherwise was good company. She was the type of friend ideal for meeting on the way to the market—full of chatter enough to make the most mundane errand pass quickly. And she'd been to Paris; although she hadn't liked it much, she had plenty of interesting stories about it.

"Come on, Miss Cooper, come on and enjoy the night with us. It's early yet!" Her friends had gone ahead without her and she looked over her shoulder at them. "I'll be there in a tick."

"I'm trying to find my friend. She was wearing a hooded cloak," Evelina pressed. Coats were more the fashion, so a full cloak would stand out.

"Wish I had a nice cloak," Mary mused.

"Are you sure you haven't seen her?"

Mary blinked, seeming to make an honest effort to focus her alcohol-soaked thoughts. "I've seen a woman like that late at night, but not tonight."

Evelina wasn't surprised. Magnus had tried to confine Serafina to the theater and assumed taking out her pin was enough, but the doll had clearly discovered that she could sneak out. Was it Magnus's assumption that he was in control blinding him to the fact, or had he always blamed his workers for being careless? Evelina had done that, when she found Serafina up and about. "When did you see this woman?"

"Your friend? Oh, it would be weeks ago now. Before I met you."

That could mean nothing. Or everything. "Mary," Evelina said slowly. "Would you take it amiss if I told you to be careful? After what happened to Annie Chapman, I can't help worrying about you."

"Oh, I'm safe enough," Mary shook her head. "Bless your heart, Miss Cooper, but I have a roof over my head—a snug little place on Dorset Street. You won't catch me in a dark alley with a stranger. I'm smarter than that."

Evelina let out her breath. "I'm glad to hear it."

"But what about you? You're out here alone in the dark."

"I won't be if I can find my friend."

"What's her name?"

Evelina turned away. "Trouble! Now catch up to your mates."

Her instincts took her south, following the same path she'd taken with Serafina during their afternoon walk. When she had just about given up, she met Gareth among a crowd of scruffy young men. He stopped, looking surprised to see her.

"What are you doing out at this hour, Miss Cooper?"

"Meeting a friend. Since when does Miss Hyacinth let you off at night?" she asked, a little alarmed by the rough look of some of his friends. They might not be entirely bad news yet, but they were certainly trying it on for size.

Gareth preened, thrusting his shoulders back and flicking

the hair out of his eyes. "I've a right to a night out now and again."

Big man with the big job, showing off to his friends. There really wasn't any harm in it. "Just be sure you're all the earlier tomorrow."

"Course. I know what's good for me, and Miss Hyacinth has a whip."

They all laughed at that. "I'm looking for a friend of mine," Evelina said.

Gareth grinned. "What's his name?"

"It's a woman. And she's wearing a hooded cloak. Have you seen a woman dressed like that?"

"Oh, aye, back there not five minutes ago." He turned and pointed down Aldgate. "Near Mitre Square. Right queer she was."

"Thanks!" Evelina started off at once.

Gareth caught her hand. "Is everything all right?"

"Yes! Now I have to go." She pulled her hand free and started running.

With a terrible certainty, she realized she had to be nearing the right place when she saw the lights in Mitre Square. Police. *Another murder.* She stopped outside the entrance to the square. It was filled with the uniforms of the City of London police. They'd crossed the line that marked the divide between the central part of London known as the Mile and the larger area patrolled by Scotland Yard and the Metropolitan Police. Various steam barons had a foothold here, but this place seemed to be under the Gold King's control. Along with the City police, she saw a handful of black-coated Yellowbacks with their extravagant guns. Evelina drew back, suddenly afraid to be seen.

"Second victim tonight," someone was saying. "There was another on the Whitechapel side earlier. Didn't get nearly so far as he did with this one. This is just—he's a bedlamite, he is."

A little farther down the way, someone was cursing and throwing up. Whatever was in the square, Evelina was absolutely certain she didn't want to see it.

Then she saw movement—the swift furl of a cape. In the

shadows along Duke Street, Serafina was hovering in the space between two buildings, hood drawn up and cloak wrapped around her. *What's she doing?* Now that Evelina had seen her, she wasn't certain how to proceed. The one thing she was sure of was that Serafina couldn't be left roaming the streets. Not after everything Evelina had seen that night.

She slowly strolled in her direction, doing her best to look utterly relaxed while her insides tried to squeeze themselves into a tiny, hard ball. "Serafina, what are you doing out here?"

The doll turned, her shoulders hunched. "I do not want to talk to you."

Evelina paused. "I'm sorry I scared you earlier, Serafina. I promise I'm not going to touch you."

"You are like him."

"No, I'm not." Evelina prayed not, and tried hard not to think of the life energy pouring out of Serafina into Magnus. "I don't want to steal from you."

"Do you promise?" It sounded oddly childlike.

"Yes." Slowly, Evelina drew near and Serafina let her. "So what are you doing?"

"I want to replace what Dr. Magnus took."

"You are looking for someone to kiss?"

Serafina shook her head. "I do not like the men here. They do not call me beautiful and bring me gifts."

Evelina could well imagine. These weren't clients of the Magnetorium, who knew that Serafina was an automaton. Unless they were completely drunk, most would be unpleasantly startled by the encounter—a few even terrified. "Then how are you feeding?"

"At night the women kiss the men—many men. I've seen them. I just need to take what I want from the women, because they must have gathered the life from all those men. After all, don't they do the same thing as me, pleasing all the men who come around?"

That didn't make sense. At the same time, it did. Horribly. Serafina had been watching the whores from the theater windows and drawing her own conclusions. "How are you taking it?"

"The way the doctor takes it from me. But I'm having trouble. They must keep it in a different place than I do, because it always drains away before I find it."

Serafina had that casing in her neck that held the whirling energy of stolen life. If she was looking for the same thing in the whores, that explained why she was slashing their throats. *Dear God!*

Then Evelina's gaze slipped down Serafina's front, and Evelina felt as if her body had turned to clay—slow, cold, and oddly clumsy.

Suddenly, everything made sense. There was the knife, now coated in gore. The front of Serafina's clothes glistened in the faint light, dark and wet. "Oh, no," Evelina whispered.

"The doctor must not know, or he will be very angry." Serafina's head tilted in a plea. "I will find other clothes, and he will never see the blood. That's what I did before, after the first time."

After the first time. How many had there been—these little incidents that Magnus had referred to with lips twisted in distaste? But it sounded like not even Magnus had the whole story about his lovely, clever, deceptive doll.

Evelina's breaths were coming in short, sharp gasps. She reached into her pocket, feeling for the revolver. She slid her hand around the grip, ready to shoot it through the pocket of her coat if she must. Serafina wasn't human, but she was breakable. A bullet through the head or heart would slow her down, if they could just get to an isolated spot. "Then let's go find you some clothes. I don't want you to get into trouble."

"Yes, please," Serafina said. "But I'm so hungry. I need someone."

"Then come," Evelina said, using the same gentle tone she would with a child. She held out her hand, as she always did, but Serafina shied away. She'd been drained once that night and, while she couldn't refuse Magnus, apparently she wasn't willing to come near anyone else.

They had started moving away from the square. Evelina's

priority was to get away from all those police and Jasper
Keating's guards. She glanced up at the cloudy sky. There
was no moon, just a rising fog. No wonder it was so dark.
She wanted light desperately, but right then darkness was
safety. People might come to the Magnetorium to see what
they pretended was a living doll. Men might pay for pleasure with one. But to be keeping company with a vessel of
black magic was quite another, especially when it was covered with blood and intent on further mayhem. Evelina
started to shake. *I'm going to have to kill her.*

Serafina walked beside her, her skirts rustling wetly like
the wings of a wounded bird. "Do you think we can find a
man, and you could make him kiss me?"

"I could," Evelina said, refusing to even picture that scene
in her mind. A few yards more, and they would be well out
of sight of the police. The sound of the gun would be a problem, but Evelina knew that she could run fast.

"But then you would want it for yourself."

There was a sound behind them, a clatter of clay pots falling. Evelina's nerves were at the snapping point. She whirled,
grabbing Serafina's arm, only to see a black and white cat
bolting through the night.

Evelina realized her mistake a split second too late.

"No!" Serafina snatched her arm away. "I said not to
touch me!"

Evelina raised the gun but Serafina moved with super-
human speed, knocking it away and locking Evelina's wrist
in a painful grip. Blind panic shot through Evelina like the
jolt from a magnetic coil. She tried to wrench away, but she
was snared. The doll was leaning close, her luxuriant hair
falling loose from its pins. It was human hair, affixed bit by
bit to the wooden scalp beneath. A strand of it near her face
had been burned away—the way Evelina herself had once
done when she grew careless with a lit candle. It was the one
flaw in Serafina's unnatural beauty.

"You lied to me!" Serafina protested, her voice tinged
with betrayal. "You want to hurt me."

Terror produced a strange lucidity. Images flashed through
Evelina's brain in rapid fire: the newspaper reports of the

Whitechapel murderer, the descriptions of the slit throats, the police in Mitre Square, and Serafina's knife. And then there was that burnt hair—and a memory of candle wax melted on the floor of Hilliard House's cloak room, where a young maid had died with her throat cut and bruises along her jaw—just like the Whitechapel victims. And next to the maid had been a woman's shoeprint in blood. The police had assumed it was hers.

"Dear Lord." Evelina had found the answer not just to the Whitechapel murders but to a mystery she'd never unraveled. "You killed Grace Child." Evelina's words were barely audible, pain robbing her voice of strength.

Serafina tilted her head. "Who was that?"

"Let me go!"

The doll's fingers twitched, squeezing harder. "I don't remember anyone named Grace. It must have been before Dr. Magnus made me better."

Evelina began to struggle again, the fingers of her free hand clawing at the doll's bruising grip. When that didn't work, she pulled away with a desperate cry, using all her weight, and Serafina let go. Evelina fell back, staggering with the sudden release. It only lasted a second, because then Serafina's hand was around her throat, the unnatural strength of her grip brutal.

The automaton drew her close, the impassive blue eyes scanning back and forth across Evelina's face, looking for some clue or meaning that only she understood. "You know something about who I was before. Tell me."

Evelina struggled to focus her vision. Her pulse crashed in her ears, a sensation of mounting pressure at war with increasing light-headedness. Her scrabbling fingers slowed, commands no longer reaching her limbs.

Serafina's grip relaxed a degree. "Tell me about Grace. I want to know."

Evelina's breath sucked in with an enormous wheeze, choking and coughing. Serafina waited through it, lovely and still. "Let me go! Please."

"Tell me." The fingers twitched around her throat again. "Tell me, Miss Cooper. I want to understand."

"She was the maid at Hilliard House," Evelina said at last. "And then there were the grooms with the horse cart. They were taking Lord Bancroft's automatons away."

A beat followed while Serafina thought. Evelina was close enough to hear the faint whir of gears and wheels inside the doll. Then she tried to swallow, but the grip around her throat was too tight.

Serafina blinked. "Yes, I remember now. Dr. Magnus asked me to kill the men. He said no one would ever accuse me of such a thing, because of what I am. But the woman simply got in the way." The fingers tightened again. "He took me apart after that. I stayed that way until the room. People are always shutting me in boxes. I don't like it. I deserve to be whole."

She took a step forward, her head tilted. Evelina had to stumble back, her hands trying to grab thin air for support. Serafina's mouth opened slightly, the expression almost a smile. "But the room changed me. I can act for myself now. I can ask questions about the things I need to know."

"What is it you want?" Evelina gasped.

She felt the knife slide into her belly a moment before pain exploded in a simultaneous rush from her toes to the roots of her hair.

"You touched me. I don't want you to take what's mine ever again," Serafina said. "And I want you to tell me where you keep the life you took. You are like Dr. Magnus, so you know exactly what I mean. You're *evil*."

A gray haze suffused Evelina's sight, robbing the dark street of form and color. Agony ripped through her, so acute that it was almost meaningless. Her senses couldn't contain it for those first few seconds—and then the aftershock set in. Wave after wave of hot pain pounded through her like a surf, sucking her under. A sound escaped her throat, but it was soft. Her damaged body had forgotten how to draw air enough to scream.

Then she was on her back, and she could breathe again. Serafina straddled her, pulling at Evelina's clothing and freeing the knife. "I'm not going to cut your throat, Miss

Cooper, not quick like the others, because then you can't tell me a thing."

Evelina moved her hands weakly, seeking something to use as a weapon, but all she found on the cold, filthy street was the sticky warmth of her own blood. She gave up, letting the pain drag her down into a murky fog.

And then the knife sliced in again. Evelina arched against it, her body tightening like the string of a bow. She could feel herself growing weaker, short of air, short of heat—and yet more blood escaped into fog-shrouded streets.

"Am I close, Miss Cooper?"

She couldn't see anymore. She could barely hear. All she could manage was a grunt of protest, a fumbling against the blade flaying her entrails. And her hand closed around the doll's.

In her weakened state, it was like opening the door onto a hurricane. Evelina had always sensed that Serafina was more human than the other dancers, but now that was abundantly clear. The soul inside the doll was not just a scrap of Dr. Magnus's life, for there was another grafted onto it— a small, stunted, and twisted thing. And it must have hidden deep inside the clockwork workings, because she hadn't truly felt it before now. But now it was out of hiding and it was terrified and enraged. The touch of it roused Evelina, like a primal need to shrink away from fire.

"Is it here?"

The knife went in a third time, but she'd gone past pain into a bright, white land beyond. Evelina lashed out, everything reduced to a feral need to survive.

Magnus hadn't taken all the life from the doll. There were remnants, scraps like the crumbs on a platter. She could use that. Greedily, Evelina sucked the life force in, hungry and aching for it. It hit her like cheap gin, sending her consciousness reeling. Howling with frustration, Serafina kept cutting, shredding life even as Evelina wrested it from her. The pain had gone from mere sensation to something beyond— a vibration, a sound that was not sound, a high, shrill scream of the soul.

"Hey!"

The voice came faintly through the haze, as if the sound had come down a long, long tunnel. It stirred a faint memory, but Evelina's mind could not fasten on it. Wordlessly, she invoked the healing spell that had healed her hand earlier that night, but it was a hopeless move. That had been a mere cut; this was wholesale destruction. Her limbs were growing cold, as if the darkness was eating her from the outside in.

"Hey!" The voice came again, this time with the pounding of running feet.

The knife jerked away and Serafina was gone, running in her turn. It should have been a mercy, for there was no more cutting, but other miseries had come. The melted-head creatures waited in the shadows, their eyeless faces turning her way. They grew more distinct as the rest of the world faded. Evelina watched them, her entire body frozen in a rictus of agony.

Deep inside, she curled around the scraps of stolen life, her dragon's hoard, and fed them like kindling to the dying spark of her existence. The running feet stopped, and someone bent over her, breath hot on her face.

"Evelina!" It was Gareth.

Her hand shot out, as if it had a will of its own, clasping his wrist. The youth was full of life, sparkling and vital and more than enough to heal her body then and there. She could smell it on Gareth's skin and wanted to rub along his hand like a cat purring for tidbits. That energy would be all good things—savory and sweet, laughter and sunrise. Her magic leapt for it, desperate for sustenance—but it was lunging at smoke. Magnus had been right. Evelina had no knowledge how to steal life. That was the one lesson she had refused to learn.

Thank the stars.

Her hand slipped away, letting Gareth go as she surrendered to the abyss.

CHAPTER THIRTY-EIGHT

BANCROFT'S BACK WAS AGAINST THE WALL. THE ENGINE that drove events in his world was powered by the struggle between himself, Keating, and Magnus. Bancroft had no magical abilities, nor did he own half of London. Coming from such a disadvantage, he had to compensate by being more ruthless than either of them. But Magnus at the moment had the advantage. He had the automatons.

If Magnus wanted Keating dead, ultimately that was fine with Bancroft. And once Keating was gone, there would be the interesting task of ridding the world of Dr. Magnus—but that would come later. One megalomaniacal despot at a time.

Bancroft had visited a different one of his clubs that night. He didn't go to the Oraculars' Club often. It was out of his way, a bit noisy, and the food was lacking. Furthermore, it wasn't the most uplifting part of town. Nevertheless, that was perfect for his needs. So was the fact that Keating ate here whenever he visited his warehouses, which—according to the club's doorman, who enjoyed a generous tip—he did regular as clockwork twice a month.

So when Keating left the club, Bancroft peeled himself from the shadows across the street and followed him. The man was guarded by a handful of his Yellowbacks. All were tall, tough men in long black coats. But just because they were there didn't mean there wouldn't be opportunity to slide in and exterminate their chief. Distractions were everywhere. And the method of death had already been provided by this Whitechapel Murderer—a knife to the throat, quick and deep. Just because Keating wasn't from the lowest rank of street whores—well, Bancroft rather liked the implied comparison.

So now he followed at a distance, hanging back enough not to be seen. The night was cold and damp, thinking hard about a fog. It made sounds echo strangely, as if every footfall were right behind one, ready to pounce. Bancroft fingered the knife sheath strapped beneath his coat. It held a long military blade he'd acquired in Austria, curved and wicked and smooth as silver butter. The hilt caressed his hand as he gripped it, giving him a confidence he badly needed.

To say the discovery of his letters had been a blow was a laughable understatement. *Alice Keating is going to pay for that.* One way or another, his son would as well. Bancroft had failed his wife, his children, and especially Anna, but that had been his private hell—the one that had driven him to both alcohol and ambition. But now the red vixen's interference had turned his secret agony to humiliation in front of his children. Shame ran toxic in his blood now, and only anger would burn it away. Anger and action—before somehow the story got out and ruined him. She'd sworn her secrecy, but what was that worth? So it made sense to bow to Magnus's command and slit the throat of the Gold King. After all, that's where Alice would run to first.

Keating stopped by the tea warehouse he owned in Mitre Square. Most men would visit their property in the daytime, but Keating worked all hours. Now Bancroft didn't try to hang back, but turned up the collar of his coat and walked past in the midnight darkness. No one would be watching for Lord Bancroft strolling along the street in a shabby coat and low-crowned hat, so that wasn't what they'd see.

This wasn't one of the dockyard warehouses guarded by huge steel automatons and miles of fencing. These buildings were ranged around the square with nothing but simple locks on the heavy doors. Bancroft turned the corner, took out his picklocks, and slipped into the building next door. It was dark inside, but he felt his way along, not willing to risk a light until he was well away from the windows, and then he struck a match just long enough to find the stairs. Using the handrail to guide him, Bancroft mounted them to the top floor and slid open the window closest to the Keating's address. Another window looked back at him from a gap between the buildings of only a few feet. Bancroft smiled. It paid to do good reconnaissance.

He wasn't as young as he used to be, but if he could get the window opposite open, it would be no problem—all right, only a moderate problem—to slide into Keating's place. Then Bancroft could sneak up on his quarry and slit his throat while all his Yellowbacks were lurking around the outside watching the street. People watched their backs and from the corners of their eyes. No one ever thought about killers descending from above. One learned interesting tidbits in the service of one's queen.

Carefully, gingerly, Bancroft tested the condition of the window frame. Death by dry rot didn't appeal. Finding it solid, he leaned out to test the distance to the other building. That wasn't so bad, but the other window was locked. He'd need a tool . . .

"Murder!" someone bellowed from the square below.

Bloody hell, that was premature. He hadn't even got started yet. Bancroft pulled his head in and strode to a window that faced into the square. An officer with the crested helmet of the City Police was already on the scene, his lantern shining on something below. *How enormously inconvenient.*

It was close enough, and at just the right angle, that Bancroft had a clear view from where he was, two floors above the storefront level. But still, he found himself squinting. He reached inside his coat and pulled out the small spyglass he carried for missions like this, pulled it open, and looked through. It was powerful, the lens pulling the scene below into sharp focus.

"Dear God." Bancroft was not a sentimental man, nor a

weak one, but he still found his gorge rising. Something un-
speakable had happened to that woman. She lay on her
back, the right leg crooked and her dress pushed up to expose the abdomen. But this killer took his business seriously. Her entrails had been pulled out and most of them
were above her right shoulder. Another piece about two feet
long looked like it had been hacked off and placed between
her body and her left arm. This wasn't murder—it was
butchery.

He moved the glass up slightly, away from the mess of her
body and toward her face. Above the woman's scarf, he
could see the throat had been slashed, and then her face
hacked to shreds. Bancroft lowered the eyeglass, unwilling
to look at more. And yet, he couldn't stop himself from ana-
lyzing what he'd seen. Swallowing hard, he lifted it again,
looking at the space around the body. Blood pooled, not
sprayed. The woman had been dead before she'd had her
abdomen ripped open—and she'd been down before her
throat was cut. He took one last look, horrified and fascinated. The killer must have been seething with rage. No one
chopped away a face unless they were in a towering fury.

That has to be the work of the Whitechapel Murderer. The
one he had been going to mimic with the murder of Keating.
A flood of distaste soured Bancroft's stomach. He would
have done a poor imitation at best, and thank the gods for
that. Assassination was one thing, this was—he kept coming back to the word *butchery,* but it fit.

*And now there are police everywhere, looking for a soli-
tary man with a knife. Good show, Bancroft.* He had to get
out of the neighborhood, and quickly. A murder like this
would bring an entire circus of police, doctors, journalists,
and the idle curious to the square. He put the spyglass away,
closed the window, and hurried down the stairs. There was
a smaller side entrance, and he slipped out that way, melting
away from the square and hurrying down an alley toward
Duke Street. He turned north and began walking briskly,
trying to cover as much ground as he could without looking
like someone on the run.

Somewhere, church bells tolled two o'clock. Bancroft was reaching that state of fatigue where he felt slightly drunk.

"Mister!" A young man was bolting in his direction.

Suddenly tense, Bancroft cast a glance over his shoulder to see if there was someone behind him. There wasn't. The lad was coming for him. Bancroft slid his hand under his coat, reaching for his knife.

"Mister, please!" He skidded to a stop a few yards away. He was in that stage between boy and man, his hair in need of a cut and his clothes one step up from rags. "I need help."

"What for?" Bancroft demanded. Did he look like a Good Samaritan?

"My friend's been stabbed."

Another stabbing victim? That was plausible enough, but it could also be a ruse to get him in a dark alley and bash him over the head. "There are police in Mitre Square."

"She won't want police." The young man gestured urgently. "I have to get her help."

"Where is she?"

"Just up here."

The lad ran ahead, vanishing into the darkness between broken streetlights. The air was growing thick with moisture, almost a mist. Bancroft kept walking, refusing to run. Viscounts didn't take orders from street rats. But this one didn't plan on giving up. Bancroft found him a dozen yards along, pointing to a crumpled body on the ground. "There!"

It was a full-grown woman, dainty enough but too big for a skinny boy to lift. Reluctantly, Bancroft went over, scanning the shadows for any additional rogues waiting to pounce. She was curled on her side, head bent and knees drawn up to her belly. He slid off a glove and touched the woman's arm. Still warm. Still a chance at life.

"Where are you planning to take her?" Bancroft asked.

"Miss Hyacinth. She'll know what to do."

"Where is she?"

The lad pointed. "Just down there."

Bancroft hesitated. This was probably some whore beaten up by a sailor. He'd left home to kill the most powerful man in London, not rescue drabs in distress. But he was still a gentleman, and when not in pursuit of nefarious aims, his instinct was to abide by a certain code of conduct. Being a bastard didn't always let one off the hook.

He tried to roll the woman—young woman, it seemed—onto her back, and then he saw the wound. Blood soaked the front of her dress, as if someone had dumped a bowl of it onto her lap. A sudden anger seized him, as if all that blood was a new enemy. His own heart started to pound.

If he was going to save her, he would have to hurry. He slid his arms under the woman's shoulders and hips, trying to lift her so that her head could rest against his shoulder. A whimper escaped her, but her head flopped to the side. Mercifully, she was unconscious.

Bancroft got to his feet, ignoring protests from his knees and back. She was light enough, but no woman was as weightless as romances would have one believe. "Which way?" he asked, but the lad was already walking backward and pointing.

"Thank you, sir, this way, sir."

Bancroft could feel blood soaking through his shirt. It was a good thing that he had already hidden a change of clothes at the bottom of the garden, just in case tonight's work got messy.

They were approaching a gas lamp, the blue globe around it lending a sepulchral air. Bancroft stole a glance down at the young girl and nearly dropped her.

He was holding Evelina Cooper half dead in his arms.

CHAPTER THIRTY-NINE

October 3, 1888

To E.C., care of The Ten Bells.
    Contact me by tomorrow, or my men will find you. Do not think you can hide.

                    —note never collected from the proprietor

London, November 8, 1888

HYACINTH'S HOUSE

3:15 p.m. Thursday

EVELINA WAS FIRST AWARE OF THE SCENT OF LAVENDER AND clean linen. And then, maybe because she smelled that crisp smell that only good bedsheets have, she felt the smooth, sleek fabric under her cheek. The mattress was soft—no lumps or hard spots—and the blankets warm. Nothing was crawling over her or biting her. In fact, she felt clean. *I've gone to Heaven.*

But then the next wave of sensation rolled in. She had a raging thirst, but when she tried to send out a message to her body to wake up and find water, the impulse died like a match in the rain. She was so very weak. And like a creeping fog, she had a gray, hazy sense that something awful had happened.

The instinct to survive sprang up, as if it had been asleep but now was on the attack. If she didn't rouse herself and accept the struggle to find water and sustenance, she would never be strong enough to keep herself safe. Tears welled up under her closed lids, leaking down her cheek into that soft, soft pillow. Somehow she knew she'd lost that fight already.

"Hey." A hand touched her cheek, brushing away the tears. "Evelina."

The voice was soft and husky and as familiar as comfortable shoes. She tried to open her eyes, but they felt so heavy. Light seeped in—brightness striped with the bars of her eyelashes—and disappeared. She tried again, and this time she got them open, wincing at the blurry brilliance of the room. Somehow, she got a hand to her face and rubbed her eyes into focus.

She was lying on her side in a bed with yellow curtains. There was striped wallpaper and white furniture, and she had no idea where she was. She'd never seen this place before.

Nick sat beside the bed, dressed in an old shirt with loose, billowing sleeves. It looked like something from his circus days. And it looked like he hadn't slept well for a very long time. He reached out, smoothing her hair back from her face. The gentle pressure of his fingers made her sink a little deeper into her pillow as tension left her body.

"How are you feeling?" he asked, his dark gaze searching her face. His eyes weren't true black, but a brown so dark they looked that way. It was only in light like this one could see the mahogany lights in them, like an exotic gem held up to the sun.

"Thirsty." The word came out as a whisper.

He turned, and poured water from a pitcher into a glass. Evelina saw that his hands were shaking slightly. He swallowed hard, the lean muscles of his throat working, but he kept his voice perfectly steady. "You're going to have to sit up."

He set the glass down again and reached to help her. Evelina tried to roll onto her back. Pain leaped up her body and she gasped, collapsing back onto the bed. *Bloody hell, what happened to me?* Fear came flooding back, along with a feeling of violation.

"Slowly," Nick said. "You were badly hurt. Your muscles have healed but they're bound to still be sore."

Evelina concentrated on breathing, moving very, very gradually this time. She felt his left arm slip behind her, the other beneath her knees, and he slid her back against a nest of pillows. She sagged back against them, feeling dizzy, but the pain was only gnawing now instead of splitting her like an ax. Nick helped her drink, and she downed the whole glass. She felt instantly better.

"Where am I?" she asked, her voice thick and rough.

A glint of mischief flickered over his face. "You're in a brothel."

"What?"

"You've taken a bed in Miss Hyacinth's house of pleasure." He grinned, teeth white in his swarthy face. "I've been praying for weeks that I'd get to say that to you."

"Weeks? What are you talking about? Is this a prank?" She'd barely said it when she saw there was an edge of panic to his smile. They'd known each other too long for him to hide it. She'd rarely seen Nick truly shaken, but he was off balance now. "Tell me."

"It's November now," he said quietly, the grin melting away. "You've been unconscious for more than a month."

"What?" Evelina looked out the window of the room. The tree outside was bare of leaves, the sky an iron gray. Shock numbed her, cold and cutting as ice, as her sense of violation returned threefold. Someone had hurt her and stolen weeks from her life. She began to shake. "How? What happened to me?"

Nick took the glass away, setting it back on the dressing table nearby, and then wrapped her in a soft knitted blanket, bundling her up like a child. "Don't you remember?" His brows drew together. "Gareth found you on the street. He said you'd been out that night, looking for someone in a panic. Something seemed off and he couldn't put it from his mind, so he decided to find out what was going on. When he found you, you'd been badly cut up."

Her hand went to her stomach. Memory flickered. The knife sliding into her, the pain. A dark street. Falling. A voice yelling—maybe Gareth's. Dizziness took her, as if the memories were a drink too potent for her weakened body.

"He saw someone standing over you, but the figure fled when he saw Gareth coming." Nick gripped her hand just a little too hard. "Two other women died that night. The boy saved your life."

No more images came. A black cloud had settled over the event, and all she had were the emotions. There had been a desperate need to find someone, but why? "I can't remember."

Nick gave a slight shake of the head. "That doesn't matter right now. You've been surviving on nothing but whatever broth we could spoon into you. The physician didn't think you were going to live, you'd lost so much blood. It's a miracle that you healed."

"I want to remember," she said, her voice rising to a shrill pitch. Some instinct said that it was very, very important that she recall what she had been doing that night. Her life depended on it. "Someone tried to kill me!"

"Hush," Nick said. "Your memories will come back. I've seen it happen before. Your body needs all your energy to heal right now. The rest will come after."

"I'm afraid," she whispered. "I'm afraid of what I don't know."

He stroked her hair. "It will pass. It's best if you don't think about it right now."

"I want to know who did this to me!"

He looked grim. "Figuring that out isn't your job. Not today, anyhow."

His words were kindly meant, but they came as a blow. She had lost control of everything. "I've always stood on my own feet. I've faced everything."

"You don't have to face this," Nick said with another caress.

That wasn't the point. She suddenly wasn't sure she had the courage. The memory of that knife in her flesh had cut away the girl who walked into Whitechapel and left a pathetic creature huddling in a strange bed. And then suddenly a terrible thought came to her. "Have you news of Uncle Sherlock?"

"Yes," Nick said. "Holmes is being watched closely by

Keating's men. I couldn't get word to him that you were here, but he's safe."

She felt her muscles ease like a fist going limp, and sank deeper into the pillows. "Thank God."

"Do you want me to send for him?" Nick asked. "I could try again to reach him."

"That would put you in danger."

"I could go," he said, though his grasp of her hand grew tighter.

"Don't leave me. I want to be wherever you are," she said before she knew she would say it. It was fear, but it was also a confession of much more.

"And I want you there, but on a pirate ship?" He frowned. "It's a dangerous place. After this, I don't know if I could stand putting you at so much risk."

Risk. Everything, even her protestations of love, were tainted by it. She pressed her hands to her face a moment, then dropped them with a sigh. "No place is safe." She tried to erase the desperation from her voice and make it sound light. "Besides, I'd look fetching with a cutlass."

The corners of his mouth twitched downward, as if he didn't know whether or not to smile. He tugged at one of her wavy, dark locks, his expression a mix of love and consternation. "I nearly went mad looking for you. What were you doing wandering the streets?"

Evelina blinked, her brain swimming. "I don't know." Images and phrases lay scattered in her mind, as if someone had dumped out a drawer. She couldn't put things in order.

Nick's hand was on hers again, holding her steady. "Did it have anything to do with Magnus and his magic? I could feel it on you, Evie. You were electric with power when I first found you. It faded away over time, but somehow it must have helped you heal. A surgeon stitched you up, but he held out no hope. He said you should never have lived."

And the memory of the workhouse fire and the sweet taste of those lives filled her. Remorse welled up, thick and bitter. Evelina squeezed her eyes shut, too weak to hold back more tears. A shuddering sob tore through her.

A sudden pain made her catch her breath, but when she

reached for the place that had hurt, there was not even a bandage. It had simply been the complaint of healing muscles. *I shouldn't have lived.* Even the beat of her heart bore witness to the fact she'd dabbled in something foul. Guilty tears spilled down her face.

"Evie?"

The urge to confess was too much. "I don't remember exactly what happened. But Magnus had books and he knows so much and he would let tidbits drop. I gobbled them up like a fool. He showed me a healing spell. It was the kind of knowledge I always wanted. But it was so, so dark."

"And yet somehow, you couldn't stop from wanting to know one morsel more," Nick finished for her.

She nodded, not able to bring herself to say another word. She couldn't even open her eyes to look at him. He knew her too well. And, she remembered what Magnus had said. Someday she would betray Nick just to learn more.

"Other girls have affairs with men, or cards, or opium. Only you would have one with black magic."

Evelina gave a gulping sob. *No, I will never go back to Magnus. It won't happen—and it will never be at the cost of anyone else.*

He leaned close, wiping away her tears with his fingertips. "You know as well as I do where that dark road leads. And yet I could kiss the sorcerer's feet for giving you the means to survive."

"I'm done with him," she said resolutely, but inside she was hollow. *Gareth found me. Did I really try to strip him of his life? Or is that a terrible hallucination? Please, please let it be nothing more than a bad dream!*

"Agreed." Nick gave a slow nod. "But remember I'm a thief. I can't throw stones."

"Oh, Nick." She closed her eyes. She didn't deserve his forgiveness, but she was damned grateful for it. She was teetering on the edge of despair and only the look in his eyes was keeping her from plunging over. "There are moments I wonder if Magnus will let me go."

"Magnus is gone. His theater is empty."

That startled her. "He's gone? Everything there? All those books?"

Nick pointed to somewhere at the foot of the bed she couldn't quite see. "Gareth found your carpetbag and tools. It was the only thing left behind."

Evelina sank back against the pillows, not sure if the news made her feel better or worse. All of a sudden, she had no energy left. Her mood plummeted. "I don't know what to think."

"He's up to something . . . but then when isn't he?"

She lifted her hand in a gesture of surrender. Nick captured it in his. The shadow of his beard had grown in, making him look even more the ruffian. "You've been bullied and stripped of everything familiar and then brutally attacked," he said quietly. "It's natural to feel as if the world is crumbling around you. But don't you worry, Evie. We've always looked after each other, and we always will."

"We will." And that's what kept them bound together. Nick was always there for her. More than anything in the world, she wanted to do the same for him.

Some of the awfulness inside her eased. She reached up, touching his face. If her journey—from a girlhood in the circus to a sickbed in a Whitechapel brothel—had been long and winding, his had been every bit as spectacular. And it was their individual voyages that had given this moment meaning, because they had come back together. They were home.

He took her hand in his, kissing her fingers. His expression was uncharacteristically vulnerable, and Evelina would have given her soul to keep that look there. A fierce, possessive warmth filled her chest.

"You should rest," he said. "Or eat something. I've been talking too much."

She was tired, but not so tired that she was willing to let Nick go. "Stay. I *want* to hear you talk."

It was hard to say if she pulled him down to her, or he drew her closer. Their lips brushed, the heat of his breath fanning her skin. A small noise of pleasure escaped him, somewhere between a moan and a growl. It roused heat deep in her belly, kindling a fire that pushed back the fear and doubt that had followed her from the depths of her healing sleep.

I'm alive. Even if that had been bought with dark magic, she was glad of it.

She slid her hand into his hair, glorying in its thickness and in the strength of the muscles under his sun-darkened skin. And then one hand wasn't enough, and she was winding both her arms around his neck. The bed sank with his added weight as he joined her there, and that felt right, too. They belonged side by side.

Slowly, because she still ached with stiffness, she rolled until she was leaning on his chest, pushing away the covers that tangled between them. With a flush of inconvenient modesty, Evelina noticed that she was wearing someone's tissue-thin chemise, and it provided as much coverage as window glass. From the look on Nick's face, he didn't mind at all. He reached up, cupping her breast in his palm. Her nipple hardened under his touch.

And her magic leaped for his. The silvery light that suddenly engulfed them was hard to see in the cool November light, but it was there, a glowing fur of power that enrobed their skin. *Oh, please, no,* she thought, afraid of the rush of destruction that was sure to follow. She grabbed at her magic, ready to haul it back under her control, but it slithered through her mental grasp as if coated in butter.

Nick never gave her the chance to worry about it. His hand slid inside the frail fabric of the chemise, sliding his thumb over the peak of her breast. Evelina's thoughts scattered as his mouth found hers again and hot desire rushed through her. The silvery light swirled around them, bright as liquid metal pouring into a new mold.

Devas began winking into sight, circling around like hummingbirds around syrup. They were tiny motes of blue, gold, and green, called by the surging energy and hungry to taste it. They were beautiful, swirling in clusters of twos and threes, like colorful stars spiraling above them.

Evelina gasped at the canopy of lights, thick as the blossoms on a tree. *If there are no devas in the East End, how far did they come?* How loudly was their passion broadcasting into the aether? The notion made her blanch.

But before she could form another thought, Nick had his shirt off, and all else crashed to nothingness. *Oh, dear God,* she thought, not sure if it was thanks or a plea for strength. Her mouth went utterly dry. He looked fit with his clothes on—without them, she could see every curve and shadow of muscle. Nick knelt on the bed, bending over her for another kiss.

The heat inside her went from a slow burn to a conflagration. Hunger of another kind—the appetite of a woman for a man—ripped through her, leaving an urgent yearning behind. She surged to her knees, wanting a better angle, more of his mouth, his tongue, of the bond he was offering her. She knew him, deep in her bones, further still into the core of her soul. All the poetry he would never say in words, he'd say with his body. And right now he was telling her a thousand things with his lips and hands.

The silver fire deepened even more, drawing the devas so close the lights covered their bodies like a cloak of stars. And then she felt their power soaking into her, healing the last shadows of hurt from her flesh. She could feel their giddy, drunken glee and it spun into her own, driving her even tighter into Nick's embrace as they fell back onto the bed, laughing.

But the alchemy of desire suddenly turned that laughter to something more predatory. Nick's power surged to the fore, lithe and sharp as a rapier. And yet he gentled it to a velvet touch, like a cat with its claws drawn in. Evelina felt it pressing against her own, urging, nudging, wanting that moment of mastery but waiting for her invitation. She lay back, her arms open to him, willing and wanting to surrender. And as he came to her, his magic washed through hers, mixing like the border of the river and sea, binding two disparate kingdoms with links that could never be broken apart.

And then she realized why the devas weren't tearing the room to shreds. *This* is what they had wanted all along. This was the wholeness that the fear and fire and engines of the barons had nearly scorched from the world.

And under that cloak of many-colored lights, Nick continued his tradition of introducing Evie Cooper to new and marvelous things.

CHAPTER FORTY

London, November 9, 1888
DORSET STREET

11:30 a.m. Friday

I was not codding dear old Boss when I gave you the tip, you'll hear about Saucy Jacky's work tomorrow double event this time number one squealed a bit couldn't finish straight off had not the time to get ears for police. thanks for keeping last letter back till I got to work again.
Jack the Ripper.

—addressed to Central News Office,
London, October 1, 1888

From hell
Mr Lusk

Sor
I send you half the Kidne I took from one women prasarvedit for you tother piece I fried an ate it was very nice. I may send you the bloody knif that took it out if you only wate a whil longer.
Signed
Catch me when you Can
Mishter Lusk.

—received by George Lusk, head of the Whitechapel
Vigilance Committee, October 16, 1888

"I wonder what our happy letter writer will send this time," Inspector Abberline muttered to Holmes as they arrived at Dorset Street about a half hour before lunch. The murder of Catherine Eddowes in Mitre Square had prompted a missive addressed "From Hell." Apparently Hell used earthly modes of delivery, for the postmark was October 15. A kidney had accompanied it, presumably that of the unfortunate Eddowes, who had been missing one of hers. Some believed it was truly hers, a few suspected medical students playing a prank.

"I had rather hoped he'd gone to the Antipodes," Abberline added. "But the Ripper is back. And by the by, speaking of unpleasant returns, the Gold King was at my door again yesterday, wanting to know about your niece. He thinks she returned to you and you're hiding her somewhere. He had the Devonshire constabulary turn over your mother's house yesterday."

"The devil he did!"

Abberline gave him a narrow look. "He says he feels responsible since she vanished after leaving his country house. But does that October date mean anything to you, Mr. Holmes?"

Frustration gnawed at Holmes. "Trust me, if I knew where Evelina was, I would know what it was to sleep again." He'd worked around the difficulty of Keating's watchdogs by having Lestrade's men ferry him to the East End once a day and either searching alongside the police or carrying on his own investigation from there. He'd found where she'd been living and where Magnus had been, but both had vanished. "There is a madman running amok. I just want her home."

"I know that, Mr. Holmes, but be aware that the longer Keating talks, the more others are listening."

"He's going to ruin me by casting suspicion my way for the disappearance of my own niece?" Holmes asked incredulously.

Abberline shrugged. "I'd find her if I were you."

"Don't insult me." Holmes looked out the window, confronted by a sudden urge to strike the man.

"I'm not. I don't like Keating in my business, and he shouldn't be in yours."

Holmes glanced at Abberline, suddenly faced with the uncomfortable feeling that the man pitied him.

The latest victim lived in a place called Miller's Court, which was a clutch of single-room rentals that led off Dorset. The passageway to get to them was less than three feet wide and twenty-six feet long. The court itself was an odd wedge shape framed by outdoor privies at one end and a communal garbage bin at the other. Six connected cottages, three to either side of the court, made up the living spaces. Each cottage had two tenants, one up and one down. The deceased—another prostitute—lived at number thirteen, on the ground floor. Her name, Holmes soon learned, was Mary Jane Kelly.

"A bit riskier, don't you think?" one of the constables said as he looked around the court. "Lots of ways someone could see a bloke coming or going."

And yet, no one had. No one ever did. All through the case, there had been witness statements, theories, sketches, and arrests, but nothing that felt right or, for that matter, stuck. "How was this one discovered?" asked Holmes.

"At ten forty-five this morning, McCarthy, the landlord, knocked on the door," Abberline replied. "When he got no answer, he reached through the broken windowpane and lifted the curtain. That's when he discovered the body. Apparently there's quite a mess."

"I deduced that from the amount of fresh vomit on the premises."

Another official was walking toward them. "Inspector Beck," Abberline said.

"They've called for the bloodhounds," Beck said. "We're not to go in until they've had a go."

"How long until they arrive?" Holmes asked.

"Hard to say. We're telling the photographers to shoot through the window."

Since there were no cameras on scene at the moment, Holmes approached the shattered pane, praying for a solid clue this time. He reached through, lifting the curtain. A quick glance told him the room was small, only about ten by twelve, with the bed on the south side of the room. And then nothing else he saw made sense. Holmes looked for a long moment, forcing himself to pick out concrete details one by one, before he could accept what was in that tiny, dingy room.

Mary Jane Kelly was naked and on her back, her body angled slightly to the left, her head turned toward the window. Like the others, her throat had been cut. In fact, from the way the blood stained the mattress, it looked like she'd been lying the other way when that had happened, and the killer had turned her around for what came next.

Her legs were spread wide, the left arm flexed across the abdomen, the right arm a little away from the body and with the fingers clenched. The arms were covered with jagged wounds. *Did this one fight?* Holmes wondered, but it was hard to tell. There was no part of the woman's flesh that hadn't been attacked with maniacal fury.

The question was more what hadn't been savaged than what had. The entire surface of her abdomen and thighs was gone, as were her breasts and much of her neck. Holmes couldn't see the particulars, but it looked like her abdominal cavity was scooped out. Spare parts were scattered here and there, with an overflow on the table by the bed. There was no way to tell what her facial features had been. Her face had been slashed in all directions, parts sliced right off. Oblique cuts ran from the lips down to the chin. *Who hated her this much? What did she represent to the killer?*

Holmes dropped the curtain, glad to give Mary Kelly back her privacy for a little while. It had been years since the sight of violence had turned his stomach, but he felt a sudden need for fresh air. Sweat slicked his skin, sticking his shirt to his back. He retreated from number thirteen.

"I'm going for a walk," he said to Abberline. The inspector took one look at his face and didn't argue.

Holmes fled the narrow passage back to Dorset Street, telling himself he was surveying the neighborhood. He would give himself two minutes, then head back in to take a closer look at the court. But the two minutes stretched to three, and he kept going, submerging himself in the noisy, vibrant scene around him. It felt good, like a hot bath after a chill. The scene in that tawdry room had struck deeper than he cared to admit.

Women gossiped outside the doorways of the tenements; men lounged on the porches. A steam tram went past on Commercial Street, heading for the markets. Life went on despite the grisly death a few dozen yards away. And it might as well, because there was no sign the deaths would ever stop. He was failing as badly as Abberline.

At the Stride murder, Holmes had been certain that there had been a connection to the Hilliard House deaths. Obviously, that meant a common link. Bancroft? The Gold King? Magnus? But that theory fell to pieces when he looked at the other deaths. He couldn't imagine any of those suspects, not even Symeon Magnus, attacking random women with that much fury. They would kill, yes, but they'd do it like they did everything else—elegantly and efficiently. In truth, he had no suspects.

Like so many of the men investigating the Whitechapel murders, Holmes was beginning to take the case personally. He knew the letters from Saucy Jack were false leads, but still the mocking, misspelled words whispered in his dreams like a music hall tune he couldn't scrub from his brain.

The only positive was that Holmes had used the case as an excuse to search as much of the area as he could over the last month. He'd started with the lodging houses, but it seemed the population was as stable as shifting sands, and few remembered the names of their current neighbors, let alone a girl who might have been there and gone. There had been hints of Evelina's presence, but they vanished as quickly as a dropped sovereign. If his niece had wanted to disappear, she'd chosen the area well.

A wave of frustration coursed through Holmes as he moved quickly down the street, doing his best to burn his own anger off so that he could summon a semblance of his usual calm. But something about the area resisted logic, as if it had given up and gone back to bed drunk.

A hand came out of a dark doorway and grabbed his sleeve. Holmes wheeled, ready to fight, but the hand let go and began to beckon instead.

"Show yourself," Holmes demanded.

"Be quiet and get in here," his brother snapped. "We have a great deal to discuss."

Reluctantly, Holmes complied. Beyond the doorway was an empty room, stinking as if a fire had cleared out the last occupants, the furniture, and most of the walls. "Is this safe?"

"Probably not," Mycroft replied. "But then few places are these days."

"I thought Keating kidnapped you from the Diogenes Club," Holmes said dryly.

"He did." Mycroft gave him a smug look. He looked haggard, but otherwise unhurt.

Holmes raised an eyebrow. "So what are you doing in Whitechapel?"

"I escaped."

"And came here?"

Mycroft waved a hand, taking in the charred walls, the mildew blackening the woodwork. "Exigent circumstances required that I break my routine."

And everyone knew Mycroft's routine was sacrosanct. Holmes refused to rise to the bait—if he did, he knew his brother would wring his tale for every nuance of drama, and Holmes wasn't in the mood. "What do you want?"

"I want to speak to you, but you're guarded as closely as a virgin queen. I'd hoped you'd turn up at this sideshow."

"If you saw what I did just now you'd be a little less flippant."

Mycroft made a face. "There is a reason I don't frequent crime scenes. It disturbs my digestion. Let us get down to business."

Holmes shrugged. "I imagine you're seeking a favor, though I can't imagine what."

"Have you no theories? No well-reasoned deductions?"

Holmes gave a dry laugh. "You know well that I'm outside the circle of your confidence."

"I'm working for the shadow government, and that means I am in deep with the Baskerville business."

"Oh, for pity's sake I already surmised that much, since you recruited me for it," Holmes snapped.

Annoyance flickered across his brother's face. "You've only seen the tip of the cat's tail."

Holmes folded his arms. "Then bring it on, whiskers and all. But speak slowly so that I might understand."

"For God's sake, pack your pride away for a moment. I haven't involved you because the level of danger is far too high." Mycroft turned away, pacing across the sooty floor.

"I've already had a bomb in my study."

"I know."

"Tell me."

Mycroft sighed. "I have worked for months gaining the confidence of the Steam Council, whispering advice, planting the seeds of doubt. I have been like a gardener sowing weeds, first with the Blue King, then with the Gold. I have played them off against one another as neatly as you please. I convinced Keating to turn a handful of King Coal's men."

"So you're the one pulling the strings of the Blue King's traitor. And somehow I got bombed in the process? Wasn't that a bit careless of you? Or were you the one who gave the order for it in the first place? King Coal is convinced someone is tampering with his minions."

Mycroft shrugged, still pacing from one wall to the other, reminding Holmes of a caged bear. "I managed to turn it around so that you weren't actually blown to bits."

It wasn't precisely an answer. Anger swept through Holmes like a hot, dry wind. "Thank you for your attention to detail."

His brother spun to face him. "It was a bit of paint and plaster. A fair price for putting the cat among the pigeons. *I* was the one dragged out of my club at gunpoint." The venom in Mycroft's voice said he hadn't expected that move.

"What happened?" Holmes softened his tone.

"Keating suspects me. Something went wrong."

"What?"

"I don't know," he snarled.

The very rarity of the statement took Holmes aback. "What about Jones? And the other one, Bingham? Do they know anything of value?" He was clutching at straws, and Mycroft's expression said so.

"They're both dead. Poison. They suffered severe hallucinations, and then their hearts stopped. There is someone in our own fold who didn't want them to speak."

Holmes felt his gut growing cold. Things were unraveling. "This is grave news. And yet you escaped the Gold King's clutches. How did you do that?"

"There is no time for the whole tale." His brother gave a wan smile. "Suffice to say there was a man of our own in Keating's employ."

"At least that is symmetry if he has one in ours."

Mycroft ignored the sally. "I have to make it back to Scotland. I need your help, and it's not for something simple like money or transportation. The Schoolmaster has seen to that much."

A cold, dry dread settled in Holmes's stomach. Although he thought he knew the answer, he asked anyhow. "What do you need?"

"Timing is everything. Right now, with these murders, we have an opportunity. It would be best if you didn't solve them quite yet."

"My conclusion is that you wrote the letters signed by the Ripper."

"Of course I did. Who knew a handful of dead whores could do so much good."

Holmes wasn't easily appalled, but that did it. "Are you mad?"

"No. Public sentiment is high."

"For rebellion?"

"For destabilization. The rebels don't have a prayer against the Steam Council if they go to war. We're not ready, and they have weapons the likes of which the world has never seen. The only hope is to break the council and turn them against one another. Keating and Scarlet target the Blue King as the greatest threat. He has allies in the Black Kingdom."

"What do you expect me to do? Keep them at each other's throats?"

"You must play a role in that."

"I have other responsibilities. Have you paused to consider that our niece is missing?"

"No," Mycroft said simply. "You're the sympathetic one in the family. I paint a larger canvas."

God help us. Anger flashed through Holmes, but it was pointless to show it. They had argued before, and he knew nothing would change no matter how he raged. He wouldn't lower himself to that again.

"I will get you word when there is something you must do," Mycroft said, as if the topic of Evelina had never come up. "But one thing above all—protect the Schoolmaster, even if it means your life. If there is a traitor among the rebels, it could come to that."

"I know," Holmes replied, the rivalry between them falling away for the moment. "I know what Baskerville means to the queen."

His brother gave him one of his rare true smiles. "If all the dominoes fall as I expect, he will save the Empire."

CHAPTER FORTY-ONE

London, November 10, 1888

HILLIARD HOUSE

9:35 a.m. Saturday

BANCROFT SAT IN HIS STUDY, WATCHING THE MINUTE HAND click forward along the enameled dial of the mantel clock. He had started at half past nine and now it was nine thirty-five. Too early for most of the family to be stirring. If someone were to ask what he was waiting for, he would have been hard-pressed to give specifics. Disaster? A thunderclap? A bullet to the head? He'd set enough potential explosions in motion, he was spoiled for choice.

He hadn't killed Jasper Keating, a direct and potent threat, but he had saved Evelina Cooper, who was another kind of threat altogether. He had even paid a physician to sew her back together. Pure folly, of course. If anyone had recognized his face, what ill fortune might have followed? And it wasn't as if he could mention finding the girl, as that would give rise to speculation as to what he'd been doing wandering the streets the night of a double murder. Better to be cautious than obliged to answer awkward questions.

And according to the doctor, against all odds, she had lived. If Bancroft had simply walked away, she would have died and ceased to be a thorn in his side forever.

But nothing was ever simple. Keating wanted to punish her. By the perverse laws that seemed to rule Bancroft's nature, that was reason enough to save the girl. And maybe it felt good to be the white knight just this once.

A light tap sounded on the door. Bancroft sighed. He knew that tap, and knew that it was hopeless to avoid that particular intruder for long. "Come in, Poppy."

The door opened, and his youngest child entered. She was the awkward one—the one who hadn't thrived at school, who had never taken an interest in being liked, and who couldn't care less if she looked or acted like a lady. As a father, he had no idea what to do with a child whose way of measuring the world was so different from his own.

And today she looked more disheveled than usual. But that was not what had his attention. It was the pinched look on her face. "Whatever is the matter?"

She didn't answer, but just held out a letter. "I went into Imogen's room and found this on her dressing table." The words came out in a hushed whisper, as if she were speaking of the dead.

Panic slammed into his diaphragm. He didn't ask what Poppy had been doing in her big sister's room. He just took the letter with a murmur of thanks.

It was addressed to *Mother and Father*. There had been a wax seal, but that had been peeled away from the paper, no doubt by Poppy. The fact that she hadn't taken the time to repair the damage said something about the urgency of the matter. *Damn and blast, it's always the obedient ones that cause the most trouble in the end.* He unfolded the paper and read, gradually rising to his feet as his gaze devoured the words.

Imogen had eloped.

EVELINA HAD AWAKENED that morning to find Nick gone and the sheets beside her unforgivably cold. She lay in bed for a little while, staring at the cracks in the plaster ceiling and missing him. Memory tangled her, making it hard to move. Memories of his mouth, his body, his magic—as long as she stayed between those sheets, she was wrapped in the sensations of their idyll. Rising from their cocoon would be a painful jolt. To be truthful, she didn't want to face the world beyond their room.

And yet sometime in those two long days between talking and resting, talking and lovemaking, and just being side by side, he'd told her that he had to leave. They were bound together in ways that had no name, but that was not the only reality. He'd stayed by her sickbed, to the consternation of his crew, but now that she was out of danger he had obligations. Urgent ones, he'd said, that he'd tell her about once she was stronger. His refusal to say anything more had sent her into fits, and Nick into smothered laughter. He'd quickly added that he would be back before the week was out, when she was just that little bit stronger, and then he would take her away forever. She trusted his word, but wished they could both stay there burrowed like rabbits down a hole.

Eventually, she'd arisen to take a long, hot bath—not the first she'd taken in the last few days, but the first she'd taken alone. Then she'd dressed in fresh clothes Hyacinth had found for her—a pale blue dress that was cut far lower in the bodice than anything she'd ever owned. She was left with the sensation of being dressed and undressed at the same time.

"You'd better be careful to stay away from the windows," her old schoolmate said. "There's been no end of people knocking on the door, looking for you."

"Me?" Evelina looked up from tugging the neckline a fraction of an inch higher.

The bath had reminded her that her flesh carried the evidence of attack. Angry scars slashed across her abdomen, puckered where the surgeon had stitched them. Nick had been careful with them, and as careful with her as if she were the most precious creature to ever walk beneath the sun, but even he couldn't buffer her from the damage. Not entirely. The sight of the wounds filled her with confusion, slowing her down until both fingers and thoughts fumbled with the simplest tasks. It was as if she'd been invaded and something vital had been stripped away.

Hyacinth was leaning against the door. Her skirts were hitched up to reveal provocatively slender calves encased in red-and-white-striped stockings and high-heeled boots. She also had a tiny white whip curled through her belt, and the fringes on the handle swayed gently as she shifted her weight.

She watched Evelina intently, as if reading her reactions and gauging how to proceed. No doubt it was a professional skill, as useful to a procuress as it was to any politician—but right now, Hyacinth looked worried for Evelina. "Your uncle was looking for you."

"My uncle?" Her spirits lifted a little, and then fell when she realized that she had let time slip past without fulfilling her end of Keating's bargain. She would have to write both the Gold King and Sherlock right away.

"Some Peelers, too. And of course, they're looking for the Whitechapel Murderer, as well. He got poor Mary Kelly yesterday."

Evelina was speechless, not sure what to say. Hyacinth was keeping her face perfectly still, but her throat was working with the effort not to cry. Despite the décolletage and extravagantly purple hair, Hyacinth was still a nineteen-year-old girl, and this wasn't the first friend she'd lost to the murders. There had been Annie Chapman, too.

Evelina bit her lip, remembering Mary's throaty laugh. "I'm sorry."

Hyacinth darted her a look that warned off any further sympathy. "We nearly lost you, too. What the fardling hell were you doing out alone at night? Some of us may need to take those risks, but you don't."

"I was looking for someone." Evelina began to comb out her damp hair. It was snarled beyond belief.

"Who?"

She remembered talking to Mary. Perhaps it was the shock of the woman's death, but it pulled something out of the dark mist that was her memory. "A woman in a cloak." It wasn't much, but it was more than she'd had before. "It had something to do with Magnus."

"Huh. Good riddance to that one. He came looking for you, too."

"You didn't—".

Hyacinth moved from the doorway, took the comb from her hand, and began to ply it herself, working from the ends of Evelina's wavy locks with brusque efficiency. "I didn't tell any of them where you were. Not even Mr. Keating's men. Who you tell is your decision to make."

"Thank you," Evelina said, impressed and infinitely grateful that her friend had stood up to them all. "For everything."

Hyacinth gave her a half smile. "There's something about this part of town that taught me to value the few friends I have. I may be a sinner, but at least I'm not a lonely one."

"Ow!" Evelina squawked as she hit a snarl.

"Did I mention they call me the Mistress of Pain?"

ABOUT HALF AN hour later, Evelina sat alone in her room, dressed and ready to face the world. Or perhaps not quite ready. She felt like a wanderer who had crossed a mountain range to find a new and strange countryside. Nick had been everything she could have dreamed of—his rough, fierce sweetness, and the unimagined pleasures he'd shown her—but now she was alone. He'd been gone just hours, and already she pined for his return like a lovesick heroine in one of Lady Bancroft's soggy romance novels. She'd always despised the women in them, with their tears and sighs, but she'd been humbled. Now she knew exactly how they felt.

Efforts to shake the morose mood only took her to darker places. Inevitably, her thoughts strayed to her attack. Images of the woman in the cape muddled with another memory, that of the murdered servant girl, Grace Child, and of the grooms who had been killed when Magnus took Lord Bancroft's automatons. She could still see Grace Child, fallen to the floor with her throat cut, her hat rolled a few steps away . . . Evelina sat bolt upright, the hair on her neck rising with icy prickles. She jerked to her feet as images came flooding back—and with them, Serafina's confession.

"Bloody hell," Evelina breathed, her face going numb with a surge of panic.

It all made sense. They hadn't found the Whitechapel Murderer because they were looking for a man. A woman could walk through the crowd of police without notice.

Back in April, hours before Grace Child was killed, Evelina had heard a man and a woman talking. The words had been faint, drowned out by other noises, but the investigators—including Uncle Sherlock—had never been able to figure out who they were. The deva in the hedge had described them as a man and his shadow. *His shadow.* A doll with a scrap of Magnus's soul might look like a shadow to a deva—a being made entirely of energy.

A sudden chill assaulted Evelina. She grabbed a shawl, wrapping it tight around her. She'd begun to feel safe in Nick's arms, but now that she knew what had held the knife, a feeling of skittishness was destroying her hard-won calm. Serafina was still at large, and her master was the Blue King's maker, impossible to touch. He might have fled the theater, but that just meant he'd become invisible. With Magnus, not even death meant that he was truly gone. *Bloody hell.*

Last April, Magnus had shown Serafina to Tobias and his friends. Tobias had tried to destroy what he'd seen—if only he had! If Serafina had accompanied Magnus that night on his first foray to get Lord Bancroft's automatons—which fit with the doll's fragmented memories—they may well have encountered Grace waiting for Lord B to meet her, and then killed the poor girl to keep her quiet about intruders in the house. What had Serafina said? *But the woman simply got in the way.*

And if Magnus had used Serafina to get the automatons from the grooms, she could have taken them by surprise. On a dark road, she'd look just like a woman out alone. Maybe one needing help. How would they know that she was monstrously strong, adept at killing, and obedient to a sorcerer bent on lifting their cargo?

Sickness flooded through Evelina, leaving her hot and sweating. She sat down quickly, suddenly alive to every ache in her body. She had felt the black oblivion of death steal upon her and now knew what those servants had felt—helpless, terrified, and betrayed.

And yet, despite everything, Evelina felt an intense pity for Serafina. Magnus had created a being stuck forever in a half-formed state, always hungry to be complete, never fully understanding what she was or where she fit. As someone who had struggled to understand her own talents, to know where she belonged in a world divided between magic and science, rich and poor, Evelina could empathize.

And dark magic could make her just as dangerous, for surely she'd struck out at Gareth in her desperation. The only mercy was that Magnus hadn't taught her how to steal life from another living being. Another week of his tutelage, and *she* might have been the monster.

A heartsick nausea swelled in Evelina's throat, making her shudder. Magnus wasn't the serpent in the garden. He was every blight, worm, scale, and fungus rolled into one, and she was sorely tempted to count herself lucky that he was gone, and simply pray that he stayed away. But in truth Magnus's disappearance meant little, and he still wanted Nick and Athena. He had to be stopped, and Serafina with him.

Her gaze fell on her carpetbag at the foot of the bed. With a sudden flurry of energy, she grabbed it, lifting it onto the bed so she could look inside. Her train case of tools for fixing clockwork was still there, as well as her few articles of clothes. It looked as if Magnus had neatly packed everything she'd arrived with back into her bag. Like so many things he did, it was hard to interpret. Why had he bothered?

Still, she was glad that he had done it. She put the train case on her lap and lifted the lid. The familiar sight and feel of her workbox comforted her, the gleam of her tools and the jingle of the metal gears and springs in their neat compartments. Something, at least, was the same as it had always been.

Then she lifted out the tray that sat on top. In the space beneath were her larger tools and half-finished projects—as well as the magical tools Gran Cooper had given her. Magnus had put them all back, including the wand.

Evelina picked it up, setting the rest of the box onto the bed beside her. *Do I dare to do this?* Her burst of confidence faltered, making the wand feel treacherous in her hand.

Magic had not been her friend of late. And yet it was the only weapon she had.

Slowly and with an unsteady step she moved to the small square of carpet in the middle of the room. Apprehension clawed up her spine, drying her mouth and robbing her of breath. *Calm, be calm.* If the snake was out there, she was going to find him with his own tricks—and where Magnus went, he'd be sure to take his mechanical helpmate.

Evelina held out her arms the way Magnus had shown her, and cast her mind down to the end of the wand and out into the aether. Now that she knew the risks, she remembered to put safeguards in place the way her Gran had taught her. She couldn't name what energies ruled this kind of spell, but she addressed them nonetheless. *Hear me, powers of the aether. There is only one question I ask. I don't want to see any fires, or disasters, or anything else. Where did Magnus and Serafina go?*

The powers must have been listening, because this time she didn't see any sweeping city panorama or a panoply of stars. All the wand showed her was a steel gray morning mottled with darker clouds, and high in that sky was a sleek black airship with a dragon-shaped prow and a balloon as black as night. And if there was any doubt as to who captained it, she could feel the sorcerer's presence shrouding it like a shimmering veil.

Magnus hadn't just left the theater. He'd left the earth behind.

CHAPTER FORTY-TWO

IMOGEN SAT ON THE EDGE OF THE COT, HER HEART PAT-patting triple time beneath her stays. She couldn't seem to stop shaking, as if she'd caught a fever. Fear wasn't something she was good with—not this kind. She could face playing the pianoforte in public, or turning her life upside down to run away with a man her parents didn't like. She'd even faced a dragon, but she'd had Evelina with her then. Being on her own and snatched from the street was far worse—especially the blindfolded part. Stumbling blind with her hands tied had underscored her loss of control in a way little else could.

She tried to think like Evelina. Her friend would have already found every weakness in the floorboards and conjured a spell to blow through them—or climbed out the window to crawl along the roof. Of course, Imogen was fairly sure they were on an airship, so there would be no blowing up or dangling from roofs. She scanned the room, trying to imagine how she could possibly make a weapon. To begin with, it wasn't much more than a cubbyhole with a bunk. If she'd tried to wave her arms, she'd rap her knuckles on the bland gray walls. For another thing, there wasn't much in there except bedding. The only battle she was likely to win was a pillow fight.

And she had no weapons with her. She'd even lost her

bonnet in the struggle. Mouse and Bird had been left—along with her suitcase—on Threadneedle Street. No one would know where she was.

A fresh wave of panic welled up inside her, bringing tears to her eyes. She shrank back on the cot, wrapping her shawl more tightly around her. *Why would anyone want to take me? I'm just another debutante. And how will Bucky ever know that I really meant to meet him?*

The door opened, and she saw who it was. She braced one hand against the wall, her jaw falling open in pure, raw shock.

"Miss Roth, I hope my crew was gentle with you." Dr. Magnus gave her a kindly smile. He was dressed, as always, in a black suit, his hair and beard neatly trimmed. He looked more like a lord than a doctor.

Imogen caught her breath. She didn't believe that smile for an instant. "As abductions go, I would have to rate it as moderately distressing."

"Such sharp thorns for a pretty flower."

"Why am I here?"

"As a bargaining chip."

"With my father?" Despite the fluttering in her stomach, she thought furiously. "What does he have that you could possibly want?"

"He is an experienced hand at games of power. There is much he could do for me, if he would just bend his will to mine."

"When my father bends, it's usually to pick up a weapon."

"Thorns and wit. Be careful how you brandish them, Miss Roth."

Imogen scowled. Her wits were the only weapon she had, and survival might depend on knowing what the blazes was going on. She grabbed at one of the thousand things that didn't make sense. "Why are you using the Blue Boys as your henchmen?" She'd seen their blue sashes right before they'd put on the blindfold.

He chuckled, as if she'd been amusing. "Why buy when one can rent—or in my case, borrow. Despite my recent turn as a puppeteer, I am a doctor of the mesmeric arts." He pressed a hand to his chest, a glint of pleasure in his eye. "And my skill lies in enhancing the traditional hypnotic approach when required."

"You mesmerized an entire crew?" She couldn't keep the incredulity from her voice.

He shrugged. "They were there, roaming about the Blue King's property like unguarded sheep. I was there, suffering Blue's idiocy and paranoia in exchange for access to his resources. It was a natural fit."

"So you spirited them away like the Pied Piper of Hamelin?"

He gave a slight bow. "Mesmerism doesn't work on every rat, but there were enough susceptible airmen in King Coal's employ to assemble a crew of willing souls."

The way he said *souls* made Imogen's flesh creep. "And I'm sure he won't miss the ship," she added, hoping for one more scrap of information.

"Oh, no, the *Wyvern* is mine. I've had it waiting for just such an occasion as this." Magnus's expression shifted back to a bland, pleasant mask as he changed topics. "But enough about that. You certainly made this encounter convenient, going off alone with a suitcase. No doubt you left a farewell note at home?"

Imogen had already thought of that, but his words sent her stomach to the floor anyhow.

"Never mind," he said. "I have written a note to your father. As soon as he meets the terms of our little agreement, I will return you and his other possessions posthaste."

"His automatons," she said, doing her best to keep her voice steady. *With the soul of my twin sister.*

He blinked, as if he hadn't expected her to know about those. "Yes. In a way it's an advantage that you are familiar with such machines."

Imogen balled her hands into fists, hiding their trembling beneath her skirts. "I can think of no uplifting reason why."

This time, his smile showed teeth. "It minimizes explanation. Allow me to introduce your companion on this journey. Serafina?"

Imogen looked toward the door, at first reassured by the

feminine name. But then what walked in made her jaw drop.
The red-haired, beautiful automaton was nothing like the
crude things her father had made years ago. But there was
the same chill that crawled over her flesh when she looked at
her. Something about her was just *wrong*. As wrong as her
nightmares.

The doll tilted her head. "I am very pleased to meet you. I
saw you on the street once before, Miss Imogen Roth."

"Charmed," said Imogen, inching back closer to the wall.

"I'm sure you'll be great company for each other." Magnus turned to go, but caught the doll's arm, giving it a shake.
"Behave yourself, sweetling. This one is mine."

Imogen had no idea what that meant, but her muscles
went rigid as steel. As soon as Magnus released her, Serafina sat in the chair that faced Imogen's bed, her blue eyes
fixed on her in a way that was both sightless and enormously
invasive. Imogen had an overwhelming urge to pull the
blanket over her head.

"You aren't going to simply leave me with her, are you?"
she gasped.

He already had one foot out the door. "Sadly, I don't have
crewmen to spare for the job. Make yourself comfortable,
but don't try to leave the room. She has orders to restrain
you if necessary. Oh, and one thing," Magnus said, pausing
to give her a sly look. "Don't let her near the cutlery."

WITH FEVERISH URGENCY, Evelina had spent the last hour
writing a detailed letter to Uncle Sherlock. There was no
question that he had to know everything she had learned.
Besides being her uncle and a consulting detective with
friends at Scotland Yard, he understood what had happened
last April. He would understand the connections Evelina
had made between Serafina, the murder of Grace Child, and
the theft of Lord Bancroft's automatons.

And then she wrote to Keating, answering his questions
as per their agreement. She had seen at least part of King
Coal's weaponry, and could tell him as much as she knew.
And she'd identified Magnus as the Blue King's maker, and

had the proof of the sorcerer's handwriting on the pages they'd taken from Mr. Juniper. Nick had brought her the papers after showing them to the Schoolmaster, but as Evelina thumbed through them, she thought long and hard about giving Keating all the Blue King's secrets. No steam baron should be allowed to rule the Empire, least of all the man who threatened the people she loved. She chose three pages to enclose with the letter as evidence. They had just enough information to support her claims without giving too much away.

But as she finished the last lines and signed the missive, the rush of energy that had kept her scribbling page after page faded. The foggy sense of guilt and helplessness that had come after Serafina's attack emerged again, leaving her drained. The doll had torn her open and looked inside, and she hadn't been able to protect herself. She hadn't been strong, or smart, or powerful enough. And if that had happened, what else might? Would she ever be truly safe? Who might she let down? *Will I betray Nick, the way Magnus predicted?*

Evelina set her pen down, letting the ink dry on the last page. She stared into nothingness, her mind remorselessly flipping through images of knife, darkness, gutter, and the cold lifeless blue of Serafina's eyes. A profound dejection swamped her, and she buried her face in her hands. She'd been able to escape those feelings as long as Nick had been with her, but now there was no protection.

Slowly, mechanically, Evelina began to fold and seal the letters, her hands taking over from her active will. The pen scratched on the cheap paper, writing out first Keating's address and then her uncle's, feeling as if an infinity of time and yet none at all had passed since she had left Paddington Station with a will to outwit the Gold King. She had achieved some of her goals and not others, and nothing had gone as she'd imagined.

She had just finished the last seal when she heard a noise at the window and looked up to see Bird sitting on the sill. With a cry of pleasure, she pulled up the sash. Bird flew in,

Mouse clambering over the sill a moment later. She picked Mouse up, cradling him in her hands. "You're dirty!"

My existence is complete. I have now clambered through gutters even the most plague-ridden rats fear to tread.

Bird gave a derisive cheep. *Make him some clockwork fleas with tiny violins.*

"Why aren't you with Imogen?" she asked. "And how did you find me?"

Trust me, said Bird, *every deva in London knows where you and the horse boy have been these last few days.*

Evelina flushed to the roots of her hair. But she had noticed devas outside, floating around the trees. If there was a way to call the devas back to this part of the city, perhaps they'd found it—and perhaps they would restore balance to the East End's unseen powers. *And maybe then I'll sleep with the lights off again.*

Mouse caught the image of the melty-head shadows in her mind. *You've seen the Others?*

She hadn't heard devas ever refer to their loathsome counterparts before, but the name made sense. "Yes."

Ah.

She wanted to know what that *ah* meant, but Bird broke in. *We have lots to tell you. Miss Imogen was having nightmares so she ran away to be with the toymaker, but two men took her before she could get there. We got left behind.* Bird flew to her shoulder, its sharp nails gripping through the shoulder of her dress. *They had the sorcerer's stink all over them.*

Mouse piped up, stretching up on its hind paws. *I was listening the whole time I was at the old house. The sorcerer has the angry old man's automatons!*

The information had come in rapid fire, and Evelina couldn't take it all in at once. Or perhaps she didn't want to. The gray fog of her mood obscured the creatures' chatter, and she could only bear to let one horrible fact reach her at a time. "Magnus said the automatons were destroyed when his house burned down!"

And you believed him? Bird asked with a ruffle of feathers.

"Good point."

And then the truth crashed over her, slicing through her defenses. Imogen was gone—snatched away when she had tried to elope with Bucky. Evelina made a despairing sound. *Magnus has her.* The thought of her gentle friend in his power was unbearable—and only part of the equation. Why was Imogen eloping now, when she had said she would not? What had made her change her mind? *How bad had things gotten since Maggor's Close?* Evelina sank back in her chair, her eyes stinging. If only she had been there.

But you weren't, said Bird in a practical tone. *So what do you do now?*

"Stop Magnus." The words came automatically, driven by logic more than by conviction. Since Serafina—who was but the shadow of Magnus—had nearly killed her, Evelina had little faith in her own power to stop him. She'd tried to unmask him as the Blue King's maker but only ended up seduced by his library and stabbed by his killer doll. A rematch didn't promise any better results.

But then ideas began to catch hold, and she sat a little straighter. She had one thing Magnus did not. She had friends and, like Hyacinth, she'd learned how very important they were.

Working with Nick had reminded her that she wasn't alone. With her light and his knowledge, they had escaped the Blue Boys at the Indifference Device. Together, they had cracked the Blue King's secrets. Last April, she had found Athena's Casket, and he had given it a home in the air. There was no reason she had to confront Magnus by herself—in fact, she was better with other people by her side.

Clearly, there were others she could call—those with ships, money, and brilliant minds. The trick would be to alert them before it was too late for Imogen. The vision she'd conjured suddenly made more sense. There was a reason the sorcerer had left London—he thought himself hidden, beyond the reach of Lord Bancroft or any others who might bring him to justice.

But you didn't count on me looking in on you, did you, Doctor? Evelina turned to Bird. "I need an air deva to carry a message to the *Red Jack*. I need Nick's help, if he's nearby. Magnus has an airship of his own—a black dragon. I'm pretty sure that's where both Imogen and the automatons will be."

Done. Bird fluttered out the window and was gone.

And if he is not nearby? asked Mouse, flicking its tail.

The creature was right. Since she didn't know what Nick's mission was, she had no idea where he might be. She needed more allies. "I need to tell my uncle and Lord Bancroft. And Tobias. They need to know what has happened to Imogen. They can help." And Tobias had access to Keating's wealth— if a solution could be bought, he would have it. Then she paused. "I should tell Bucky Penner, but I don't know where to find him."

I do. Mouse scampered across the desk to sit by her inkwell. *I know where he makes his toys.*

"Excellent." If enough people knew what Magnus really was and the things he had done, he wouldn't escape so easily this time. Purpose gave her energy again, and she pulled the stack of writing paper toward her. "I have more letters to write. I'll send them by runner."

The little steel mouse sat up on its hind legs, twitching its whiskers. *Be careful what you say. Once you send your letters, there will be no going back. Magnus got away with hiding in plain sight because he is a showman, but he won't after this and he will hold you responsible. And knowing what he is begs the question of how you recognize magic when you see it. Choose your words with care.*

There were times she forgot just how old and wise Mouse was. "You're right."

Of course I am.

A mix of emotions coursed through Evelina—frustration top of the list. She restlessly tapped the pen as she pondered what to say, wishing she could simply insert her knowledge into another's brain. Language took too long, and time was everything. "We'll solve this faster if I bring everyone to one place and we make our plans together."

I agree in principle, said Mouse. *But if you must do this,*

*have your escape routes ready. When you throw a party
there's no telling who might decide to attend.*

"I KNOW YOU, Miss Imogen Roth," said the doll in her odd
mechanical voice.

At first Imogen had thought the doll was programmed as
some sort of tasteless joke, but slowly she'd come to understand that it was thinking on its own. "I'm not sure how,"
said Imogen in a voice that quavered shamefully.

"You do not know me?"

"How would I? Where would we have met?"

The doll's fingers clenched. "I saw you leaning on your
man as I walked down the street with Miss Cooper."

Imogen started. *Evelina!* But what did she have to do with
any of this? "Do you know where Miss Cooper is?"

The doll's face remained expressionless, but her voice
swelled with satisfaction. "She pretended to be my friend,
but she wanted to take what I had. She was just like the doctor, so I turned the tables and looked inside her instead.
With her own knife, too."

Suddenly the jibe about cutlery made awful sense, even if
the rest of the words were a jumble. "You . . . cut her open?"

The imagery from her nightmares surged forward, foul
and macabre. Horror swept in on its wake, crushing her
lungs. Imogen tried to speak, but only a strangled noise
came out.

The doll was leaning forward, managing to look intense
despite her utterly bland face. "The doctor was not pleased
by what I did to Miss Cooper. He told me not to do such a
thing again. He caught me in my bloody clothes, and if he
were not in a hurry to leave, I think he would have taken me
apart and put me back in my box. But he didn't have time for
that."

Evelina. This creature had killed Evelina, the best friend
she would ever have. Imogen stared at the automaton, refusing to let herself believe.

"He locked me in a room beneath the theater where he
keeps his money. It was dark and lined with steel not even I

could break. He said he was putting his treasure in a vault."
Serafina lifted her chin. "He left me there for weeks while
he made his plans to launch this ship."

And he should have left you there until the end of days.

"But I found one more life," said Serafina. "I got away one
last time when all our things were being loaded. This one
had a room, nice and private. But I looked and looked and
still didn't find what I was looking for."

This is the Whitechapel Murderer. A doll. Imogen knew
exactly which event Serafina was talking about, though
after the double murder she had begun to take laudanum to
help her sleep. At least she hadn't had to watch her best
friend die. She herself would probably die before many
more hours passed. Strange, but she felt almost calm—or at
least the surface of her mind was. It was like standing on ice
with a raging torrent below.

"And what do you do with this life?" she asked.

"I'm hungry for it, just like the doctor and Miss Cooper. It
makes me whole and brings me peace." Serafina's head
tilted. "But you should know that."

"Why? Why would I know such a thing?"

The doll folded her hands in her lap. Imogen saw the fingers move, beautifully jointed but somehow not right. The
motion was insectile, like spider's legs.

Serafina studied her. "When I knew it was you the doctor
wanted, I asked him to tell me how I came to be. He never
tells me everything, but this is what I could piece together.
Do you want to hear it?"

Imogen gave a mute nod.

"Very well. I was locked away for a long time in a dead
place. It could not be anything but a prison, because a
human soul needs life to cling to. You must understand this
is why I first invaded your dreams. I was desperate for light
and air, and even your nightmares were a miracle of relief to
me."

My nightmares? The automaton's words sent something
through Imogen—a resonance like the breeze over a wind
harp, but one that was made of old bones. Knowledge was

rising inside her, familiar and old but far from welcome. "Go on."

"Dr. Magnus didn't prepare my vessel well enough the first time. But when he made his new automatons, he put a tiny piece of his own life inside them. That's why they can move and talk."

"They can?" Imogen asked in a dull voice, terrified of where this was leading.

"Certainly, but not as well as I can. I am the prima ballerina."

The way she said it brought a shudder from deep inside Imogen. Despite the thing's inhuman voice, she recognized that preening, smug lilt to the words.

"So when he took me out of your father's old automaton and put me into Serafina, I had a good place to go. I could attach myself properly. I—or as much of me as he could salvage by then—could be in the world again. It's better now, even if I am always hungry."

"Tobias spoke of a doll named Serafina," Imogen murmured. "When Magnus came to our house last spring."

"That was before I joined the ballet. This"—the automaton made a gesture that encompassed her body—"has been walking the world for years, but I was reborn inside it. I made Serafina something special."

"Oh, God." The resonance had become a tremor as facts began fitting together.

"Why are you shaking?" Serafina asked. "Are you cold? Are you afraid, Miss Imogen Roth?"

"No." Her throat started to clog with tears, her eyes brimming and blurry. A shrill whimper escaped before she could cover her mouth. A tremor of hysteria began to bubble up, shuddering through her. She held her eyes open as wide as she could, holding the tears in.

But her eyes filled and Imogen blinked, wetness hot on her cheeks.

"Why are you crying?" the doll asked, leaning even closer to see. Mocking her.

"It was you in my dreams?" She knew it was, but she had

to hear this *thing* say it. A blind anger was stirring—one she thought she'd buried along with childhood memories.

"Yes. We have been sharing the night for so, so long—but I am afraid it has been one-sided. Whenever I slept, you forgot all about me. But whenever I woke it was a simple matter to step into your nightmares—as easy as slipping on a coat. Poor, weak Imogen."

"But you're an automaton!"

"Is that all I am?"

Imogen's insides gave a wrench of fresh terror. "What gives you the right to take over my dreams?"

"Right? There is nothing *right* in what happened to me!" Serafina snapped, and this time it was a very human snarl. "All I want is what you have. You got everything!"

Imogen's hands crept toward her ears. A primal instinct urged her to cover them so that she would not hear one word more.

But the doll kept talking. "Looking out through your dreams was bad enough, seeing everything I'd missed, but then I saw you on the street. My eyes did not know you but some other part of me did."

"How?" Her hands were almost to her ears, but she was not quite fast enough.

The doll caught her wrists before she could raise her arms any further. "Sister, I would know you anywhere."

Imogen made a nonsense noise, but it held a world of horror.

"How I hate you!" cried Anna. "You got well again."

CHAPTER FORTY-THREE

November 10, 1888

2:13 p.m. Saturday

NICCOLO, SAID ATHENA, *A MESSENGER APPROACHES.*

Nick stood at the prow of the *Red Jack,* his spyglass trained on the early afternoon sky. Striker stood at Nick's side, leaning against the ship's rail with the same slouch he'd use at the counter at the Saracen's Head. "What is it? You have that the-ship's-talking-to-me frown."

"Incoming message," he said, sliding the spyglass closed. "An ash rook."

"Oh, bloody hell, I hate those things."

They'd left London at first light and now they were on their way back from delivering Mycroft Holmes to another vessel headed north. The man had looked far less composed than the last trip he'd made aboard the *Red Jack*—and this time he kept to himself, barely speaking the entire trip. Nick's curiosity had been at full throttle, but no amount of coaxing or liquor had made the man talk. He didn't think it was lack of trust. Mycroft Holmes had been plunged deep in thought, obviously working out some complex problem.

Even without the spyglass, Nick could see the rook clearly now. From the single square of metal laced about its neck, it was Talfryn sporting the rewards of his first mission. Striker had pierced and filed the square of brass himself, despite his supposed distaste for the birds.

Talfryn flapped toward them, wings eating the air with

steady, relentless beats. Then the rook gave a hollow croak and landed in the rigging with a huge commotion of feathers.

Somehow the rooks always knew to land above Striker. He darted back with a split second to spare before the bird splatted the deck. He cursed, checking his boots just in case. The rook croaked again, bobbing its hooked black beak at its own joke. Bird humor, Nick had observed, wasn't particularly sophisticated.

Captain Niccolo, fair winds.

"Fair winds, Talfryn."

The devas below send word to the horse boy.

Nick straightened in alarm. Only Evelina's creatures called him that. When he spoke, his reply came out tight with apprehension. "What word?"

There is a sorcerer's ship as black as my own feathers. He has a hostage, a beautiful maid who is as fair as the devas' mistress is dark. The dark one bids you rescue her sister-friend.

"Imogen Roth?" Nick said in surprise. "Why is she hostage?"

I do not know.

But that answer didn't matter. If word had come to him from the devas, then Evelina had sent it—and that was enough for Nick. "Where is this ship?"

Turn your vessel to the southwest, the rook said.

Athena had heard the message as well, because the ship began to turn its head.

"Hey!" Digby's exasperated shout rose from the helm. "Why do I even bother?"

"Many thanks," said Nick to the bird. There was only one sorcerer it could be. *Magnus.* The name alone made him bare his teeth. "Summon your flock and be ready for war."

The rook was already in flight again, laughing into the wind. *Dark winds ahead, Captain Niccolo, but we will be ready.*

Rooks came to the ship three times that afternoon, relaying information about where the black ship sailed. It seemed to be circling London in a loose oval, but far enough out not to attract too much attention. It was dusk when the *Red Jack* drew near enough for Nick to settle down for a closer look, the last sun fading from the sky in ragged orange streaks.

Nick didn't use his magic much, unless he was going into battle. Knives were his weapon of choice, for show as well as for fighting. Once, he had earned his bread and meat by showing off his skill with blades. By contrast, he never drew a gun or prepared a spell without very specific reasons. That way, his allies and enemies always knew when he was out of patience.

He hadn't even used his powers to find the *Leaping Hind,* but that raid had been everyday business, at least to begin with. This was different. This was an innocent life in Magnus's clutches, and he'd pull out every trick he had to save the young woman.

He took his silver shaving bowl, filled it half full of water, and settled cross-legged on the deck with it in front of him. Then he poured rum onto the surface of the water, and with a word called flame. The spirits caught with a hot blue fire that would last longer than it had any right to. Such was magic. It only ever needed a suggestion from the physical plane. *Air and fire, show me the black ship.*

The crew stood at a respectful distance, watching. He could see their black outlines against an indigo sky, the flames reflecting off the metal on Striker's coat, the lenses of Digby's goggles. Their lives depended in part on what Nick could convince the air to show them, but more than that, they needed to believe their captain was magic. He was their luck, and luck was everything to men of the air.

And the black ship took shape in the flames, a ferocious dragon at its prow. And there was the *Red Jack,* smaller and sleeker, still some distance away but with the advantage of height. They could stoop like a hawk and take them from above. *Air and fire, take me to her.*

And the wind subtly shifted, aiming the pirate ship like an arrow from a bow. Athena bound her own strength to the powers Nick summoned, forming a web of elemental force that spanned the planes of body and spirit. He set the bowl aside, leaving the devas to do their work. He poured an extra measure of rum into the flames, letting them leap high. *With thanks.*

There were some spells that drained strength, but sighting a quarry never failed to energize Nick. He got to his feet. "Ready the grappling hooks. We have work to do."

"There she is!" Striker called, looking through the spyglass. "She's called the *Wyvern*. Fardlin' hell, she's magnificent."

Nick ran to the side and took the glass from him. He adjusted the tube, bringing the vessel into focus. She was indeed a large, beautiful ship, the dragon prow a fierce, snarling thing with fire in its eyes. The double helix of an aether distiller glowed green in the darkness. Not a hydrogen ship then. They could use their guns. "I'd sooner just blow her out of the sky, but there's a hostage."

"What do you want to do?"

"Paralyze her."

Striker shook his head. "We used all the stopwatch beetles on the *Hind*." That was his name for the tiny clockwork gadgets that swarmed the deck and immobilized any machines made of metal. "I haven't had time to make more. I had to play captain while you were being bloody Florence Nightingale."

Nick grunted. "Then we get the hostage and blow the ship out of the sky."

"Is that actually a plan?" Striker said with a sarcastic bite. "I'm just asking in case I'm missing the details."

Nick snapped the spyglass shut, addressing the crew as a group. "We don't know what we're going to find. Not with magic involved. I'll take two men. The rest stay here. We're down there for fifteen minutes, and then we're back here and gone. No exceptions."

Beadle nodded and began issuing orders. Within seconds, all the group had dispersed except Striker and Digby.

"I wish we'd got that bastard sorcerer the last time," Striker muttered, crossing to a weapons locker.

"Seems we didn't kill him enough," Nick said, shrugging.

"Let him try these on for size." Striker passed out weapons. The barrels looked like three metal oranges glued together with twisty blue and green tubes. Nick hadn't seen them before.

"Have you tested these?" he asked suspiciously.

Striker gave him an innocent look. "Of course. My honor's on the line."

Nick bit his tongue at that one and holstered his regular weapon as well, just in case. Striker had his own sense of right and wrong, but it obeyed different rules.

They were coming in toward the *Wyvern* at an oblique angle from the stern. With the devas' help, it was possible to silence the engines and make an approach that was not only close to invisible, especially against the darkening sky, but also silent.

The grapples were fired and caught. Digby tugged on one experimentally. "We got 'er."

Nick hopped up on the rail, testing the line himself. It was good. Then he grabbed the bar on the pulley, ready to go—but he paused, a thousand misgivings sliding around his bones. He couldn't put a name to what he felt, but it turned him cold.

"What's wrong?" said Striker.

There were a dozen ways Nick could have answered, none of them helpful. Foreboding? Superstition? None of that would help Imogen Roth, especially when he couldn't even say what it was he feared. So instead he jumped off the rail, sliding down to the black ship below. A few seconds later, Striker and Digby followed.

Nick dropped to the deck. It was dark and unfamiliar, and the first thing he wanted to know was where the watch was. He crept a few paces, looking around as he heard the other two land softly behind him. Then Nick spotted the watchman. So did Striker. They exchanged glances and Striker gestured, pointing out the blue sash that identified the Blue Boys. Nick nodded, filing away that information.

But as they approached, the airman seemed slow to react, his movements dreamlike and clumsy. *Mesmerized, and not in the usual way.* Nick's scalp prickled, feeling the aura of sorcery around the man. Magnus was using the Blue Boys to man his ship, and they hadn't volunteered. It might be a problem. A crew of mindless drones didn't always behave as one expected.

"Who—" The word only half emerged before Striker silenced the man with a blow and lowered the limp body to the deck. It was good to know blunt force still worked despite the magic.

"Now we need to find the prisoners," Nick murmured.

Digby pointed to a door. "My money's there. That's where the cabins would be on a ship like this."

Since Digby had been an airman longest, Nick took his word for it. He advanced on silent feet, pulled the door open, and stepped inside a tiny corridor. Each of the doors had a minuscule window, and he began ghosting along, searching for damsels in distress.

EVELINA CHOSE THE workshop of the Magnetorium as the meeting site, and then got there before the appointed time. Nick had been right—the place was empty except for the tables and the workbench. It was dark outside, and the shadows clung to the rafters and corners, making the vast space seem small. She remembered that the last time she'd been there, the Others had watched her with empty eyes. They weren't there now though she could still smell the stench of sorcery.

She circled the space, lighting what lamps and candles she could find. It was good to have a job to do, because it would be all too easy to give in and let the enormity of what had happened pull her under. As she reached up for a lantern on a high shelf, the scars on her stomach pulled.

The wounds reminded her that she had nearly been killed, and she was organizing a battle against the evil that had created her attacker. Was she ready to take responsibility for what would happen if her plans failed and Magnus turned on her friends? The idea of it robbed her of breath, and she leaned against the workbench, momentarily dizzy. Her strength wasn't back yet. All she had was her willpower.

She heard the creak of the wooden door behind her. She turned. "Uncle Sherlock!"

He was tall and neat as ever, his tall hat and black coat impeccable, but his face was haggard. "Great Scot, Evelina!"

It was all he said before she flung her arms around his neck. She couldn't remember ever embracing her uncle before—he just wasn't the type to welcome it—but she didn't care. He must not have, either, because he held her tight for a long, breathless moment, telling her without words how worried he'd been.

"There is much I have to say to you, girl, but it can wait. Obviously, I received your letter," he said once she finally let him go. "I informed Scotland Yard of what I could. They know the Whitechapel Murderer is on the doctor's ship."

"Excellent."

"How do you mean to stop Magnus?" That was Uncle Sherlock, going directly to the problem at hand.

"I sent word to Nick's ship," she said, smoothing her skirts. "I don't know if he'll reach it in time, or if he will be able to overpower Magnus by himself. We need help."

She'd said the last words just as the door banged open. Holmes stiffened.

"That's why I am here." It was Jasper Keating, silver haired and patrician, with an entourage of black-coated Yellowbacks trailing in his wake. Evelina froze, anger and loathing taking her strength for an instant. She'd written him with his answers, but certainly hadn't invited him to this meeting. "I thought you couldn't come to the Blue King's territory," she said, struggling to keep her voice calm.

Keating harrumphed, sounding a bit like an offended bull seal. "Today, it is worth the risk. Imogen Roth is a relation by marriage. I have an interest in her welfare." He cast a narrow-eyed look at Holmes. "And of course you pointed the way, Detective. All we had to do was follow you."

Uncle Sherlock made a noise that sounded suspiciously like a growl, but he didn't reply.

The Gold King turned to Evelina. "Very good of you to call this meeting, my dear. And I must say I truly enjoyed your letter. Exactly what I wanted, though I'm very sorry that you were injured in the process of collecting my information. You won't go unrewarded. Well done, Evelina."

The use of her first name was an intimacy she'd never granted. She recoiled inside, but kept her face still. The sight of Keating brought back the impotence she'd felt in his study at Maggor's Close. He'd all but held her hostage then, and no doubt meant to turn this situation to his own ends. *Reward?* Fury broke through the dark fog of her mood. She clenched her fists, wanting to scream at him to leave. But the truth was, they might well need his wealth and resources to capture Magnus far more than they needed anything she had to offer.

"I have been invited to participate by Scotland Yard," said Keating grandly. "Thank you for giving them notice, Holmes, they were all the more ready when I announced that I was there to put my resources at their disposal. They have their ships in the air, as do I. Together, we will bring down the *Wyvern*. My own son is participating in the rescue."

"That would be *my* son," said Lord Bancroft quietly, entering from the front of the theater. He dropped the cigarette he was smoking to the floor and crushed it into the dust. "And *my* daughter. And under the circumstances, I think most of the credit goes to Miss Cooper for having the presence of mind to notify us of Imogen's whereabouts. None of the rest of us knew where to start looking."

The two men glared at each other, hatred barely concealed. Evelina's nerves itched with the hostility crackling in the air.

"I rather expected that we would discuss what had to be done," Holmes broke in, entirely courteous for once, "but you appear to have preempted us, Mr. Keating, if there are ships already in the sky."

"No time to waste in affairs like this," the Gold King replied.

Evelina heard the door close, and everyone turned that way. It was Bucky Penner, his expression saying that he knew very well he wasn't welcome—but he wasn't about to leave.

"What are you doing here?" Lord Bancroft snapped.

"I invited him, too," said Evelina. "Imogen would want it."

Bucky pulled off his hat, giving a slight bow. His eyes had

the look of someone who has suffered a bad shock, but his manners were beyond reproach. "I am here to offer whatever assistance it is in my power to offer."

"If it hadn't been for you, Imogen would still be safely at home," Bancroft snapped.

Bucky nodded once, saying nothing. Evelina stiffened, wanting to fly to his defense, but Holmes put a gloved hand on her arm, a gesture of both support and warning. Fortunately, the warning wasn't needed. Bancroft made a sour face, and contented himself with ignoring the young man.

While they had been talking, the Yellowbacks set up a contraption on the workbench. The device looked vaguely familiar.

"What is that?" Bancroft demanded.

Keating gave a satisfied quirk of the lips. "A communications device that Tobias has been perfecting."

Now Evelina knew where she had seen it before. "I remember that. It looks like a version of that device Aragon Jackson had at the garden party last spring."

Bancroft's face darkened at the memory, and Bucky shifted, no doubt remembering as well. Keating had used it to torture one of Lord B's upstairs maids.

"But it has become so much more than a mere means of sending an electrical signal through space," Keating said. "Now it's a machine for ground-to-air aether telegraphy."

Despite herself, Evelina was fascinated. "You can speak to your ships from here?"

"Just like a telegraph, but there is no wire."

Just like the devices Nick found in the Saracen's Head. There was no doubt that the Gold King had been spying on the rebels. Evelina chewed her thumbnail, wishing Nick were there.

For a moment, the entire company stood motionless while one of Keating's men connected the last few parts of the machine together and tapped out a message. A moment later, somebody began tapping one back. Evelina tensed.

"What is it saying?" Bancroft snapped.

The operator was a young man in a checked suit. He cleared his throat, visibly nervous about the whole business.

"The *Helios*—that's Mr. Keating's ship—has sighted the black ship, and also another vessel that has already reached the target. It's the *Red Jack*."

"The pirate ship." Keating chuckled, and it wasn't a pleasant sound. "Fancy that. I believe my stolen casket is on board. I knew that if I had you in my sights long enough, Evelina, somehow you'd manage to draw the pirates out of hiding."

"How dare you!" Evelina cried, forgetting herself. She had known Magnus wanted to use her to get to Nick, but she hadn't anticipated this. "Use me, but leave Nick out of this!"

Holmes motioned her to silence, but Keating merely laughed. "Oh, Miss Cooper, I never miss an opportunity to multiply the value of a situation. And Magnus and I have old business to settle."

"No," Bancroft said quickly. "That's my daughter he has. Magnus has *business* with me, and I know my claim is older."

"Perhaps," Keating said with a wave. "No doubt there is something you have to offer him, but he has always wanted Athena's Casket as much as I do. I can offer him more if it comes to bargaining."

Bancroft bridled, obviously displeased despite all logic to have his role in the drama diminished. But Evelina leaned on her uncle's arm, strength ebbing to make room for despair as she contemplated Keating's words. It was true, the Gold King and Magnus both wanted Athena—they had ever since the casket had been dug from beneath Greek soil and shipped to London months before. She didn't doubt that they desired the deva enough to kill for it.

And she had been the one to summon Nick right into their trap. "Oh, no," she whispered, closing her eyes against Keating's mocking stare.

AS HE PACED down the ship's corridor, Nick paused at each door, looking through the tiny windows. The first few rooms were dark, yielding no information. But the next one showed light, so he peered through at an angle, making sure his own face wasn't visible to whoever was inside. With a mix of alarm and satisfaction, he glimpsed a fair-haired woman struggling with an attacker he couldn't see.

His booted foot broke the lock with a single blow, sending the door crashing inward. He slid inside the room, his Striker-made weapon up and ready to fire. "Hold!"

He recognized Imogen Roth in an instant, but unexpectedly her attacker was another woman. That caught him off guard just long enough for the red-haired female to swing around in the tiny cabin and knock him on the shoulder. He gave a surprised grunt. She was no taller than he was, but was enormously strong. He bounced against the wall, cracking his head hard enough to make the room spin.

Nick swore as his weapon flew from his hand, bouncing onto the drab blankets. He stumbled, righting himself and bashing his shin on the edge of the cot. Crew quarters weren't meant for combat. He righted himself just as Miss Roth lunged for the weapon. The redhead darted forward at the same instant. If they struggled for the gun, that wasn't going to end well.

"Stop!" He pulled his revolver, aiming it at the aggressor. The redhead turned to him, her movements not quite right. Nick's jaw dropped, astonishment blanking his thoughts for an instant. *An automaton!* It opened its mouth wide in a mockery of a smile that looked more like a hungry leer. The thing gathered into itself like a serpent and sprang.

Bloody hell! He put a bullet between its eyes, porcelain face shattering, spewing hair and clockwork and shards of glass. The sound was terrible, whatever gave the thing voice dying in a wheeze. The body fell to the floor with a clatter, more bits and pieces scattering as it crashed.

Miss Roth made a strangled cry, turning a pasty white. "She was trying to . . . to . . . take my life."

"Are you hurt?" Nick demanded.

"No. And neither is she."

He was about to ask what she meant, but then the automaton started to pull itself to its hands and knees. Nick shuddered, his dinner crawling back up his throat. The doll was broken, and shouldn't have been able to move—but Nick didn't give that a second thought. He didn't care about the why, he simply wanted to be gone.

"Miss Roth? I'm Nick."

But Imogen Roth had Striker's weapon, and was pointing it at the lurching automaton. "I know who you are."

"Come on!" Nick urged. "We have to leave."

"I can't," she said, sighting down the weapon. For a pale, thin thing, she had steady hands. "That's my sister."

That made no sense. "What?"

The automaton got to its feet, sparks flying from the shattered head. Red hair spilled from the remains of the skull like blood, the face reduced to a plane of rattling gears. The limbs jerked spasmodically, but still the arms reached for Miss Roth, fingers clutching.

Miss Roth pulled the trigger with a heartbroken cry. The weapon made a peculiar sound, and a bolt of green and blue light blossomed out its end. The automaton blew out the door and into the passage with a splintering crash. Miss Roth dropped the weapon to the cot, backing away from it as if it might turn and sink fangs into her flesh. Nick saw the wide-eyed shock on her face, and knew he didn't understand the whole of it, but there was no time for questions.

"Come on." He grabbed Miss Roth and Striker's weapon and ran. Someone would have heard the shots and Nick needed to get them back to the *Red Jack*. She trailed after him, skittering past the twitching wreck of the automaton.

"How did you know I was here?" She asked after a few strides. Tears were streaming down her cheeks, but her mouth was set in a determined line.

"Evelina sends her regards."

Miss Roth looked at him sharply, pale gray eyes searching his face. "She's not dead?"

Nick shook his head. "She was badly hurt, miss, but she's fine."

Miss Roth sucked in her breath, but she kept pace with him, which was all he cared about right then. He made it to the door that led out to the deck when he knew something had gone wrong. He'd brought two men, but there were a lot more fighting. Ash rooks were diving out of the dark, metal collars flashing. Swords and guns were in play, men cursing, sometimes screaming in pain. He felt Imogen shrink closer to him, her fingers trembling in fright.

"Trust me," he said gently. "I'll see you safe."

She nodded, all business. "And I won't hold you back, if I can help it." In that moment, Nick understood what Evelina saw in her friend.

"But if you can burn that automaton," she added, swallowing hard as if she were fighting down more than fear, "I'd greatly appreciate it. I don't think gunshots will kill it, and I need it to be thoroughly dead."

It was animated by magic, Nick guessed. "Don't worry, I'm planning on burning this whole fardling ship and Magnus along with it."

"Good," Miss Roth said in her quiet way. "And thank you for saving me."

Slowly, they went through the door to the deck. He took her arm and drew her close, shielding her with his body as he looked for Striker and Digby. The battle was all too familiar—blood, noise, and the stink of gunpowder.

He recognized Yellowbacks, and that meant one of Keating's ships had to be there. That spelled big trouble for the *Jack* as long as she was grappled alongside Magnus's ship, waiting for the landing party. The Yellowbacks were well armed and disciplined, the best brutes that Keating's money could buy, and their ships were typically heavy with cannons.

By contrast, the *Wyvern*'s mesmerized crew were poor fighters, if the number of dead and wounded was any indication. That meant there was little fighting to be done before Keating's men turned their attention to the *Jack*.

Nick took a few steps toward the grappling lines, Miss Roth close behind. They hadn't gone far when he heard a shout.

"Imogen!"

They both turned. Nick saw a fair-haired man barreling his way through the melee, pausing only to club someone over the head in passing. He was flanked by two Yellowbacks, but ordered them aside when he was a few yards away.

"Tobias!" Miss Roth cried.

Nick stared in astonishment. *First a demonic automaton, and now this.*

Tobias Roth bore down on them like an avenging angel. Nick's first thought was to shoot him on principle. His second was that he had Roth's sister by the hand.

"Imogen!" Roth bellowed again.

"I'm here," Miss Roth replied, this time sounding slightly impatient.

"Unhand my sister!" Roth demanded.

Really? "Take her," Nick said. "I only came to see her safe."

"You—you're Evelina's friend," Roth said, looking suddenly confused.

"Yes."

Roth grabbed his sister, pushing her behind him as if Nick might try to keep her. But then he hesitated. "Thank you for saving her."

Nick gave a slight bow. "Just get her away from here and be quick about it."

Then Roth licked his lips. "You need to go. Word just came through to the *Helios* that Keating wants your ship." Then he turned and pulled his sister after him, shepherding her through the throng.

Nick watched them go with mixed feelings. Imogen Roth belonged with her family, but her brother, by the mere act of breathing, made Nick's hackles rise. Still, he didn't need to be told twice to leave. He'd done what he'd come to do.

"To the *Jack*!" he roared, lunging through the fray. The fight seemed to be breaking up, with Keating's men running toward their own ladders. They'd come up from the other side, sandwiching the *Wyvern* between her attackers. When it came to avoiding enemy ships, Magnus was uncharacteristically careless. *Unless he wanted to get caught. But why?*

Striker was at his side. "Look." He pointed. There were a handful of other ships closing in, two bearing the Gold King's markings, the others Scotland Yard's.

"Bugger," Nick said. "Come on, Digby!"

Where was the helmsman? Worry stabbed him, but then

he saw Digby's lanky form loping along the deck, a grin on his face. They pelted for safety. Poole had already run down ladders and they grabbed them, scrambling to leave the black ship. The ash rooks swept in, swooping down on anyone who tried to open fire.

The landing party reached the ladders, but not before the Gold King's ship fired its cannons into the *Wyvern*. The grappling lines jerked loose, sending the *Red Jack* into a sideways drift. The ladders swung free through the air. Nick held on with every muscle he could bring to bear, waiting out the sickening vertigo. Digby whooped, but Striker's roar of fright and fury trailed through the empty sky as his ladder swayed through open space, ash rooks circling around him.

Barely a moment later, Nick started to climb again, fighting the motion while trying to find secure holds for his hands and feet. The ship couldn't fight with crew hanging over the side, and they were clearly in for a battle. Before long, he felt Poole's hand close around his wrist and pull him up. Nick somersaulted over the side with a grunt, rolling smoothly to his feet.

"Status?" he asked Beadle.

The first mate was grim, but professional as ever. "Both ships are turning on us, sir. The others are closing in."

"On us?" Nick cast a panicked glance at the *Wyvern*. Beadle was right. The black ship was on fire, but her gun ports were open. The *Helios* was distancing herself from the black ship, but positioning for an attack on Nick. Tobias Roth hadn't lied—he'd tried to warn Nick.

Damnation! He took stock. Digby was on board, and Poole was dumping Striker to the floor like a sack of meal. Nick turned to Beadle. "Prepare to respond."

The words had barely left his mouth before the first cannon shots from the *Wyvern* ripped through the gondola, throwing him through the air.

CHAPTER FORTY-FOUR

"NO!" CRIED EVELINA. "NO, YOU CAN'T FIRE ON NICK! HE went to save Imogen!"

The Gold King looked at her as if she were no more than a puppy tugging at his shoelaces. "Of course I can attack. The *Red Jack* is a pirate ship. It's crewed by felons."

And nobody cared if they died. Evelina looked wildly around the room, but only Bucky looked sympathetic. A muscle jumped in Uncle Sherlock's jaw, but that was the sole sign of emotion in his face. That meant he was thinking furiously, but he had no immediate solutions. There was no help in the room.

The communications device went into a flurry of clicks, and the operator gave his report. "The *Red Jack* has fired on the *Wyvern*. Dr. Magnus's ship is entirely engulfed in flame. The police ships are closing in on the wreck, but the *Helios* is in pursuit of the *Red Jack*." The young man looked up, chewing his lip. "They say it shouldn't be a long chase. The *Jack* has been badly hit."

"Tell the *Helios* to prepare to board," Keating said. "And come to think of it, tell them to bring me my old street-keeper if they find him. I have a score to settle with Mr. Striker."

The Gold King's calm orders, edged with malice, crushed the air from Evelina's body. She listened, barely believing one man could hold so many lives at such low cost. She'd met many of the crew the day of the market, and had watched them drink and laugh. She remembered sitting with Striker outside the Saracen's Head, listening to his rough voice. They were people, not just counters on a board.

She pressed a hand to her stomach, feeling the echo of the knife wounds beneath her palm. Her breath came short and uneven, her skin going cold and clammy at once. If she had felt helpless before, she felt it a hundred times more now, with no means to save the man she loved. She knew why her uncle couldn't speak—there was nothing to say. Nick was a pirate. No law protected him. All other ships were duty bound to bring down the *Red Jack,* the lives of the crew forfeit. Anything less was treason.

She leaned against one of the worktables, fighting a light-headed sensation of falling. *Nick.* He'd just been holding her in his arms, his lips on hers, his hands on her body. And now he was about to be blown from the air. Magnus had predicted that she would deliver Nick to his enemies; the sorcerer had just been wrong about how. The earth seemed to dissolve beneath her feet, as if not even the soil could be relied on. *It was me who begged Nick to come. I drew him into this trap.*

It was up to her to protect him.

"I know you want Athena's Casket. If you spare the pirates, I can offer you something better than the device," Evelina said quickly, throwing down the gauntlet.

Her uncle gave her a warning look, his features sharp with alarm. "Evelina, no," said Holmes, his voice hard. "Forgive me, but there is nothing you can do. If you take my advice on nothing else, take it now."

"I can't," she whispered. "I brought Nick into this. I have to get him out."

Bucky and Lord Bancroft stared, as if she'd taken leave of her senses. Maybe she had.

"You have something better?" asked Keating. "What have you been hiding all this time, Evelina?"

All the eyes in the room were on her. She could feel the weight of those gazes. Bancroft looked pitying, but Keating was the worst. He looked like he'd suspected something all along, and now he saw his chance. Evelina bowed her head. She'd felt vague, almost helpless since waking from her attack. Now the feeling crawled over her, shock and exhaustion plucking at her will with teasing fingers. It was hard to think. "I just want to save them."

"You've proven yourself more than once, so I'm prepared to entertain an offer. You've earned that much," Keating said. "But it would mean whatever you give me will be exclusively mine to use. I wonder what that could possibly be?"

Me. And the moment I step over this line, you'll know I'm a magic user and you'll have the power to kill me in a thousand unpleasant ways. But where would hiding get her? One way or the other, she was already in Keating's sights.

"I forbid it," said Holmes, taking Evelina's arm as if he meant to shake her. "You've shut me out from the start of this affair. Slow down and let me find a better solution. In the name of your mother, my sister, I beg you."

That made her flinch. "There's no time. Nick is going to die."

His voice grew hoarse with frustration. "Do you really think anything you do now is going to save him?"

"I have to try."

"Evelina, no."

But still she fixed her gaze on the Gold King. "What I have to say is for private discussion."

"Then come." Keating waved toward the door that led to the front of the theater. "Let us be private."

She nodded, trying to extract her arm from her uncle's grip. Holmes balked, but two of the Yellowbacks flanked him. Her uncle gave her a desperate look. "Don't do this!"

"I have to," she said, pulling free. "It's Nick's life if I don't."

"It's your life if you do." Her uncle's face closed then, shutting her out, showing nothing. "That's worth something to me, even if it means little to you."

And she loved him dearly in that moment, for all the good it did them. "It's mine to give. Please, respect that."

Her uncle's face grew pale. Keating made an impatient movement, and the Yellowbacks rattled their weapons. Evelina started forward, but Holmes followed her, refusing to be cowed. "I am her legal guardian," he said. "Nothing can be agreed to without my consent. If you insist on a bargain, at least I can make sure it is an equitable one."

"Please yourself." Keating led the way from backstage to the front of the house. "If you think you can outwit me in a business deal."

"No, don't come." She laid a palm on her uncle's chest. "I need to bear this on my own conscience."

When she drew away, a Yellowback's weapon took the place of her hand, pressing into Holmes's chest. And so it was that her uncle stayed, and she followed Keating alone.

Evelina was barely aware that she was walking. She was about to do the one thing she had always guarded against, the one thing any who possessed the Blood dreaded above all else, and she found that she was not afraid—at least not yet. After Serafina's knife, perhaps there was little worse that anyone could do.

When Keating reached the first row of plush seats, he sat down, spreading his arms along the backs of the neighboring chairs. He tilted his head, the dim light catching at his silver hair. "What precisely do you have to offer, Miss Cooper?"

Still standing, Evelina looked down at the Gold King, recalling their interview after he'd caught her with Tobias. They had come full circle, but this time she had invited him to the table. Anger welled up, sharp as one of Nick's blades. Evelina's fingers twitched, aching to make fists. She could tell Keating that she had the ability to blend magic and machinery, but there was no value in giving her trump card away up front. She would bargain low, and see what would tempt him. "You know from my report that Magnus is a sorcerer. I studied with him. I studied *magic* with him."

Keating's eyes opened wider, a sure sign of interest. He regarded her with his amber gaze, a leopard in repose. "And what did you learn?"

"I repaired his living automatons. I learned how he gathered his power. I read his books."

She saw his breath catch at "power." A pang of something—not quite satisfaction, but close—eased the pressure in her chest.

Keating blinked. "What else?" He said the words precisely, as if bored, but there was no hiding the subtle tension in his shoulders.

"I learned how to see what is happening at a distance. That is how I found his ship. Do these talents interest you, Mr. Keating?"

"Perhaps. With your mechanical talents, would what you learned put me on an even footing with the Blue King?"

"Perhaps," she echoed, fairly certain she was lying. Her magic was still nothing compared to Magnus's—but she wasn't interested in playing fair with the Gold King. "Perhaps more, with a little time."

"Play me false and you know what will happen. Magic users do not live long in the Empire."

Evelina's heart began to pound. The reality of what she'd done was catching up with her. She thought of Crowleyton, of what he'd done to Tobias. Of what he'd done to his own daughter. There was no mercy in Jasper Keating, and she'd just oversold herself. "All I ask is that you save Nick and his crew. Let them go. Do what you must with me."

"Do you think I'm going to lock you in an attic like a mad relation?" Keating scoffed.

"Don't you lock up your victims in secret laboratories and put them to the knife?"

He burst into laughter. "Oh, Evelina, what you must take me for!"

She flushed. She knew the laboratories weren't a myth, so she wasn't sure why he was mocking her. "I don't think you'll let me roam free."

"No," he crossed his legs. "I don't suppose I'll do that."

"Then what?"

"I'm not sure. You are of more use to me in Society than out of it, but I cannot let you go wherever you wish. You've just made yourself too valuable."

Her mouth went dry. His words terrified her, but at the same time this was better than she had hoped. But what kind of a life would he allow her?

He gave her a long look, his amber eyes dark in the theater's murky light. "What shall I do with you, Evelina? How shall I inspire you to excel at what I need?"

Perhaps he was already succeeding, because she suddenly had an idea. "I wish to attend college."

One eyebrow raised. "You did say that you wished to continue your education, but how does that help me?"

"It is a regulated environment, secure enough in its way," she suggested. "And I can use the resources of an educational institution to research whatever task you assign to me."

"Very good," Keating mused. "An improved mind is always more useful. And a break from general society would be appropriate, given recent events. After that, a slow introduction back into fashionable company would seem natural. A pretty young woman would be of use to me in drawing rooms as well as laboratories."

For a young gentlewoman who had gone missing for several months, rejoining the ton would be impossible without a protector like the Gold King. What he was offering her was not, technically speaking, a bad offer. She had wanted college. In time, she could rejoin Society. And she could use her magic, at least in a limited way.

If this future could have come to her any other way, she would have been jubilant. As it was, she felt ill. Was this what Tobias had gone through, surrendering what he loved to buy safety for his family?

Keating rose, clearly feeling that he had won. "But I would have approval over your social contacts. I have standards where my employees are concerned." He turned his amber gaze on her. "No rebels or pirates."

Anger crackled through her, leaving her cheeks hot. She'd save Nick, but she'd lose him—at least as long as Keating had her on a leash. But he'd be alive.

One of the Yellowbacks appeared from the workshop. "The *Helios* is ready to fire on your word, sir."

She buried her face in her hands, trying to drag her thoughts into some kind of useful order. She raised her eyes to encounter Keating's hard expression. There was no real choice now that Keating knew her secret. He'd get her one way or another, just as he had trapped her at Maggor's Close.

Keating raised his eyebrows, his question plain.

She closed her eyes, shutting out her captor's face. "Save the ship. I'll do whatever you ask."

THE *WYVERN* WAS ablaze, but so was the *Red Jack*.

"Take her down!" Beadle screamed at Digby, who was doing his best to keep control of a ship steered by a panicking deva. The tail propeller was gone.

Striker and Nick were the only two worrying about defenses, because everyone else was trying to ensure something was left to defend. The stink of burning wood and fuel surrounded them, the sky lit by orange wraiths of flame. Men were fighting the fires, but a chunk had been torn out of the hull, and that chunk had held their stores of water. They'd also lost two of their cannons. Nick could see the forward gun portals of the *Helios* open. While he was staring at those, a hot harpoon arched into the sky, trailing flame with a sound like tearing cloth. It sailed over the *Red Jack*.

"Surrender!" someone shouted from the *Helios*. They were close enough that Nick could hear the faint cry.

Is this it? Is this how it all starts spiraling down to the earth? Evelina's face flickered through his mind, and he cursed violently, loss and fear bringing a moment of weakness.

Striker fired his odd gun at the *Helios*. It made a *cra-ch-ch-ack* sound, green and blue lights flaring, and a chunk the size of a dinner plate flew off the enemy's hull. Nick swore again, but this time it was a good curse.

Then another harpoon flew, and hit smack into the *Jack*'s remaining patch of deck. Flame gushed from the oily substance released from the harpoon's head. He heard Athena's scream of terror.

And just like that, the *Red Jack* was done. As one, he and Striker lowered their weapons.

"Abandon ship! Save yourselves if you can!" Nick yelled, and bolted for Athena, where she was secured at the prow.

He leapt over the fire, feeling his ankle scorch, and shoved his way through the crew, who were scrambling for parachutes. He skidded to a halt right before the panel where

Athena was secured and undid the bolts with shaking fingers. The cover dropped away and he reached inside, his hands gentle despite his haste. She was just a cube of metal, rusted and warped as if in a fire—no wonder she hated flames. He'd sewn her cube into a kind of sling that he'd worn for the first while they were together. Until she had adopted the *Red Jack* for her own.

I don't like fire, she said plaintively.

It's all right. I'm here. He slipped the handle of the sling across his shoulders, pulling his jacket over her for added protection. Now for a parachute.

Nick turned, and there was Magnus, tall and gaunt, his eyes wild and his clothes scorched and ragged. Surprise would have staggered Nick, but too much had happened for that. They just stared at each other, the flames roaring like the wind in sails. Nick might have asked how the sorcerer had got there, but it didn't really matter.

"Give it to me," said Magnus. "Give me the device, and you can save yourself. Resist, and you know what I can do to you."

Nick remembered the paralyzing pain of their last encounter well enough, but Athena was his to protect. "Bugger off."

Magnus gave a derisive huff, and lifted his hand. But Nick flung his own power, knocking the sorcerer backward. Then he lifted Striker's gun.

"That won't kill me!" Magnus scoffed, scrambling to his feet.

Nick tried anyway, but Magnus was too fast. The gun flew from his hand as Magnus leapt, knocking Nick's back against the rail. Pain flared as his spine crashed into hard oak. Nick flailed, his feet lifting off the deck. A cry escaped his throat as his legs went numb.

Magnus was taller, and every bit as strong. He shifted his grip, bracing his forearm under Nick's chin and choking him. Heat flared, searing the inside of his nose and mouth with the few breaths he managed to take. Magnus's clothes began to smoke.

Nick kicked, but he was blacking out, the pulse in his

head pounding like a drum. The stars above blurred and smeared across his vision, melting to a silver rain. He tried lashing out, jamming his fingers in Magnus's eyes and throat, but the sorcerer seemed impervious to pain, only choking Nick harder.

He was just about gone when he finally fumbled a knife from his wrist sheath and slid it in the sweet spot between Magnus's ribs, driving up toward the heart. With a roar of anguish, Magnus released him, staggering back two steps, shock and outrage painting his features in the ungodly orange light of flames. The sorcerer grabbed the knife hilt with both hands, mouth wide in a curse.

And then the powder stores erupted, blowing the *Red Jack* to splinters. Blown forward, Magnus smashed into Nick, knocking the air from his lungs and sweeping him headfirst over the side. Deaf, stunned, Nick dropped in a dead fall through the darkness, slowly wheeling over and over, tossed by the blast. He felt Magnus's fingers on his arm, the clutch of something dreaded but at least familiar. And then they were gone, too, peeled away by the rushing air.

Well, I always figured a fall would get me. It didn't matter if it was from a horse or a high wire or a ship. He just hoped it would be quick. *I wonder if the boys made it away in time.*

And then he thought of Evie, and his heart snagged there like a leaf catching on the bank of a running stream, clinging as long and hard as he could against the force pulling him away.

The wind flattened and pulled at the flesh of his face, clawed at his hair and clothes, made it impossible to see or breathe. Beadle had always told him to grab a parachute before anything else.

Should've listened.

EVELINA AND HOLMES followed Keating back to the main group. Bucky rose from where he was slumped against the workbench, his face anxious.

"Tell the *Helios* to stand down," Keating commanded. "Return to base."

The operator nodded. "Very good, sir. They're already on their way."

"What do you mean?" the Gold King demanded. "I just gave the order."

The young man blinked. "It was on the orders of young Mr. Roth. The battle was over."

"What do you mean? No one had authority to fire without my leave!"

"I'm sorry, sir. The captain pursued the attack, sir, as he had a clear advantage."

Evelina sucked in a breath. "What does that mean?"

"And then young Mr. Roth persuaded him to return to base. It seems Miss Roth fell gravely ill."

"What happened?" Bucky demanded. Lord Bancroft said nothing, but the same question was clear on his face.

The young operator was beginning to wear the expression of a hunted rabbit. Too many people were staring at him, demanding answers. "It came on her in the midst of the battle, just as the *Wyvern* was destroyed. That ship's lost sir, all hands gone."

"Where is the *Red Jack*?" Keating thundered. "Where is my device?"

"I'm sorry, sir," said the operator in a small voice. "That ship was utterly destroyed as well. Not a plank remaining."

In that moment, Evelina was sure that she had died.

CHAPTER FORTY-FIVE

AND THE BLOWS WOULD NOT STOP COMING. AFTER LEAVING the Magnetorium, Evelina had gone to Hilliard House. There, numb with misery, Evelina sat at Imogen's bedside through the night, sometimes with Tobias or Alice, but often alone. Evelina had always been Imogen's most capable nurse, and the household was relieved to let her take charge until the morning.

Lord and Lady Bancroft, Alice and Tobias, and especially Poppy were dumbstruck by Imogen's sudden illness. Bucky Penner was devastated. The only positive note was that Tobias rallied to give and take comfort from his old friend. Tragedy buried whatever tension had grown between them; Imogen would have been glad.

As dawn arrived, she remained beneath the lace-trimmed covers, seemingly asleep and lovely as ever. There was no injury, no visible sign of illness. Imogen's breathing went on, as did her heartbeat. But Evelina knew, as no one else could, that her friend's soul had fled. Imogen's body was there, but she was not.

Mouse and Bird sat on the bedside table, to every eye but Evelina's just clever ornaments made to amuse. In truth, the devas watched over the still, pale form. They would be Evelina's eyes and ears after she'd made her good-byes and surrendered herself to the Gold King.

* * *

"SO WHAT HAVE you learned from any of this?" Holmes asked her later that afternoon, after she'd had a few fitful hours of sleep.

Evelina's first instinct was to retreat from the study and go hide downstairs with Mrs. Hudson. She already knew this wasn't going to be a pleasant conversation, for anger still showed in the white lines around Holmes's mouth. She'd explained her reasons for going to Whitechapel, but he was still too furious to accept them. In truth, she couldn't blame him. She could imagine how wrongheaded her actions appeared from his perspective—but he hadn't been in that room at Maggor's Close with Keating weaving his web of threats and coercion.

"Pray tell, niece, what was gained by leaving me in the dark?" Holmes went on in icy tones. "Or do you think I am so utterly incompetent that I require a schoolgirl to take charge of my safety? Is that why you chose to bargain with Keating on your own? Is there no plane of reality in which I might have improved the outcome?"

She flinched at that, her spine rigid as a board as she sat down across from her uncle. Keating hadn't saved Nick and his men, but he had insisted that his intent was good—so the terms of the bargain held. Keating had might on his side, and he would force Evelina to keep her half of the deal. Whether that was just or logical didn't matter, and no one tried to dispute it. As a self-proclaimed user of magic, her life was forfeit anyhow.

Evelina looked at the clock. In another quarter hour, Keating's coach would take her to college—her trunks were still packed from her trip to the shooting party, and the Gold King was anxious to have her under his control. There was barely time to say farewell. She had longed for an education, but not like this. Not like a prison sentence, with her heart breaking for all her losses.

She glanced around the Baker Street study. The window had been replaced, and new china was on the table. The room had been repaired, but she was not. She had just lost two of the people she loved best, and her entire body ached with spent emotion. When she had arrived home from Hilliard House, she had cried until she felt bruised. Now there was nothing left, as if, like Serafina, she had nothing but sawdust inside.

Holmes must have read her mood, because his face lost some of its ire. "Evelina?"

"I'm sorry," she said miserably.

"Did you learn anything of use in all this?"

"Did I learn anything?" she repeated with surprise. "Are you talking about my time with Magnus or the dire consequences of trusting anything Jasper Keating has to say?"

"Theorize," her uncle prompted. "And don't be flippant. How did we end up here, where we are in this moment?"

She sighed. "You heard Keating. I think that Magnus probably kidnapped Imogen for two reasons. There was his old feud with Bancroft, but taking Imogen made another trap possible. He wanted Athena's Casket."

She didn't mention Magnus's prediction that her lust for dark magic would eventually tempt her to betray Nick. With Magnus gone and the *Red Jack* in ashes, that wasn't even possible anymore. The damage was already done.

"Keating did almost the same thing," she added. "Either one could have held me hostage and forced Nick to give up Athena, but instead I blithely asked him to save Imogen, never thinking what that meant. I was a fool. Nick being Nick went straight to the *Wyvern*. If Keating's men hadn't shot down the *Red Jack,* Magnus would have tried for it."

Holmes nodded. "What else?"

"I put myself in Keating's power and the *Red Jack* was destroyed anyway. I asked Nick for help and it killed him. I deserve the bargain I made."

For the first time, Holmes looked sympathetic. "Don't say that. You don't know that Nick is gone."

Tears flooded Evelina's vision, her eyes stinging with fresh grief. "How could he have survived?" She wiped her cheeks impatiently, aware that her uncle was uncomfortable with tears. The emotional fog that had filled her with exhaustion was finally receding, replaced by anger so vibrant she could barely hold it in.

"I don't know," Holmes said. "But the last time we sat like this, we turned over the remaining clues of the Grace Child murder. You found the answers, despite the obscurity of the case. I've learned to have faith in slim chances."

"What answers do we lack this time? Besides how to find Nick, if he still lives, and save Imogen." As if that was not more than enough.

Holmes nodded. "Someone poisoned Jones and Bingham, even while they were in rebel custody. The rebels have a traitor in their midst. So does the Blue King. My assumption was that it was Mycroft, but I am not sure it was entirely his work. I have yet to solve that mystery."

Evelina blinked. "You know far more about the resistance than you're letting on. Are you involved? Do you know who the Schoolmaster is? He seems to have a lot of influence for someone so young."

He gave her an enigmatic look. "I know something of the players in the Baskerville affair, and I think you are better off under Keating's protection than out in the cold right now. Say what you wish about the Gold King, but he looks after what's his, and dangerous times are coming."

"I don't want his protection. I want his entrails as boot-laces."

"I can sympathize, but I repeat my point. It is only a matter of time before you may be grateful of shelter. Rebellions are not for young ladies, however much they may aspire to the status of hoyden."

"Keating put me in shackles."

"But tasteful ones."

There were silver bracelets on her wrists, plain and slender, almost elegant, but impossible to remove. And they were equipped with an aetheric signaling device. As long as she wore them, the Yellowbacks knew where she was.

Any hope of flight had been crushed as soon as she saw the mark the bracelets bore: Her Majesty's Laboratories, where those of the Blood were committed for scientific experimentation. It was a less than subtle reminder of what might happen if she crossed her employer.

Holmes's expression was grave. For once, her uncle wasn't reading the paper or fiddling with his pipe. He was looking at her very seriously, and it made her twitch. It really was like Bird said: *I can see him thinking about unbolting my hide so he can see what makes my gears turn.* "Don't mistake me, Evelina. I want your freedom almost as much as you want it. But you know how much it hurts to lose the ones you hold dear, so I cannot help but desire your safety more than anything else. Be patient and leave the battle to others. Live to see the Empire free."

"And if there's anything that can be done to find Nick or help Imogen . . ."

"It shall be done. Trust me on that."

"You're getting downright sentimental, Uncle," she said, trying to keep her tone light though her throat ached with unshed tears.

The corner of his mouth twitched. "What else did you learn in Whitechapel? You were in some extremely challenging circumstances."

Evelina swallowed, feeling the stir of dark hunger inside her. There was a little bit of her that was grateful for the restraint of Keating's bracelets. "I learned that I can be tempted."

Sherlock gave a brief flicker of a smile. "Everyone can. It's just a matter of who will admit to it, and who whistles in the dark, and who will make that weakness their weapon."

"Weapon?"

"One has to understand the nature of a fatal flaw before one can find it in others. Know yourself, to know your enemy." Holmes's eyes grew hard.

Evelina felt the heat of anger again. "Keating regards me as an interesting toy."

"Then use his mistake."

"I wish I could, but I'm useless. Imogen and Nick are dead or in mortal peril, and I'm about to be enslaved. Last spring I was worried about what gloves to wear. What can I do against Keating?"

"Always go with the white, and stay safe." Holmes made a steeple of his fingers. "Arm yourself against every eventuality and survive. There is only one thing to do once you have such distinguished enemies. Wait and watch. And when your moment comes, you make them pay dearly. Difficult times do not last."

She finished his favorite piece of advice. "Difficult, obstinate, and impertinent people do."

And then she heard the sound of feet on the stairs, and a sharp, commanding rap.

"Ah," said Holmes. "Your coach is here. Then this is good-bye."

IMOGEN DIDN'T FEEL right. It wasn't that she felt physically ill—she was fine that way. It was just that everything felt odd. Disconnected. Almost as if she'd gone shopping and left a parcel behind but couldn't recall what it was.

Then she realized that she was lying on a very pretty pink and green carpet. It was soft, but she was on the floor, so she got to her feet, shaking out her skirts. Had she fainted? And where was she? *This has to be another dream.*

Except somehow she knew it wasn't. With a pang of uneasiness—the creeping, crawly kind one gets from a frightening novel—she looked around. The room was a small study, pleasant enough and nicely furnished, and with a case of books that looked very old and musty indeed. She'd never seen this place in her life.

Until she went to the window and lifted the curtain. Imogen sucked in her breath, her fingers crushing the soft fabric. She had expected to see a garden, or a meadow, or some bit of landscape. Instead, she saw the stairs descending from the bedrooms of her house to the second-floor landing. The perspective was confusing, to say the least. *There's no study on this side of the stairway, so how am I standing in it?*

And then it slowly dawned on her that it wasn't just the perspective and angle that was strange, but also the scale. For things to look the way they did, she would have to be as tiny as a china figurine.

And she would have to be inside the longcase clock that Dr. Magnus built.

She looked again, and then reasoned everything through again, her mind resisting an illogic as relentless as an incoming tide. In a sudden surge of terror, Imogen began pounding on the window—the inside of the clock face—and screamed.

Evelina Cooper's adventures
reach their explosive conclusion in

A STUDY IN ASHES

Book 3 of The Baskerville Affair
by

EMMA JANE HOLLOWAY

Be sure not to miss the final, thrilling chapter,
which will hit shelves soon!

Turn the page for a special preview.

And, for any desiring bonus content,
check out the exclusive, FREE e-short
"The Steamspinner Mutiny," currently available on
www.facebook.com/emmajane.holloway.

Not to mention, for those who missed it,
the FREE e-short "The Strange and Alarming Courtship
of Miss Imogen Roth," being the tale of Imogen's secret
engagement to one Buckingham Penner.

"YOU ARE NOT WELCOME HERE," SAID THE MAN IN THE QUI-
etly understated brown suit. "Forgive my blunt speech, but I
cannot make it any more plain. Those of us on the faculty
have established policies."

Those of us on the faculty. That meant this man who had
interrupted her work was a professor. Evelina Cooper gripped
her notebook until her knuckles hurt, wishing it were heavy
enough to knock reason into his head. Surely he could see
the equipment in this place was infinitely superior to what
they had at the Ladies' College? And what harm was there
in her using it? She wasn't in anyone's way.

The man waited for her to acknowledge his words—
no doubt expecting swift obedience—but Evelina couldn't
look at him. A painful knot lodged at the back of her throat,
like a stillborn wail of frustration.

"I am happy to assist you in clearing away this equipment," he offered, "and we'll say no more about this incident."

Stubbornness made her stall, and she fiddled with the
photograph slipping out from between the pages of her
book, tucking it back into place. It was of her uncle Sherlock, his likeness no doubt at home between the ruled pages
of formulae and lecture notes. *If someone had tried to toss
Sherlock Holmes out of a lab, he would have knocked the
offender down.* But young ladies were expected to be meek
and mild.

Marginal politeness was a more attainable goal. "Your
offer of assistance is kind, sir, and yet I don't understand
why I can't use this facility."

"I think you do. None of the sciences are required for a Lady's Certificate of Arts." He swept a hand around the laboratory. "Therefore, all this is unnecessary for students of the female college."

"I protest that logic, sir." It came out stiff with displeasure, but Evelina knew she had lost.

"Miss, be reasonable."

"I am perfectly reasonable, sir, which is why I am astonished by this restriction." Evelina twisted her silver bracelets around, fingers alive with agitation.

Her gaze searched the high-ceilinged room, though there was nothing to find in the gray shadows. The laboratory, with its rows of tables and shelves of gleaming equipment, was empty this early in the morning. Most of the students were still groping for their second cup of tea. The fact that the door to the lab had been locked hadn't slowed her down for more than half a minute.

He gave her a hard look from under beetling eyebrows. He wasn't one of the creaky old dons of the University of Camelin—not yet, anyhow—but he had perfected the glower. "Perhaps you should consider something in the line of elocution or moral philosophy."

Evelina bit her tongue. *Do my morals appear to need philosophy, sir? Outside of picking the lock, that is?*

The man harrumphed at her silence. "Domestic management, then. Or maybe literature." He pronounced the latter with a curl of the lip.

Evelina looked away before her temper led her down a regrettable path. She had powers this man had no idea about. She could command spirits of earth and tree. She had dabbled in sorcery and tasted death magic. She had nearly bled to death in a Whitechapel gutter and had made enemies and allies of some of the most powerful men in Mayfair—one of whom had bound her magic to his service with those pretty silver bracelets. And yet she couldn't get a seat in a proper chemistry class.

At last, she let out a sigh. "I am an eager student of languages and literature, but I am here to study science."

"A worthy ambition," said the man. He might have bottled

the tone and put it on the shelf next to the other dangerous acids. "But perhaps the practical work is a little beyond your scope."

Bugger that. Evelina's equipment was already set up to begin her exercise. Surely, if she got through it without a mistake, he would see she had a right to be there?

The exercise was of intermediate difficulty, a standard every serious student in the field was expected to know. She reached for the striker and, with a deft movement, lit the gas in the burner. A pale flame sprang to life, and she settled her flask of solution into place. Much depended on getting the exact proportion of alcohol to pure water, and then adding just the right amount of several organic compounds, but she'd measured carefully. "Your kind concerns about my abilities are unfounded, Professor . . .?" She let the question dangle. The man hadn't given her his name.

But he knew hers. "Miss Cooper," he snapped, "turn down that flame at once!"

Months of frustration made her balk. She stiffened her posture and stood her ground. "I am here to study science. Therefore, I require access to equipment and materials."

More specifically, she was there to learn the connection between science and magic. Evelina's mother had been gentry, the younger sister of Sherlock and Mycroft Holmes, but Evelina's father had been a commoner and a carrier of magic. She'd yearned all her life to make sense of these two opposing legacies, because surely everything was ruled by the same natural laws. If she understood those, there was much she might understand about herself.

But first she had to learn the basics, which was why she had wanted a higher education. Of any place, a university should have been eager to throw open the doors to new ideas, but all she'd met with so far was a wall of cold displeasure. Never mind telling them about her magic—they still hadn't seen past the fact that she wore petticoats.

There was a tense moment of silence as the gas hissed and bubbles formed at the base of the liquid. The solution heated quickly, but not fast enough to calm her mounting temper. She could hear Professor No-name's quick, irritated breathing as he hovered uncertainly at her elbow—flummoxed by her insubordination but too outraged to back away.

She felt her stomach coil into an aching knot. Her fingers crushed the heavy, dark fabric of her skirts until she forced them to uncurl and pick up a glass wand, ready to stir her concoction. She kept her features deliberately bland, hoping that as long as she reined in her mood, she would have the upper hand. *That always works for Uncle Sherlock.*

Finally, No-name spoke. "I will say this one last time. Students of the Ladies' College of London are not permitted to use the Sir Henry John Bickerton Laboratory for the Advancement of Chemical Science."

"But are we not part of the university, along with the other colleges?" Evelina asked tightly. "I believe our tuition flows to the greater institution." Except that the students resident at the Ladies' College experienced shorter academic terms, had access to fewer courses, and were only granted an L.C.A. rather than a proper bachelor's degree.

"The young men will someday attain positions of economic importance, whereas women will not. Squandering resources where they will never amount to anything is simply poor management."

Evelina couldn't stop herself from making a derisive huff as she measured out grains of crystalized aether onto a scale. The lime green sand pattered into the steel pan. "Perhaps a sound understanding of the volatile properties of sodium bicarbonate will assist me to perfect my muffins, Professor . . ." She let the name dangle once more, this time more rudely.

"Professor Bickerton. This is my laboratory, young lady."

That surprised her enough that she spun to face him, spilling grains of aether onto the tabletop. *This dead squib is the mighty Bickerton?* If he'd made assumptions about her, she'd done the same to him. She smoothed her skirts with her free hand, a little flustered. The man held one of the most important faculty chairs at Camelin. "Sir!"

He adopted a lecturing stance, his hands clasped behind his back. "And I note you are attempting the reconstitution of crystalized aether into liquid form. What industries require liquid aether, Miss Cooper?"

Her brain stalled for a moment, but then lurched forward awkwardly, like a poorly maintained engine. "Aeronautics, primarily. Also weapons manufacturing, cartography and exploration, and some forms of advanced telegraphy."

"You neglected to mention submersibles and a few branches of agriculture. Do you plan a career in any of these fields, Miss Cooper?"

"No, sir." She felt her cheeks heat.

"As I thought," he said with a twist of his mustached lip. "And what is the most salient point about liquid aether in the laboratory, Miss Cooper?"

She answered quickly, eager to redeem herself. "Aether is stable, which is why it has replaced hydrogen as the fuel of choice for dirigibles. But it takes a steady, high heat to ignite it. Ergo, one must be careful to regulate the temperature to avoid combustion."

"Indeed. And the fact that your solution is at a rolling boil demonstrates your inability to translate theory into safe practice." He chose that moment to make a grab for the jar of salts.

"I would have turned down the heat!" *If you hadn't distracted me!* Already on edge, Evelina jerked at his movement, snatching the open container out of reach. Their hands collided and a thick plume of green salts flew into the air, coating the entire table and plopping into the bubbling solution.

"Bloody hell," she cursed before she could stop herself. Boiling aether equaled an explosion.

She felt Professor Bickerton's grip on her arm and was wheeling around to protest when he pulled her under the heavy oak table. She opened her mouth to argue, but the professor's weight shifted away, and then he was scrabbling at the floor, shutting off the valve that supplied gas to the worktables.

Terror made her entire body clench into a ball. Instinctively, Evelina raised her hands over her face. She squeezed her eyes closed as Professor Bickerton drew her closer, sheltering her with his arm. And then, right above them, the aether dissolved and came to a boil. She knew the moment it happened because the skin of her face went tight and her ears popped. Then a blast of light turned Evelina's vision red through her eyelids—followed by the crash of glass and the rustling rush of flame. She felt rather than saw the rush of air like a wing sweeping across the laboratory, brushing everything in its path aside.

When Evelina uncoiled moments or years later, she felt deaf and blind, and her entire body was shaking. She scrambled out from under the table, boot heels catching in her skirts. Pages of her notebook fluttered to the floor like glowing feathers. With a pang, she thought of her photograph, but there was no chance it had survived.

Green flames licked across the work surface above, but her apparatus had been the only equipment in the path of destruction. In truth, the scene wasn't as bad as she'd expected, and that helped tame her panic. She stopped, gathering her wits and looking around for the heavy copper-sided fire extinguisher. The air was choking, the smoke heavy with the minty scent of aether distillate.

There! She lunged toward where the extinguisher sat at the front of the room. It was heavy, three gallons of liquid in a solid metal canister, but she heaved it onto a nearby table and depressed the plunger. Inside a vial of sulfuric acid broke and mixed with sodium bicarbonate to create a carbon dioxide propellant that pressurized the water. Evelina aimed the hose at the flaming table, nearly catching Professor Bickerton as he rose.

She saw his eyes widen, his finger point. Her eyes followed the direction of the gesture and suddenly understood his wordless yelp of dismay. The flames were slithering around the fallen jar of aether salts where she had dropped it, and the container was open and still half full. If a generous pinch had done this much damage, what would twenty times that do?

Her throat closed as if a giant fist had clenched around it. She aimed the spray of water in the direction of the jar, hoping to at least stem the tide of destruction. The hose jumped in her hand, alive with pressure, but it wasn't enough. With a hungry green flame, the fire licked toward the jar, dancing along the worktable like an evil spirit. Somewhere outside the room, a bell was clanging. They were no longer the only ones aware of this catastrophe.

Her eyes met the professor's and she saw his face turn chalk white. He dove for the door and she took her cue, dropping the hose and leaping toward the exit. They nearly collided.

"Run!" Evelina cried, and she pushed the man ahead of her. Cold certainty said they wouldn't make it out in time.

She turned at the last moment to summon her magic. She needed power, and she needed it fast; there was no time to summon a deva or weave a spell. That meant the more dangerous option of grabbing the fear-fueled energy already inside her and using sorcery.

She shuddered as the dark side of her power reared up, savage and ready to fight. It whispered of hunger, sliding through her with the deadly ease of a serpent—but it held the strength she needed. Evelina was backing away, aware that Professor Bickerton was almost through the door and yelling at her in confusion. He would have no idea what she was about to do, and with luck would never figure it out.

She raised her hands just as the contents of the jar ignited, sending shards and fire and crystallized aether in every direction. The shield of her power surged into place in time to deflect the shower of glass. Force jolted the shield, numbing her arms with the blow. She stumbled, falling to one knee, and braced for what came next, sending a fresh wave of magic surging forward. It wavered as it encountered the resistance of the bracelets, but steadied a second later; the shield held. She reeled, giddy with the sensation.

Then the aether exploded in earnest, the airborne crystals finding flame. Glass shattered throughout the room, the combustion crushing beakers and retorts, flasks and tubes, and a bank of locked cases filled with myriad substances in stoppered vials. The glass doors of the chemical stores burst in spinning shards, seeming to splash like water through the smoking air. Then the eruption of chemicals met a storm of fire, and the hammer of expanding gasses smashed into her protective shield and hurled Evelina through the air.

She landed outside the laboratory door, her back smacking against the hard ground. A wave of sick dizziness rose up, making her head spin as a blast of heat raked over her skin. She rolled over, her hands over her head as the ground shuddered with an explosion. Hands grabbed her, hauling her to her feet and dragging her across the lawn. Her shoulder joints protested as she tripped on her hems and went down, slamming her palms into the ground. Her relentless rescuer heaved her back into a forward stagger.

"No, no, please, let me sit down," she murmured, but she couldn't hear her own voice. The blast had done something to her ears.

A fit of coughing took Evelina, her eyes and nose streaming from the fog of chemical stink. She fished for her pocket handkerchief, dimly aware that it was Professor Bickerton at her side. She was glad he was all right—even if his face was a peculiar shade of outraged purple as he shouted at her.

And then she began to understand part of what he was saying, because he was repeating it over and over again. "You foolish girl!" He was so angry, he was spewing saliva.

Evelina stopped, the will to move her feet deserting her. The incident hadn't been entirely her fault, but she could tell he was going to make it sound that way. She shut her eyes, exhausted. It was abundantly clear that she shouldn't have defied the man—and yet even now she recoiled at the idea of meekly abandoning her equipment and crawling away.

"I will see you expelled!" Bickerton finished with a roar loud enough to penetrate her stunned hearing.

Expelled! Her eyes snapped open. She clutched at her bracelets, knowing they bound her to this place for her own safety—because the alternatives for a magic-user like her weren't good.

"You cannot!" she protested.

"Take note and learn, Miss Cooper." Then he turned on his heel and went to speak to the horde of men arriving to deal with the disaster.

Expulsion? What will Keating say? What will he do to me?

Jasper Keating, the man they called the Gold King, had soldered the bracelets around her wrist—a mark of his patronage and her prison. Wherever she went, the bracelets signaled her presence to Keating's minions, making her easy to find. They also delivered a painful shock if she strayed out of bounds. She was his property as surely as if she were in chains.

He'd allowed her to attend the university as long as she never left the grounds. The arrangement was generous, given that the alternatives for someone with magical Blood were execution or a short, brutal future as a laboratory rat. And now—at least as far as public opinion went—she'd shown that his generosity was misplaced. Her patron did not like being in the wrong.

Another small explosion went off inside the burning building, letting out a cloud of stink and sparks. Evelina sank to the ground with a noise halfway between a groan and curse. *Mr. Keating is going to be very displeased indeed.*

TWO DAYS LATER, Evelina left the Ladies' College and crossed the University of Camelin grounds toward the New Hall, which looked as if it was at least three hundred years old. Plane trees lined the narrow, cobbled road, their wide leaves giving a dry rustle in the light breeze. Though the air was cool, the afternoon sun and the rising slope of the path made her warm, and she paused to catch her breath.

She had been here nearly a year. The weather brought back the previous autumn, when Keating had first forced her into his service. The job had taken her into the slums of Whitechapel, but it had also reunited her with her childhood sweetheart, Nick. She turned her face up to the sunlight, feeling its warmth even as her chest tightened with grief. After so many years of coming together and parting over and over, Nick had finally become her lover. And then came the battle that had changed everything. She'd traded her freedom to save Nick's airship from Keating's guns, but her sacrifice had come to nothing. Nick was dead, she was a prisoner, and the last year had been the loneliest of her life.

And alone she would go to face the consequences of the laboratory accident. Despondent, she began walking again, the soft soles of her boots scuffing on the cobbles. To her right were the mellow stone arches of Fullman College, to her left Usher College with Witherton House and its regal gardens behind. Gowned faculty clustered around the buildings like crows, but this close to the heart of the university they were an almost exclusively male flock. The Ladies' College of London was at the bottom of the hill, secure behind high walls. It was part of the university, and not.

Rather like her—and based on Professor Bickerton's harangue after the explosion, soon she wouldn't be part of Camelin at all. If this summons to the vice-chancellor's office unfolded as she suspected it would, her academic career would set before the sun did. *And then what?* What would happen? Would she go back to working as a spy, or something worse? She couldn't bring that future into focus. Every time she tried, her breath grew short. For now, it was better not to think about it at all.

Evelina noticed several conversations breaking off as curious faces turned her way. She looked over her shoulder, making sure there was nothing behind her that was attracting attention. That gave her a view of the lower campus, the blackened shell of the laboratory conspicuous against the pastoral green. Sick, cold dread settled in her gut, driving out the warmth of the sun. She tucked in her chin, letting the brim of her hat hide her face as she marched the remaining distance to the entrance of the New Hall. The watching faces followed her as if pulled by a magnetic force. *There goes the silly woman who blew up the laboratory.* As she neared the door, she shuddered, the touch of their gazes an almost palpable pressure along her spine.

Once inside she mounted the stairs to the offices, her stomach a leaden ball of apprehension. Marie Antoinette could not have felt less doomed as she climbed the scaffold. But Evelina bravely knocked and entered the vice-chancellor's chambers. When the young man who was his secretary rose to show her into the inner sanctum, she followed him with her gloved hands clasped nervously at her waist. The decor did nothing to lighten the mood; the walls were covered in dark walnut paneling made darker still by age. As she crossed the faded carpet, the smell of old tobacco rose up, tickling her nose. Three men were ranged in a conversational semicircle of oxblood leather chairs. In her anxiety, she had half-imagined a judge's bench and uniformed guards, so the informality was a relief.

They rose as she entered. Bickerton was one, and another was old, white-whiskered Sir William Fillipott, the vice-chancellor. The older man bowed, his manners as always impeccable. "Miss Cooper, how gracious of you to join us."

"Sir." She curtsied, long training helping her to fall into the ritual of pleasantries. She'd always gotten along with Sir William, and hoped that counted for something now.

"You have met Professor Bickerton." The vice-chancellor gave a rueful smile, and then indicated the third member of his party. "And this is young James, our new chair of mathematics. I have asked him to observe and record this meeting."

Sir William patted the mathematician's shoulder with a fond, fatherly gesture. The man nodded politely to Evelina, adjusting a small clockwork device that inscribed a squiggling code onto a wax cylinder. She had seen the police use similar equipment for taking statements. The brass contraption with its whirling gears was not the latest technology, but it was advanced for Camelin, steeped as it was in tradition.

The young professor had nutmeg brown hair and a tidy mustache. His lean build and fastidious air reminded Evelina of Uncle Sherlock. She was sure she'd seen his face before, though she could not remember where. On the campus? She didn't think so. Memory itched at her like a healing cut.

Sir William gestured toward another chair, arranged to face the three men. "Please, Miss Cooper, have a seat."

"I'm sure you know why you are here, Miss Cooper," Bickerton began. "What do you think will be the outcome of this interview?" The man gave a hint of a smile, and she didn't like it one little bit.

Evelina sat with all the grace she could muster. When she opened her mouth to speak, her throat was so tight she could barely breathe. She cleared it as delicately as she could and tried again. "I would not presume to anticipate your judgment."

Sir William frowned, both at her and Bickerton. "Even if no one was seriously injured and even if it was accidental, this was a grave occurrence. Can you please tell me, Miss Cooper, why you were in that laboratory?"

Bickerton snorted, but Evelina was grateful to Sir William for asking. "The Ladies' College does not have as good a facility or equipment. Nor does it offer the same level of instruction in the sciences. What we get are shorter, less demanding classes that do not teach us nearly as well."

The vice-chancellor's bushy white brows shot up. "And so you took it upon yourself to break into our laboratory and help yourself to the men's equipment?"

Bickerton leaned forward. "A criminal act, I might point out."

"Let the girl speak," said Sir William.

"If no one was willing to instruct me at the level I desired, it seemed I must help myself to advance." Even as she said it, Evelina felt her cheeks heat, alarm trickling through her insides. It sounded so high-handed, but solving the problem on her own had been a natural response. "At the time, it did not seem so rash an act."

"Let me assure you, it was extremely rash." Sir William's tone was dry. "I know the destruction of the lab was not your intent, but bad action inevitably leads to bad results. For shame, Miss Cooper—for you clearly *did* intend to flout our rules, and see what came of it."

And yet it really had seemed like a reasonable solution. In the last year and a half, she'd been in too many dire situations, with her life on the line, to bother with rules. Yet somehow that recklessness had trickled down to her everyday conduct. One wouldn't have thought it possible, given the restraints on her freedom, but there it was. Her goal was to learn everything she could to understand her powers in a scientific light. The lock on the laboratory door had just been another obstacle to overcome and she had conquered it. Such a will to succeed might be heroic, but she had to admit that it hadn't been smart.

"There is no apology that I can make that will be sufficient to the situation," she said, meaning every word. "And yet I do apologize. I am wholeheartedly sorry."

The transcription device whirred and bobbled, writing down her guilt and contrition. The professor operating it watched her with cool, appraising eyes.

"Prettily said, Miss Cooper," Sir William replied, "but Professor Bickerton has requested your expulsion, and he is within his rights to do so."

She drew breath, ready to launch into her defense, but Sir William held up a quelling hand. "However, there are a number of factors that come into play, including the wishes of your patron."

"Does he know?" she asked meekly.

Now she felt her fingers tremble, and she clasped them in her lap. Jasper Keating could buy the University of Camelin a dozen times over, but he could also crush her like a gnat. She couldn't assume anything, least of all his tolerance for failure. The last time she'd worked for him, she'd nearly been killed. If he lost interest in her, he could order her death in an eyeblink.

"Mr. Keating is aware of what has happened." Sir William reached behind him and picked up a letter from the desk, unfolding it slowly with the thumb and fingers of one hand. He glanced down at it and let the paper curl shut again, his expression carefully neutral. "He responded in no uncertain terms."

Nerves made her temper grow sharp. She fingered her bracelets, picturing her patron's hard, patrician face. "And?"

"You are a fortunate young woman. He is desirous that you remain here."

She might have been relieved, but the way Sir William said it left room for doubt. She inched forward on her s͏

"You said there were a number of factors. What are the others?"

"We must consider the wishes of the governing body of this institution. The chancellor in particular."

She understood. Some would align with Bickerton, and yet others dared not offend the Gold King. He owned too many important men and could easily scuttle university endowments. *And here I am, the cause of discord.* That would come back to haunt her for sure. "I assume then, it will take time before my fate is decided?"

"It will be discussed at the end of the month, during our usual meeting."

As Sir William spoke, Bickerton looked like he'd swallowed one of his own chemical preparations. "An unnecessary waste of time in my opinion. I say make the decision now."

Part of her agreed. Waiting for judgment would be excruciating. The mere thought of it gnawed her insides. "Is there nothing I can do to redeem myself?"

Sir William frowned, his lined face stern and sad. "It is a question of principle. Mr. Keating has offered a sum in recompense for the damage to our facility, but there is more at stake than mere money. The sovereignty and dignity of our institution are at stake."

Evelina lowered her eyes, staring at her gloves. She'd put on clean ones to come here, but somehow still managed to get a smudge of ink on one finger. She curled her hand closed to hide it. *How am I going to get out of this?*

Sir William leaned forward, his hands on his knees. "My advice to you in this interval is to behave as a lady ought, to study what you are assigned and not to rearrange the natural boundaries of custom to suit yourself."

Feeling suddenly ill, Evelina slowly sat back in her chair. It was a simple command, and yet unpalatable. She was already confined to the campus. He was taking away the one ~~liberty~~ the university offered—the freedom to learn.

"~~And~~ you will confine yourself to the precincts of the La~~dies' Co~~llege. You are to remain within its walls."

~~S~~he looked up, meeting Sir William's stern gaze

and Bickerton's mocking smirk. "Not leave the college?" Her voice was high and incredulous. "Not even to walk the rest of the campus?"

"It will spare the feelings of the faculty if they know you are not loose upon the grounds," Sir William replied. "Especially since locks are apparently no obstacle to you."

Unless of course I'm trying to escape altogether. But the bracelets took care of that.

"I see," she said faintly. Bloody hell, she would be penned into a tiny area, just the quadrangle and the buildings around it. She lifted her chin, her face numb with dismay. "That is going to make my world a very small one."

"But at least it is still a foothold at Camelin," Sir William said gravely. "Do not slip again, Miss Cooper, lest you fall entirely. The University Council will make its decision in the fullness of time, and how you adapt to these rules will count for much."

"Or perhaps not at all," Bickerton added tightly.

"Professor," Sir William chided, "let penitence do its work."

Evelina bowed her head, her rueful anger an open wound. If it weren't for the bracelets and the threat the Gold King posed to her loved ones, she would have simply walked away. She'd disappeared once; she could do it again. "I will do my best, Sir William. You may rely on that."

"Very well. And now it is time that you retired to meditate upon your actions." Sir William rose, the others following his lead. "James here will escort you to your rooms."

"Miss." The man switched off his device and rose. Then he gave an almost mocking bow and held out his arm.

Evelina felt her eyes widen in shock. Now she remembered where she'd seen the man before. *It's Mr. Juniper!* She had seen him almost a year ago, when she'd been sneaking through the compound where the Blue King kept his war machines hidden. Juniper was the Blue King's man of business, and therefore one of Keating's bitter enemies.

The memory brought a fresh flood of loss, remembering her hand in Nick's as they crept unseen through enemy territory. Her body tensed as she clamped down hard on emotions. Nick was gone, and she had to focus on the threat in front of her. *Does Juniper recognize me? Does he know it was me who stole the designs for the Blue King's weapons?*

She could feel the three men watching her, and quickly hid her confusion. "Then I will bid you good day, gentlemen," she said with a neat curtsey.

The men bowed—Bickerton with a perfunctory jerk, Sir William with gravity. Steeling herself, she took Mr. Juniper's arm and let him lead her from the room and down the stairs.

Juniper gave a small, cold smile as they left the New Hall. "I see that I am familiar to you, Miss Cooper. No doubt your association with Mr. Keating has acquainted you with many players surrounding the Steam Council."

"Only in a modest way." If he believed that she knew him through Keating, it was far safer than the truth.

He led her along the path with a casual air, as if they were just out for a stroll. In the afternoon sun, his face seemed pale to the point of translucence, blue veins visible beneath the fine skin of his temples. "And so here we are. Academia makes strange bedfellows."

She couldn't argue with that. "How did you come to be here?"

"Ambition," he said, without the least embarrassment. "I have been working on a binomial theorem. Perhaps I shall publish a treatise. A university chair gives me credibility in a way that a steam baron's patronage could not."

It still seemed a strange leap from managing a steam baron's business affairs, especially since the Blue King held sway in the poorest parts of the city. "It seems you are a man of hidden talents."

"We share that quality in common, though your abilities are far more controversial than mine. Oh, yes," he said, smiling at her fresh surprise, "I know what those bracelets you wear mean. Most students just think they're prisoners who are chained in fact, bound to do Keating's bidding finally chooses to crook his finger."

Evelina was speechless for a long moment. "How do you know about that?"

Juniper narrowed his eyes. "Think about it. The public version is that you are a ward of sorts to Mr. Keating. No mention of magic is made in the official records. Still, you must know by now that you are watched, and not just by the university gossips and Keating's pet thugs."

"What do you mean by that?" She tried to pull away, but he grasped her more tightly, keeping her arm linked through his.

"Word of your talents has gotten out, Miss Cooper. There are those on the Steam Council who know where you are." He stopped walking. They were almost to the gates of the Ladies' College, but still far enough away that no one else was close enough to hear his words. "Both you and Bickerton should have been blown to pieces. Is he even aware that you must have saved his life with your powers? How did you do it, Miss Cooper? I've always wanted to know how sorcery works."

Evelina shielded her eyes from the sun, studying his sharp features. He might have been handsome but for an unpleasant glitter in his eyes. "Are you really here for your theorem, or did the Blue King send you?"

His smile made her pulse skip, and not in a good way. "I have my eye on many interests, Miss Cooper. The steam barons are like Titans. They will go to war with one another before long."

"I think that is common knowledge."

"Perhaps." He finally released her arm. "In any event, creatures like you and I will be looking to our own survival once it happens."

She almost smiled. "Are we not doing so now?"

"A valid point, Miss Cooper. You are as astute as you are troublesome." A flock of birds flashed across the sun, their wings casting a fluttering shadow. Juniper looked up, seeming almost uneasy. "Nevertheless, I would be very careful to watch my back if I were you."

"I always do." Juniper was trying to lay the groundwork for something, with his dark observations and half-confide and she wasn't having any of it. She began walking again, returning the conversation to safer territory. "But my chief concern at the moment is my education. I have to say the entire college experience has been a severe disappointment."

His bright eyes darted toward her. "How so?"

"I've been to one finishing school already. I did not come here to learn flower arranging and domestic economy."

Juniper looked away, laughing softly to himself. "Then allow me to do you a favor, Miss Cooper, in the name of equitable education. Tutors can be arranged, as can a modest amount of scientific equipment. As a member of the faculty, I will gladly provide you with anything that is not poisonous or combustible. For the time being, that should satisfy your needs and those of the administration both." He pulled out a silver case and extracted a calling card. "Make a list of what you need and send it to me. I will do what I can to ease the burden of good behavior."

She took the card from him, still wary. "And why would you do me this favor?"

"Because someday I may need one from you. I am still at the start of my career and building my capital. Do not look for complications where they do not exist." He gave a slight bow. "And here we are at your gate. Good day, Miss Cooper."

"Good day, Mr. Juniper."

"Ah." He gave a slight grin—a real one this time—gesturing toward the card. "I do not use that name here. Arnold Juniper has nothing to do with my career as a professor of mathematics."

Evelina inclined her head. "I stand corrected, sir. It seems a nom de guerre is de rigueur these days."

"As is schoolroom French."

"Touché."

And with a last tip of his tall hat, Mr. Juniper left her there, his tall, slim frame elegant in the mellow sunshine.

last Evelina turned to enter the gates to the Ladies'
of London. Reluctance seized her, but there was no
obey. She shivered as the lock clanged behind
like the snap of iron jaws. *Here I am, and*